The Spectator

Richard Steele, Joseph Addison, Richard Steele, Joseph Addison

Copyright © BiblioLife, LLC

This book represents a historical reproduction of a work originally published before 1923 that is part of a unique project which provides opportunities for readers, educators and researchers by bringing hard-to-find original publications back into print at reasonable prices. Because this and other works are culturally important, we have made them available as part of our commitment to protecting, preserving and promoting the world's literature. These books are in the "public domain" and were digitized and made available in cooperation with libraries, archives, and open source initiatives around the world dedicated to this important mission.

We believe that when we undertake the difficult task of re-creating these works as attractive, readable and affordable books, we further the goal of sharing these works with a global audience, and preserving a vanishing wealth of human knowledge.

Many historical books were originally published in small fonts, which can make them very difficult to read. Accordingly, in order to improve the reading experience of these books, we have created "enlarged print" versions of our books. Because of font size variation in the original books, some of these may not technically qualify as "large print" books, as that term is generally defined; however, we believe these versions provide an overall improved reading experience for many.

THE

SPECTATOR,

IN EIGHT VOLUMES.

VOL. II

PHILADELPHIA

PRINTED FOR SAMUEL F. BRADFORD, NO. 4, SOUTH
THIRD-STREET, AND JOHN CONRAD & CO. NO. 30,
CHESNUT-STREET.

1803.

TO THE RIGHT HONOURABLE

CHARLES LORD HALIFAX.

My Lord,

Similitude of manners and studies is usually mentioned as one of the strongest motives to affection and esteem, but the passionate veneration I have for your Lordship, I think, flows from an admiration of qualities in you, of which, in the whole course of these papers, I have acknowledged myself incapable. While I busy myself as a stranger upon earth, and can pretend to no other than being a looker-on, you are conspicuous in the busy and polite world, both in the world of men and that of letters. While I am silent and unobserved in public meetings, you are admired by all that approach you, as the life and genius of the conversation. What a happy conjunction of different talents meets in him whose whole discourse is at once animated by the strength and force of reason, and adorned with all the graces and embellishments of wit? When learning irradiates common life, it is then in its highest use and perfection; and it is to such as your Lordship, that the sciences owe the esteem which they have with the active part of mankind. Knowledge of books in recluse men, is like that sort of lanthorn which hides him who carries it, and serves only to pass through secret and gloomy paths of his own, but in the possession of a man of business, it is as a torch in the hand of one who is willing and able to shew those who are bewildered, the way which leads to their prosperity and welfare. A generous concern for your country, and a passion for every thing which is truly great and noble, are what actuate all your life and actions; and I hope you will forgive me that I have an ambition this book may be placed in the library of so good a judge of what is valuable, in that library where the choice is such, that it will not be a disparagement to be the meanest author in it. Forgive me, my Lord, for taking this occasion of telling all the world how ardently I love and honour you, and that I am, with the utmost gratitude for all your favours,

 My Lord,

  Your Lordship's most obliged,

   most obedient, and

    most humble Servant,

     THE SPECTATOR.

THE SPECTATOR.

No. LXXXI.   SATURDAY, JUNE 2, 1711.

Qualis ubi audito venantum murmure tigris
Horruit in maculas......   STATIUS.

As when the tigress hears the hunter's din,
A thousand angry spots defile her skin

ABOUT the middle of last winter I went to see an opera at the theatre in the Hay-market, where I could not but take notice of two parties of very fine women, that had placed themselves in the opposite side-boxes, and seemed drawn up in a kind of battle array one against another. After a short survey of them, I found they were patched differently, the faces on one hand being spotted on the right side of the forehead, and those upon the other on the left. I quickly perceived that they cast hostile glances upon one another, and that their patches were placed in those different situations, as party signals to distinguish friends from foes. In the middle boxes, between these two opposite bodies, were several ladies who patched indifferently on both sides of their faces, and seemed to sit there with no other intention but to see the opera. Upon inquiry I found, that the body of Amazons on my right hand were whigs, and those on my left tories, and that those who had placed themselves in the middle boxes were a neutral party, whose faces had not yet declared themselves. These last, however, as I afterwards found, diminished daily, and took their party with one side or the other; insomuch that I observed in several of them, the patches, which were before dispersed equally, are now all gone over to the whig or tory side of the face. The censorious say, that the men, whose hearts are aimed at, are very often the occasion that one part of the face is thus dishonoured, and lies under a kind of disgrace, while the other is so much set off and adorned by the owner; and that the patches turn to the right or to the left, according to the principles of the man who is most in favour. But whatever may be the motives of a few fantastical coquettes, who do not patch for the public good so much as for their own private advantage, it is certain, that there are several women of honour, who patch out of principle, and with an eye to the interest of their country. Nay, I am informed that some of them adhere so stedfastly to their party, and are so far from sacrificing their zeal for the public, to their passion for any particular person, that in a late draught of marriage articles a lady has stipulated with her husband, that, whatever his opinions are, she shall be at liberty to patch on which side she pleases.

I must here take notice that Rosalinda, a famous whig partizan, has most unfortunately a very beautiful mole on the tory part of her forehead, which being very conspicuous, has occasioned many mistakes, and given a handle to her enemies to misrepresent her face, as though it had revolted from the whig interest. But, whatever this natural patch may seem to intimate, it is well known that her notions of government are still the same. This unlucky mole, however, has misled several coxcombs, and, like the hanging out of false colours, made some of them converse with Rosalinda in what they thought the spirit of her party, when on a sudden she has given them an unexpected fire, that has sunk them all at once. If Rosalinda is unfortunate in her mole, Nigranilla is as unhappy in a pimple, which forces her, against her inclinations, to patch on the whig side.

I am told that many virtuous matrons, who formerly have been taught to believe that this artificial spotting of the face was unlawful, are now reconciled, by a zeal for their cause, to what they could not be prompted by a concern for their beauty. This way of declaring war upon one another, puts me in mind of what is reported of the tigress, that several spots rise in her skin when she is angry, or, as Mr. Cowley has imitated the verses that stand as the motto of this paper,

' She swells with angry pride,
' And calls forth all her spots on ev'ry side.'

When I was in the theatre the time above-mentioned, I had the curiosity to count the patches on both sides, and found the tory patches to be about twenty stronger than the whig; but to make amends for this small inequality, I the next morning found the whole puppet-show filled with faces spotted after the whiggish manner. Whether or no the ladies had retreated hither in order to rally their forces, I cannot tell; but the next night they came in so great a body to the opera, that they out-numbered the enemy.

This account of party patches will, I am afraid, appear improbable to those who live at a distance from the fashionable world; but as it is a distinction of a very singular nature, and what perhaps may never meet with a parallel, I think I should not have discharged the office of a faithful *Spectator*, had I not recorded it.

I have, in former papers, endeavoured to expose this party-rage in women, as it only serves to aggravate the hatreds and animosities that reign among men, and in a great measure deprives the fair sex of those peculiar charms with which nature has endowed them.

When the Romans and Sabines were at war, and just upon the point of giving battle, the women who were allied to both of them, interposed with so many tears and entreaties, that they prevented the mutual slaughter which threatened both parties, and united them together in a firm and lasting peace.

I would recommend this noble example to our British ladies, at a time when their country is torn with so many unnatural divisions, that if they continue, it will be a misfortune to be born in it. The Greeks thought it so improper for women to interest themselves in competitions and contentions, that for this reason, among others, they forbade them, under pain of death, to be present at the Olympic games, notwithstanding these were the public diversions of all Greece.

As our English women excel those of all nations in beauty, they should endeavour to outshine them in all other accomplishments proper to the sex, and to distinguish themselves as tender mothers, and faithful wives, rather than as furious partizans. Female virtues are of a domestic turn. The family is the proper province for private women to shine in. If they must be shewing their zeal for the public, let it not be against those who are perhaps of the same family, or at least of the same religion or nation, but against those who are the open, professed, undoubted enemies of their faith, liberty, and country. When the Romans were pressed with a foreign enemy, the ladies voluntarily contributed all their rings and jewels to assist the government under a public exigence; which appeared so laudable an action in the eyes of their countrymen, that from thenceforth it was permitted by a law to pronounce public orations at the funeral of a woman in praise of the deceased person, which until that time was peculiar to men. Would our English ladies, instead of sticking on a patch against those of their own country, shew themselves so truly public-spirited, as to sacrifice every one her necklace against the common enemy, what decrees ought not to be made in favour of them?

Since I am recollecting upon this subject such passages as occur to my memory out of ancient authors,

I cannot omit a sentence in the celebrated funeral oration of Pericles, which he made in honour of those brave Athenians that were slain in a fight with the Lacedemonians. After having addressed himself to the several ranks and orders of his countrymen, and shown them how they should behave themselves in the public cause, he turns to the female part of his audience, " And as for you (says he), I shall advise you in very few words: aspire only to those virtues that are peculiar to your sex, follow your natural modesty, and think it your greatest commendation not to be talked of one way or other."

C.

No. LXXXII   MONDAY, JUNE 4.

. . . Caput domina venale sub hasta.   Juv.

His fortune's ruin'd, and himself a slave

Passing under Ludgate the other day, I heard a voice bawling for charity, which I thought I had somewhere heard before. Coming near to the grate, the prisoner called me by my name, and desired I would throw something into the box: I was out of countenance for him, and did as he bid me, by putting in half a crown. I went away, reflecting upon the strange constitution of some men, and how meanly they behave themselves in all sorts of conditions. The person who begged of me is now, as I take it, fifty; I was well acquainted with him till about the age of twenty-five, at which time a good estate fell to him by the death of a relation. Upon coming to this unexpected good fortune, he ran into all the extravagancies imaginable, was frequently in drunken disputes, broke drawer's heads, talked and swore loud, was unmannerly to those above him, and insolent to those below him. I could not but remark, that it was the same baseness of spirit which worked in his behaviour in both fortunes, the same little mind was insolent in riches, and shameless in poverty. This accident made me muse upon the circumstance of being in debt in general, and solve in my mind what tempers were most apt to fall into this error of life, as well as the misfortune it must needs be to languish under such pressures. As for my myself, my natural aversion to that sort of conversation which makes a figure with the generality of mankind, exempts me from any temptations to expense; and all my business lies within a very narrow compass, which is only to give an honest man who takes care of my estate proper vouchers for his quarterly payments to me, and observe what linen my laundress brings and takes away with her once a-week: my steward brings his receipts ready for my signing; and I have a pretty implement with the respective names of shirts, cravats, handkerchiefs, and stockings, with proper numbers to know how to reckon with my laundress. This being almost all the business I have in the world for the care of my own affairs, I am at full leisure to observe upon what others do with relation to their equipage and economy.

When I walk the streets, and observe the hurry about me in this town,

' Where, with like haste, thro' diff'rent ways they run,
' Some to undo, and some to be undone;' *Cooper's Hill.*

I say, when I behold this vast variety of persons and humours, with the pains they both take for the accomplishment of the ends mentioned in the above verses of Denham, I cannot much wonder at the endeavour after gain, but am extremely astonished that men can be so insensible of the danger of running into debt. One would think it impossible a man who is given to contract debts should know, that his creditor has, from that moment in which he transgresses payment, so much as that demand comes to in his debtor's honour, liberty, and fortune. One would think he did not know, that his creditor can say the worst thing imaginable of him, to wit, *That he is unjust*, without defamation; and can seize his person, without being guilty of an assault. Yet such is the loose and abandoned turn of some men's minds, that they can live under these constant apprehensions, and still go on to increase the cause of them. Can there be a more low and servile condition than to be ashamed or afraid to see any one man breathing? yet he that is much in debt, is in that condition with relation to twenty different people. There are, indeed, circumstances wherein men of honest natures may become liable to debts, by some unadvised behaviour in any great point of their life, or mortgaging a man's honesty as a security for that of another, and the like; but these instances are so particular and circumstantiated, that they cannot come within general considerations; for one such case as one of these, there are ten, where a man, to keep up a farce of retinue and grandeur, within his own house, shall shrink at the expectation of surly demands at his doors. The debtor is the creditor's criminal, and all the officers of power and state, whom we behold make so great a figure, are no other than so many persons in authority to make good his charge against him. Human society depends upon his having the vengeance law allots him; and the debtor owes his liberty to his neighbour as much as the murderer does his life to his prince.

Our gentry are, generally speaking, in debt; and many families have put it into a kind of method of being so from generation to generation. The father mortgages when the son is very young, and the boy is to marry as soon as he is at age, to redeem it, and find portions for his sisters. This, forsooth, is no great inconvenience to him; for he may wench, keep a public table, or feed dogs, like a worthy English gentleman, until he has out-run half his estate, and leave the same incumbrance upon his first born; and so on, till one man of more vigour than ordinary goes quite through the estate, or some man of sense comes into it, and scorns to have an estate in partnership, that is to say, liable to the demand or insult of any man living. There is my friend Sir Andrew, though for many years a great and general trader, was never the defendant in a law-suit, in all the perplexity of business, and the iniquity of mankind at present: no one had any colour for the least complaint against his dealings with him. This is certainly as uncommon, and in its proportion as laudable, in a citizen, as it is in a general never to have suffered a disadvantage in fight. How different from this gentleman is Jack Truepenny, who has been an old acquaintance of Sir Andrew and myself from boys, but could never learn our caution. Jack has a whorish unresisting good nature, which makes him incapable of having a property in any thing. His fortune, his reputation, his time, and his capacity, are at any man's service that comes first. When he was at school he was whipped thrice a-week for faults he took upon himself to excuse others; since he came into the business of the world, he has been arrested twice or thrice a year for debts he had nothing to do with, but as surety for others; and I remember when a friend of his had suffered in the vice of the town, all the physic his friend took was conveyed to him by Jack, and inscribed, ' A bolus or an electuary for Mr. Truepenny.' Jack had a good estate left him, which came to nothing; because he believed all who pretended to demands upon it. This easiness and credulity destroy all the other merit he has; and he has all his life been a sacrifice to others, without ever receiving thanks, or doing one good action.

I will end this discourse with a speech which I heard Jack make to one of his creditors (of whom he deserved gentler usage), after lying a whole night in custody at his suit.

'SIR,
'Your ingratitude for the many kindnesses I have done you, shall not make me unthankful for the good you have done me, in letting me see there is such a man as you in the world. I am obliged to you for the diffidence I shall have all the rest of my life: " I shall hereafter trust no man so far as to be in his debt."
R.

No. LXXXIII. TUESDAY, JUNE 5.

——Animum pictura pascit inani
VIRGIL

And with an empty picture feeds his mind
DRYDEN

WHEN the weather hinders me from taking my diversions without doors, I frequently make a little party with two or three select friends, to visit any thing curious that may be seen under covert. My principal entertainments of this nature are pictures, insomuch, that when I have found the weather set in to be very bad, I have taken a whole day's journey to see a gallery that is furnished by the hands of great masters. By this means, when the heavens are filled with clouds, when the earth swims in rain, and all nature wears a lowering countenance, I withdraw myself from these uncomfortable scenes, into the visionary worlds of art, where I meet with shining landscapes, gilded triumphs, beautiful faces, and all those other objects that fill the mind with gay ideas, and disperse that gloominess which is apt to hang upon it in those dark disconsolate seasons.

I was some weeks ago in a course of these diversions, which had taken such an entire possession of my imagination, that they formed in it a short morning's dream; which I shall communicate to my reader rather as the first sketch and outlines of a vision, than as a finished piece.

I dreamt that I was admitted into a long spacious gallery which had one side covered with pieces of all the famous painters who are now living, and the other with the works of the greatest masters that are dead.

On the side of the living, I saw several persons busy in drawing, colouring, and designing; on the side of the dead painters, I could not discover more than one person at work, who was exceeding slow in his motions, and wonderfully nice in his touches.

I was resolved to examine the several artists that stood before me, and accordingly applied myself to the side of the living. The first I observed at work in this part of the gallery was Vanity, with his hair tied behind him in a ribband, and dressed like a Frenchman. All the faces he drew were very remarkable for their smiles, and a certain smirking air which he bestowed indifferently on every age and degree of either sex. The *toujours gai* appeared even in his judges, bishops, and privy-counsellors: In a word, all his men were petits maitres, and all his women coquettes. The drapery of his figures was extremely well suited to his faces, and was made up of all the glaring colours that could be mixed together, every part of the dress was in a flutter, and endeavoured to distinguish itself above the rest.

On the left hand of Vanity stood a laborious workman, who I found was his humble admirer, and copied after him. He was dressed like a German, and had a very hard name that sounded something like Stupidity.

The third artist that I looked over was Fantasque, dressed like a Venetian scaramouch. He had an excellent hand at chimera, and dealt very much in distortions and grimaces. He would sometimes affright himself with the phantoms that flowed from his pencil. In short, the most elaborate of his pieces was at best but a terrifying dream; and one could say nothing more of his finest figures than that they were agreeable monsters.

The fourth person I examined was very remarkable for his hasty hand, which left his picture so unfinished, that the beauty in the picture (which was designed to continue as a monument of it to posterity) faded sooner than in the person after whom it was drawn. He made so much haste to dispatch his business, that he neither gave himself time to clean his pencils, nor mix his colours. The name of this expeditious workman was Avarice.

Not far from this artist I saw another of a quite different nature, who was dressed in the habit of a Dutchman, and known by the name of Industry. His figures were wonderfully laboured: If he drew the portraiture of a man, he did not omit a single hair in his face; if the figure of a ship, there was not a rope among the tackle that escaped him. He had likewise hung a great part of the wall with night-pieces, that seemed to show themselves by the candles which were lighted up in several parts of them; and were so inflamed by the sun-shine which accidentally fell upon them, that at first sight I could scarcely forbear crying out, Fire.

The five foregoing artists were the most considerable on this side the gallery; there were indeed several others whom I had not time to look into. One of them, however, I could not forbear observing, who was very busy in retouching the finest pieces, though he produced no originals of his own. His pencil aggravated every feature that was before overcharged, loaded every defect, and poisoned every colour it touched. Though this workman did so much mischief on the side of the living, he never turned his eye towards that of the dead. His name was Envy.

Having taken a cursory view of one side of the gallery, I turned myself to that which was filled by the works of those great masters that were dead; when immediately I fancied myself standing before a multitude of spectators, and thousands of eyes looking upon me at once; for all before me appeared so like men and women, that I almost forgot they were pictures. Raphael's figures stood in one row, Titian's in another, Guido Rheni's in a third. One part of the wall was peopled by Hannibal Carrache, another by Corregio, and another by Rubens. To be short, there was not a great master among the dead who had not contributed to the embellishment of this side of the gallery. The persons that owed their being to these several masters, appeared all of them to be real and alive, and differed among one another only in the variety of their shapes, complexions, and clothes, so that they looked like different nations of the same species.

Observing an old man (who was the same person I before mentioned, as the only artist that was at work on this side of the gallery) creeping up and down from one picture to another, and retouching all the fine pieces that stood before me, I could not but be very attentive to all his motions. I found his pencil was so very light, that it worked imperceptibly, and after a thousand touches, scarce produced any visible effect in the picture on which he was employed. However, as he busied himself incessantly, and repeated touch after touch, without rest or intermission, he wore off insensibly every little disagreeable gloss that hung upon a figure. He also added such a beautiful brown to the shades, and mellowness to the colours, that he made every picture appear more perfect than when it came fresh from the master's pencil. I could not forbear looking upon the face of this ancient workman, and immediately, by the long lock of hair upon his forehead, discovered him to be Time.

Whether it were because the thread of my dream was at an end I cannot tell, but upon my taking a survey of this imaginary old man, my sleep left me.

No. LXXXIV. WEDNESDAY, JUNE 6.

..... Quis talia fando
Myrmidonum, Dolopumve, aut duri miles Ulyssei,
Temperet a lachrymis?   VIRG.

Who can such woes relate, without a tear,
As stern Ulysses must have wept to hear?

LOOKING over the old manuscripts wherein the private actions of Pharamond are set down by way of table-book, I found many things which gave me great delight; and as human life turns upon the same principles and passions in all ages, I thought it very proper to take minutes of what passed in that age, for the instruction of this. The antiquary who lent me these papers, gave me a character of Eucrate, the favourite of Pharamond, extracted from an author who lived in that court. The account he gives both of the prince and this his faithful friend, will not be improper to insert here, because I may have occasion to mention many of their conversations, into which these memorials of them may give light.

" Pharamond, when he had a mind to retire for an hour or two from the hurry of business and fatigue of ceremony, made a signal to Eucrate, by putting his hand to his face, placing his arm negligently on a window, or some such action as appeared indifferent to all the rest of the company. Upon such notice, unobserved by others, (for their entire intimacy was always a secret) Eucrate repaired to his own apartment to receive the king. There was a secret access to this part of the court, at which Eucrate used to admit many whose mean appearance in the eyes of the ordinary waiters and door keepers made them be repulsed from other parts of the palace. Such as these were let in here by the order of Eucrate, and had audiences of Pharamond. This entrance Pharamond called " The Gate of the Unhappy;" and the tears of the afflicted who came before him, he would say, were bribes received by Eucrate; for Eucrate had the most compassionate spirit of all men living, except his generous master, who was always kindled at the least affliction which was communicated to him. In the regard for the miserable, Eucrate took particular care, that the common forms of distress, and the idle pretenders to sorrow, about courts, who wanted only supplies to luxury, should never obtain favour by his means: but the distresses which arise from the many inexplicable occurrences that happen among men, the unaccountable alienation of parents from their children, cruelty of husbands to their wives, poverty occasioned from shipwreck or fire, the falling out of friends, or such other terrible disasters, to which the life of man is exposed; in cases of this nature, Eucrate was the patron; and enjoyed this part of the royal favour so much without being envied, that it was never inquired into by whose means, what no one else cared for doing, was brought about.

'One evening when Pharamond came into the apartment of Eucrate, he found him extremely dejected; upon which he asked (with a smile which was natural to him) " What, is there any one too miserable to be relieved by Pharamond, that Eucrate is melancholy? I fear there is, answered the favourite: a person without, of a good air, well dressed, and though a man in the strength of his life, seems to faint under some inconsolable calamity: all his features seem suffused with agony of mind; but I can observe in him, that it is more inclined to break away in tears than rage. I asked him what he would have? he said he would speak to Pharamond. I desired his business, he could hardly say to me, "Eucrate, carry me to the king, my story is not to be told twice; I fear I shall not be able to speak it at all." Pharamond commanded Eucrate to let him enter; he did so, and the gentleman approached the king with an air which spoke him under the greatest concern in what manner to demean himself. The king, who had a quick discerning, relieved him from the oppression he was under; and with the most beautiful complacency said to him, " Sir, do not add, to that load of sorrow I see in your countenance, the awe of my presence: think you are speaking to your friend· if the circumstances of your distress will admit of it, you shall find me so." To whom the stranger: " Oh excellent Pharamond, name not a friend to the unfortunate Spinamont. I had one, but he is dead by my own hand; but, oh Pharamond, though it was by the hand of Spinamont, it was by the guilt of Pharamond. I come not, oh excellent prince, to implore your pardon; I come to relate my sorrow, a sorrow too great for human life to support: from henceforth shall all occurrences appear dreams or short intervals of amusement, from this one affliction, which has seized my very being: pardon me, oh Pharamond! if my griefs give me leave, that I lay before you, in the anguish of a wounded mind, that you, good as you are, are guilty of the generous blood spilt this day by this unhappy hand: oh that it had perished before that instant!" ' Here the stranger paused, and recollecting his mind, after some little meditation, he went on in a calmer tone and gesture as follows:

" There is an authority due to distress, and as none of the human race is above the reach of sorrow, none should be above the hearing the voice of it, I am sure Pharamond is not. Know then, that I have this morning unfortunately killed, in a duel, the man whom of all men living I most loved. I command myself too much in your royal presence, to say, Pharamond, give me my friend! Pharamond has taken him from me! I will not say, shall the merciful Pharamond destroy his own subjects? Will the father of his country murder his people? But the merciful Pharamond does destroy his subjects, the father of his country does murder his people! Fortune is so much the pursuit of mankind, that all glory and honour is in the power of a prince, because he has the distribution of their fortunes. It is therefore the inadvertency, negligence, or guilt of princes, to let any thing grow into custom which is against their laws. A court can make fashion and duty walk together; it can never, without the guilt of a court, happen, that it shall not be unfashionable to do what is unlawful. But, alas! in the dominions of Pharamond, by the force of a tyrant custom, which is mis-named a point of honour, the duellist kills his friend whom he loves, and the judge condemns the duellist, while he approves his behaviour. Shame is the greatest of all evils; what avail laws, when death only attends the breach of them, and shame obedience to them? As for me, oh Pharamond, were it possible to describe the nameless kinds of compunctions and tendernesses I feel, when I reflect upon the little accidents in our former familiarity, my mind swells into sorrow which cannot be resisted enough to be silent in the presence of Pharamond!" With that he fell into a flood of tears, and wept aloud. "Why should not Pharamond hear the anguish he only can relieve others from in time to come? Let him hear from me, what they feel who have given death by the false mercy of his administration, and form to himself the vengeance called for by those who have perished by his negligence." R.

No. LXXXV. THURSDAY, JUNE 7.

Interdum specrosa locis, morataque recte
Fabula, nullius veneris, sine pondere et arte,
Valdius oblectat populum, meliusque moratur,
Quam versus inopes rerum, nugæque canoræ
       HORACE.

Sometimes in rough and undigested plays,
We meet with such a lucky character,
As, being humour'd right, and well pursu'd,
Succeeds much better than the shallow verse,
And chiming trifles of more studious pens
       ROSCOMMON.

IT is the custom of the Mahometans, if they see any printed or written paper upon the ground, to take it up and lay it aside carefully, as not knowing but it may contain some piece of their Alcoran. I must confess I have so much of the Mussulman in me, that I cannot forbear looking into every printed paper which comes in my way, under whatsoever despicable circumstances it may appear; for as no mortal author, in the ordinary fate and vicissitude of things, knows to what use his works may, some time or other be applied, a man may often meet with very celebrated names in a paper of tobacco. I have lighted my pipe more than once with the writings of a prelate; and know a friend of mine, who, for these several years, has converted the essays of a man of quality into a kind of fringe for his candlesticks. I remember, in particular, after having read over a poem of an eminent author on a victory, I met with several fragments of it upon the next rejoicing day, which had been employed in squibs and crackers, and by that means celebrated its subject in a double capacity. I once met with a page of Mr. Baxter under a Christmas pye. Whether or no the pastry-cook had made use of it through chance or waggery, for the defence of that superstitious viande, I know not; but, upon the perusal of it, I conceived so good an idea of the author's piety, that I bought the whole book. I have often profited by these accidental readings, and have sometimes found very curious pieces, that are either out of print, or not to be met with in the shops of our London booksellers. For this reason, when my friends take a survey of my library, they are very much surprised to find, upon the shelf of folios, two long band-boxes standing upright among my books, until I let them see that they are both of them lined with deep erudition and abstruse literature. I might likewise mention a paper-kite, from which I have received great improvement; and a hat-case, which I would not exchange for all the beavers in Great-Britain. This my inquisitive temper, or rather impertinent humour of prying into all sorts of writing, with my natural aversion to loquacity, gives me a good deal of employment when I enter any house in the country; for I cannot for my heart leave a room, before I have thoroughly studied the walls of it, and examined the several printed papers which are usually pasted upon them. The last piece that I met with upon this occasion gave me a most exquisite pleasure. My reader will think I am not serious, when I acquaint him that the piece I am going to speak of was the old ballad of the " Two Children in the Wood," which is one of the darling songs of the common people, and has been the delight of most Englishmen in some part of their age.

This song is a plain simple copy of nature, destitute of the helps and ornaments of art. The tale of it is a pretty tragical story, and pleases for no other reason but because it is a copy of nature. There is even a despicable simplicity in the verse; and yet because the sentiments appear genuine and unaffected, they are able to move the mind of the most polite reader with inward meltings of humanity and compassion. The incidents grow out of the subject, and are such as are the most proper to excite pity, for which reason the whole narration has something in it very moving, notwithstanding the author of it (whoever he was) has delivered it in such an abject phrase and poorness of expression, that the quoting any part of it would look like a design of turning it into ridicule. But though the language is mean, the thoughts, as I have before said, from one end to the other, are natural, and therefore cannot fail to please those who are not judges of language, or those who, notwithstanding they are judges of language, have a true and unprejudiced taste of nature. The condition, speech, and behaviour of the dying parents, with the age, innocence, and distress of the children, are set forth in such tender circumstances, that it is impossible for a reader of common humanity not to be affected with them. As for the circumstance of the Robin-red-breast, it is indeed a little poetical ornament, and to shew the genius of the author, amidst all his simplicity, it is just the same kind of fiction which one of the greatest of the Latin poets has made use of upon a parallel occasion; I mean that passage in Horace, where he describes himself, when he was a child, fallen asleep in a desert wood, and covered with leaves by the turtles that took pity on him.

> Me fabulosæ Vulture in Apulo,
> Altricis extra limen Apuliæ,
>   Ludo fatigatumque somno
>   Fronde nova puerum palumbes
> Texere———   Hor.

> In lofty Vulture's rising grounds,
> Without my nurse Apulia's bounds,
> When young and tir'd with sport and play,
> And bound with pleasing sleep I lay,
> Doves cover'd me with myrtle boughs   Creech.

I have heard that the late lord Dorset, who had the greatest wit tempered with the greatest candour, and was one of the finest critics, as well as the best poets of his age, had a numerous collection of old English ballads, and took a particular pleasure in the reading of them. I can affirm the same of Mr. Dryden, and know several of the most refined writers of our present age who are of the same humour.

I might likewise refer my reader to Moliere's thoughts on this subject, as he has expressed them in the character of the Misanthrope; but those only who are endowed with a true greatness of soul and genius, can divest themselves of the little images of ridicule, and admire nature in her simplicity and nakedness. As for the little conceited wits of the age, who can only shew their judgment by finding fault, they cannot be supposed to admire these productions which have nothing to recommend them but the beauties of nature, when they do not know how to relish even those compositions that, with all the beauties of nature, have also the additional advantage of art.

No LXXXVI   FRIDAY, JUNE 8.

Heu quam difficile est crimen non prodere vultu!
                                        OVID

How in the looks does conscious guilt appear!
                                        ADDISON

THERE are several arts which all men are in some measure masters of, without having been at the pains of learning them. Every one that speaks or reasons is a grammarian and a logician, though he may be wholly unacquainted with the rules of grammar or logic, as they are delivered in books and systems. In the same manner, every one is in some degree a master of that art which is generally distinguished by the name of physiognomy; and naturally forms to himself the character or fortune of a stranger from the features and lineaments of his face. We are no sooner presented to any one we never saw before, but we are immediately struck with the idea of a proud, a reserved, an affable, or a good-natured man; and upon our first going into a company of strangers, our benevolence or aversion, awe or contempt, rises naturally towards several particular persons, before we have heard them speak a single word, or so much as know who they are.

Every passion gives a particular cast to the countenance, and is apt to discover itself in some feature or other. I have seen an eye curse for half an hour together, and an eyebrow call a man a scoundrel. Nothing is more common than for lovers to complain, resent, languish, despair, and die in dumb show. For my own part, I am so apt to frame a notion of every man's humour or circumstances by his looks, that I have sometimes employed myself from Charing-cross to the Royal Exchange in drawing the characters of those who have passed by me. When I see a man with a sour rivelled face, I cannot forbear pitying his wife; and when I meet with an open ingenuous countenance, think on the happiness of his friends, his family and relations.

I cannot recollect the author of a famous saying to a stranger who stood silent in his company, " Speak that I may see thee." But, with submission, I think we may be better known by our looks than by our words, and that a man's speech is much more easily disguised than his countenance. In this case, however, I think the air of the whole face is much more expressive than the lines of it: the truth of it is, the air is generally nothing else but the inward disposition of the mind made visible.

Those who have established physiognomy into an art, and laid down rules of judging mens' tempers by their faces, have regarded the features much more than the air. Martial has a pretty epigram on this subject:

> Crine ruber, niger ore, brevis pede, lumine læsus·
> Rem magnam præstas Zoile, si bonus es.

> Thy beard and head are of a diff'rent dye;
> Short of one foot, distorted in an eye
> With all these tokens of a knave complete,
> Should'st thou be honest, thou'rt a dev'lish cheat.

I have seen a very ingenious author on this subject, who founds his speculations on the supposition, that as a man hath in the mould of his face a remote likeness to that of an ox, a sheep, a lion, a hog, or any other creature, he hath the same resemblance in the frame of his mind, and is subject to those passions which are predominant in the creature that appears in his countenance. Accordingly he gives the prints of several faces that are of a different mould, and by a little overcharging the likeness, discovers the figures of these several kinds of brutal faces in human features. I remember in the life of the famous Prince of Condé, the writer observes, the face of that prince was like the face of an eagle, and that the prince was very well pleased to be told so. In this case, therefore, we may be sure, that he had in his mind some general implicit notion of this art of physiognomy, which I have just now mentioned; and that when his courtiers told him his face was made like an eagle's, he understood them in the same manner as if they had told him, there was something in his looks which shewed him to be strong, active, piercing, and of a royal descent. Whether or no the different motions of the animal spirits, in different passions, may have any effect on the mould of the face when the lineaments are pliable and tender, or whether the same kind of souls require the same kind of habitations, I shall leave to the consideration of the curious. In the mean time, I think nothing can be more glorious than for a man to give the lie to his face, and to be an honest, just, good-natured man, in spite of all those marks and signatures which nature seems to have set upon him for the contrary. This very often happens among those who, instead of being exasperated by their own looks, or envying the looks of others, apply themselves entirely to the cultivating of their minds, and getting those beauties which are more lasting and more ornamental. I have seen many an amiable piece of deformity, and have observed a certain cheerfulness in as bad a system of features as ever was clapped together, which hath appeared more lovely than all the blooming charms of an insolent beauty. There is a double praise due to virtue, when it is lodged in a body that seems to have been prepared for the reception of vice, in many such cases the soul and the body do not seem to be fellows.

Socrates was an extraordinary instance of this nature. There chanced to be a great physiognomist in his time at Athens, who had made strange discoveries of men's tempers and inclinations by their outward appearances. Socrates's disciples, that they might put this artist to the trial, carried him to their master, whom he had never seen before, and did not know he was then in company with him. After a short examination of his face, the physiognomist pronounced him the most lewd, libidinous, drunken old fellow that he had ever met with in his whole life. Upon which the disciples all burst out a-laughing, as thinking they had detected the falsehood and vanity of his art. But Socrates told them, that the principles of his art might be very true, notwithstanding his present mistake; for that he himself was naturally inclined to those particular vices which the physiognomist had discovered in his countenance, but that he had conquered the strong dispositions he was born with by the dictates of philosophy.

We are indeed told by an ancient author, that Socrates very much resembled Silenus in his face, which we find to have been very rightly observed from the statues and busts of both that are still extant; as well as on several antique seals and precious stones, which are frequently enough to be met with in the cabinets of the curious. But however observations of this nature may sometimes hold, a wise man should be particularly cautious how he gives credit to a man's outward appearance. It is an irreparable injustice we are guilty of towards one another, when we are prejudiced by the looks and features of those whom we do not know. How often do we conceive hatred against a person of worth, or fancy a man to be proud or ill natured by his aspect, whom we think we cannot esteem too much when we are acquainted with his real character? Dr. Moore, in his admirable System of Ethics, reckons this particular inclination to take a prejudice against a man for his looks among the smaller vices in morality, and, if I remember, gives it the name of a Prosopolepsia. L.

No. LXXXVII. SATURDAY, JUNE 9.

.........Nimiùm ne crede colori. VIRGIL.

Trust not too much to an enchanting face.
                                    DRYDEN.

It has been the purpose of several of my speculations to bring people to an unconcerned behaviour, with relation to their persons, whether beautiful or defective. As the secrets of the Ugly Club were exposed to the public, that men might see there were some noble spirits in the age, who were not at all displeased with themselves upon considerations which they had no choice in; so the discourse concerning idols tended to lessen the value people put upon themselves from personal advantages and gifts of nature. As to the latter species of mankind, the beauties, whether male or female, they are generally the most untractable people of all others. You are so excessively perplexed with the particularities in their behaviour, that to be at ease, one would be apt to wish there were no such creatures. They expect so great allowances, and give so little to others, that they who have to do with them find in the main, a man with a better person than ordinary, and a beautiful woman, might be very happily changed for such to whom nature has been less liberal. The handsome fellow is usually so much a gentleman, and the fine woman hath something so becoming, that there is no enduring either of them. It has therefore been generally my choice to mix with cheerful ugly creatures, rather than gentlemen who are graceful enough to omit or do what they please, or beauties who have charms enough to do and say what would be disobliging in any but themselves.

Diffidence and presumption upon account of our persons are equally faults, and both arise from the want of knowing, or rather endeavouring to know ourselves, and for what we ought to be valued or neglected. But indeed, I did not imagine these little considerations and coquetries could have the ill consequence as I find they have by the following letters of my correspondents, where it seems beauty is thrown into the account, in matters of sale, to those who receive no favour from the charmers.

'June 4.

'Mr Spectator,

'After I have assured you I am in every respect one of the handsomest young girls about town—I need be particular in nothing but the make of my face, which has the misfortune to be exactly oval. This I take to proceed from a temper that naturally inclines me both to speak and to hear.

'With this account you may wonder how I can have the vanity to offer myself as a candidate, which I now do, to a society, where the Spectator and Hecatissa have been admitted with so much applause. I do not want to be put in mind how very defective I am in every thing that is ugly: I am too sensible of my own unworthiness in this particular, and therefore I only propose myself as a foil to the Club.

'You see how honest I have been to confess all my imperfections, which is a great deal to come from a woman, and what I hope you will encourage with the favour of your interest.

'There can be no objection made on the side of the matchless Hecatissa, since it is certain I shall be in no danger of giving her the least occasion of jealousy, and then a joint-stool in the very lowest place at the table is all the honour that is coveted by

'Your most humble
'and obedient servant,
'ROSALINDA!'

'P. S. I have sacrificed my necklace to put into the public lottery against the common enemy. And last Saturday, about three o'clock in the afternoon, I began to patch indifferently on both sides of my face.'

'LONDON, JUNE 7, 1711.

'MR. SPECTATOR,

'UPON reading your late dissertation concerning idols, I cannot but complain to you that there are, in six or seven places of this city, coffee-houses kept by persons of that sisterhood. These idols sit and receive all day long the adoration of the youth within such and such districts. I know in particular, goods are not entered as they ought to be at the custom-house, nor law-reports perused at the Temple, by reason of one beauty who detains the young merchants too long near 'Change, and another fair one who keeps the students at her house when they should be at study. It would be worth your while to see how the idolaters alternately offer incense to their idols, and what heart burnings arise in those who wait for their turn to receive kind aspects from those little thrones, which all the company, but these lovers, call the bars. I saw a gentleman turn as pale as ashes, because an idol turned the sugar into a tea-dish for his rival, and carelessly called the boy to serve him, with a "Sirrah! Why don't you give the gentleman the box to please himself?" Certain it is, that a very hopeful young man was taken with leads in his pockets, below bridge, where he intended to drown himself, because his idol would wash the dish in which she had but just drank tea, before she would let him use it.

'I am, Sir, a person past being amorous, and do not give this information out of envy or jealousy, but I am a real sufferer by it. These lovers take any thing for tea and coffee; I saw one yesterday surfeit to make his court; and all his rivals, at the same time loud in the commendation of liquors that went against every body in the room that was not in love. While these young fellows resign their stomachs with their hearts, and drink at the idol in this manner, we who come to do business, or talk politics, are utterly poisoned. They have also drams for those who are more enamoured than ordinary; and it is very common for such as are too low in constitution to ogle the idol upon the strength of tea, to fluster themselves with warmer liquors, thus all pretenders advance, as fast as they can, to a fever or a diabetes. I must repeat to you, that I do not look with an evil eye upon the profit of the idols, or the diversions of the lovers; what I hope from this remonstrance is, only, that we plain people may not be served as if we were idolaters; but that from the time of publishing this in your paper, the idols would mix ratsbane only for their admirers, and take more care of us who do not love them.

'I am Sir,
'Your's,

R.
'T. T.'

No. LXXXVIII. MONDAY, JUNE 11.

Quid domini faciant, audent cum talia fures?
VIRGIL.

What will not masters do, when servants thus presume?

MAY 30, 1711.

'MR SPECTATOR,

'I HAVE no small value for your endeavours to lay before the world what may escape their observation, and yet highly conduces to their service. You have, I think, succeeded very well on many subjects, and seem to have been conversant in very different scenes of life. But in the considerations of mankind, as a Spectator, you should not omit circumstances which relate to the inferior part of the world, any more than those which concern the greater. There is one thing in particular which I wonder you have not touched upon, and that is, the general corruption of manners in the servants of Great-Britain. I am a man that has travelled and seen many nations, but have for seven years last past resided constantly in London, or within twenty miles of it. In this time I have contracted a numerous acquaintance among the best sort of people, and have hardly found one of them happy in their servants. This is matter of great astonishment to foreigners, and all such as have visited foreign countries, especially since we cannot but observe, that there is no part of the world where servants have those privileges and advantages as in England; they have no where else such plentiful diet, large wages, or indulgent liberty: There is no place wherein they labour less, and yet where they are so little respectful, more wasteful, more negligent, or where they so frequently change their masters. To this I attribute, in a great measure, the frequent robberies and losses which we suffer on the high road and in our own houses. That, indeed, which gives me the present thought of this kind, is, that a careless groom of mine has spoiled me the prettiest pad in the world with only riding him ten miles; and I assure you, if I were to make a register of all the horses I have known thus abused by negligence of servants, the number would mount a regiment. I wish you would give us your observations, that we may know how to treat these rogues, or that we masters may enter into measures to reform them. Pray give us a speculation in general about servants, and you make me

'Your's,

'Philo-Britannicus.'

'P. S. Pray do not omit the mention of grooms in particular.'

This honest gentleman who is so desirous that I should write a satire upon grooms, has a great deal of reason for his resentment; and I know no evil which touches all mankind so much as this of the misbehaviour of servants.

The complaint of this letter runs wholly upon men servants; and I can attribute the licentiousness which has at present prevailed among them, to nothing but what a hundred before me have ascribed it to, the custom of giving board wages. This one instance of false economy is sufficient to debauch the whole nation of servants, and makes them as it were but for some part of their time in that quality. They are either attending in places where they meet and run into clubs, or else, if they wait at taverns, they eat after their masters, and reserve their wages for other occasions. From hence it arises, that they are but in a lower degree what their masters themselves are; and usually affect an imitation of their manners: and you have in liveries, beaux, fops, and coxcombs, in as high perfection as among people that keep equipages. It is a common humour among the retinue of people of quality, when they are in their revels, that is, when they are out of their master's sight, to assume in a humorous way the names and titles of those whose liveries they wear. By which means characters and distinctions become so familiar to them, that it is to this among other causes, one may impute a certain insolence among our servants, that they take no notice of any gentleman, though they know him ever so well, except he is an acquaintance of their master's.

My obscurity and taciturnity leave me at liberty, without scandal, to dine, if I think fit, at a common ordinary, in the meanest as well as the most sumptuous house of entertainment. Falling in the other day at a victualling-house near the House of Peers, I heard the maid come down and tell the landlady at the bar, that my Lord Bishop swore he would throw her out at the window, if she did not bring up more mild beer, and that my Lord Duke would have a double mug of purl. My surprise was increased, in hearing loud and rustic voices speak and answer to each other upon the public affairs, by the names of the most illustrious of our nobility, until of a sudden one came running in, and cried the house was rising. Down came all the company together, and away! the alehouse was immediately filled with clamour, and scoring one mug to the Marquis of such a place, oil and vinegar to such an Earl, three quarts to my new Lord for wetting his title, and so forth. It is a thing too notorious to mention the crowds of servants, and their insolence, near the courts of justice, and the stairs towards the supreme assembly, where there is an universal mockery of all order, such riotous clamour and licentious confusion, that one would think the whole nation lived in jest, and there were no such things as rule and distinction among us.

The next place of resort, wherein the servile world are let loose, is at the entrance of Hyde-Park, while the gentry are at the ring. Hither people bring their lacquies out of state, and here it is that all they say at their tables, and act in their houses, is communicated to the whole town. There are men of wit in all conditions of life; and mixing with these people at their diversions, I have heard coquettes and prudes as well rallied, and insolence and pride exposed (allowing for their want of education), with as much humour and good sense as in the politest companies. It is a general observation, that all dependants run in some measure into the manners and behaviour of those whom they serve: you shall frequently meet with lovers and men of intrigue among the lacquies, as well as at White's, or in the side-boxes. I remember some years ago an instance of this kind. A footman to a captain of the guards used frequently, when his master was out of the way, to carry on amours and make assignations in his master's clothes. The fellow had a very good person, and there are very many women that think no further than the outside of a gentleman: besides which, he was almost as learned a man as the colonel himself: I say, thus qualified, the fellow could scrawl billet-doux so well, and furnish a conversation on the common topics, that he had, as they call it, a great deal of good business on his hands. It happened one day that coming down a tavern stairs in his master's fine guard-coat, with a well-dressed woman masked, he met the colonel coming up with other company: but with a ready assurance he quitted his lady, came up to him, and said, " Sir, I know you have too much respect for yourself to cane me in this honourable habit: but you see there is a lady in the case, and I hope on that score also you will put off your anger till I have told you all another time." After a little pause the colonel cleared up his countenance, and with an air of familiarity whispered his man apart, " Sirrah, bring the lady with you to ask pardon for you," then aloud, " Look to it, Will, I'll never forgive you else." The fellow went back to his mistress, and telling her with a loud voice and an oath, " that was the honestest fellow in the world," conveyed her to a hackney coach.

But the many irregularities committed by servants in the places above-mentioned, as well as in the theatres, of which masters are generally the occasions, are too various not to need being resumed on another occasion. R.

No. LXXXIX. TUESDAY, JUNE 12.

Petite hinc, juvenesque senesque,
Finem animo certum, miserisque viatica canis
Cras hoc fiet. Idem cras fiet. Quid? quasi magnum,
Nempe diem donas? sed cum lux altera venit,
Jam cras hesternum consumpsimus; ecce aliud cras
Egerit hos annos, et semper paulum erit ultra
Nam quamvis prope te, quamvis temone sub uno;
Vertentem sese frustra sectabere canthum.
PERS.

Pers. From thee both old and young, with profit, learn
The bounds of good and evil to discern.
Corn. Unhappy he who does this work adjourn,
And to to-morrow would the search delay
His lazy morrow will be like to-day.
Pers. But is one day of ease too much to borrow?
Corn. Yes sure: for yesterday was once to-morrow,
That yesterday is gone, and nothing gain'd,
And all thy fruitless days will thus be drain'd;
For thou hast more to-morrows yet to ask,
And wilt be ever to begin thy task;
Who, like the hindmost chariot-wheels, art curst,
Still to be near, but ne'er to reach the first.

As my correspondents upon the subject of love are very numerous, it is my design, if possible, to range them under several heads, and address myself to them at different times. The first branch of them, to whose service I shall dedicate this paper, are those that have to do with women of dilatory tempers, who are for spinning out the time of courtship to an immoderate length, without being able either to close with their lovers, or to dismiss them. I have many letters by me filled with complaints against this sort of women. In one of them no less a man than a brother of the coif tells me, that he began his suit *vicesimo nono Caro-*

li secundi, before he had been a twelvemonth at the Temple, that he prosecuted it for many years after he was called to the bar, that at present he is a serjeant at law, and notwithstanding he hoped that matters would have been long since brought to an issue, the fair one still demurs. I am so well pleased with this gentleman's phrase, that I shall distinguish this sect of women by the title of " Demurrers." I find by another letter from one who calls himself Thyrsis, that his mistress has been demurring above these seven years. But among all my plaintiffs of this nature, I most pity the unfortunate Philander, a man of a constant passion and plentiful fortune, who sets forth that the timorous and irresolute Sylvia has demurred till she is past child-bearing. Strephon appears by his letter to be a very choleric lover, and irrevocably smitten with one that demurs out of self-interest. He tells me with great passion that she has bubbled him out of his youth, that she drilled him on to five and fifty, and that he verily believes she will drop him in his old age, if she can find her account in another. I shall conclude this narrative with a letter from honest Sam Hopewell, a very pleasant fellow, who it seems has at last married a demurrer; I must only premise, that Sam, who is a very good bottle-companion, has been the diversion of his friends upon account of his passion ever since the year one thousand six hundred and eighty-one.

' DEAR SIR,

' You know very well my passion for Mrs Martha, and what a dance she has led me, she took me out at the age of two-and-twenty, and dodged with me above thirty years. I have loved her till she has grown as grey as a cat, and am with much ado become the master of her person, such as it is at present. She is however, in my eye, a very charming old woman. We often lament that we did not marry sooner, but she has nobody to blame for it but herself. You know very well that she would never think of me while she had a tooth in her head. I have put the date of my passion " Anno amoris trigesimo primo" instead of a posy on my wedding-ring. I expect you should send me a congratulatory letter, or, if you please, an epithalamium upon this occasion.

'Mrs. Martha's and your's eternally,
'SAM HOPEWELL.'

In order to banish an evil out of the world, that does not only produce great uneasiness to private persons, but has also a very bad influence on the public, I shall endeavour to show the folly of demurrage, from two or three reflections, which I earnestly recommend to the thoughts of my fair readers.

First of all, I would have them seriously think on the shortness of their time. Life is not long enough for a coquette to play all her tricks in. A timorous woman drops into her grave before she has done deliberating. Were the age of man the same that it was before the flood, a lady might sacrifice half a century to a scruple, and be two or three ages in demurring. Had she nine hundred years good, she might hold out to the conversion of the Jews before she thought fit to be prevailed upon. But, alas! she ought to play her part in haste, when she considers that she is suddenly to quit the stage, and make room for others.

In the second place, I would desire my female readers to consider, that as the term of life is short, that of beauty is much shorter. The finest skin wrinkles in a few years, and loses the strength of its colouring so soon, that we have scarce time to admire it. I might embellish this subject with roses and rainbows, and several other ingenious conceits, which I may possibly reserve for another opportunity.

There is a third consideration which I would likewise recommend to a demurrer, and that is, the great danger of her falling in love when she is about threescore, if she cannot satisfy her doubts and scruples before that time. There is a kind of latter spring that sometimes gets into the blood of an old woman, and turns her into a very odd sort of an animal. I would therefore have the demurrer consider what a strange figure she will make, if she chances to get over all difficulties, and comes to a final resolution in that unseasonable part of her life.

I would not however be understood, by any thing I have here said, to discourage that natural modesty in the sex, which renders a retreat from the first approaches of a lover both fashionable and graceful: all that I intend is, to advise them, when they are prompted by reason and inclination, to demur only out of form, and so far as decency requires. A virtuous woman should reject the first offer of marriage, as a good man does that of a bishopric; but I would advise neither the one nor the other to persist in refusing what they secretly approve. I would in this particular propose the example of Eve to all her daughters, as Milton has represented her in the following passage, which I cannot forbear transcribing entire, though only the twelve last lines are to my present purpose.

"The rib he form'd and fashion'd with his hands;
Under his forming hands a creature grew,
Man-like, but diff'rent sex so lovely fair!
That what seem'd fair in all the world seem'd now
Mean, or in her summ'd up, in her contain'd,
And in her looks, which from that time infus'd
Sweetness into my heart, unfelt before
And in all things from her air inspir'd
The spirit of love and amorous delight.
"She disappear'd, and left me dark! I wak'd
To find her, or for ever to deplore
Her loss, and other pleasures all abjure.
When out of hope, behold her! not far off,
Such as I saw her in my dream, adorn'd

With what all earth or heav'n could bestow
To make her amiable. On she came,
Led by her heavenly Maker, though unseen,
And guided by his voice, nor uninform'd
Of nuptial sanctity, and marriage rites;
Grace was in all her steps, heav'n in her eye,
In every gesture, dignity and love!
I, overjoy'd, could not forbear aloud—
" This turn hath made amends; thou hast fulfill'd
Thy words, Creator bounteous and benign!
Giver of all things fair! but fairest this
Of all thy gifts, nor enviest. I now see
Bone of my bone, flesh of my flesh, myself.
" She heard me thus, and though divinely brought,
Yet innocence, and virgin modesty,
Her virtue, and the conscience of her worth,
That would be woo'd, and not unsought be won,
Not obvious, not obtrusive, but retir'd
The more desirable: or to say all,
Nature herself, though pure of sinful thought,
Wrought in her so, that seeing me she turn'd;
I follow'd her, she what was honour knew,
And with obsequious majesty approv'd
My pleaded reason. To the nuptial bow'r
I led her blushing like the morn"— L.

No XC. WEDNESDAY, JUNE 13.

— Magnus sine viribus ignis
Incassum furit . . VIRG.

In vain he burns, like hasty stubble fires. DRYDEN

THERE is not in my opinion, a consideration more effectual to extinguish inordinate desires in the soul of man, than the notions of Plato and his followers upon that subject. They tell us, that every passion which has been contracted by the soul during her residence in the body, remains with her in a separate state; and that the soul in the body, or out of the body, differs no more than the man does from himself when he is in his house, or in open air. When therefore the obscene passions in particular have once taken root, and spread themselves in the soul, they cleave to her inseparably, and remain in her for ever, after the body is cast off and thrown aside. As an argument to confirm this their doctrine, they observe, that a lewd youth who goes on in a continued course of voluptuousness, advances by degrees into a libidinous old man; and that the passion survives in the mind when it is altogether dead in the body; nay, that the desire grows more violent, and (like all other habits) gathers strength by age, at the same time that it has no power of executing its own purposes. If, say they, the soul is the most subject to these passions at a time when it has the least instigations from the body, we may well suppose she will still retain them when she is entirely divested of it. The very substance of the soul is festered with them, the gangrene is gone too far to be ever cured; the inflammation will rage to all eternity.

In this, therefore (say the Platonists), consists the punishment of a voluptuous man after death: he is tormented with desires which it is impossible for him to gratify, solicited by a passion that has neither objects nor organs adapted to it: he lives in a state of invincible desire and impotence, and always burns in the pursuit of what he always despairs to possess. It is for this reason (says Plato) that the souls of the dead appear frequently in cemeteries, and hover about the places where their bodies are buried, as still hankering after their old brutal pleasures, and desiring again to enter the body that gave them an opportunity of fulfilling them.

Some of our most eminent divines have made use of this Platonic notion, so far as it regards the substance of our passions after death, with great beauty and strength of reason. Plato indeed carries the thought very far, when he grafts upon it his opinion of ghosts appearing in places of burial. Though I must confess if one did believe that the departed souls of men and women wandered up and down in these lower regions, and entertained themselves with the sight of their species, one could not devise a more proper hell for an impure spirit than that which Plato has touched upon.

The ancients seem to have drawn such a state of torments in the description of Tantalus, who was punished with the rage of an eternal thirst, and set up to the chin in water that fled from his lips whenever he attempted to drink it.

Virgil, who has cast the whole system of Platonic philosophy, so far as it relates to the soul of man, into beautiful allegories, in the sixth book of his Æneid gives us the punishment of a voluptuary after death, not unlike that which we are here speaking of.

> Lucent genialibus altis
> Aurea fulcra toris, epulæque ante ora paratæ
> Regifico luxu. Furiarum maxima juxta
> Accubat, et manibus prohibet contingere mensas;
> Exurgitque facem attollens, atque intonat ore.
> VIRG.

> They lie below on golden beds display'd,
> And genial feasts with regal pomp are made:
> The queen of furies by their side is set,
> And snatches from their mouths th' untasted meat,
> Which if they touch, her hissing snakes she rears,
> Tossing her torch, and thund'ring in their ears.
> DRYDEN.

That I may a little alleviate the severity of this my speculation (which otherwise may lose me several of my polite readers), I shall translate a story that has been quoted upon another occasion by one of the most learned men of the present age, as I find it in the original. The reader will see it is not foreign to my present subject, and I dare say will think it a lively representation of a person lying under the torments of such a kind of Tantalism or Platonic hell, as that which we have now under consideration. Monsieur Pontignan, speaking of a love adventure that happened to him in the country, gives the following account of it.

"When I was in the country last summer, I was often in company with a couple of charming women, who had all the wit and beauty one could desire in female companions, with a dash of coquetry, that, from time to time gave me a great many agreeable torments. I was, after my way, in love with both of them, and had such frequent opportunities of pleading my passion to them when they were asunder, that I had reason to hope for particular favours from each of them. As I was walking one evening in my chamber with nothing about me but my night-gown, they both came into my room, and told me they had a very pleasant trick to put upon a gentleman that was in the same house, provided I would bear a part in it. Upon this they told me such a plausible story, that I laughed at their contrivance, and agreed to do whatever they should require of me. They immediately began to swaddle me up in my night-gown with long pieces of linen, which they folded about me till they had wrapped me in above an hundred yards of swathe: my arms were pressed to my sides, and my legs closed together by so many wrappers, one over another, that I looked like an Egyptian mummy. As I stood bolt-upright upon one end in this antique figure, one of the ladies burst out a-laughing. "And now, Pontignan," says she, "we intend to perform the promise that we find you have extorted from each of us. You have often asked the favour of us, and I dare say you are a better bred cavalier than to refuse to go to bed to two ladies that desire it of you." After having stood a fit of laughter, I begged them to uncase me, and do with me what they pleased. "No, no," said they, "we like you very well as you are;" and upon that ordered me to be carried to one of their houses, and put to bed in all my swaddles. The room was lighted up on all sides, and I was laid very decently between a pair of sheets, with my head (which was indeed the only part I could move) upon a very high pillow; this was no sooner done, but my two female friends came into bed to me in their finest night-clothes. You may easily guess at the condition of a man that saw a couple of the most beautiful women in the world undressed and in bed with him, without being able to stir hand or foot. I begged them to release me, and struggled all I could to get loose, which I did with so much violence, that about midnight they both leaped out of the bed, crying out they were undone. But seeing me safe, they took their posts again, and renewed their raillery. Finding all my prayers and endeavours were lost, I composed myself as well as I could; and told them, that if they would not unbind me, I would fall asleep between them, and by that means disgrace them for ever: but, alas! this was impossible; could I have been disposed to it, they would have prevented me by several little ill-natured caresses and endearments which they bestowed upon me. As much devoted as I am to womankind, I would not pass such another night, to be master of the whole sex. My reader will doubtless be curious to know what became of me the next morning. Why truly my bed-fellows left me about an hour before day, and told me, if I would be good and lie still, they would send some body to take me up as soon as it was time for me to rise; accordingly, about nine o'clock in the morning, an old woman came to unswathe me. I bore all this very patiently, being resolved to take my revenge of my tormentors, and to keep no measures with them as soon as I was at liberty; but upon asking my old woman what was become of the two ladies, she told me she believed they were by that time within sight of Paris, for that they went away in a coach-and-six before five o'clock in the morning.' L.

No. XCI. THURSDAY, JUNE 14.

In furias ignemque ruunt, amor omnibus idem
                                VIRG.

... They rush into the flame,
For love is lord of all, and is in all the same
                                DRYDEN.

Though the subject I am now going upon would be much more properly the foundation of a comedy, I cannot forbear inserting the circumstances which pleased me in the account a young lady gave me of the loves of a family in town, which shall be nameless; or rather, for the better sound and elevation of the history, instead of Mr. and Mrs. such-a-one, I shall call them by feigned names. Without further preface, you are to know that within the liberties of the city of Westminster lives the lady Honoria, a widow about the age of forty, of a healthy constitution, gay temper, and elegant person. She dresses a little too much like a girl, affects a childish fondness in the tone of her voice, sometimes a pretty sullenness in the leaning of her head, and now and then a downcast of her eyes on her fan; neither her imagination nor her health would ever give her to know that she is turned of twenty; but that in the midst of these pretty softnesses, and airs of delicacy and attraction, she has a tall daughter within a fortnight of fifteen, who impertinently comes into the room, and towers so much towards woman, that her mother is always checked by her presence, and every charm of Honoria droops at the entrance of Flavia. The agreeable Flavia would be what she is not, as well as her mother Honoria; but all their beholders are more partial to an affectation of what a person is growing up to, than of what has been already enjoyed, and is gone for ever. It is therefore allowed to Flavia to look forward, but not to Honoria to look back. Flavia is no way dependent on her mother with relation to her fortune, for which reason they live almost upon an equality in conversation: and as Honoria has given Flavia to understand, that it is illbred to be always calling mother, Flavia is as well pleased never to be called child. It happens by this means, that these ladies are generally rivals in all places where they appear, and the words mother and daughter never pass between them but out of spite. Flavia one night at a play, observing Honoria draw the eye of several in the pit, called to a lady who sat by her, and bid her ask her mother to lend her her snuff-box for one moment. Another time, when a lover of Honoria was on his knees, beseeching the favour to kiss her hand, Flavia, rushing into the room, kneeled down by him and asked her blessing. Several of these contradictory acts of duty have raised between them such a coldness, that they generally converse, when they are in mixed company, by way of talking at one another, and not to one another. Honoria is ever complaining of a certain sufficiency in the young women of this age, who assume to themselves an authority of carrying all things before them, as if they were possessors of the esteem of mankind, and all who were but a year before them in the world were neglected or deceased. Flavia, upon such a provocation, is sure to observe, that there are people who can resign nothing, and know not how to give up what they know they cannot hold; that there are those who will not allow youth their follies, not because they are themselves past them, but because they love to continue in them. These beauties rival each other on all occasions, not that they have always had the same lovers, but each has kept up a vanity to shew the other the charms of her lover. Dick Crastin and Tom Tulip, among many others, have of late been pretenders to this family: Dick to Honoria, Tom to Flavia. Dick is the only surviving beau of the last age, and Tom almost the only one that keeps up that order of men in this.

I wish I could repeat the little circumstances of a conversation of the four lovers, with the spirit in which the young lady I had my account from represented it at a visit where I had the honour to be present; but it seems Dick Crastin the admirer of Honoria, and Tom Tulip the pretender to Flavia, were purposely admitted together by the ladies, that each might shew the other that her lover had the superiority in the accomplishments of that sort of creature whom the sillier part of women call a fine gentleman. As this age has a much more gross taste in courtship, as well as in every thing else, than the last had, these gentlemen are instances of it in their different manner of application. Tulip is ever making allusions to the vigour of his person, the sinewy force of his make; while Crastin professes a wary observation of the turns of his mistress's mind. Tulip gives himself the air of a resistless ravisher, Crastin practises that of a skilful lover. Poetry is the inseparable property of every man in love; and as men of wit write verses on those occasions, the rest of the world repeat the verses of others. These servants of the ladies were used to imitate their manner of conversation, and allude to one another, rather than interchange discourse in what they said when they met. Tulip the other day seized his mistress's hand, and repeated out of Ovid's "Art of Love,"

> " 'Tis I can in soft battles pass the night,
> Yet rise next morning vigorous for the fight,
> Fresh as the day, and active as the light."

Upon hearing this, Crastin, with an air of defiance, played Honoria's fan, and repeated,

> " Sedley has that prevailing gentle art,
> That can, with a resistless charm impart
> The loosest wishes to the chastest heart;

Raise such a conflict, kindle such a fire,
Between declining virtue, and desire,
Till the poor vanquish'd maid dissolves away
In dreams all night, in sighs and tears all day."

When Crastin had uttered these verses, with a tenderness which at once spoke passion and respect, Honoria cast a triumphant glance at Flavia, as exulting in the elegance of Crastin's courtship, and upbraiding her with the homeliness of Tulip's. Tulip understood the reproach, and in return began to applaud the wisdom of old amorous gentlemen, who turned their mistress's imagination as far as possible from what they had long themselves forgot, and ended his discourse with a sly commendation of the doctrine of platonic love: at the same time he ran over, with a laughing eye, Crastin's thin legs, meagre looks, and spare body. The old gentleman immediately left the room with some disorder, and the conversation fell upon untimely passion, after love, and unseasonable youth. Tulip sung, danced, moved before the glass, led his mistress half a minuet, hummed

"Celia the fair, in the bloom of fifteen"

when there came a servant with a letter to him, which was as follows:

'SIR,

'I UNDERSTAND very well what you meant by your mention of platonic love. I shall be glad to meet you immediately in Hyde-park, or behind Montague-house, or attend you to Barn-elms, or any other fashionable place that is fit for a gentleman to die in, that you shall appoint for, Sir,

'Your most humble servant,
'RICHARD CRASTIN.'

Tulip's colour changed at the reading of this epistle; for which reason his mistress snatched it to read the contents. While she was doing so, Tulip went away, and the ladies now agreeing in a common calamity, bewailed together the dangers of their lovers. They immediately dressed to go out, and took hackneys to prevent mischief; but, after alarming all parts of the town, Crastin was found by his widow in his pumps at Hyde-park, which appointment Tulip never kept, but made his escape into the country. Flavia tears her hair for his inglorious safety, curses and despises her charmer, is fallen in love with Crastin: which is the first part of the history of the Rival Mother

R.

No. XCII. FRIDAY, JUNE 15.

...... Convivæ propè dissentire videntur,
Proscentes vario multùm diversa palato;
Quid dem? Quid non dem? ....
HORACE.

IMITATED.

..... What would you have me do,
When out of twenty I can please not two?
One likes the pheasant's wing, and one the leg,
The vulgar boil, the learned roast an egg
Hard task to hit the palate of such guests.
POPE.

Looking over the late packets of letters which have been sent to me, I found the following one.

'Mr. Spectator,

'Your paper is a part of my tea-equipage; and my servant knows my humour so well, that calling for my breakfast this morning (it being past my usual hour,) she answered, the Spectator was not yet come in, but that the tea-kettle boiled, and she expected it every moment. Having thus in part signified to you the esteem and veneration which I have for you, I must put you in mind of the catalogue of books which you have promised to recommend to our sex: for I have deferred furnishing my closet with authors, till I receive your advice in this particular, being your daily disciple and humble servant.

'LEONORA.'

In answer to my fair disciple, whom I am very proud of, I must acquaint her, and the rest of my readers, that since I have called out for help in my catalogue of a lady's library, I have received many letters upon that head, some of which I shall give an account of.

In the first class I shall take notice of those which come to me from eminent booksellers, who every one of them mention with respect the authors they have printed, and consequently have an eye to their own advantage more than to that of the ladies. One tells me, that he thinks it absolutely necessary for women to have true notions of right and equity, and that therefore they cannot peruse a better book than 'Dalton's Country Justice:' another thinks they cannot be without " the Complete Jockey." A third observing the curiosity and desire of prying into secrets, which he tells me is natural to the fair sex, is of opinion this female inclination, if well directed, might turn very much to their advantage, and therefore recommends to me, " Mr. Mede upon the Revelations." A fourth lays it down as an unquestionable truth, that a lady cannot be thoroughly accomplished who has not read " the Secret Treaties and Negociations of Marshal D'Estrades." Mr. Jacob Tonson junior is of opinion, that " Bayle's Dictionary" might be of very great use to the ladies, in order to make them general scholars. Another, whose name I have forgotten, thinks it highly proper that every woman with child should read " Mr. Wall's History of Infant Baptism;" as another is very importunate with me to recommend to all my female readers " the Finishing Stroke; being a Vindication of the Patriarchal Scheme, &c."

In the second class I shall mention books which are recommended by husbands, if I may believe the writers of them. Whether or no they are real husbands or personated ones I cannot tell, but the books they recommend are as follow: " A Paraphrase on the History of Susanna." " Rules to keep Lent." " The Christian's Overthrow Prevented." " A Dissuasive from the Playhouse." " The Virtues of Camphire, with Directions to make Camphire Tea." " The Pleasures of a Country-Life." " The Government of the Tongue." A letter from Cheapside, desires me that I would advise all young wives to make themselves mistresses of " Wingate's Arithmetic," and concludes with a postscript, that he hopes I will not forget " the Countess of Kent's Receipts."

I may reckon the ladies themselves as a third class among these my correspondents and privy-counsellors. In a letter from one of them, I am advised to place " Pharamond" at the head of my catalogue, and if I think proper to give the second place to " Cassandra." Coquetilla begs me not to think of nailing women upon their knees with manuals of devotion, nor of scorching their faces with books of housewifery. Florella desires to know if there are any books written against prudes, and entreats me, if there are, to give them a place in my library. Plays of all sorts have their several advocates: " All for Love" is mentioned in above fifteen letters; " Sophonisba," or " Hannibal's Overthrow," in a dozen; " the Innocent Adultery" is likewise highly approved of; " Mithridates King of Pontus" has many friends, " Alexander the Great," and

"Aurengzebe," have the same number of voices; but "Theodosius," or "the Force of Love," carries it from all the rest.

I should, in the last place, mention such books as have been proposed by men of learning, and those who appear competent judges of this matter, and must here take occasion to thank A. B. whoever it is that conceals himself under those two letters, for his advice upon this subject: but as I find the work I have undertaken to be very difficult, I shall defer the executing of it till I am further acquainted with the thoughts of my judicious contemporaries, and have time to examine the several books they offer to me, being resolved, in an affair of this moment, to proceed with the greatest caution.

In the meanwhile, as I have taken the ladies under my particular care, I shall make it my business to find out, in the best authors ancient and modern, such passages as may be for their use, and endeavour to accommodate them as well as I can to their taste; not questioning but the valuable part of the sex will easily pardon me, if, from time to time, I laugh at those little vanities and follies which appear in the behaviour of some of them, and which are more proper for ridicule than a serious censure. Most books being calculated for male readers, and generally written with an eye to men of learning, makes a work of this nature the more necessary; besides, I am the more encouraged, because I flatter myself that I see the sex daily improving by these my speculations. My fair readers are already deeper scholars than the beaux: I could name some of them who talk much better than several gentlemen that make a figure at Will's, and as I frequently receive letters from the 'fine ladies' and 'pretty fellows,' I cannot but observe that the former are superior to the others, not only in the sense but in the spelling. This cannot but have a good effect upon the female world, and keep them from being charmed by those empty coxcombs that have hitherto been admired among the women, though laughed at among the men.

I am credibly informed that Tom Tattle passes for an impertinent fellow, that Will Trippet begins to be smoked, and that Frank Smoothly himself is within a month of a coxcomb, in case I think fit to continue this paper. For my part, as it is my business in some measure to detect such as would lead astray weak minds by their false pretences to wit and judgment, humour and gallantry, I shall not fail to lend the best lights I am able to the fair sex for the continuation of these their discoveries. L.

No. XCIII. SATURDAY, JUNE 16.

………..Spatio brevi
Spem longam reseces dum loquimur, fugerit invida
Ætas carpe diem, quàm minimum credula postero
HOR.

    Be wise, cut off long cares
      From thy contracted span
E'en whilst we speak, the envious time
      Doth make swift haste away,
Then seize the present, use thy prime,
      Nor trust another day   CREECH.

WE all of us complain of the shortness of time, saith Seneca, and yet have much more than we know what to do with. Our lives, says he, are spent either in doing nothing at all, or in doing nothing to the purpose, or in doing nothing that we ought to do: we are always complaining our days are few, and acting as though there would be no end of them. That noble philosopher has described our inconsistency with ourselves in this particular, by all those various turns of expression and thought which are peculiar to his writings.

I often consider mankind as wholly inconsistent with itself in a point that bears some affinity to the former. Though we seem grieved at the shortness of life in general, we are wishing every period of it at an end. The minor longs to be at age, then to be a man of business, then to make up an estate, then to arrive at honours, then to retire. Thus, although the whole of life is allowed by every one to be short, the several divisions of it appear long and tedious. We are for lengthening our span in general, but would fain contract the parts of which it is composed. The usurer would be very well satisfied to have all the time annihilated that lies between the present moment and next quarter-day. The politician would be contented to lose three years of his life, could he place things in the posture which he fancies they will stand in, after such a revolution of time. The lover would be glad to strike out of his existence all the moments that are to pass away before the happy meeting. Thus, as fast as our time runs, we should be very glad in most part of our lives that it ran much faster than it does. Several hours of the day hang upon our hands, nay we wish away whole years; and travel through time as through a country filled with many wild and empty wastes, which we would fain hurry over, that we may arrive at those several little settlements or imaginary points of rest which are dispersed up and down in it.

If we divide the life of most men into twenty parts, we shall find that at least nineteen of them are mere gaps and chasms, which are neither filled with pleasure nor business. I do not however include in this calculation, the life of those men who are in a perpetual hurry of affairs, but of those only who are not always engaged in scenes of action; and I hope I shall not do an unacceptable piece of service to these persons, if I point out to them certain methods for the filling up their empty spaces of life. The methods I shall propose to them are as follow:

The first is the exercise of virtue, in the most general acceptation of the word. That particular scheme which comprehends the social virtues, may give employment to the most industrious temper, and find a man in business more than the most active station of life. To advise the ignorant, relieve the needy, comfort the afflicted, are duties that fall in our way almost every day of our lives. A man has frequent opportunities of mitigating the fierceness of a party, of doing justice to the character of a deserving man; of softening the envious, quieting the angry, and rectifying the prejudiced, which are all of them employments suited to a reasonable nature, and bring great satisfaction to the person who can busy himself in them with discretion.

There is another kind of virtue that may find employment for those retired hours in which we are altogether left to ourselves, and destitute of company and conversation; I mean that intercourse and communication which every reasonable creature ought to maintain with the great Author of his being. The man who lives under an habitual sense of the Divine Presence keeps up a perpetual cheerfulness of temper, and enjoys every moment the satisfaction of thinking himself in company with his dearest and best of friends. The time never lies heavy upon him: It is impossible for him to be alone. His thoughts and passions are the most busied at such hours, when those of other men are the most inactive. He no sooner steps out of the world but his heart burns with devotion, swells with hope, and triumphs in the consciousness of that presence which every where surrounds him; or, on the contrary, pours out its fears, its sorrows, its apprehensions, to the great Supporter of its existence.

I have here only considered the necessity of a man's being virtuous, that he may have something to do, but if we consider further, that the exercise of virtue is not only an amusement for the time it lasts, but that its influence extends to those parts of our existence which lie beyond the grave, and that our whole eternity is to take its colour from those hours which we here employ in virtue or in vice, the argument redoubles upon us, for putting in practice this method of passing away our time.

When a man has but a little stock to improve, and has opportunities of turning it all to good account, what shall we think of him, if he suffers nineteen parts of it to lie dead, and perhaps employs even the twentieth to his ruin or disadvantage? But because the mind cannot be always in its fervours, nor strained up to a pitch of virtue, it is necessary to find out proper employments for it in its relaxations.

The next method therefore that I would propose to fill up our time, should be useful and innocent diversions. I must confess I think it is below reasonable creatures to be altogether conversant in such diversions as are merely innocent, and have nothing else to recommend them, but that there is no hurt in them. Whether any kind of gaming has even thus much to say for itself, I shall not determine: but I think it is very wonderful to see persons of the best sense passing away a dozen hours together in shuffling and dividing a pack of cards, with no other conversation but what is made up of a few game-phrases, and no other ideas but those of black or red spots ranged together in different figures. Would not a man laugh to hear any one of this species complaining that life is short?

The stage might be made a perpetual source of the most noble and useful entertainments, were it under proper regulations.

But the mind never unbends itself so agreeably as in the conversation of a well-chosen friend. There is indeed no blessing of life that is any way comparable to the enjoyment of a discreet and virtuous friend. It eases and unloads the mind, clears and improves the understanding, engenders thoughts and knowledge, animates virtue and good resolutions, sooths and allays the passions, and finds employment for most of the vacant hours of life.

Next to such an intimacy with a particular person, one would endeavour after a more general conversation with such as are able to entertain and improve those with whom they converse, which are qualifications that seldom go asunder.

There are many other useful amusements of life, which one would endeavour to multiply, that one might on all occasions have recourse to something, rather than suffer the mind to lie idle, or run adrift with any passion that chances to rise in it.

A man that has a taste for music, painting, or architecture, is like one that has another sense when compared with such as have no relish for those arts. The florist, the planter, the gardener, the husbandman, when they are only as accomplishments to the man of fortune, are great reliefs to a country life, and many ways useful to those who are possessed of them.

But of all the diversions of life, there is none so proper to fill up his empty spaces as the reading of useful and entertaining authors. But this I shall only touch upon, because it in some measure interferes with the third method, which I shall propose in another paper, for the employment of our dead inactive hours, and which I shall only mention in general to be the pursuit of knowledge. L.

No. XCIV. MONDAY, JUNE 18.

.... Hoc est
Vivere bis, vitâ posse priore frui. MART.

The present joys of life we doubly taste,
By looking back with pleasure on the past.

The last method which I proposed in my Saturday's paper, for filling up those empty spaces of life which are so tedious and burdensome to idle people, is the employing ourselves in the pursuit of knowledge. I remember Mr. Boyle, speaking of a certain mineral, tells us, That a man may consume his whole life in the study of it, without arriving at the knowledge of all its qualities. The truth of it is, there is not a single science, or any branch of it, that might not furnish a man with business for life, though it were much longer than it is.

I shall not here engage on those beaten subjects of the usefulness of knowledge, nor of the pleasure and perfection it gives the mind, nor on the methods of attaining it, nor recommend any particular branch of it; all which have been the topics of many other writers: but shall indulge myself in a speculation that is more uncommon, and may therefore perhaps be more entertaining.

I have before shewn how the unemployed parts of life appear long and tedious, and shall here endeavour to shew how those parts of life which are exercised in study, reading, and the pursuits of knowledge, are long but not tedious; and by that means discover a method of lengthening our lives, and at the same time of turning all the parts of them to our advantage.

Mr Locke observes, 'that we get the idea of time, or duration, by reflecting on that train of ideas which succeed one another in our minds: that for this reason, when we sleep soundly without dreaming, we have no perception of time, or the length of it, whilst we sleep; and that the moment wherein we leave off to think, till the moment we begin to think again, seems to have no distance.' To which the author adds, ' And so I doubt not but it would be to a waking man, if it were possible for him to keep only idea in his mind, without variation, and the succession of others; and we see, that one who fixes his thoughts very intently on one thing, so as to take but little notice of the succession of ideas that pass in his mind whilst he is taken up with that earnest contemplation, lets slip out of his account a good part of that duration, and thinks that time shorter than it is.'

We might carry this thought farther, and consider a man as, on one side, shortening his time, by thinking on nothing, or but a few things; so, on the other, as lengthening it, by employing his thoughts on many subjects, or by entertaining a quick and constant succession of ideas. Accordingly monsieur Mallebranche, in his " Inquiry after Truth," which was published several years before Mr. Locke's " Essay on Human Understanding," tells us, That it is possible some creatures may think half an hour as long as we do a thousand years; or look upon that space of duration which we call a minute, as an hour, a week, a month, or a whole age.

This notion of monsieur Mallebranche is capable of some little explanation from what I have quoted out of Mr. Locke: for, if our notion of time is produced by our reflecting on the succession of ideas in our mind, and this succession may be infinitely accelerated or retarded, it will follow, that different beings may have different notions of the same parts of duration, according as their ideas, which we suppose are equally distinct in each of them, follow one another in a greater or less degree of rapidity.

There is a famous passage in the Alcoran, which looks as if Mahomet had been possessed of the notion we are now speaking of. It is there said, That the angel Gabriel took Mahomet out of his bed one morning to give him a sight of all things in the seven heavens, in paradise, and in hell, which the prophet took a distinct view of; and after having held ninety thousand conferences with God, was brought back again to his bed. All this, says the Alcoran, was transacted in so small a space of time, that Mahomet at his return found his bed still warm, and took up an earthen pitcher (which was thrown down at the very instant that the angel Gabriel carried him away,) before the water was all spilt.

There is a very pretty story in the Turkish Tales which relates to this passage of that famous impostor, and bears some affinity to the subject we are now upon. A sultan of Egypt, who was an infidel, used to laugh at this circumstance in Mahomet's life, as what was altogether impossible and absurd: but conversing one day with a great doctor in the law, who had the gift of working miracles, the doctor told him he would quickly convince him of the truth of this passage in the history of Mahomet, if he would consent to do what he would desire of him. Upon this the sultan was directed to place himself by a huge tub of water, which he did accordingly; and as he stood by the tub amidst a circle of his great men, the holy man bid him plunge his head into the water, and draw it up again: the king accordingly thrust his head into the water, and at the same time found himself at the foot of a mountain on a sea-shore. The king immediately began to rage against his doctor for this piece of treachery and witchcraft; but at length, knowing it was in vain to be angry, he set himself to think on proper methods for getting a livelihood in this strange country: accordingly he applied himself to some people whom he saw at work in a neighbouring wood. These people conducted him to a town that stood at a little distance from the wood, where, after some adventures, he married a woman of great beauty and fortune. He lived with this woman so long, that he had by her seven sons and seven daughters. he was afterwards reduced to great want, and forced to think of plying in the streets as a porter for his livelihood. One day as he was walking alone by the sea-side, being seized with many melancholy reflections upon his former and his present state of life, which had raised a fit of devotion in him, he threw off his clothes with a design to wash himself, according to the custom of the Mahometans, before he said his prayers.

After his first plunge into the sea, he no sooner raised his head above the water, but he found himself standing by the side of the tub, with the great men of his court about him, and the holy man at his side. He immediately upbraided his teacher for having sent him on such a course of adventures, and betrayed him into so long a state of misery and servitude; but was wonderfully surprised when he heard that the state he had talked of was only a dream and delusion; that he had not stirred from the place where he then stood, and that he had only dipped his head into the water, and immediately taken it out again.

The Mahometan doctor took this occasion of instructing the sultan, that nothing was impossible with God; and that he, with whom a thousand years are but as one day, can, if he please, make a single day, nay a single moment, appear to any of his creatures as a thousand years.

I shall leave my reader to compare these eastern fables with the notions of those two great philosophers whom I have quoted in this paper; and shall only, by way of application, desire him to consider how we may extend life beyond its natural dimensions, by applying ourselves diligently to the pursuits of knowledge.

The hours of a wise man are lengthened by his ideas, as those of a fool are by his passions: the time of the one is long, because he does not know what to do with it, so is that of the other, because he distinguishes every moment of it with useful or amusing thoughts: or, in other words, because the one is always wishing it away, and the other always enjoying it

How different is the view of past life, in the man who is grown old in knowledge and wisdom, from that of him who is grown old in ignorance and folly? The latter is like the owner of a barren country, that fills his eye with the prospect of naked hills and plains, which produce nothing either profitable or ornamental, the other beholds a beautiful and spacious landscape, divided into delightful gardens, green meadows, fruitful fields, and can scarce cast his eye on a single spot of his possessions, that is not covered with some beautiful plant or flower. L.

No. XCV TUESDAY, JUNE 19.

Curæ leves loquuntur, ingentes stupent. SENEC.

Light sorrows speak, great grief is dumb

HAVING read the two following letters with much pleasure, I cannot but think the good sense of them will be as agreeable to the town, as any thing I could say either on the topics they treat of, or any other They both allude to former papers of mine, and I do not question but the first, which is upon inward mourning, will be thought the production of a man who is well acquainted with the generous yearnings of distress in a manly temper, which is above the relief of tears. A speculation of my own on that subject I shall defer till another occasion.

The second letter is from a lady of a mind as great as her understanding. There is perhaps something in the beginning of it which I ought in modesty to conceal; but I have so much esteem for this correspondent, that I will not alter a tittle of what she writes, though I am thus scrupulous at the price of being ridiculous.

' Mr. Spectator,

' I was very well pleased with your discourse upon general mourning, and should be obliged to you if you would enter into the matter more deeply, and give us your thoughts upon the common sense the ordinary people have of the demonstrations of grief, who prescribe rules and fashions to the most solemn affliction; such as the loss of the nearest relations and dearest friends. You cannot go to visit a sick friend, but some impertinent waiter about him observes the muscles of your face, as strictly as if they were prognostics of his death or recovery. If he happens to be taken from you, you are immediately surrounded with numbers of these spectators, who expect a melancholy shrug of your shoulders, a pathetical shake of your head, and an expressive distortion of your face, to measure your affection and value for the deceased, but there is nothing, on these occasions, so much in their favour as immoderate weeping. As all their passions are superficial, they imagine the seat of love and friendship to be placed visibly in the eyes: they judge what stock of kindness you had for the living by the quantity of tears you pour out for the dead; so that if one body wants that quantity of salt-water another abounds with, he is in great danger of being thought insensible or ill-natured; they are strangers to friendship, whose grief happens not to be moist enough to wet such a parcel of handkerchiefs. But experience has told us that nothing is so fallacious as that outward sign of sorrow; and the natural history of our bodies will teach us that this flux of the eyes, this faculty of weeping, is peculiar only to some constitutions. We observe in the tender bodies of children, when crossed in their little wills and expectations, how dissolvable they are into tears. If this were what grief is in men, nature would not be able to support them in the excess of it for one moment. Add to this observation, how quick is their transition from this passion to that of their joy! I will not say we see often, in the next tender things to children, tears shed without much grieving. Thus it is common to shed tears without much sorrow, and as common to suffer much sorrow without shedding tears. Grief and weeping are indeed frequent companions; but, I believe, never in their highest excesses. As laughter does not proceed from profound joy, so neither does weeping from profound sorrow. The sorrow which appears so easily at the eyes, cannot have pierced deeply into the heart. The heart distended with grief, stops all the passages for tears or lamentations.

'Now, Sir, what I would incline you to in all this is, that you would inform the shallow critics and observers upon sorrow, that true affliction labours to be invisible, that it is a stranger to ceremony, and that it bears in its own nature a dignity much above the little circumstances which are affected under the notion of decency. You must know, Sir, I have lately lost a dear friend, for whom I have not yet shed a tear; and for that reason your animadversions on that subject would be the more acceptable to,

'Sir,
   'Your most humble servant,
      'B. D.'

JUNE 15.

'MR. SPECTATOR,

'As I hope there are but few that have so little gratitude as not to acknowledge the usefulness of your pen, and to esteem it a public benefit; so I am sensible, be that as it will, you must nevertheless find the secret and incomparable pleasure of doing good, and be a great sharer in the entertainment you give. I acknowledge our sex to be much obliged, and I hope improved, by your labours, and even your intentions more particularly for our service. If it be true, as it is sometimes said, that our sex have an influence on the other, your paper may be a yet more general good. Your directing us to reading is certainly the best means to our instruction; but I think, with you, caution in that particular very useful, since the improvement of our understandings may or may not be of service to us, according as it is managed. It has been thought we are not generally so ignorant as ill-taught, or that our sex does so often want wit, judgment, or knowledge, as the right application of them: you are so well bred, as to say your fair readers are already deeper scholars than the beaux, and that you could name some of them that talk much better than several gentlemen that make a figure at Will's. This may possibly be, and no great compliment, in my opinion, even supposing your comparison to reach Tom's and the Grecian: Surely you are too wise to think that a real commendation of a woman. Were it not rather to be wished we improved in our own sphere, and approved ourselves better daughters, wives, mothers, and friends?

'I cannot but agree with the judicious trader in Cheapside (though I am not at all prejudiced in his favour) in recommending the study of arithmetic; and must dissent even from the authority which you mention, when it advises the making our sex scholars. Indeed a little more philosophy, in order to the subduing our passions to our reason, might be sometimes serviceable, and a treatise of that nature I should approve of, even in exchange for "Theodosius," or "The Force of Love;" but as I well know you want not hints, I will proceed no further than to recommend the Bishop of Cambray's "Education of a Daughter," as it is translated into the only language I have any knowledge of, though perhaps very much to its disadvantage. I have heard it objected against that piece, that its instructions are not of general use, but only fitted for a great lady; but I confess, I am not of that opinion, for I don't remember that there are any rules laid down for the expenses of a woman, in which particular only, I think a gentlewoman ought to differ from a lady of the best fortune, or highest quality, and not in their principles of justice, gratitude, sincerity, prudence, or modesty. I ought perhaps to make an apology for this long epistle; but as I rather believe you a friend to sincerity than ceremony, shall only assure you I am,

'Sir,

'Your most humble servant,

T   'ANNABELLA.'

No XCVI. WEDNESDAY, JUNE 20.

———Amicum
Mancipium domino, et frugi. Hor.

The faithful servant, and the true. Creech.

'Mr Spectator,

'I have frequently read your discourse upon servants, and as I am one myself, have been much offended that in that variety of forms wherein you considered the bad, you found no place to mention the good. There is, however, one observation of your's I approve, which is, that there are men of wit and good sense among all orders of men, and that servants report most of the good or ill which is spoken of their masters. That there are men of sense who live in servitude, I have the vanity to say I have felt, to my woeful experience. You attribute very justly the source of our general iniquity to board-wages, and the manner of living out of a domestic way; but I cannot give you my thoughts on this subject, any way so well, as by a short account of my own life, to this the forty-fifth year of my age: that is to say, from my being first a foot-boy at fourteen, to my present station of a nobleman's porter in the year of my age above-mentioned.

'Know then, that my father was a poor tenant to the family of Sir Stephen Rackrent. Sir Stephen put me to school, or rather made me follow his son Harry to school, from my ninth year; and there, though Sir Stephen paid something for my learning, I was used like a servant, and was forced to get what scraps of learning I could by my own industry, for the schoolmaster took very little notice of me. My young master was a lad of very sprightly parts, and my being constantly about him, and loving him, was no small advantage to me. My master loved me extremely, and has often been whipped for not keeping me at a distance. He used always to say, that when he came to his estate, I should have a lease of my father's tenement for nothing. I came up to town with him to Westminster-school; at which time he taught me, at night, all he learnt, and put me to find out words in the dictionary, when he was about his exercise. It was the will of Providence, that Mr. Harry was taken very ill of a fever, of which he died within ten days after his first falling sick. Here was the first sorrow I ever knew; and I assure you, Mr. Spectator, I remember the beautiful action of the sweet youth in his fever, as fresh as if it were yesterday. If he wanted any thing, it must be given him by Tom. When I let any thing fall, through the grief I was under, he would cry, Do not beat the poor boy; give him some more julep for me, nobody else shall give it me. He would strive to hide his being so bad, when he saw I could not bear his being in so much danger, and comforted me, saying, Tom, Tom, have a good heart. When I was holding a cup at his mouth, he fell into convulsions; and at this very time I heard my dear master's last groan. I was quickly turned out of the room, and left to sob and beat my head against the wall at my leisure. The grief I was in was inexpressible, and every body thought it would have cost me my life. In a few days, my old lady, who was one of the house-wives of the world, thought of turning me out of doors, because I put her in mind of her son. Sir Stephen proposed putting me apprentice, but my lady, being an excellent manager, would not let her husband throw away his money in acts of charity. I had sense enough to be under the utmost indignation, to see her discard with so little concern, one her son had loved so much; and went out of the house to ramble wherever my feet would carry me.

'The third day after I left Sir Stephen's family, I was strolling up and down the walks in the Temple. A young gentleman of the house, who (as I heard him say afterwards) seeing me half starved and well dressed, thought me an equipage ready to his hand, after very little inquiry more than " Did I want a master?" bid me follow him. I did so, and in a very little while, thought myself the happiest creature in this world. My time was taken up in carrying letters to wenches, or messages to young ladies of my master's acquaintance. We rambled from tavern to tavern, to the playhouse, the mulberry-garden, and all places of resort; where my master engaged every night in some new amour, in which, and drinking, he spent all his time when he had money. During these extravagancies, I had the pleasure of lying on the stairs of a tavern half a night, playing at dice with other servants, and the like idlenesses. When my master was moneyless, I was generally employed in transcribing amorous pieces of poetry, old songs, and new lampoons. This life held till my master married, and he had then the prudence to turn me off, because I was in the secret of his intrigues.

'I was utterly at a loss what course to take next; when at last I applied myself to a fellow-sufferer, one of his mistresses, a woman of the town. She happening at that time to be pretty full of money, clothed me from head to foot, and knowing me to be a sharp fellow, employed me accordingly. Sometimes I was to go abroad with her, and when she had pitched upon a young fellow she thought for her turn, I was dropped as one she could not trust. She would often cheapen goods at the New-Exchange; and when she had a mind to be attacked, she would send me away on an errand. When an humble servant and she were beginning a parley, I came immediately, and told her Sir John was come home; then she would order another coach to prevent being dogged. The lover makes signs to me as I get behind the coach; I shake my head it was impossible: I leave my lady at the next turning, and follow the cully to know how to fall in his way on another occasion. Besides good offices of this nature, I write all my mistress's love-letters; some from a lady that saw such a gentleman in such a place in such a coloured coat, some shewing the terror she was in of a jealous old husband, others explaining that the severity of her parents was such (though her fortune was settled) she was willing to run away with such a one, though she knew he was but a younger brother In a word, my half-education and love of idle books, made me out-write all that made love to her by way of epistle; and as she was extremely cunning, she did well enough in company by a skilful affectation of the greatest modesty. In the midst of all this I was surprised with a letter from her and a ten pound note.

'HONEST TOM.

'You will never see me more I am married to a very cunning country gentleman, who might possibly guess something if I keep you still, therefore farewel.'

" When this place was lost also in marriage, I was resolved to go among quite another people for the future; and got in butler to one of those families where there is a coach kept, three or four servants, a clean house, and a good general outside upon a small estate. Here I lived very comfortably for some time, till I unfortunately found my master, the very gravest man alive, in the garret with the chambermaid I knew the world too well to think of staying there, and the next day pretended to have received a letter out of the country that my father was dying, and got my discharge with a bounty for my discretion.

" The next I lived with was a peevish single man, whom I staid with for a year and a half. Most part of the time I passed very easily; for when I began to know him, I minded no more than he meant what he said; so that one day in good humour he said, ' I was the best man he ever had, by my want of respect to him.'

"These, Sir, are the chief occurrences of my life; and I will not dwell upon very many other places I have been in, where I have been the strangest fellow in the world, where nobody in the world had such servants as they, where sure they were the unluckiest people in the world in servants, and so forth. All I mean by this representation is, to show you that we poor servants are not (what you called us too generally) all rogues; but that we are what we are, according to the example of our superiors. In the family I am now in, I am guilty of no one sin but lying; which I do with a grave face in my gown and staff every day I live, and almost all day long, in denying my lord to impertinent suitors, and my lady to unwelcome visitants. But, Sir, I am to let you know, that I am, when I can get abroad, a leader of the servants. I am he that keeps time with beating my cudgel against the boards in the gallery at an opera; I am he that is touched so properly at a tragedy, when the people of quality are staring at one another during the most important incidents; when you hear in a crowd a cry in the right place, a hum where the point is touched in a speech, or a huzza set up where it is the voice of the people, you may conclude it is begun, or joined by,

"Sir,

"Your more than humble servant,

T

"THOMAS TRUSTY."

No. XCVII. THURSDAY, JUNE 21.

Projecêre animas.......   VIRG.
They prodigally threw their souls away.

Among the loose papers which I have frequently spoken of heretofore, I find a conversation between Pharamond and Eucrate upon the subject of duels, and the copy of an edict issued in consequence of that discourse.

Eucrate argued, That nothing but the most severe and vindictive punishment, such as placing the bodies of the offenders in chains, and putting them to death by the most exquisite torments, would be sufficient to extirpate a crime which had so long prevailed, and was so firmly fixed in the opinion of the world as great and laudable. but the King answered, that indeed instances of ignominy were necessary in the cure of this evil: but considering that it prevailed only among such as had a nicety in their sense of honour, and that it often happened that a duel was fought to save appearances to the world, when both parties were in their hearts in amity and reconciliation to each other; it was evident, that turning the mode another way would effectually put a stop to what had being only as a mode: that to such persons, poverty and shame were torments sufficient: that he would not go further in punishing in others, crimes which he was satisfied he himself was most guilty of, in that he might have prevented them by speaking his displeasure sooner. Besides which the King said, he was in general averse to tortures, which was putting human nature itself, rather than the criminal, to disgrace; and that he would be sure not to use this means where the crime was but an ill effect arising from a laudable cause, the fear of shame. The King, at the same time, spoke with much grace upon the subject of mercy, and repented of many acts of that kind which had a magnificent aspect in the doing, but dreadful consequences in the example. Mercy to particulars, he observed, was cruelty in the general: that though a prince could not revive a dead man by taking the life of him who killed him, neither could he make reparation to the next that should die by the evil example; or answer to himself for the partiality, in not pardoning the next as well as the former offender. " As for me (says Pharamond), I have conquered France, and yet have given laws to my people: the laws are my methods of life; they are not a diminution but a direction to my power. I am still absolute to distinguish the innocent and the virtuous, to give honours to the brave and generous. I am absolute in my goodwill; none can oppose my bounty or prescribe rules for my favour. While I can, as I please, reward the good, I am under no pain that I cannot pardon the wicked; for which reason (continued Pharamond), I will effectually put a stop to this evil, by exposing no more the tenderness of my nature to the importunity of having the same respect to those who are miserable by their fault, and those who are so by their misfortune. Flatterers (concluded the King smiling), repeat to us princes, that we are heaven's vicegerents, let us be so, and let the only thing out of our power be to do ill."

Soon after the evening wherein Pharamond and Eucrate had this conversation, the following edict was published.

PHARAMOND'S EDICT AGAINST DUELS

' PHARAMOND, KING OF THE GAULS, TO ALL HIS LOVING SUBJECTS SENDETH GREETING.

' WHEREAS it hath come to our royal notice and observation, that in contempt of all laws, divine and human, it is of late become a custom among the nobility and gentry of this our kingdom, upon slight and trivial, as well as great and urgent provocations, to invite each other into the field, there by their own hands, and of their own authority, to decide their controversies by combat; we have thought fit to take the said custom into our royal consideration, and find, upon inquiry into the usual causes, whereon such fatal decisions have arisen, that by this wicked custom, maugre all the precepts of our holy religion, and the rules of right reason, the greatest act of the human mind, forgiveness of injuries, is become vile and shameful. that the rules of good society and virtuous conversation are hereby inverted, that the loose, the vain, and the impudent, insult the careful, the discreet, and the modest, that all virtue is suppressed, and all vice supported, in the one act of being capable to dare to the death. We have also further, with great sorrow of mind, observed that this dreadful action, by long impunity, (our royal attention being employed upon matters of more general concern,) is become honourable, and the refusal to engage in it ignominious. In these our royal cares and inquiries, we are yet further made to understand, that the persons of most eminent worth and most hopeful abilities, accompanied with the strongest passion for true glory, are such as are most liable to be involved in the dangers arising from this licence. Now taking the said premises into our serious consideration, and well weighing that all such emergencies (wherein the mind is incapable of commanding itself, and where the injury is too sudden or too exquisite to be borne) are particularly provided for by laws heretofore enacted; and that the qualities of less injuries, like those of ingratitude, are too nice and delicate to come under general rules; we do resolve to blot this fashion, or wantonness of anger, out of the minds of our subjects, by our royal resolutions declared in this edict as follows:

"No person who either sends or accepts a challenge, or the posterity of either, though no death ensues thereupon shall be, after the publication of this our edict, capable of bearing office in these our dominions.

"The person who shall prove the sending or receiving a challenge, shall receive to his own use and property the whole personal estate of both parties; and their real estate shall be immediately vested in the next heir of the offenders in as ample manner as if the said offenders were actually deceased.

"In cases where the laws (which we have already granted to our subjects) admit of an appeal for blood; when the criminal is condemned by the said appeal, he shall not suffer death, but his whole estate, real, mixed, and personal, shall from the hour of his death be vested in the next heir of the person whose blood he spilt.

"That it shall not hereafter be in our royal power, or that of our successors, to pardon the said offences, or restore the offenders in their estates, honour, or blood for ever.

"Given at our court at Blois, the 8th of February, 420, in the second year of our reign." T

No. XCVIII. FRIDAY, JUNE 22.

... Tanta est quærendi cura decoris

Juv

So studiously their persons they adorn

There is not so variable a thing in nature as a lady's head-dress: within my own memory I have known it rise and fall above thirty degrees. About ten years ago it shot up to a very great height, insomuch that the female part of our species were much taller than the men. The women were of such an enormous stature, that 'we appeared as grasshoppers before them.' At present the whole sex is in a manner dwarfed and shrunk into a race of beauties that seems almost another species. I remember several ladies, who were once very near seven feet high, that at present want some inches of five: How they came to be thus curtailed I cannot learn; whether the whole sex be at present under any penance which we know nothing of, or whether they have cast their head-dresses in order to surprise us with something in that kind which shall be entirely new, or whether some of the tallest of the sex, being too cunning for the rest, have contrived this method to make themselves appear sizeable, is still a secret, though I find most are of opinion, they are at present like trees new lopped and pruned, that will certainly sprout up and flourish with greater heads than before. For my own part, as I do not love to be insulted by women who are taller than myself, I admire the sex much more in their present humiliation, which has reduced them to their natural dimensions, than when they had extended their persons and lengthened themselves out into formidable and gigantic figures. I am not for adding to the beautiful edifices of nature, nor for raising any whimsical superstructure upon her plans: I must therefore repeat it, that I am highly pleased with the coiffure now in fashion, and think it shews the good sense which at present very much reigns among the valuable part of the sex. One may observe, that women in all ages have taken more pains than men to adorn the outside of their heads: and indeed I very much admire that those female architects, who raise such wonderful structures out of ribbands, lace, and wire, have not been recorded for their respective inventions. It is certain there has been as many orders in these kinds of building, as in those which have been made of marble, sometimes they rise in the shape of a pyramid, sometimes like a tower, and sometimes like a steeple. In Juvenal's time, the building grew by several orders and stories, as he has very humorously described it.

> Tot premit ordinibus, tot adhuc compagibus altum
> Ædificat caput: Andromachen à fronte videbis,
> Post minor est: aliam credas.... Juv.

> With curls on curls they build their heads before,
> And mount it with a formidable tow'r,
> A giantess she seems; but look behind,
> And then she dwindles to the pigmy kind.
> Dryden.

But I do not remember, in any part of my reading, that the head-dress aspired to so great an extravagance as in the fourteenth century; when it was built up in a couple of cones or spires, which stood so excessively high on each side of the head, that a woman, who was but a pigmy without her head-dress, appeared like a Colossus upon putting it on. Monsieur Paradin says, "That these old-fashioned fontanges rose an ell above the head; that they were pointed like steeples, and had long loose pieces of crape fastened to the tops of them, which were curiously fringed, and hung down their backs like streamers."

The women might possibly have carried this Gothic building much higher, had not a famous monk, Thomas Conecte by name, attacked it with great zeal and resolution. This holy man travelled from place to place to preach down this monstrous commode; and succeeded so well in it, that as the magicians sacrificed their books to the flames upon the preaching of an apostle, many of the women threw down their head-dresses in the middle of his sermon, and made a bonfire of them within sight of the pulpit. He was so renowned, as well for the sanctity of his life as his manner of preaching, that he had often a congregation of twenty thousand people; the men placing themselves on the one side of his pulpit, and the women on the other, that appeared (to use the similitude of an ingenious writer) like a forest of cedars with their heads reaching to the clouds. He so warmed and animated the people against this monstrous ornament, that it lay under a kind of persecution, and, whenever it appeared in public, was pelted down by the rabble, who flung stones at the persons that wore it. But, notwithstanding this prodigy vanished while the preacher was among them, it began to appear again some months after his departure, or to tell it in Monsieur Paradin's own words, the women " that, like snails in a fright, had drawn in their horns, shot them out again as soon as the danger was over." This extravagance of the womens' head-dresses in that age is taken notice of by Monsieur d'Argentié in his history of Bretagne, and by other historians, as well as the person I have here quoted.

It is usually observed, that a good reign is the only proper time for making of laws against the exorbitance of power; in the same manner an excessive head-dress may be attacked the most effectually when the fashion is against it. I do therefore recommend this paper to my female readers by way of prevention.

I would desire the fair sex to consider how impossible it is for them to add any thing that can be ornamental to what is already the master-piece of nature. The head has the most beautiful appearance, as well as the highest station, in a human figure. Nature has laid out all her art in beautifying the face: she has touched it with vermilion, planted in it a double row of ivory, made it the seat of smiles and blushes, lighted it up and enlivened it with the brightness of the eyes, hung it on each side with curious organs of sense, given it airs and graces that cannot be described, and surrounded it with such a flowing shade of hair as sets all its beauties in the most agreeable light. In short, she seems to have designed the head as the cupola to the most glorious of her works; and when we load it with such a pile of supernumerary ornaments, we destroy the symmetry of the human figure, and foolishly contrive to call off the eye from great and real beauties, to childish gewgaws, ribbands, and bonelace. L.

No. XCIX. SATURDAY, JUNE 23.

....Turpi secernis honestum   Hor.

You know to fix the bounds of right and wrong.

The club, of which I have often declared myself a member, were last night engaged in a discourse upon that which passes for the chief point of honour among men and women; and started a great many hints upon the subject, which I thought were entirely new. I shall therefore methodise the several reflections that arose upon this occasion, and present my reader with them for the speculation of this day; after having premised, that if there is any thing in this paper which seems to differ with any passage of last Thursday's, the reader will consider this as the sentiments of the club, and the other as my own private thoughts, or rather those of Pharamond.

The great point of honour in men is courage, and in women chastity. If a man loses his honour in one rencounter, it is not impossible for him to regain it in another; a slip in a woman's honour is irrecoverable. I can give no reason for fixing the point of honour to these two qualities, unless it be that each sex sets the greatest value on the qualification which renders them the most amiable in the eyes of the contrary sex. Had men chosen for themselves, without regard to the opinions of the fair sex, I should believe the choice would have fallen on wisdom or virtue; or had women determined their own point of honour, it is probable that wit or good nature would have carried it against chastity.

Nothing recommends a man more to the female sex than courage; whether it be that they are pleased to see one who is a terror to others fall like a slave at their feet, or that this quality supplies their own principal defect, in guarding them from insults, and avenging their quarrels, or that courage is a natural indication of a strong and sprightly constitution. On the other side, nothing makes a woman more esteemed by the opposite sex than chastity; whether it be that we always prize those most who are hardest to come at, or that nothing besides chastity, with its collateral attendants, truth, fidelity, and constancy, gives the man a property in the person he loves, and consequently endears her to him above all things.

I am very much pleased with a passage in the inscription on a monument erected in Westminster-Abbey to the late duke and duchess of Newcastle; " Her name was Margaret Lucas, youngest sister to the lord Lucas of Colchester; a noble family, for all the brothers were valiant, and all the sisters virtuous."

In books of chivalry, where the point of honour is strained to madness, the whole story runs on chastity and courage. The damsel is mounted on a white palfrey, as an emblem of her innocence; and, to avoid scandal, must have a dwarf for her page. She is not to think of a man, till some misfortune has brought a knight-errant to her relief. The knight falls in love; and did not gratitude restrain her from murdering her deliverer, would die at her feet by her disdain. However, he must waste many years in the desert before her virgin-heart can think of a surrender. The knight goes off, attacks every thing he meets that is bigger and stronger than himself, seeks all opportunities of being knocked on the head, and, after seven years rambling, returns to his mistress, whose chastity has been attacked in the mean time by giants and tyrants, and undergone as many trials as her lover's valour.

In Spain, where there are still great remains of this romantic humour, it is a transporting favour for a lady to cast an accidental glance on her lover from a window, though it be two or three stories high; as it is usual for the lover to assert his passion for his mistress in single combat with a mad bull.

The great violation of the point of honour from man to man, is giving the lie. One may tell another he whores, drinks, blasphemes, and it may pass unresented; but to say he lies, though but in jest, is an affront that nothing but blood can expiate. The reason perhaps may be, because no other vice implies a want of courage so much as the making of a lie; and therefore telling a man he lies, is touching him in the most sensible part of honour, and indirectly calling him a coward. I cannot omit, under this head, what Herodotus tells us of the ancient Persians, that from the age of five years to twenty, they instruct their sons only in three things, to manage the horse, to make use of the bow, and to speak truth.

The placing the point of honour in this false kind of courage, has given occasion to the very refuse of mankind, who have neither virtue nor common sense, to set up for men of honour. An English peer, who has not been long dead, used to tell a pleasant story of a French gentleman that visited him early one morning at Paris, and, after great professions of respect, let him know that he had it in his power to oblige him; which, in short, amounted to this, that he believed he could tell his lordship the person's name who jostled him as he came out from the opera; but before he would proceed, he begged his lordship that he would not deny him the honour of making him his second. The English lord, to avoid being drawn into a very foolish affair, told him, that he was under engagements for his two next duels to a couple of particular friends. Upon which the gentleman immediately withdrew, hoping his lordship would not take it ill if he meddled no farther in an affair from whence he himself was to receive no advantage.

The beating down this false notion of honour, in so vain and lively a people as those of France, is deservedly looked upon as one of the most glorious parts of their present king's reign. It is pity but the punishment of these mischievous notions should have in it some particular circumstances of shame and infamy; that those who are slaves to them may see, that instead of advancing their reputations, they lead them to ignominy and dishonour.

Death is not sufficient to deter men who make it their glory to despise it; but if every one that fought a duel were to stand in the pillory, it would quickly lessen the number of these imaginary men of honour, and put an end to so absurd a practice.

When honour is a support to virtuous principles, and runs parallel with the laws of God and our country, it cannot be too much cherished and encouraged: but when the dictates of honour are contrary to those of religion and equity, they are the greatest depravations of human nature, by giving wrong ambitions and false ideas of what is good and laudable, and should therefore be exploded by all governments, and driven out as the bane and plague of human society.   L.

No. C. MONDAY, JUNE 25.

Nil ego contulerim jucundo sanus amico. HOR.

The greatest blessing is a pleasant friend.

A MAN advanced in years, that thinks fit to look back upon his former life, and calls that only life which was passed with satisfaction and enjoyment, excluding all parts which were not pleasant to him, will find himself very young, if not in his infancy. Sickness, ill-humour, and idleness, will have robbed him of a great share of that space we ordinarily call our life. It is therefore the duty of every man that would be true to himself, to obtain, if possible, a disposition to be pleased, and place himself in a constant aptitude for the satisfactions of his being. Instead of this, you hardly see a man who is not uneasy in proportion to his advancement in the arts of life. An affected delicacy is the common improvement we meet with in those who pretend to be refined above others; they do not aim at true pleasures themselves, but turn their thoughts upon observing the false pleasures of other men. Such people are valetudinarians in society, and they should no more come into company than a sick man should come into the air: if a man is too weak to bear what is a refreshment to men in health, he must still keep his chamber. When any one in Sir Roger's company, complains he is out of order, he immediately calls for some posset-drink for him; for which reason that sort of people, who are ever bewailing their constitution in other places, are the cheerfullest imaginable when he is present.

It is a wonderful thing, that so many, and they not reckoned absurd, shall entertain those with whom they converse, by giving them the history of their pains and aches, and imagine such narrations, their quota of the conversation. This is, of all other, the meanest help to discourse, and a man must not think at all, or think himself very insignificant, when he finds an account of his head-ach, answered by another's asking what news in the last mail? Mutual good humour is a dress we ought to appear in whenever we meet, and we should make no mention of what concerns ourselves, without it be of matters wherein our friends ought to rejoice: but indeed there are crowds of people who put themselves in no method of pleasing themselves or others; such are those whom we usually call indolent persons. Indolence is, methinks, an intermediate state between pleasure and pain, and very much unbecoming any part of our life, after we are out of the nurse's arms. Such an aversion to labour, creates a constant weariness, and one should think would make existence itself a burden. The indolent man descends from the dignity of his nature, and makes that being which was rational, merely vegetative: his life consists only in the mere increase and decay of a body, which, with relation to the rest of the world, might as well have been uninformed, as the habitation of a reasonable mind.

Of this kind is the life of that extraordinary couple Harry Tersett and his Lady. Harry was, in the days of his celibacy, one of those pert creatures who have much vivacity and little understanding; Mis Rebecca Quickly, whom he married, had all that the fire of youth and a lively manner could do towards making an agreeable woman. These two people, of seeming merit, fell into each other's arms; and passion being sated, and no reason or good sense in either to succeed it, their life now is at a stand; their meals are insipid, and their time tedious; their fortune has placed them above care, and their loss of taste, reduced them below diversion. When we talk of these as instances of inexistence, we do not mean that, in order to live, it is necessary we should always be in jovial crews, or crowned with chaplets of roses, as the merry fellows among the ancients are described; but it is intended, by considering these contraries to pleasure, indolence, and too much delicacy, to show that it is prudent to preserve a disposition in ourselves to receive a certain delight in all we hear and see.

This portable quality of good humour seasons all the parts and occurrences we meet with, in such a manner that there are no moments lost; but they all pass with so much satisfaction, that the heaviest of loads (when it is a load), that of time, is never felt by us. Varilas has this quality to the highest perfection, and communicates it wherever he appears: the sad, the merry, the severe, the melancholy, shew a new cheerfulness when he comes amongst them. At the same time no one can repeat any thing that Varilas has ever said that deserves repetition; but the man has that innate goodness of temper, that he is welcome to every body, because every man thinks he is so to him. He does not seem to contribute any thing to the mirth of the company; and yet, upon reflection, you find it all happened by his being there. I thought it was whimsically said of a gentleman, that if Varilas had wit, it would be the best wit in the world. It is certain, when a well corrected lively imagination and good breeding, are added to a sweet disposition, they qualify it to be one of the greatest blessings, as well as pleasures, of life.

Men would come into company with ten times the pleasure they do, if they were sure of hearing nothing which should shock them, as well as expected what would please them. When we know every person that is spoken of is represented by one who has no ill-will, and every thing that is mentioned described by one that is apt to set it in the best light, the entertainment must be delicate; because the cook has nothing brought to his hand but what is the most excellent in its kind. Beautiful pictures are the entertainments of pure minds, and deformities of the corrupted. It is a degree towards the life of angels, when we enjoy conversation wherein there is nothing presented but in its excellence, and a degree towards that of demons, wherein nothing is shewn but in its degeneracy.

T

No. CI. TUESDAY, JUNE 6.

Romulus, et Liber pater, et cum Castore Pollux,
Post ingentia facta, deorum in templa recepti,
Dum terras hominumque colunt genus, aspera bella
Componunt, agros assignant, oppida condunt,
Ploravere suis non respondere favorem
Speratum meritis........ Hor.

IMITATED.

Edward and Henry, now the boast of fame,
And virtuous Alfred, a more sacred name,
After a life of gen'rous toils endur'd,
The Gaul subdu'd, or property secur'd,
Ambition humbled, mighty cities storm'd,
Our laws establish'd, and the world reform'd,
Clos'd their long glories with a sigh, to find
Th' unwilling gratitude of base mankind. Pope.

'CENSURE (says a late ingenious author) is the tax a man pays to the public for being eminent.' It is a folly for an eminent man to think of escaping it, and a weakness to be affected with it. All the illustrious persons of antiquity, and indeed of every age in the world, have passed through this fiery persecution. There is no defence against reproach but obscurity:

it is a kind of concomitant to greatness, as satires and invectives were an essential part of a Roman triumph.

If men of eminence are exposed to censure on one hand, they are as much liable to flattery on the other. If they receive reproaches which are not due to them, they likewise receive praises which they do not deserve. In a word, the man in a high post is never regarded with an indifferent eye, but always considered as a friend or an enemy. For this reason, persons in great stations have seldom their true characters drawn till several years after their deaths. Their personal friendships and enmities must cease, and the parties they were engaged in be at an end, before their faults or their virtues can have justice done them. When writers have the least opportunities of knowing the truth, they are in the best disposition to tell it.

It is therefore the privilege of posterity to adjust the characters of illustrious persons, and to set matters right between those antagonists, who, by their rivalry for greatness, divided a whole age into factions. We can now allow Cæsar to be a great man, without derogating from Pompey, and celebrate the virtues of Cato, without detracting from those of Cæsar. Every one that has been long dead, has a due proportion of praise allotted him; in which, whilst he lived, his friends were too profuse, and his enemies too sparing.

According to Sir Isaac Newton's calculations, the last comet that made its appearance in 1680, imbibed so much heat by its approaches to the sun, that it would have been two thousand times hotter than redhot iron, had it been a globe of that metal, and that supposing it as big as the earth, and at the same distance from the sun, it would be fifty thousand years in cooling, before it recovered its natural temper. In the like manner, if an Englishman considers the great ferment into which our political world is thrown at present, and how intensely it is heated in all its parts, he cannot suppose it will cool again in less than three hundred years. In such a tract of time it is possible that the heats of the present age may be extinguished, and our several classes of great men represented under their proper characters. Some eminent historian may then probably arise that will not write *recentibus odiis*, (as Tacitus expresses it) with the passions and prejudices of a contemporary author, but make an impartial distribution of fame among the great men of the present age.

I cannot forbear entertaining myself very often with the idea of such an imaginary historian describing the reign of Anne the first, and introducing it with a preface to his reader, that he is now entering upon the most shining part of the English story. The great rivals in fame will be then distinguished according to their respective merits, and shine in their proper points of light. Such an one (says the historian) though variously represented by the writers of his own age, appears to have been a man of more than ordinary abilities, great application, and uncommon integrity; nor was such an one (though of an opposite party and interest) inferior to him in any of these respects. The several antagonists who now endeavour to depreciate one another, and are celebrated or traduced by different parties, will then have the same body of admirers, and appear illustrious in the opinion of the whole British nation. The deserving man, who can now recommend himself to the esteem of but half his countrymen, will then receive the approbation and applauses of a whole age.

Among the several persons that flourish in this glorious reign, there is no question but such a future historian as the person of whom I am speaking, will make mention of the men of genius and learning, who have now any figure in the British nation. For my own part, I often flatter myself with the honourable mention which will then be made of me, and have drawn up a paragraph in my own imagination, that

I fancy will not be altogether unlike what will be found in some page or other of this imaginary historian

It was under this reign, says he, that the Spectator, published those little diurnal essays which are still extant. We know very little of the name or person of this author, except only that he was a man of a very short face, extremely addicted to silence, and so great a lover of knowledge, that he made a voyage to Grand Cairo for no other reason but to take the measure of a pyramid. His chief friend was one Sir Roger de Coverley, a whimsical country knight, and a Templar, whose name he has not transmitted to us. He lived as a lodger at the house of a widow-woman, and was a great humourist in all parts of his life. This is all we can affirm with any certainty of his person and character. As for his speculations, notwithstanding the several obsolete words, and obscure phrases of the age in which he lived, we still understand enough of them to see the diversions and characters of the English nation in his time: not but that we are to make allowance for the mirth and humour of the author, who has doubtless strained many representations of things beyond the truth. For if we interpret his words in their literal meaning, we must suppose that women of the first quality used to pass away whole mornings at a puppet-show: that they attested their principles by their patches: that an audience would sit out an evening to hear a dramatical performance written in a language which they did not understand: that chairs and flower-pots were introduced as actors upon the British stage: that a promiscuous assembly of men and women were allowed to meet at midnight in masques within the verge of the court, with many improbabilities of the like nature. We must, therefore, in these and the like cases, suppose that these remote hints and allusions aimed at some certain follies which were then in vogue, and which at present we have not any notion of. We may guess by several passages in the speculations, that there were writers who endeavoured to detract from the works of this author; but as nothing of this nature is come down to us, we cannot guess at any objections that could be made to his paper. If we consider his style with that indulgence which we must show to old English writers, or if we look into the variety of his subjects with those several critical dissertations, moral reflections,

* * * * * * * * * *
* * * * * * * * *
* * * * * * * * *
* * * * * * * * *

The following part of the paragraph is so much to my advantage, and beyond any thing I can pretend to, that I hope my readers will excuse me for not inserting it.

L

No. CII. WEDNESDAY, JUNE 27.

Lusus animo debent aliquando dari,
Ad cogitandum melior ut redeat tibi.

PHAEDR.

The mind ought sometimes to be diverted, that it may return the better to thinking.

I do not know whether to call the following letter a satire upon coquettes, or a representation of their several fantastical accomplishments, or what other title to give it, but as it is, I shall communicate it to the public. It will sufficiently explain its own intention; so that I shall give it my readers at length, without either preface or postcript.

'Mr. SPECTATOR,

'WOMEN are armed with fans as men with swords, and sometimes do more execution with them. To the end therefore that ladies may be entire mistresses of the weapon which they bear, I have erected an academy for the training up of young women in the exercise of the Fan, according to the most fashionable airs and motions that are now practised at court. The ladies who carry fans under me are drawn up twice a-day in my great hall, where they are instructed in the use of their arms, and exercised by the following words of command,

> 'Handle your fans,
> 'Unfurl your fans,
> 'Discharge your fans,
> 'Ground your fans,
> 'Recover your fans,
> 'Flutter your fans.

'By the right observation of these few plain words of command, a woman of a tolerable genius, who will apply herself diligently to her exercise for the space of but one half year, shall be able to give her fan all the graces that can possibly enter into that little modish machine.

'But to the end that my readers may form to themselves a right notion of this exercise, I beg leave to explain it to them in all its parts. When my female regiment is drawn up in array, with every one her weapon in her hand, upon my giving the word to "handle their fans," each of them shakes her fan at me with a smile, then gives her right-hand woman a tap upon the shoulder, then presses her lips with the extremity of her fan, then lets her arms fall in an easy motion, and stands in readiness to receive the next word of command. All this is done with a close fan and is generally learned in the first week.

'The next motion is that of "unfurling the fan;" in which are comprehended several little flirts and vibrations, as also gradual and deliberate openings, with many voluntary fallings asunder in the fan itself, that are seldom learned under a month's practice. This part of the exercise pleases the spectators more than any other, as it discovers on a sudden an infinite number of Cupids, garlands, altars, birds, beasts, rainbows, and the like agreeable figures, that display themselves to view, whilst every one in the regiment holds a picture in her hand.

Upon my giving the word to "discharge their fans," they give one general crack that may be heard at a considerable distance when the wind sits fair. This is one of the most difficult parts of the exercise, but I have several ladies with me, who at their first entrance could not give a pop loud enough to be heard at the further end of a room, who can now "discharge a fan" in such a manner that it shall make a report like a pocket-pistol. I have likewise taken care (in order to hinder young women from letting off their fans in wrong places or unsuitable occasions) to show upon what subject the crack of a fan may come in properly. I have likewise invented a fan, with which a girl of sixteen, by the help of a little wind which is inclosed about one of the largest sticks, can make as loud a crack as a woman of fifty with an ordinary fan.

'When the fans are thus discharged, the word of command in course is to "ground their fans." This teaches a lady to quit her fan gracefully when she throws it aside, in order to take up a pack of cards, adjust a curl of hair, replace a falling pin, or apply herself to any other matter of importance. This part of the exercise, as it only consists in tossing a fan with an air upon a long table (which stands by for that purpose) may be learned in two day's time as well as in a twelvemonth.

'When my female regiment is thus disarmed, I generally let them walk about the room for some time, when on a sudden (like ladies that look upon their watches after a long visit) they all of them hasten to their arms, catch them up in a hurry, and place themselves in their proper stations upon my calling out " recover your fans." This part of the exercise is not difficult, provided a woman applies her thoughts to it.

'The " fluttering of the fan" is the last, and indeed the masterpiece of the whole exercise, but if a lady does not mispend her time, she may make herself mistress of it in three months. I generally lay aside the dog-days and the hot time of the summer for the teaching this part of the exercise; for as soon as ever I pronounce " flutter your fans," the place is filled with so many zephyrs and gentle breezes as are very refreshing in that season of the year, though they might be dangerous to ladies of a tender constitution in any other.

'There is an infinite variety of motions to be made use of in the " flutter of a fan." there is the angry flutter, the modest flutter, the timorous flutter, the confused flutter, the merry flutter, and the amorous flutter. Not to be tedious, there is scarce any emotion in the mind which does not produce a suitable agitation in the fan; insomuch, that if I only see the fan of a disciplined lady, I know very well whether she laughs, frowns, or blushes. I have seen a fan so very angry, that it would have been dangerous for the absent lover who provoked it to have come within the wind of it; and at other times so very languishing, that I have been glad for the lady's sake the lover was at a sufficient distance from it. I need not add, that a fan is either a prude or coquette, according to the nature of the person who bears it. To conclude my letter, I must acquaint you, that I have from my own observations compiled a little treatise for the use of my scholars, entitled the " Passions of the fan," which I will communicate to you if you think it may be of use to the public. I shall have a general review on Thursday next; to which you shall be very welcome, if you will honour it with your presence.

'I am, &c.

'P. S. I teach young gentlemen the whole art of gallanting a fan.

'N. B. I have several little plain fans made for this use, to avoid expense.'   L.

No. CIII. THURSDAY, JUNE 28.

——— Sibi quivis
Speret idem, sudet multum, frustraque laboret,
Ausus idem ———   HOR.

All men will try, and hope to write as well,
And not (without much pains) be undeceiv'd.
             ROSCOMMON.

My friend the Divine, having been used with words of complaisance (which he thinks could be properly applied to no one living, and I think could be only spoken of him, and that in his absence), was so extremely offended with the excessive way of speaking civilities among us, that he made a discourse against it at the club; which he concluded with this remark, That he had not heard one compliment made in our society since its commencement. Every one was pleased with his conclusion; and as each knew his good will to the rest, he was convinced that the many professions of kindness and service which we ordinarily meet with, are not natural where the heart is well inclined; but are a prostitution of speech, seldom intended to mean any part of what they express, never to mean all they express. Our reverend friend, upon this topic, pointed out to us two or three paragraphs on this subject in the first sermon of the first volume of the late Archbishop's posthumous works. I do not know that I ever read any thing that pleased me more; and as it is the praise of Longinus, that he speaks of the sublime in a style suitable to it, so one may say of this author upon sincerity, that he abhors any pomp of rhetoric on this occasion, and treats it with a more than ordinary simplicity, at once to be a preacher and an example. With what command of himself does he lay before us, in the language and temper of his profession, a fault, which, by the least liberty and warmth of expression, would be the most lively wit and satire? But his heart was better disposed, and the good man chastised the great wit in such a manner, that he was able to speak as follows:

'Amongst too many other instances of the great corruption and degeneracy of the age wherein we live, the great and general want of sincerity in conversation, is none of the least. The world is grown so full of dissimulation and compliment, that men's words are hardly any signification of their thoughts; and if any man measure his words by his heart, and speak as he thinks, and do not express more kindness to every man than men usually have for any man, he can hardly escape the censure of want of breeding. The old English plainness and sincerity, that generous integrity of nature and honesty of disposition, which always argues true greatness of mind, and is usually accompanied with undaunted courage and resolution, is in a great measure lost amongst us: there hath been a long endeavour to transform us into foreign manners and fashions, and to bring us to a servile imitation of none of the best of our neighbours, in some of the worst of their qualities. The dialect of conversation is now-a-days so swelled with vanity and compliment, and so surfeited, as I may say, of expressions of kindness and respect, that if a man that lived an age or two ago, should return into the world again, he would really want a dictionary to help him to understand his own language, and to know the true intrinsic value of the phrase in fashion, and would hardly at first believe at what a low rate the highest strains and expressions of kindness imaginable, do commonly pass in current payment: and when he should come to understand it, it would be a great while before he could bring himself, with a good countenance and a good conscience, to converse with men upon equal terms, and in their own way.

' And in truth it is hard to say whether it should more provoke our contempt or our pity, to hear what solemn expressions of respect and kindness will pass between men, almost upon no occasion, how great honour and esteem they will declare for one, whom perhaps, they never saw before, and how entirely they are all on the sudden devoted to his service and interest, for no reason how infinitely and eternally obliged to him, for no benefit, and how extremely they will be concerned for him, yea, and afflicted too, for no cause. I know it is said, in justification of this hollow kind of conversation, that there is no harm, no real deceit, in compliment, but the matter is well enough, so long as we understand one another; *et verba valent ut nummi,* " words are like money," and when the current value of them is generally understood, no man is cheated by them. This is something, if such words were any thing, but being brought into the account, they are mere cyphers. However, it is still a just matter of complaint, that sincerity and plainness are out of fashion, and that our language is running into a lie, that men have almost quite perverted the use of speech, and made words to signify nothing, that the greatest part of the conversation of mankind is little else but driving a trade of dissimulation, insomuch, that it would make a man heartily sick and weary of the world, to see the little sincerity that is in use and practice among men.'

When the vice is placed in this contemptible light, he argues unanswerably against it, in words and thoughts so natural, that any man who reads them would imagine he himself could have been the author of them.

'If the show of any thing be good for any thing, I am sure sincerity is better, for why does any man dissemble, or seem to be that which he is not, but because he thinks it good to have such a quality as he pretends to? For to counterfeit and dissemble, is to put on the appearance of some real excellency. Now the best way in the world to seem to be any thing, is really to be what he would seem to be. Besides, that it is many times as troublesome to make good the pretence of a good quality, as to have it; and if a man have it not, it is ten to one but he is discovered to want it; and then all his pains and labour to seem to have it is lost.'

In another part of the same discourse he goes on to shew, that all artifice must naturally tend to the disappointment of him that practises it.

'Whatsoever convenience may be thought to be in falsehood and dissimulation, it is soon over: but the inconvenience of it is perpetual, because it brings a man under an everlasting jealousy and suspicion, so that he is not believed when he speaks truth, nor trusted when perhaps he means honestly. When a man hath once forfeited the reputation of his integrity, he is set fast; and nothing will then serve his turn, neither truth nor falsehood.' R.

No. CIV. FRIDAY, JUNE 29.

.. ..Qualis equos Threissa fatigat
Harpalyce   VIR®

With such array Harpalyce bestrode
Her Thracian courser.   DRYDEN.

IT would be a noble improvement, or rather a recovery of what we call good breeding, if nothing were to pass among us for agreeable, which was the least transgression against that rule of life called decorum, or a regard to decency. This would command the respect of mankind, because it carries in it deference to their good opinion; as humility lodged in a worthy mind, is always attended with a certain homage, which no haughty soul, with all the arts imaginable, will ever be able to purchase. Tully says, Virtue and decency are so nearly related, that it is difficult to separate them from each other, but in our imagination. As the beauty of the body always accompanies the health of it, so certainly is decency concomitant to virtue: as beauty of body, with an agreeable carriage, pleases the eye, and that pleasure consists in that we observe all the parts with a certain elegance are proportioned to each other; so does decency of behaviour, which appears in our lives, obtain the approbation of all with whom we converse, from the order, consistency, and moderation of our words and actions. This flows from the reverence we bear towards every good man, and to the world in general: for to be negligent of what any one thinks of you, does not only shew you arrogant, but abandoned. In all these considerations we are to distinguish how one virtue differs from another: as it is the part of justice never to do violence, it is of modesty never to commit offence. In this last particular, lies the whole force of what is called decency: to this purpose that excellent moralist above-mentioned, talks of decency, but this quality is more easily comprehended by an ordinary capacity, than expressed with all his eloquence. This decency of behaviour, is generally transgressed among all orders of men, nay, the very women, though themselves created as it were for ornament, are often very much mistaken in this ornamental part of life. It would, methinks, be a short rule for behaviour, if every young lady in her dress, words, and actions, were only to recommend herself as a sister, daughter, or wife, and make herself the more esteemed in one of those characters. The care of themselves with regard to the families in which women are born, is the best motive for their being courted to come into the alliance of other houses. Nothing can promote this end more than a strict preservation of decency. I should be glad if a certain equestrian order of ladies, some of whom one meets in an evening at every outlet of the town, would take this subject into their serious consideration. In order thereunto, the following letter may not be wholly unworthy their perusal.

' Mr. Spectator,

' Going lately to take the air, in one of the most beautiful evenings this season has produced, as I was admiring the serenity of the sky, the lively colours of the fields, and the variety of the landscape every way around me, my eyes were suddenly called off from these inanimate objects, by a little party of horsemen I saw passing the road. The greater part of them escaped my particular observation, by reason that my whole attention was fixed on a very fair youth, who rode in the midst of them, and seemed to have been dressed by some description in a romance. His features, complexion, and habit, had a remarkable effeminacy, and a certain languishing vanity appeared in his air: his hair, well curled and powdered, hung to a considerable length on his shoulders, and was wantonly tied, as if by the hands of his mistress, in a scarlet ribband, which played like a streamer behind him: he had a coat and waistcoat of blue camlet, trimmed and embroidered with silver, a cravat of the finest lace, and wore, in a smart cock, a little beaver hat edged with silver, and made more sprightly by a feather. His horse, too, which was a pacer, was adorned after the same airy manner, and seemed to share in the vanity of the rider. As I was pitying the luxury of this young person, who appeared to me to have been educated only as an object of sight, I perceived on my nearer approach, and as I turned my eyes downward, a part of the equipage I had not observed before, which was a petticoat of the same with the coat and waistcoat. After this discovery, I looked again on the face of the fair Amazon who had thus deceived me, and thought those features which had before offended me by their softness, were now strengthened into as improper a boldness; and though her eyes, nose and mouth, seemed to be formed with perfect symmetry, I am not certain whether she, who in appearance was a very handsome youth, may not be, in reality, a very indifferent woman.

'There is an objection which naturally presents itself against these occasional perplexities and mixtures of dress, which is, that they seem to break in upon that propriety and distinction of appearance in which the beauty of different characters is preserved, and if they should be more frequent than they are at present, would look like turning our public assemblies into a general masquerade. The model of this Amazonian hunting-habit for ladies, was, as I take it, first imported from France, and well enough expresses the gaiety of a people who are taught to do any thing, so it be with an assurance; but I cannot help thinking it sits awkwardly yet on our English modesty. The petticoat is a kind of incumbrance upon it; and if the Amazons should think fit to go on in this plunder of our sex's ornaments, they ought to add to their spoils, and complete their triumph over us, by wearing the breeches

'If it be natural to contract insensibly the manners of those we imitate, the ladies who are pleased with assuming our dresses will do us more honour than we deserve, but they will do it at their own expense Why should the lovely Camilla deceive us in more shapes than her own, and affect to be represented in her picture with a gun and a spaniel; while her elder brother, the heir of a worthy family, is drawn in silks like his sister? The dress and air of a man are not well to be divided; and those who would not be content with the latter, ought never to think of assuming the former. There is so large a portion of natural agreeableness among the fair sex of our island, that they seem betrayed into these romantic habits, without having the same occasion for them with their inventors All that needs to be desired of them is, that they would be themselves, that is, what Nature designed them; and to see their mistake when they depart from this, let them look upon a man who affects the softness and effeminacy of a woman, to learn how their sex must appear to us, when approaching to the resemblance of a man.

'I am, Sir,

T   Your most humble servant.'

No. CV. SATURDAY, JUNE 30.

>   Id arbitror
>   Ad prime in vita esse utile, ne quid nimis.
>   TER.

I take it to be a principal rule of life, not to be too much addicted to any one thing.

My friend Will Honeycomb values himself very much upon what he calls the knowledge of mankind, which has cost him many disasters in his youth; for Will reckons every misfortune that he has met with among the women, and every rencounter among the men, as parts of his education, and fancies he should never have been the man he is, had not he broke windows, knocked down constables, disturbed honest people with his midnight serenades, and beat up a lewd woman's quarters, when he was a young fellow. The engaging in adventures of this nature Will calls the studying of mankind, and terms this knowledge of the town, the knowledge of the world. Will ingenuously confesses, that for half his life his head ached every morning with reading of men over-night; and at present comforts himself under certain pains which he endures from time to time, that without them he could not have been acquainted with the gallantries of the age. This Will looks upon as the learning of a gentleman, and regards all other kinds of science as the accomplishments of one whom he calls a scholar, a bookish man, or a philosopher.

For these reasons, Will shines in mixed company, where he has the discretion not to go out of his depth, and has often a certain way of making his real ignorance appear a seeming one. Our club however has frequently caught him tripping, at which times they never spare him. For as Will often insults us with his knowledge of the town, we sometimes take our revenge upon him by our knowledge of books.

He was last week producing two or three letters which he writ in his youth to a coquette lady. The raillery of them was natural and well enough for a mere man of the town; but, very unluckily, several of the words were wrong spelled. Will laughed this off at first as well as he could; but finding himself pushed on all sides, and especially by the templar, he told us with a little passion, that he never liked pedantry in spelling, and that he spelled like a gentleman, and not like a scholar: upon this Will had recourse to his old topic of shewing the narrow-spiritedness, the pride and ignorance of pedants, which he carried so far, that upon my returning to my lodgings, I could not forbear throwing together such reflections as occurred to me upon that subject.

A man who has been brought up among books, and is able to talk of nothing else, is a very indifferent companion, and what we call a pedant. But, methinks, we should enlarge the title, and give it every one that does not know how to think out of his profession and particular way of life.

What is a greater pedant than a mere man of the town? Bar him the play-houses, a catalogue of the reigning beauties, and an account of a few fashionable distempers that have befallen him, and you strike him dumb. How many a pretty gentleman's knowledge lies all within the verge of the court? He will tell you the names of the principal favourites, repeat the shrewd sayings of a man of quality, whisper an intrigue that is not yet blown upon by common fame; or if the sphere of his observations is a little larger than ordinary, will perhaps enter into all the incidents, turns, and revolutions, in a game of ombre. When he has gone thus far, he has shewn you the whole circle of his accomplishments, his parts are drained, and he is disabled from any further conversation. What are these but rank pedants? and yet these are the men who value themselves most on their exemption from the pedantry of colleges.

I might here mention the military pedant, who always talks in a camp, and is storming towns, making lodgements, and fighting battles from one end of the year to the other. Every thing he speaks smells of gunpowder. If you take away his artillery from him, he has not a word to say for himself. I might likewise mention the law pedant, that is perpetually putting cases, repeating the transactions of Westminster-Hall, wrangling with you upon the most indifferent circumstances of life, and not to be convinced of the distance of a place, or of the most trivial point in conversation, but by dint of argument. The state pedant is wrapt up in news, and lost in politics. If you mention either of the kings of Spain or Poland, he talks very notably; but if you go out of the Gazette you drop him.

In short, a mere courtier, a mere soldier, a mere scholar, a mere any thing, is an insipid pedantic character, and equally ridiculous.

Of all the species of pedants which I have mentioned, the book pedant is much the most supportable: he has at least an exercised understanding, and a head which is full though confused, so that a man who converses with him may often receive from him hints of things that are worth knowing, and what he may possibly turn to his own advantage, though they are of little use to the owner. The worst kind of pedants among learned men, are such as are naturally endowed with a very small share of common sense, and have read a great number of books without taste or distinction.

The truth of it is, learning, like travelling, and all other methods of improvement, as it finishes good sense, so it makes a silly man ten thousand times more insufferable, by supplying variety of matter to his impertinence, and giving him an opportunity of abounding in absurdities

Shallow pedants cry up one another much more than men of solid and useful learning. To read the titles they give an editor, or collator of a manuscript, you would take him for the glory of the commonwealth of letters, and the wonder of his age, when perhaps upon examination you find that he has only rectified a Greek particle, or laid out a whole sentence in proper commas

They are obliged indeed to be thus lavish of their praises, that they may keep one another in countenance; and it is no wonder if a great deal of knowledge, which is not capable of making a man wise, has a natural tendency to make him vain and arrogant.

L.

No. CVI. MONDAY, JULY 2.

——Hinc tibi copia
Manabit ad plenum, benigno
Ruris honorum opulenta cornu   HOR.

——Here to thee shall plenty flow,
And all her riches show,
To raise the honour of the quiet plain
CREECH

HAVING often received an invitation from my friend Sir Roger de Coverley to pass away a month with him in the country,—I last week accompanied him thither, and am settled with him for some time at his country-house, where I intend to form several of my ensuing speculations. Sir Roger, who is very well acquainted with my humour, lets me rise and go to bed when I please, dine at his own table, or in my chamber, as I think fit, sit still and say nothing without bidding me be merry. When the gentlemen of the country come to see him, he only shews me at a distance. As I have been walking in his fields, I have observed them stealing a sight of me over a hedge, and have heard the knight desiring them not to let me see them, for that I hated to be stared at.

I am the more at ease in Sir Roger's family, because it consists of sober and staid persons: for as the knight is the best master in the world, he seldom changes his servants; and as he is beloved by all about him, his servants never care for leaving him by this means his domestics are all in years, and grown old with their master. You would take his valet de chambre for his brother, his butler is grey-headed, his groom is one of the gravest men that I have ever seen, and his coachman has the looks of a privy-counsellor. You see the goodness of the master even in the old house-dog, and in a grey pad that is kept in the stable with great care and tenderness out of regard to his past services, though he has been useless for several years.

I could not but observe, with a great deal of pleasure, the joy that appeared in the countenances of these ancient domestics upon my friend's arrival at his country seat. Some of them could not refrain from tears at the sight of their old master; every one of them pressed forward to do something for him, and seemed discouraged if they were not employed. At the same time the good old knight, with a mixture of the father and the master of the family, tempered the inquiries after his own affairs with several kind questions relating to themselves. This humanity and good nature engages every body to him; so that when he is pleasant upon any of them, all his family are in good humour, and none so much as the person whom he diverts himself with: on the contrary, if he coughs, or betrays any infirmity of old age, it is easy for a stander-by to observe a secret concern in the looks of all his servants.

My worthy friend has put me under the particular care of his butler, who is a very prudent man, and, as well as the rest of his fellow-servants, wonderfully desirous of pleasing me, because they have often heard their master talk of me as of his particular friend.

My chief companion, when Sir Roger is diverting himself in the woods or the fields, is a very venerable man who is ever with Sir Roger, and has lived at his house in the nature of a chaplain above thirty years. This gentleman is a person of good sense and some learning, of a very regular life and obliging conversation: he heartily loves Sir Roger, and knows that he is very much in the old knight's esteem; so that he lives in the family rather as a relation than a dependent.

I have observed in several of my papers, that my friend Sir Roger, amidst all his good qualities, is something of an humourist; and that his virtues, as well as imperfections, are as it were tinged by a certain extravagance, which makes them particularly HIS, and distinguishes them from those of other men. This cast of mind, as it is generally very innocent in itself, so it renders his conversation highly agreeable, and more delightful than the same degree of sense and virtue would appear in their common and ordinary colours. As I was walking with him last night, he asked me how I liked the good man whom I have just now mentioned? and, without staying for my answer, told me, that he was afraid of being insulted with Latin and Greek at his own table, for which reason he desired a particular friend of his at the university to find him out a clergyman rather of plain sense than much learning, of a good aspect, a clear voice, a sociable temper, and, if possible, a man that understood a little of back-gammon. My friend, says Sir Roger, found me out this gentleman, who, besides the endowments required of him, is, they tell me, a good scholar, though he does not shew it. I have given him the parsonage of the parish, and because I know his value, have settled upon him a good annuity for life. If he outlives me, he shall find that he was higher in my esteem than perhaps he thinks he is. He has now been with me thirty years; and though he does not know I have taken notice of it, has never in all that time asked any thing of me for himself, though he is every day soliciting me for something in behalf of one or other of my tenants his parishioners. There has not been a law suit in the parish since he has lived among them. If any dispute arises, they apply themselves to him for the decision; if they do not acquiesce in his judgment, which I think never happened above once or twice at most, they appeal to me. At his first settling with me, I made him a present of all the good sermons which have been printed in English, and only begged of him that every Sunday he would pronounce one of them in the pulpit. Accordingly he has digested them into such a series, that they follow one another naturally, and make a continued system of practical divinity.

As Sir Roger was going on in his story, the gentleman we were talking of, came up to us; and upon the knight's asking him who preached to-morrow (for it was Saturday night), told us, the bishop of St. Asaph in the morning, and Dr. South in the afternoon. He then shewed us a list of preachers for the whole year; where I saw with a great deal of pleasure archbishop Tillotson, bishop Saunderson, Dr. Barrow, Dr. Calamy, with several living authors who have published discourses of practical divinity. I no sooner saw this venerable man in the pulpit, but I very much approved of my friend's insisting upon the qualifications of a good aspect and a clear voice; for I was so charmed with the gracefulness of his figure and delivery, as well as with the discourses he pronounced, that I think I never passed any time more to my satisfaction. A sermon repeated after this manner, is like the composition of a poet in the mouth of a graceful actor.

I could heartily wish that more of our country-clergy would follow this example; and instead of wasting their spirits in laborious compositions of their own, would endeavour after a handsome elocution, and all those other talents that are proper to enforce what has been penned by greater masters. This would not only be more easy to themselves, but more edifying to the people.
L.

No. CVII.   TUESDAY, JULY 3.

*Æsopo ingentem statuam posuere Attici,
Servumque collocârunt æterna in basi,
Patere honoris scirent ut cuncti viam*

PHÆDR.

The Athenians erected a large statue to Æsop, and placed him, though a slave, on a lasting pedestal, to shew that the way to honour lies open indifferently to all.

THE reception, manner of attendance, undisturbed freedom and quiet, which I meet with here in the country, has confirmed me in the opinion I always had, that the general corruption of manners in servants is owing to the conduct of masters. The aspect of every one in the family carries so much satisfaction, that it appears he knows the happy lot which has befallen him in being a member of it. There is one particular which I have seldom seen but at Sir Roger's: it is usual in all other places, that servants fly from the parts of the house through which their master is passing; on the contrary, here they industriously place themselves in his way, and it is on both sides, as it were, understood as a visit, when the servants appear without calling. This proceeds from the humane and equal temper of the man of the house, who also perfectly well knows how to enjoy a great estate, with such economy as ever to be much beforehand. This makes his own mind untroubled, and consequently unapt to vent peevish expressions, or give passionate or inconsistent orders to those about him. Thus, respect and love go together, and a certain cheerfulness in the performance of their duty is the particular distinction of the lower part of this family. When a servant is called before his master, he does not come with an expectation of hearing himself rated for some trivial fault, threatened to be stripped, or used with any other unbecoming language, which mean masters often give to worthy servants, but it is often to know, what road he took that he came so readily back according to order, whether he passed by such a ground, if the old man who rents it is in good health, or whether he gave Sir Roger's love to him, or the like

A man who preserves a respect, founded on his benevolence to his dependents, lives rather like a prince than a master in his family; his orders are received as favours rather than duties, and the distinction of approaching him is part of the reward for executing what is commanded by him

There is another circumstance in which my friend excels in his management, which is the manner of rewarding his servants. he has ever been of opinion, that giving his cast clothes to be worn by valets has a very ill effect upon little minds, and creates a silly sense of equality between the parties, in persons affected only with outward things. I have heard him often pleasant on this occasion, and describe a young gentleman abusing his man in that coat, which a month or two before was the most pleasing distinction he was conscious of in himself. He would turn his discourse still more pleasantly upon the ladies' bounties of this kind, and I have heard him say he knew a fine woman, who distributed rewards and punishments in giving becoming or unbecoming dresses to her maids

But my good friend is above these little instances of good-will, in bestowing only trifles on his servants a good servant to him is sure of having it in his choice very soon of being no servant at all. As I before observed, he is so good an husband, and knows so thoroughly that the skill of the purse is the cardinal virtue of this life, I say, he knows so well that frugality is the support of generosity, that he can often spare a large fine when a tenement falls, and give that settlement to a good servant who has a mind to go into the world, or make a stranger pay the fine to that servant, for his more comfortable maintenance, if he stays in his service.

A man of honour and generosity considers it would be miserable to himself to have no will but that of another, though it were of the best person breathing, and for that reason goes on as fast as he is able to put his servants into independent livelihoods. The greatest part of Sir Roger's estate is tenanted by persons who have served himself or his ancestors. It was to me extremely pleasant to observe the visitants from several parts to welcome his arrival into the country: and all the difference that I could take notice of between the late servants who came to see him, and those who staid in the family, was, that these latter were looked upon as finer gentlemen and better courtiers.

This manumission, and placing them in a way of livelihood, I look upon as only what is due to a good servant, which encouragement will make his successor be as diligent, as humble, and as ready as he was. There is something wonderful in the narrowness of those minds which can be pleased, and be barren of bounty to those who please them.

One might, on this occasion, recount the sense that great persons in all ages have had of the merit of their dependents, and the heroic services which men have done their masters in the extremity of their fortunes; and shewn to their undone patrons, that fortune was all the difference between them, but as I design this my speculation only as a gentle admonition to thankless masters, I shall not go out of the occurrences of common life, but assert it as a general observation, that I never saw, but in Sir Roger's family, and one or two more, good servants treated as they ought to be. Sir Roger's kindness extends to their children's children; and this very morning he sent his coachman's grandson apprentice. I shall conclude this paper with an account of a picture in his gallery, where there are many which will deserve my future observation.

At the very upper end of this handsome structure I saw the portraiture of two young men standing in a river, the one naked, the other in a livery. The person supported seemed half dead, but still so much alive as to shew in his face exquisite joy and love towards the other. I thought the fainting figure resembled my friend Sir Roger; and looking at the butler, who stood by me, for an account of it, he informed me, that the person in the livery was a servant of Sir Roger's, who stood on the shore while his master was swimming, and observing him taken with some sudden illness, and sink under water, jumped in and saved him. He told me, Sir Roger took off the dress he was in as soon as he came home, and by a great bounty at that time, followed by his favour ever since, had made him master of that pretty seat which we saw at a distance as we came to this house. I remembered indeed Sir Roger said, there lived a very worthy gentleman, to whom he was highly obliged, without mentioning any thing further Upon my looking a little dissatisfied at some part of the picture, my attendant informed me that it was against Sir Roger's will, and at the earnest request of the gentleman himself, that he was drawn in the habit in which he had saved his master.   R

No. CVIII. WEDNESDAY, JULY 4.

Gratis anhelans, multa agendo nihil agens.
                                    PHÆDR.

Out of breath to no purpose, and very busy about nothing.

As I was yesterday morning walking with Sir Roger before his house, a country fellow brought him a huge fish, which, he told him Mr. William Wimble had caught that very morning, and that he presented it, with his service to him, and intended to come and dine with him. At the same time he delivered a letter, which my friend read to me as soon as the messenger left him.

'SIR ROGER,

'I DESIRE you to accept of a jack, which is the best I have caught this season. I intend to come and stay with you a week, and see how the perch bite in the Black River. I observed, with some concern, the last time I saw you upon the bowling-green, that your whip wanted a lash to it; I will bring half a dozen with me that I twisted last week, which I hope will serve you all the time you are in the country. I have not been out of the saddle for six days last past, having been at Eaton with Sir John's eldest son. He takes to his learning hugely. I am,
  'Sir,
    'Your humble servant,
      'WILL WIMBLE.'

This extraordinary letter, and message that accompanied it, made me very curious to know the character and quality of the gentleman who sent them; which I 'found to be as follows. Will Wimble is younger brother to a baronet, and descended of the ancient family of the Wimbles. He is now between forty and fifty; but being bred to no business, and born to no estate, he generally lives with his elder brother as superintendant of his game. He hunts a pack of dogs better than any man in the country, and is very famous for finding out a hare. He is extremely well versed in all the little handicrafts of an idle man: he makes a May-fly to a miracle, and furnishes the whole country with anglerods. As he is a good-natured officious fellow, and very much esteemed upon account of his family, he is a welcome guest at every house, and keeps up a good correspondence among all the gentlemen about him. He carries a tulip-root in his pocket from one to another, or exchanges a puppy between a couple of friends that live perhaps in the opposite sides of the county. Will is a particular favourite of all the young heirs, whom he frequently obliges with a net that he has weaved, or a setting dog that he has 'made' himself. He now and then presents a pair of garters of his own knitting to their mothers or sisters; and raises a great deal of mirth among them, by inquiring as often as he meets them, "how they wear?" These gentleman-like manufactures and obliging little humours make Will the darling of the country.

Sir Roger was proceeding in the character of him, when we saw him make up to us with two or three hazel twigs in his hand that he had cut in Sir Roger's woods as he came through them in his way to the house. I was very much pleased to observe on one side the hearty and sincere welcome with which Sir Roger received him, and on the other the secret joy which his guest discovered at sight of the good old knight. After the first salutes were over, Will desired Sir Roger to lend him one of his servants to carry a set of shuttle-cocks he had with him in a little box, to a lady that lived about a mile off, to whom it seems he had promised such a present for above this half year. Sir Roger's back was no sooner turned, but honest Will began to tell me of a large cock-pheasant that he had sprung in one of the neighbouring woods, with two or three other adventures of the same nature. Odd and uncommon characters are the game that I look for, and most delight in; for which reason I was as much pleased with the novelty of the person that talked to me, as he could be for his life with the springing of a pheasant, and therefore listened to him with more than ordinary attention.

In the midst of his discourse the bell rung to dinner, where the gentleman I have been speaking of had the pleasure of seeing the huge jack he had caught served up for the first dish in a most sumptuous manner. Upon our sitting down to it, he gave us a long account how he had hooked it, played with it, foiled it, and at length drew it out upon the bank, with several other particulars that lasted all the first course. A dish of wild-fowl that came afterwards furnished conversation for the rest of the dinner, which concluded with a late invention of Will's for improving the quail-pipe.

Upon withdrawing into my room, after dinner, I was secretly touched with compassion towards the honest gentleman that had dined with us; and could not but consider, with a great deal of concern, how so good an heart and such busy hands were wholly employed in trifles, that so much humanity should be so little beneficial to others, and so much industry so little advantageous to himself. The same temper of mind and application to affairs, might have recommended him to the public esteem, and have raised his fortune in another station of life. What good to his country, or himself, might not a trader or merchant have done with such useful, though ordinary qualifications?

Will Wimble's is the case of many a younger brother of a great family, who had rather see their children starve like gentlemen, than thrive in a trade or profession that is beneath their quality. This humour fills several parts of Europe with pride and beggary. It is the happiness of a trading nation, like ours, that the younger sons, though incapable of any liberal art or profession, may be placed in such a way of life as may perhaps enable them to vie with the best of their family: accordingly we find several citizens that were launched into the world with narrow fortunes, rising, by an honest industry, to greater estates than those of their elder brothers. It is not improbable but Will was formerly tried at divinity, law, or physic, and that, finding his genius did not lie that way, his parents gave him up at length to his own inventions. But certainly, however improper he might have been for studies of a higher nature, he was perfectly well turned for the occupations of trade and commerce. As I think this is a point which cannot be too much inculcated, I shall desire my reader to compare what I have here written, with what I have said in my twenty-first speculation.

L.

No. CIX. THURSDAY, JULY 5.

Abnormis sapiens.. .. Hor.

Of plain good sense, untutor'd in the schools

I WAS this morning walking in the gallery, when Sir Roger entered at the end opposite to me, and advancing towards me, said he was glad to meet me among his relations the De Coverleys, and hoped I liked the conversation of so much good company, who were as silent as myself. I knew he alluded to the pictures; and as he is a gentleman who does not a little value himself upon his ancient descent, I expected he would give me some account of them. We were now arrived at the upper end of the gallery, when the knight faced towards one of the pictures; and as we stood before it, he entered into the matter, after his blunt way, of saying things as they occur to his imagination, without regular introduction, or care to preserve the appearance of chain of thought.

' It is, said he, worth while to consider the force of dress, and how the persons of one age, differ from those of another, merely by that only. One may observe also, that the general fashion of one age has been followed by one particular set of people in another, and by them preserved from one generation to another. Thus, the vast-jetting coat and small bonnet, which was the habit in Harry the Seventh's time, is kept on in the yeomen of the guard; not without a good and politic view, because they look a foot taller and a foot and a half broader; besides that, the cap leaves the face expanded, and consequently more terrible, and fitter to stand at the entrance of pallaces.

' This predecessor of ours, you see, is dressed after this manner, and his cheeks would be no larger than mine, were he in a hat as I am. He was the last man that won a prize in the tilt-yard, which is now a common street before Whitehall. You see the broken lance that lies there by his right foot; he shivered that lance of his adversary all to pieces; and bearing himself, look you, Sir, in this manner, at the same time he came within the target of the gentleman who rode against him, and taking him with incredible force before him on the pommel of the saddle, he in that manner rid the tournament over, with an air that shewed he did it rather to perform the rule of the lists than expose his enemy: however, it appeared he knew how to make use of a victory, and with a gentle trot, he marched up to a gallery where their mistress sat, for they were rivals, and let him down with laudable courtesy, and pardonable insolence. I do not know but it might be exactly where the coffee-house is now.

'You are to know, this my ancestor was not only of a military genius, but fit also for the arts of peace, for he played on the bass-viol, as well as any gentleman at court; you see where his viol hangs by his basket-hilt sword. The action at the tilt-yard, you may be sure won the fair lady, who was a maid of honour, and the greatest beauty of her time; here she stands the next picture. You see, Sir, my great great great grand-mother, has on the new fashioned petticoat, except that the modern is gathered at the waist; my grand-mother appears as if she stood in a large drum, whereas the ladies now walk as if they were in a go-cart. For all this lady was bred at court, she became an excellent country wife; she brought ten children: and when I shew you the library, you shall see in her own hand, allowing for the difference of the language, the best receipt now in England, both for a hasty-pudding and a white pot.

'If you please to fall back a little, because it is necessary to look at the three next pictures at one view; these are three sisters. She on the right hand, who is so very beautiful, died a maid; the next to her, still handsomer, had the same fate against her will; this homely thing in the middle, had both their portions added to her own, and was stolen by a neighbouring gentleman, a man of stratagem and resolution; for he poisoned three mastiffs to come at her, and knocked down two deer stealers in carrying her off. Misfortunes happen in all families: the theft of this romp and so much money was no great matter to our estate. But the next heir who possessed it, was this soft gentleman, whom you see there. observe the small buttons, the little boots, the laces, the slashes about his clothes, and above all, the posture he is drawn in, (which to be sure was his own chusing). you see he sits with one hand on a desk writing, and looking as it were another way, like an easy writer or a sonneteer: he was one of those who had too much wit to know how to live in the world, he was a man of no justice, but great good manners; he ruined every body that had any thing to do with him, but never said a rude thing in his life. the most indolent person in the world, he would sign a deed that passed away half his estate with his gloves on, but would not put on his hat before a lady if it were to save his country. He is said to be the first that made love by squeezing the hand. He left the estate with ten thousand pounds debt upon it: but however, by all hands I have been informed, that he was every way the finest gentleman in the world. That debt lay heavy on our house for one generation, but it was retrieved by a gift from that honest man you see there, a citizen of our name, but nothing at all akin to us. I know Sir Andrew Freeport has said behind my back, that this man was descended from one of the ten children of the maid of honour I shewed you above; but it was never made out. We winked at the thing indeed, because money was wanting at that time.'

Here I saw my friend a little embarrassed, and turned my face to the next portraiture.

Sir Roger went on with his account of the gallery in the following manner. ' This man (pointing to him I looked at) I take to be the honour of our house, Sir Humphrey de Coverley; he was in his dealings as punctual as a tradesman, and as generous as a gentleman.

' He would have thought himself as much undone by breaking his word, as if it were to be followed by bankruptcy. He served his country as knight of this shire to his dying day. He found it no easy matter to maintain an integrity in his words and actions, even in things that regarded the offices that were incumbent upon him, in the care of his own affairs and relations of life, and therefore dreaded, though he had great talents, to go into employments of state, where he must be exposed to the snares of ambition. Innocence of life, and great ability, were the distinguishing parts of his character; the latter, he had often observed, had led to the destruction of the former, and used frequently to lament that Great and Good had not the same signification. He was an excellent husbandman, but had resolved not to exceed such a degree of wealth; all above it he bestowed in secret bounties, many years after the sum he aimed at for his own use was attained. Yet he did not slacken his industry, but, to a decent old age, spent the life and fortune which was superfluous to himself, in the service of his friends and neighbours.'

Here we were called to dinner, and Sir Roger ended the discourse of this gentleman, by telling me, as we followed the servant, that his ancestor was a brave man, and narrowly escaped being killed in the civil wars; 'For (said he) he was sent out of the field upon a private message the day before the battle of Worcester.' The whim of narrowly escaping by having been within a day of danger, with other matters above-mentioned, mixed with good sense, left me at a loss whether I was more delighted with my friend's wisdom or simplicity. R

No. CX. FRIDAY, JULY 6.

Horror ubique animos, simul ipsa silentia terrent.
VIRG.

All things are full of horror and affright,
And dreadful ev'n the silence of the night
DRYDEN.

AT a little distance from Sir Roger's house, among the ruins of an old abbey, there is a long walk of aged elms; which are shot up so very high, that when one passes under them, the rooks and crows that rest upon the tops of them seem to be cawing in another region. I am very much delighted with this sort of noise, which I consider as a kind of natural prayer to that Being who supplies the wants of his whole creation, and who, in the beautiful language of the Psalms, ' feedeth the young ravens that call upon him.' I like this retirement the better, because of an ill report it lies under of being haunted; for which reason, as I have been told in the family, no living creature ever walks in it besides the chaplain. My good friend the butler desired me, with a very grave face, not to venture myself in it after sun-set, for that one of the footmen had been almost frightened out of his wits by a spirit that appeared to him in the shape of a black horse without an head, to which he added, that about a month ago, one of the maids coming home late that way, with a pail of milk upon her head, heard such a rustling among the bushes, that she let it fall.

I was taking a walk in this place last night between the hours of nine and ten, and could not but fancy it one of the most proper scenes in the world for a ghost to appear in. The ruins of the abbey are scattered up and down on every side, and half covered with ivy and elder bushes, the harbours of several solitary birds which seldom make their appearance till the dusk of the evening. The place was formerly a church-yard, and has still several marks in it of graves and burying-places. There is such an echo among the old ruins and vaults, that if you stamp but a little louder than ordinary, you hear the sound repeated. At the same time the walk of elms, with the croaking of the ravens, which from time to time are heard from the tops of them, looks exceeding solemn and venerable. These objects naturally raise seriousness and attention; and when night heightens the awfulness of the place, and pours out her supernumerary horrors upon every thing in it, I do not at all wonder that weak minds fill it with spectres and apparitions.

Mr. Locke, in his chapter of the Association of Ideas, has very curious remarks, to show how, by the prejudice of education, one idea often introduces into the mind a whole set that bear no resemblance to one another in the nature of things. Among several examples of this kind, he produces the following instance. ' The ideas of goblins and sprites have really no more 'to do with darkness than light; yet let but a foolish ' maid inculcate these often on the mind of a child, and ' raise them there together, possibly he shall never be ' able to separate them again so long as he lives; but ' darkness shall ever afterwards bring with it those ' frightful ideas, and they shall be so joined, that he can ' no more bear the one than the other.'

As I was walking in this solitude, where the dusk of the evening conspired with so many other occasions of terror, I observed a cow grazing not far from me, which an imagination that is apt to startle might easily have construed into a black horse without a head; and I dare say the poor footman lost his wits upon some such trivial occasion.

My friend Sir Roger has often told me, with a good deal of mirth, that at his first coming to his estate he found three parts of his house altogether useless; that the best room in it had the reputation of being haunted, and by that means was locked up; that noises had been heard in his long gallery, so that he could not get a servant to enter it after eight o'clock at night; that the door of one of his chambers was nailed up, because there went a story in the family that a butler had formerly hanged himself in it; and that his mother, who lived to a great age, had shut up half the rooms in the house, in which either her husband, a son, or a daughter had died. The Knight seeing his habitation reduced to so small a compass, and himself in a manner shut out of his own house, upon the death of his mother ordered all the apartments to be flung open, and exorcised by his chaplain, who lay in every one after another, and by that means dissipated the fears which had so long reigned in the family.

I should not have been thus particular upon these ridiculous horrors, did not I find them so very much prevail in all parts of the country. At the same time I think a person who is thus terrified with the imagination of ghosts and spectres, much more reasonable than one who, contrary to the reports of all historians sacred and profane, ancient and modern, and to the traditions of all nations, thinks the appearance of spirits fabulous and groundless. could not I give myself up to this general testimony of mankind, I should to the relations of particular persons who are now living, and whom I cannot distrust in other matters of fact. I might here add that not only the historians, to whom we may join the poets, but likewise the philosophers of antiquity, have favoured this opinion. Lucretius himself, though by the course of his philosophy he was obliged to maintain that the soul did not exist separate from the body, makes no doubt of the reality of apparitions, and that men have often appeared after their death. This I think very remarkable: he was so pressed with the matter of fact, which he could not have the confidence to deny, that he was forced to account for it by one of the most absurd unphilosophical notions that was ever started. He tells us, that the surfaces of all bodies are perpetually flying off from their respective bodies, one after another; and that these surfaces or thin cases that included each other whilst they were joined in the body, like the coats of an onion, are sometimes seen entire when they were separated from it; by which means we often behold the shapes and shadows of persons who are either dead or absent.

I shall dismiss this paper with a story out of Josephus, not so much for the sake of the story itself, as for the moral reflections with which the author concludes it, and which I shall here set down in his own words. ' Glaphyra the daughter of king Archelaus, after the death of her two first husbands (being married to a third, who was brother to her first husband, and so passionately in love with her that he turned off his former wife to make room for this marriage), had a very odd kind of dream. She fancied that she saw her first husband coming towards her, and that she embraced him with great tenderness; when, in the midst of the pleasure which she expressed at the sight of him, he reproached her after the following manner: " Glaphyra (says he,) thou hast made good the old saying, That women are not to be trusted. Was not I the husband of thy virginity? Have I not children by thee? How couldst thou forget our loves so far as to enter into a second marriage, and after that into a third; nay, to take for thy husband a man who has so shamelessly crept into the bed of his brother? However, for the sake of our past loves, I shall free thee from thy present reproach, and make thee mine for ever." Glaphyra told this dream to several women of her acquaintance, and died soon after. I thought this story might not be impertinent in this place, wherein I speak of those kings; besides that, the example deserves to be taken notice of, as it contains a most certain proof of the immortality of the soul, and of divine Providence. If any man thinks these facts incredible, let him enjoy his own opinion to himself, but let him not endeavour to disturb the belief of others, who, by instances of this nature, are excited to the study of virtue.'

L

No. CXI.   SATURDAY, JULY 7.

.... Inter silvas academi quærere verum
Hor.

To search for truth in academic groves.

The course of my last speculation led me insensibly into a subject upon which I always meditate with great delight, I mean the immortality of the soul. I was yesterday walking alone in one of my friend's woods, and lost myself in it very agreeably, as I was running over in my mind the several arguments that establish this great point, which is the basis of morality, and the source of all the pleasing hopes and secret joys that can arise in the heart of a reasonable creature. I considered those several proofs drawn,

First, From the nature of the soul itself, and particularly its immateriality; which, though not absolutely necessary to the eternity of its duration, has, I think, been evidenced to almost a demonstration.

Secondly, From its passions and sentiments, as particularly from its love of existence, its horror of annihilation, and its hopes of immortality, with that secret satisfaction which it finds in the practice of virtue, and that uneasiness which follows in it upon the commission of vice.

Thirdly, From the nature of the supreme Being, whose justice, goodness, wisdom, and veracity, are all concerned in this great point.

But among these and other excellent arguments for the immortality of the soul, there is one drawn from the perpetual progress of the soul to its perfection, without a possibility of ever arriving at it; which is a hint that I do not remember to have seen opened and improved by others who have written on this subject, though it seems to me to carry great weight with it. How can it enter into the thoughts of man, that the soul, which is capable of such immense perfections, and of receiving new improvements to all eternity, shall fall away into nothing almost as soon as it is created? Are such abilities made for no purpose? A brute arrives at a point of perfection that he can never pass: in a few years he has all the endowments he is capable of; and were he to live ten thousand more, would be the same thing he is at present. Were a human soul thus at a stand in her accomplishments, were her faculties to be full blown, and incapable of farther enlargements, I could imagine it might fall away insensibly, and drop at once into a state of annihilation. But can we believe a thinking being, that is in a perpetual progress of improvements, and travelling on from perfection to perfection, after having just looked abroad into the works of its Creator, and made a few discoveries of his infinite goodness, wisdom, and power, must perish at her first setting out, and in the very beginning of her inquiries?

A man, considered in his present state, seems only sent into the world to propagate his kind. He provides himself with a successor, and immediately quits his post to make room for him.

>............Hæres
Hæredem alterius, velut unda supervenit undam.
Hor.

.......Heir crowds heir, as in a rolling flood
Wave urges wave.
Creech.

He does not seem born to enjoy life, but to deliver it down to others. This is not surprising to consider in animals, which are formed for our use, and can finish their business in a short life. The silk-worm, after having spun her task, lays her eggs and dies. But a man can never have taken in his full measure of knowledge, has not time to subdue his passions, establish his soul in virtue, and come up to the perfection of his nature, before he is hurried off the stage. Would an infinitely wise Being make such glorious creatures for so mean a purpose? Can he delight in the production of such abortive intelligences, such short-lived reasonable beings? Would he give us talents that are not to be exerted? Capacities that are never to be gratified? How can we find that wisdom which shines through all his works, in the formation of man, without looking on this world as only a nursery for the next, and believing that the several generations of rational creatures, which rise up and disappear in such quick successions, are only to receive their first rudiments of existence here, and afterwards to be transplanted into a more friendly climate, where they may spread and flourish to all eternity?

There is not, in my opinion, a more pleasing and triumphant consideration in religion than this, of the perpetual progress which the soul makes towards the perfection of its nature, without ever arriving at a period in it. To look upon the soul as going on from strength to strength, to consider that she is to shine for ever with new accessions of glory, and brighten to all eternity; that she will be still adding virtue to virtue, and knowledge to knowledge... carries in it something wonderfully agreeable to that ambition which is natural to the mind of man. Nay, it must be a prospect pleasing to God himself, to see his creation for ever beautifying in his eyes, and drawing nearer to him, by greater degrees of resemblance.

Methinks this single consideration, of the progress of a finite spirit to perfection, will be sufficient to extinguish all envy in inferior natures, and all contempt in superior. That cherubim, which now appears as a god to a human soul, knows very well that the period will come about in eternity, when the human soul shall be as perfect as he himself now is, nay, when she shall look down upon that degree of perfection as much as she now falls short of it. It is true, the higher nature still advances, and by that means preserves his distance and superiority in the scale of being; but he knows that high howsoever the station is of which he stands possessed at present, the inferior nature will at length mount up to it, and shine forth in the same degree of glory.

With what astonishment and veneration may we look into our own souls, where there are such hidden stores of virtue and knowledge, such inexhausted sources of perfection! We know not yet what we shall be, nor will it ever enter into the heart of man to conceive the glory that will be always in reserve for him. The soul, considered with its Creator, is like one of those mathematical lines that may draw nearer to another for all eternity without a possibility of touching it. and can there be a thought so transporting, as to consider ourselves in these perpetual approaches to Him, who is not only the standard of perfection, but of happiness? L

No. CXII. MONDAY, JULY 9.

'Αθανάτους μὲν πρῶτα θεὸς, νόμω ὡς διάκειται,
Τιμᾶ......... PYTHAG.

First, in obedience to thy country's rights,
Worship th' immortal gods.

I AM always very well pleased with a country Sunday, and think, if keeping holy the seventh day were only a human institution, it would be the best method that could have been thought of for the polishing and civilizing of mankind. It is certain the country people would soon degenerate into a kind of savages and barbarians, were there not such frequent returns of a stated time in which the whole village meet together with their best faces, and in their cleanliest habits, to converse with one another upon indifferent subjects, hear their duties explained to them, and join together in adoration of the supreme Being. Sunday clears away the rust of the whole week, not only as it refreshes in their minds the notions of religion, but as it puts both the sexes upon appearing in their most agreeable forms, and exerting all such qualities as are apt to give them a figure in the eye of the village. A country fellow distinguishes himself as much in the church-yard as a citizen does upon the 'Change; the whole parish-politics being generally discussed in that place either after sermon or before the bell rings.

My friend Sir Roger being a good church-man, has beautified the inside of his church with several texts of his own choosing; he has likewise given a handsome pulpit-cloth, and railed in the communion-table at his own expense. He has often told me, that at his coming to his estate, he found his parishioners very irregular;

and that in order to make them kneel and join in their responses, he gave every one of them a hassoc and a common-prayer book: and at the same time employed an itinerant singing-master, who goes about the country for that purpose, to instruct them rightly in the tunes of the Psalms, upon which they now very much value themselves, and indeed out-do most of the country churches that I have ever heard.

As Sir Roger is landlord to the whole congregation, he keeps them in very good order, and will suffer nobody to sleep in it besides himself; for if by chance he has been surprised into a short nap at sermon, upon recovering out of it, he stands up and looks about him, and if he sees any body else nodding, either wakes them himself, or sends his servants to them. Several other of the old knight's particularities break out upon these occasions: sometimes he will be lengthening out a verse in the singing Psalms half a minute after the rest of the congregation have done with it, sometimes, when he is pleased with the matter of his devotion he pronounces Amen three or four times to the same prayer, and sometimes stands up when every body else is upon their knees, to count the congregation, or see if any of his tenants are missing.

I was yesterday very much surprised to hear my old friend, in the midst of the service, calling out to one John Matthews to mind what he was about, and not disturb the congregation. This John Matthews, it seems, is remarkable for being an idle fellow, and at that time was kicking his heels for his diversion. This authority of the knight, though exerted in that odd manner which accompanies him in all circumstances of life, has a very good effect upon the parish, who are not polite enough to see any thing ridiculous in his behaviour; besides that, the general good sense and worthiness of his character make his friends observe those little singularities as foils that rather set off than blemish his good qualities.

As soon as the sermon is finished, nobody presumes to stir till Sir Roger is gone out of the church. The knight walks down from his seat in the chancel between a double row of his tenants, that stand bowing to him on each side: and every now and then inquires how such an one's wife, or mother, or son, or father do, whom he does not see at church, which is understood as a secret reprimand to the person that is absent.

The chaplain has often told me, that upon a catechising day, when Sir Roger has been pleased with a boy that answers well, he has ordered a bible to be given him next day for his encouragement: and sometimes accompanies it with a flitch of bacon to his mother. Sir Roger has likewise added five pounds a-year to the clerk's place, and, that he may encourage the young fellows to make themselves perfect in the church-service, has promised, upon the death of the present incumbent, who is very old, to bestow it according to merit.

The fair understanding between Sir Roger and his chaplain, and their mutual concurrence in doing good, is the more remarkable, because the very next village is famous for the differences and contentions that rise between the parson and the esquire, who live in a perpetual state of war. The parson is always preaching at the esquire, and the esquire to be revenged on the parson never comes to church. The esquire has made all his tenants atheists and tithe-stealers, while the parson instructs them every Sunday in the dignity of his order, and insinuates to them, in almost every sermon, that he is a better man than his patron. In short, matters are come to such an extremity, that the esquire has not said his prayers, either in public or private, this half year, and that the parson threatens him, if he does not mend his manners, to pray for him in the face of the whole congregation.

Feuds of this nature, though too frequent in the country, are very fatal to the ordinary people; who are so used to be dazzled with riches, that they pay as much deference to the understanding of a man of an estate, as of a man of learning; and are very hardly brought to regard any truth, how important soever it may be, that is preached to them, when they know there are several men of five hundred a-year who do not believe it.

L

No. CXIII. TUESDAY, JULY 10.

.——Hærent infixi pectore vultus   VIRG.

Her looks were deep imprinted in his heart.

In my first description of the company in which I pass most of my time, it may be remembered that I mentioned a great affliction which my friend Sir Roger had met with in his youth, which was no less than a disappointment in love. It happened this evening that we fell into a very pleasing walk at a distance from his house: as soon as we came into it, 'It is (quoth the good old man, looking round him with a smile) very hard that any part of my land should be settled upon one who has used me so ill as the perverse widow did; and yet I am sure I could not see a sprig of any bough of this whole walk of trees, but I should reflect upon her and her severity. She has certainly the finest hand of any woman in the world. You are to know this was the place wherein I used to muse upon her, and by that custom, I can never come into it but the same tender sentiments revive in my mind, as if I had actually walked with that beautiful creature under these shades. I have been fool enough to carve her name on the bark of several of these trees, so unhappy is the condition of men in love, to attempt the removing of their passion by the methods which serve only to imprint it deeper. She has certainly the finest hand of any woman in the world.'

Here followed a profound silence; and I was not displeased to observe my friend falling so naturally into a discourse which I had ever before taken notice he industriously avoided. After a very long pause, he entered upon an account of this great circumstance in his life, with an air which I thought raised my ideas of him above what I had ever had before, and gave me the picture of that cheerful mind of his, before it received that stroke which has ever since affected his words and actions. But he went on as follows.

' I came to my estate in my twenty-second year, and resolved to follow the steps of the most worthy of my ancestors, who have inhabited this spot of earth before me, in all the methods of hospitality and good neighbourhood, for the sake of my fame; and in country sports and recreations, for the sake of my health. In my twenty-third year I was obliged to serve as sheriff of the county, and in my servants, officers, and whole equipage, indulged the pleasure of a young man (who did not think ill of his own person) of taking that public occasion of shewing my figure and behaviour to advantage. You may easily imagine to yourself what appearance I made, who am pretty tall, ride well, and was very well dressed, at the head of a whole county, with music before me, a feather in my hat, and my horse well bitted. I can assure you I was not a little pleased with the kind looks and glances I had from all the balconies and windows as I rode to the hall where the assizes were held. But when I came there, a beautiful creature in a widow's habit sat in court, to hear the event of a cause concerning her dower. This commanding creature (who was born for the destruction of all who behold her) put on such a resignation in her countenance, and bore the whispers of all around the court, with such a pretty uneasiness, I warrant you, and then recovered herself from one eye to another, till she was perfectly confused, by meeting something so wistful in all she encountered, that at last, with a murrain to her, she cast her bewitching eye upon me. I no sooner met it, but I bowed, like a great surprised booby; and knowing her cause to be the first which came on, I cried, like a captivated calf, as I was, make way for the defendant's witnesses. This sudden partiality, made all the county immediately see the sheriff also was become a slave to the fine widow. During the time her cause was upon trial, she behaved herself, I warrant you, with such a deep attention to her business, took opportunities to have little billets handed to her counsel, then would be in such a pretty confusion, occasioned, you must know, by acting before so much company, that not only I, but the whole court, was prejudiced in her favour, and all that the next heir to her husband had to urge, was thought so groundless and frivolous, that when it came to her counsel to reply, there was not half so much said as every one besides in the court thought he could have urged to her advantage. You must understand, Sir, this perverse woman is one of those unaccountable creatures that secretly rejoice in the admiration of men, but indulge themselves in no farther consequences. Hence it is that she has ever had a train of admirers, and she removes from her slaves in town to those in the country, according to the seasons of the year. She is a reading lady, and far gone in the pleasures of friendship, she is always accompanied by a confidant, who is witness to her daily protestations against our sex, and consequently a bar to her first steps towards love, upon the strength of her own maxims and declarations.

'However, I must needs say, this accomplished mistress of mine has distinguished me above the rest, and has been known to declare Sir Roger de Coverly was the tamest and most humane of all the brutes in the country. I was told she said so by one who thought he rallied me; but upon the strength of this slender encouragement, of being thought least detestable, I made new liveries, new-paired my coach-horses, sent them all to town to be bitted, and taught to throw their legs well, and move all together, before I pretended to cross the country, and wait upon her. As soon as I thought my retinue suitable to the character of my fortune and youth, I set out from hence to make my addresses. The particular skill of this lady, has ever been to inflame your wishes, and yet command respect. To make her mistress of this art, she has a greater share of knowledge, wit, and good sense, than is usual even among men of merit. Then she is beautiful beyond the race of women. If you will not let her go on with a certain artifice with her eyes, and the skill of beauty, she will arm herself with her real charms, and strike you with admiration instead of desire. It is certain that if you were to behold the whole woman, there is that dignity in her aspect, that composure in her motion, that complacency in her manner, that if her form makes you hope, her merit makes you fear. But then again, she is such a desperate scholar, that no country gentleman can approach her without being a jest. As I was going to tell you, when I came to her house, I was admitted to her presence with great civility; at the same time she placed herself to be first seen by me in such an attitude as I think you call the posture of a picture, that she discovered new charms, and I at last came towards her with such an awe as made me speechless. This she no sooner observed, but she made her advantage of it, and began a discourse to me concerning love and honour, as they both are followed by pretenders, and the real votaries to them. When she discussed these points in a discourse, which I verily believe was as learned as the best philosopher in Europe could possibly make, she asked me whether she was so happy as to fall in with my sentiments on these important particulars. Her confidant sat by her, and upon my being in the least confusion and silence, this malicious aid of hers, turning to her, says, I am very glad to observe Sir Roger pauses upon this subject, and seems resolved to deliver all his sentiments upon the matter when he pleases to speak. They both kept their countenances, and after I had sat half an hour meditating how to behave before such profound casuists, I rose up and took my leave. Chance has since that time very often thrown me in her way, and she as often has directed a discourse to me which I do not understand. This barbarity has kept me ever at a distance from the most beautiful object my eyes ever beheld. It is thus also she deals with all mankind, and you must make love to her, as you would conquer the sphynx, by posing her. But were she like other women, and that there were any talking to her, how constant must the pleasure of that man be who could converse with a creature. But, after all, you may be sure her heart is fixed on some one or other, and yet I have been credibly informed;... but who can believe half that is said? After she had done speaking to me, she put her hand to her bosom and adjusted her tucker. Then she cast her eyes a little down, upon my beholding her too earnestly. They say she sings excellently: her voice in her ordinary speech has something in it inexpressibly sweet. You must know I dined with her at a public table the day after I first saw her, and she helped me to some tansy, in the eye of all the gentlemen in the country, she has certainly the finest hand of any woman in the world. I can assure you, Sir, were you to behold her, you would be in the same condition; for as her speech is music, her form is angelic. But I find I grow irregular while I am talking of her; but indeed it would be stupidity to be unconcerned at such perfection. Oh the excellent creature! she is as inimitable to all women, as she is inaccessible to all men.'

I found my friend begin to rave, and insensibly led him towards the house, that we might be joined by some other company; and am convinced that the widow is the secret cause of all that inconsistency which appears in some parts of my friend's discourse, though he has so much command of himself as not directly to mention her, yet according to that of Martial, which one knows not how to render into English, *Dum tacet, hanc loquitur.* I shall end this paper with that whole epigram, which represents, with much humour, my honest friend's condition.

> Quicquid agit Rufus, nihil est, nisi Nævia Rufo,
> Si gaudet, si flet, si tacet, hanc loquitur.
> Cœnat, propinat, poscit, negat, annuit, una est
> Nævia, si non sit Nævia, mutus erit.
> Scriberet hesternâ patri cùm luce salutem,
> Nævia lux, inquit, Nævia numen, ave.   MAR.

> Let Rufus weep, rejoice, stand, sit or walk,
> Still he can nothing but of Nævia talk;
> Let him eat, drink, ask questions or dispute,
> Still he must speak of Nævia, or be mute.
> He writ to his father, ending with this line,
> I am, my lovely Nævia, ever thine.

R

No. CXIV.   WEDNESDAY, JULY 11.

> ... Paupertatis pudor et fuga .....   HOR.

> The dread of nothing more,
> Than to be thought necessitous and poor.   POOLY.

ECONOMY in our affairs, has the same effect upon our fortunes, which good breeding has upon our conversation. There is a pretending behaviour in both cases, which, instead of making men esteemed, renders them both miserable and contemptible. We had yesterday at Sir Roger's a set of country-gentlemen, who dined with him; and after dinner, the glass was taken, by those who pleased, pretty plentifully. Among others I observed a person of a tolerable good aspect, who seemed to be more greedy of liquor than any of the company, and yet, methought, he did not taste it with delight. As he grew warm, he was suspicious of every thing that was said; and as he advanced towards being fuddled, his humour grew worse. At the same time his bitterness seemed to be rather an inward dissatisfaction in his own mind, than any dislike he had taken to the company. Upon hearing his name, I knew him to be a gentleman of a considerable fortune in this county, but greatly in debt. What gives the unhappy man this peevishness of spirit, is, that his estate is dipped, and is eating out with usury; and yet he has not the heart to sell any part of it. His proud stomach, at the cost of restless nights, constant inquietudes, danger of affronts, and a thousand nameless inconveniencies, preserves this canker in his fortune, rather than it shall be said he is a man of fewer hundreds a year, than he has been commonly reputed. Thus he endures the torment of poverty to avoid the name of being less rich. If you go to his house, you see great plenty; but served in a manner that shews it is all unnatural, and that the master's mind is not at home. There is a certain waste and carelessness in the air of every thing, and the whole appears but a covered indigence, a magnificent poverty. That neatness and cheerfulness which attends the table of him who lives within compass, is wanting, and exchanged for a libertine way of service in all about him.

This gentleman's conduct, though a very common way of management, is as ridiculous as that officer's would be who had but few men under his command, and should take the charge of an extent of country rather than of a small pass. To pay for, personate, and keep in a man's hands a greater estate than he really has, is, of all others, the most unpardonable vanity, and must in the end reduce the man who is guilty of it to dishonour. Yet if we look round us in any county of Great Britain, we shall see many in this fatal error; if that may be called by so soft a name which proceeds from a false shame of appearing what they really are, when the contrary behaviour would in a short time advance them to the condition which they pretend to.

Laertes has fifteen hundred pounds a year, which is mortgaged for six thousand pounds: but it is impossible to convince him that, if he sold as much as would pay off that debt, he would save four shillings in the pound, which he gives for the vanity of being the reputed master of it. Yet if Laertes did this, he would, perhaps, be easier in his own fortune; but then Irus, a fellow of yesterday, who has but twelve hundred a year, would be his equal. Rather than this shall be, Laertes goes on to bring well-born beggars into the world, and every twelvemonth charges his estate with at least one year's rent more by the birth of a child.

Laertes and Irus are neighbours, whose way of living are an abomination to each other. Irus is moved by the fear of poverty, and Laertes by the shame of it. Though the motive of action is of so near affinity in both, and may be resolved into this, 'that to each of them poverty is the greatest of all evils,' yet are their manners very widely different. Shame of poverty makes Laertes launch into unnecessary equipage, vain expense, and lavish entertainments; fear of poverty makes Irus allow himself only plain necessaries, appear without a servant, sell his own corn, attend his labourers, and be himself a labourer. Shame of poverty makes Laertes go every day a step nearer to it; and fear of poverty stirs up Irus to make every day some further progress from it.

These different motives produce the excesses which men are guilty of in the negligence of and provision for themselves. Usury, stock-jobbing, extortion, and oppression, have their seed in the dread of want; and vanity, riot, and prodigality, from the shame of it: but both these excesses are infinitely below the pursuit of a reasonable creature. After we have taken care to command so much as is necessary for maintaining ourselves in the order of men suitable to our character, the care of superfluities is a vice no less extravagant than the neglect of necessaries would have been before.

Certain it is that they are both out of Nature, when she is followed with reason and good sense. It is from this reflection that I always read Mr. Cowley with the greatest pleasure: his magnanimity is as much above that of other considerable men as his understanding; and it is a true distinguishing spirit in the elegant author who published his works, to dwell so much upon the temper of his mind, and the moderation of his desires: by this means he has rendered his friend as amiable as famous. That state of life which bears the face of poverty with Mr. Cowley's "Great Vulgar" is admirably described; and it is no small satisfaction to those of the same turn of desire, that he produces the authority of the wisest men of the best age of the world to strengthen his opinion of the ordinary pursuits of mankind.

It would, methinks, be no ill maxim of life, if, according to that ancestor of Sir Roger whom I lately mentioned, every man would point to himself what sum he would resolve not to exceed. He might, by this means, cheat himself into a tranquillity on this side of that expectation, or convert what he should get above it to nobler uses than his own pleasures or necessities. This temper of mind would exempt a man from an ignorant envy of restless men above him, and a more inexcusable contempt of happy men below him. This would be sailing by some compass, living with some design; but to be eternally bewildered in prospects of future gain, and putting on unnecessary armour against improbable blows of fortune, is a mechanic being which has not good sense for its direction, but is carried on by a sort of acquired instinct towards things below our consideration and unworthy our esteem. It is possible that the tranquillity I now enjoy at Sir Roger's may have created in me this way of thinking, which is so abstracted from the common relish of the world; but as I am now in a pleasing arbour, surrounded with a beautiful landscape, I find no inclination so strong as to continue in these mansions, so remote from the ostentatious scenes of life, and am at this present writing philosopher enough to conclude with Mr. Cowley;

> " If e'er ambition did my fancy cheat
> With any wish so mean as to be great
> Continue, Heav'n, still from me to remove
> The humble blessings of that life I love."

T

No. CXV. THURSDAY, JULY 12.

....Ut sit mens sana in corpore sano   Juv.

A healthy body and a mind at ease.

Bodily labour is of two kinds, either that which a man submits to for his livelihood, or that which he undergoes for his pleasure. The latter of them generally changes the name of labour for that of exercise, but differs only from ordinary labour as it rises from another motive.

A country life abounds in both these kinds of labour, and for that reason gives a man a greater stock of health, and consequently a more perfect enjoyment of himself, than any other way of life. I consider the body as a system of tubes and glands, or to use a more rustic phrase, a bundle of pipes and strainers, fitted to one another after so wonderful a manner as to make a proper engine for the soul to work with. This description does not only comprehend the bowels, bones, tendons, veins, nerves and arteries, but every muscle and every ligature, which is a composition of fibres, that are so many imperceptible tubes or pipes interwoven on all sides with invisible glands or strainers.

This general idea of a human body, without considering it in the niceties of anatomy, lets us see how absolutely necessary labour is for the right preservation of it. There must be frequent motions and agitations, to mix, digest, and separate the juices contained in it, as well as to clear and cleanse that infinitude of pipes and strainers of which it is composed, and to give their solid parts a more firm and lasting tone. Labour or exercise ferments the humours, casts them into their proper channels, throws off redundancies, and helps nature in those secret distributions, without which the body cannot subsist in its vigour, nor the soul act with cheerfulness.

I might here mention the effects which this has upon all the faculties of the mind, by keeping the understanding clear, the imagination untroubled, and refining those spirits that are necessary for the proper exertion of our intellectual faculties during the present laws of union between soul and body. It is to a neglect in this particular that we must ascribe the spleen, which is so frequent in men of studious and sedentary tempers, as well as the vapours to which those of the other sex are so often subject.

Had not exercise been absolutely necessary for our well-being, Nature would not have made the body so proper for it, by giving such an activity to the limbs, and such a pliancy to every part, as necessarily produce those compressions, extensions, contortions, dilatations, and all other kinds of motions that are necessary for the preservation of such a system of tubes and glands as has been before mentioned. And that we might not want inducements to engage us in such an exercise of the body as is proper for its welfare, it is so ordered, that nothing valuable can be procured without it. Not to mention riches and honour, even food and raiment are not to be come at without the toil of the hands and sweat of the brows. Providence furnishes materials, but expects that we should work them up ourselves. The earth must be laboured before it gives its increase, and when it is forced into its several products, how many hands must they pass through before they are fit for use? Manufactures, trade, and agriculture, naturally employ more than nineteen parts of the species in twenty; and as for those who are not obliged to labour, by the condition in which they are born, they are more miserable than the rest of mankind, unless they indulge themselves in that voluntary labour which goes by the name of exercise

My friend Sir Roger has been an indefatigable man in business of this kind, and has hung several parts of his house with the trophies of his former labours. The walls of his great hall are covered with the horns of several kinds of deer that he has killed in the chace, which he thinks the most valuable furniture of his house, as they afford him frequent topics of discourse, and shew that he has not been idle. At the lower end of the hall is a large otter's skin stuffed with hay, which his mother ordered to be hung up in that manner, and the knight looks upon with great satisfaction, because it seems he was but nine years old when his dog killed him. A little room adjoining to the hall is a kind of arsenal filled with guns of several sizes and inventions, with which the knight has made great havoc in the woods, and destroyed many thousands of pheasants, partridges, and woodcocks. His stable doors are patched with noses that belonged to foxes of the knight's own hunting down. Sir Roger shewed me one of them, that, for distinction sake, has a brass nail struck through it, which cost him about fifteen hours riding, carried him through half a dozen counties, killed him a brace of geldings, and lost above half his dogs. This the knight looks upon as one of the greatest exploits of his life. The perverse widow, whom I have given some account of, was the death of several foxes, for Sir Roger has told me, that in the course of his amours he patched the western door of his stable. Whenever the widow was cruel, the foxes were sure to pay for it. In proportion as his passion for the widow abated, and old age came on, he left off fox-hunting; but a hare is not yet safe that sits within ten miles of his house.

There is no kind of exercise which I would so recommend to my readers of both sexes as this of riding, as there is none which so much conduces to health, and is every way accommodated to the body, according to the idea which I have given of it. Dr Sydenham is very lavish in its praises, and if the English reader will see the mechanical effects of it described at length, he may find them in a book published not many years since under the title of Medicina Gymnastica. For my own part, when I am in town, for want of these opportunities, I exercise myself an hour every morning upon a dumb-bell that is placed in a corner of my room; and pleases me the more, because it does every thing I require of it in the most profound silence. My landlady and her daughters are so well acquainted with my hours of exercise, that they never come into my room to disturb me while I am ringing.

When I was some years younger than I am at present, I used to employ myself in a more laborious diversion, which I learned from a Latin treatise on exercises, that is written with great erudition, it is there called the σκιομαχία, or the fighting with a man's own shadow, and consists in the brandishing of two short sticks grasped in each hand, and loaden with plugs of lead at either end. This opens the chest, exercises the limbs, and gives a man all the pleasure of boxing without the blows. I could wish that several learned men would lay out that time which they employ in controversies and disputes about nothing, in this method of fighting with their own shadows. It might conduce very much to evaporate the spleen, which makes them uneasy to the public as well as to themselves.

To conclude, as I am a compound of soul and body, I consider myself as obliged to a double scheme of duties; and think I have not fulfilled the business of the day, when I do not thus employ the one in labour and exercise, as well as the other in study and contemplation. L.

No. CXVI. FRIDAY, JULY 13.

...... Vocat ingenti clamore Cithæron,
Taygetique canes .....   VIRG.

The echoing hills and chiding hounds invite

Those who have searched into human nature observe, that nothing so much shews the nobleness of the soul, as that its felicity consists in action. Every man has such an active principle in him, that he will find out something to employ himself upon in whatever place or state of life he is posted. I have heard of a gentleman who was under close confinement in the Bastile seven years; during which he amused himself in scattering a few small pins about his chamber, gathering them up again, and placing them in different figures on the arm of a great chair. He often told his friends afterwards, that unless he had found out this piece of exercise, he verily believed that he should have lost his senses.

After what has been said, I need not inform my readers that Sir Roger, with whose character I hope they are at present pretty well acquainted, has in his youth gone through the whole course of those rural diversions which the country abounds in, and which seem to be extremely well suited to that laborious industry a man may observe here in a far greater degree than in towns and cities. I have before hinted at some of my friend's exploits; he has in his youthful days taken forty coveys of partridges in a season, and tired many a salmon with a line consisting but of a single hair. The constant thanks and good wishes of the neighbourhood always attended him, on account of his remarkable enmity towards foxes, having destroyed more of those vermin in one year than it was thought the whole country could have produced. Indeed the knight does not scruple to own among his most intimate friends, that in order to establish his reputation this way, he has secretly sent for great numbers of them out of other counties, which he used to turn loose about the country by night, that he might the better signalize himself in their destruction the next day. His hunting horses were the finest and best managed in all these parts: his tenants are still full of the praises of a gray stone horse that unhappily staked himself several years since, and was buried with great solemnity in the orchard.

Sir Roger being at present too old for fox-hunting, to keep himself in action, has disposed of his beagles, and got a pack of stop-hounds. What these want in speed, he endeavours to make amends for by the deepness of their mouths, and the variety of their notes, which are suited in such manner to each other, that the whole cry makes up a complete concert. He is so nice in this particular, that a gentleman having made him a present of a very fine hound the other day, the knight returned it by the servant with a great many expressions of civility, but desired him to tell his master, that the dog he had sent was indeed a most excellent bass, but that at present he only wanted a counter tenor. Could I believe my friend had ever read Shakspeare, I should certainly conclude he had taken the hint from Theseus in The Midsummer Night's Dream

> "My hounds are bred out of the Spartan kind,
> So flu'd, so sanded, and their heads are hung
> With ears that sweep away the morning dew.
> Crook-knee'd and dew-lap'd like Thessalian bulls,
> Slow in pursuit, but match'd in mouths like bells,
> Each under each—a cry more tuneable
> Was never halloo'd to, nor cheer'd with horn."

Sir Roger is so keen at this sport, that he has been out almost every day since I came down; and upon the chaplain's offering to lend me his easy pad, I was prevailed on yesterday morning to make one of the company. I was extremely pleased, as we rode along, to observe the general benevolence of all the neighbourhood towards my friend. The farmers' sons thought themselves happy if they could open a gate for the good old knight as he passed by, which he generally requited with a nod or a smile, and a kind inquiry after their fathers or uncles.

After we had rid about a mile from home, we came upon a large heath, and the sportsmen began to beat. They had done so for some time, when, as I was at a little distance from the rest of the company, I saw a hare pop out from a small furze-brake almost under my horse's feet. I marked the way she took, which I endeavoured to make the company sensible of by extending my arm, but to no purpose, till Sir Roger, who knows that none of my extraordinary motions are insignificant, rode up to me, and asked me, If puss was gone that way? Upon my answering Yes, he immediately called in the dogs, and put them upon the scent. As they were going off, I heard one of the country fellows muttering to his companion, 'That it was a wonder they had not lost all their sport, for want of the silent gentleman's crying, Stole away.'

This, with my aversion to leaping hedges, made me withdraw to a rising ground, from whence I could have the pleasure of the whole chace, without the fatigue of keeping in with the hounds. The hare immediately threw them above a mile behind her, but I was pleased to find, that instead of running straight forwards, or, in hunter's language, " flying the country," as I was afraid she might have done, she wheeled about, and described a sort of circle round the hill where I had taken my station, in such a manner as gave me a very distinct view of the sport. I could see her first pass by, and the dogs some time afterwards unravelling the whole track she had made, and following her through all her doubles. I was at the same time delighted in observing that deference which the rest of the pack paid to each particular hound, according to the character he had acquired amongst them. If they were at a fault, and an old hound of reputation opened but once, he was immediately followed by the whole cry; while a raw dog, or one who was a noted liar, might have yelped his heart out, without being taken notice of.

The hare now, after having squatted two or three times, and been put up again as often, came still nearer to the place where she was at first started. The dogs pursued her, and these were followed by the jolly Knight, who rode upon a white gelding, encompassed by his tenants and servants, and cheering his hounds with all the gaiety of five-and-twenty. One of the sportsmen rode up to me, and told me, that he was sure the chase was almost at an end, because the old dogs, which had hitherto lain behind, now headed the pack. The fellow was in the right. Our hare took a large field just under us, followed by the full cry " in view." I must confess, the brightness of the weather, the cheerfulness of every thing around me, the "chiding" of the hounds, which was returned upon us in a double echo from two neighbouring hills, with the hallooing of the sportsmen, and the sounding of the horn, lifted my spirits into a most lively pleasure, which I freely indulged, because I was sure it was innocent. If I was under any concern, it was on account of the poor hare, that was now quite spent, and almost within the reach of her enemies, when the huntsman getting forward, threw down his pole before the dogs. They were now within eight yards of that game, which they had been pursuing for almost as many hours; yet, on the signal before mentioned, they all made a sudden stand, and though they continued opening as much as before, durst not once attempt to pass beyond the pole. At the same time Sir Roger rode forward, and alighting, took up the hare in his arms, which he soon after delivered up to one of his servants, with an order, if she could be kept alive, to let her go in his great orchard, where, it seems, he has several of those prisoners of war, who live together in a very comfortable captivity. I was highly pleased to see the discipline of the pack, and the good nature of the Knight, who could not find in his heart to murder a creature that had given him so much diversion.

As we were returning home I remembered that Monsieur Paschal, in his most excellent discourse on "The Misery of Man," tells us, that "all our endeavours after greatness proceed from nothing but a desire of being surrounded by a multitude of persons and affairs that may hinder us from looking into ourselves, which is a view that we cannot bear." He afterwards goes on to shew, that our love of sports comes from the same reason, and is particularly severe upon hunting. "What (says he), unless it be to drown thought, can make men throw away so much time and pains upon a silly animal, which they might buy cheaper in the market?" The foregoing reflection is certainly just, when a man suffers his whole mind to be drawn into his sports, and altogether loses himself in the woods, but does not affect those who propose a far more laudable end from this exercise, I mean "The preservation of health, and keeping all the organs of the soul in a condition to execute her orders." Had that incomparable person, whom I last quoted, been a little more indulgent to himself in this point, the world might probably have enjoyed him much longer; whereas, through too great an application to his studies in his youth, he contracted that ill habit of body which, after a tedious sickness, carried him off in the fortieth year of his age; and the whole history we have of his life till that time, is but one continued account of the behaviour of a noble soul, struggling under innumerable pains and distempers.

For my own part, I intend to hunt twice a-week during my stay with Sir Roger; and shall prescribe the moderate use of this exercise to all my country friends, as the best kind of physic for mending a bad constitution, and preserving a good one.

I cannot do this better than in the following lines out of Dryden.

> " The first physicians by debauch were made;
> Excess began, and sloth sustains the trade
> By chace our long-liv'd fathers earn'd their food;
> Toil strung the nerves, and purify'd the blood,
> But we their sons, a pamper'd race of men,
> Are dwindled down to threescore years and ten
> Better to hunt in fields for health unbought,
> Than fee the doctor for a nauseous draught
> The wise for cure on exercise depend
> God never made his work for man to mend "

X

No CXVIII. SATURDAY, JULY 14.

———Ipsi sibi somnia fingunt   VIRG.

Their own imaginations they deceive.

THERE are some opinions in which a man should stand neuter, without engaging his assent to one side or the other. Such a hovering faith as this, which refuses to settle upon any determination, is absolutely necessary in a mind that is careful to avoid errors and prepossessions. When the arguments press equally on both sides, in matters that are indifferent to us, the safest method is to give up ourselves to neither.

It is with this temper of mind that I consider the subject of witchcraft. When I hear the relations that are made from all parts of the world, not only from Norway and Lapland, from the East and West Indies, but from every particular nation in Europe, I cannot forbear thinking that there is such an intercourse and commerce with evil spirits, as that which we express by the name of witchcraft. But when I consider that the ignorant and credulous parts of the world abound most in these relations, and that the persons among us who are supposed to engage in such an infernal commerce, are people of a weak understanding and crazed imagination, and at the same time reflect upon the many impostures and delusions of this nature that have been detected in all ages, I endeavour to suspend my belief till I hear more certain accounts than any which have yet come to my knowledge. In short, when I consider the question, whether there are such persons in the world as those we call witches? my mind is divided between the two opposite opinions; or rather, (to speak my thoughts freely) I believe in general that there is and has been such a thing as witchcraft; but, at the same time can give no credit to any particular instance of it.

I am engaged in this speculation by some occurrences which I met with yesterday, which I shall give my reader an account of at large. As I was walking with my friend Sir Roger by the side of one of his woods, an old woman applied herself to me for my charity. Her dress and figure put me in mind of the following description in Otway....

> "In a close lane as I pursu'd my journey,
> I spy'd a wrinkled hag, with age grown double,
> Picking dry sticks, and mumbling to herself
> Her eyes with scalding rheum were gall'd and red,
> Cold palsy shook her head, her hands seem'd wither'd;
> And on her crooked shoulders had she wrapp'd
> The tatter'd remnant of an old strip'd hanging,
> Which serv'd to keep her carcase from the cold;
> So there was nothing of a piece about her.
> Her lower weeds were all o'er coarsely patch'd
> With different colour'd rags, black, red, white, yellow,
> And seem'd to speak variety of wretchedness."

As I was musing on this description, and comparing it with the object before me, the knight told me, that this very old woman had the reputation of a witch all over the country, that her lips were observed to be always in motion, and that there was not a switch about her house which her neighbours did not believe had carried her several hundreds of miles. If she chanced to stumble, they always found sticks or straws that lay in the figure of a cross before her. If she made any mistake at church, and cried Amen in a wrong place, they never failed to conclude that she was saying her prayers backwards. There was not a maid in the parish that would take a pin of her, though she should offer a bag of money with it. She goes by the name of Moll White, and has made the country ring with several imaginary exploits which are palmed upon her.

If the dairy-maid does not make her butter come so soon as she would have it, Moll White is at the bottom of the churn. If a horse sweats in the stable, Moll White has been upon his back. If a hare makes an unexpected escape from the hounds, the huntsman curses Moll White. Nay (says Sir Roger), I have known the master of the pack, upon such an occasion, send one of his servants to see if Moll White had been out that morning.'

This account raised my curiosity so far, that I begged my friend Sir Roger to go with me into her hovel, which stood in a solitary corner under the side of the wood. Upon our first entering, Sir Roger winked to me, and pointed at something that stood behind the door, which, upon looking that way, I found to be an old broomstaff. At the same time he whispered me in the ear to take notice of a tabby cat that sat in the chimney corner, which, as the Knight told me, lay under as bad a report as Moll White herself, for besides that Moll is said often to accompany her in the same shape, the cat is reported to have spoken twice or thrice in her life, and to have played several pranks above the capacity of an ordinary cat.

I was secretly concerned to see human nature in so much wretchedness and disgrace, but at the same time, could not forbear smiling to hear Sir Roger, who is a little puzzled about the old woman, advising her, as a justice of peace, to avoid all communication with the devil, and never to hurt any of her neighbour's cattle. We concluded our visit with a bounty which was very acceptable.

In our return home, Sir Roger told me that old Moll had been often brought before him for making children spit pins, and giving maids the night-mare; and that the country people would be tossing her into a pond, and trying experiments with her every day, if it was not for him and his chaplain.

I have since found, upon inquiry, that Sir Roger was several times staggered with the reports that had been brought him concerning this old woman, and would frequently have bound her over to the county sessions, had not his chaplain, with much ado, persuaded him to the contrary.

I have been the more particular in this account, because I hear there is scarce a village in England that has not a Moll White in it. When an old woman begins to dote, and grow chargeable to a parish, she is generally turned into a witch, and fills the whole country with extravagant fancies, imaginary distempers, and terrifying dreams. In the mean time, the poor wretch that is the innocent occasion of so many evils, begins to be frighted at herself, and sometimes confesses secret commerce and familiarities, that her imagination forms in a delirious old age. This frequently cuts off charity from the greatest objects of compassion, and inspires people with a malevolence towards those poor decrepid parts of our species, in whom human nature is defaced by infirmity and dotage. L.

No CXVIII. MONDAY, JULY 16.

——Hæret lateri lethalis arundo. VIRG.

The fatal dart
Sticks in his side, and rankles in his heart. DRYDEN.

THIS agreeable seat is surrounded with so many pleasing walks, which are struck out of a wood, in the midst of which the house stands, that one can hardly ever be weary of rambling from one labyrinth of delight to another. To one used to live in a city, the charms of the country are so exquisite, that the mind is lost in a certain transport which raises us above ordinary life, and yet is not strong enough to be inconsistent with tranquillity. This state of mind was I in, ravished with the murmur of waters, the whisper of breezes, the singing of birds; and whether I looked up to the heavens, down on the earth, or turned to the prospects around me, still struck with new sense of pleasure; when I found by the voice of my friend, who walked by me, that we had insensibly strolled into the grove sacred to the widow. This woman (says he) is, of all others, the most unintelligible; she either designs to marry, or she does not. What is the most perplexing of all, is, that she does not either say to her lovers she has any resolution against that condition of life in general, or that she banishes them; but, conscious of her own merit, she permits their addresses, without fear of any ill consequence, or want of respect, from their rage or despair She has that in her aspect, against which it is impossible to offend. A man whose thoughts are constantly bent upon so agreeable an object, must be excused if the ordinary occurrences in conversation are below his attention. I call her indeed perverse, but, alas! why do I call her so? Because her superior merit is such, that I cannot approach her without awe, that my heart is checked by too much esteem: I am angry that her charms are not more accessible, that I am more inclined to worship than salute her: how often have I wished her unhappy, that I might have an opportunity of serving her; and how often troubled in that very imagination at giving her the pain of being obliged? Well, I have led a miserable life in secret upon her account; but fancy she would have condescended to have some regard for me, if it had not been for that watchful animal her confidant.

Of all persons under the sun (continued he, calling me by my name) be sure to set a mark upon confidants:

they are of all people the most impertinent. What is most pleasant to observe in them, is, that they assume to themselves the merit of the persons whom they have in their custody. Oresilla is a great fortune, and in wonderful danger of surprises, therefore full of suspicions of the least indifferent thing, particularly careful of new acquaintance, and of growing too familiar with the old. Themista, her favourite woman, is every whit as careful of whom she speaks to, and what she says. Let the ward be a beauty, her confidant shall treat you with an air of distance: let her be a fortune, and she assumes the suspicious behaviour of her friend and patroness. Thus it is that very many of our unmarried women of distinction are to all intents and purposes married, except the consideration of different sexes. They are directly under the conduct of their whisperer; and think they are in a state of freedom, while they can prate with one of these attendants of all men in general, and still avoid the man they most like. You do not see one heiress in an hundred whose fate does not turn upon this circumstance of choosing a confidant. Thus it is that the lady is addressed to, presented and flattered, only by proxy, in her woman. In my case, how is it possible that—Sir Roger was proceeding in his harangue, when we heard the voice of one speaking very importunately, and repeating these words, " What, not one smile?" We followed the sound till we came to a close thicket, on the other side of which we saw a young woman sitting, as it were, in a personated sullenness just over a transparent fountain. Opposite to her stood Mr. William, Sir Roger's master of the game. The knight whispered me, " Hist, these are lovers." The huntsman looking earnestly at the shadow of the young maiden in the stream.. " Oh, thou dear picture, if thou couldst remain there in the absence of that fair creature whom you represent in the water, how willingly could I stand here satisfied for ever, without troubling my dear Betty herself with any mention of her unfortunate William, whom she is angry with: but alas! when she pleases to be gone, thou wilt also vanish—Yet let me talk to thee while thou dost stay. Tell my dearest Betty thou dost not more depend upon her than does her William: her absence will make away with me as well as thee. If she offers to remove thee, I'll jump into these waves to lay hold on thee; herself, her own dear person, I must never embrace again. Still do you hear me without one smile—It is too much to bear."... He had no sooner spoke these words, but he made an offer of throwing himself into the water, at which his mistress started up, and at the next instant he jumped across the fountain, and met her in an embrace. She, half recovering from her fright, said, in the most charming voice imaginable, and with a tone of complaint, " I thought how well you would drown yourself. No, no, you won't drown yourself till you have taken your leave of Susan Holiday." The huntsman, with a tenderness that spoke the most passionate love, and with his cheek close to her's, whispered the softest vows of fidelity in her ear, and cried, " Dont, my dear, believe a word Kate Willow says, she is spiteful, and makes stories, because she loves to hear me talk to herself for your sake." " Look you there" (quoth Sir Roger), " do you see there, all mischief comes from confidants! but let us not interrupt them; the maid is honest, and the man dares not be otherwise, for he knows I loved her father. I will interpose in this matter, and hasten the wedding. Kate Willow is a witty mischievous wench in the neighbourhood, who was a beauty; and makes me hope I shall see the perverse widow in her condition. She was so flippant with her answers to all the honest fellows that came near her, and so very vain of her beauty, that she has valued herself upon her charms till they are ceased. She therefore now makes it her business to prevent other young women from being more discreet than she was herself: however, the saucy thing said the other day well enough, " Sir Roger and I must make a match, for we are both despised by those we loved:" the hussy has a great deal of power wherever she comes, and has her share of cunning.

However, when I reflect upon this woman, I do not know whether in the main I am the worse for having loved her: whenever she is recalled to my imagination, my youth returns, and I feel a forgotten warmth in my veins. This affliction in my life has streaked all my conduct with a softness of which I should otherwise have been incapable. It is, perhaps, owing to this dear image in my heart, that I am apt to relent, that I easily forgive, and that many desirable things are grown into my temper, which I should not have arrived at by better motives than the thought of being one day her's. I am pretty well satisfied such a passion as I have had is never well cured: and between you and me, I am often apt to imagine it has had some whimsical effect upon my brain: for I frequently find, that in my most serious discourse I let fall some comical familiarity of speech, or odd phrase, that makes the company laugh: however, I cannot but allow she is a most excellent woman. When she is in the country I warrant she does not run into dairies, but reads upon the nature of plants; she has a glass bee-hive, and comes into the garden out of books to see them work, and observe the policies of their commonwealth. She understands every thing. I would give ten pounds to hear her argue with my friend Sir Andrew Freeport about trade. No, no, for all she looks so innocent as it were, take my word for it she is no fool.

T

No CXIX. TUESDAY, JULY 17.

*Urbem quam dicunt Romam, Melibœe, putavi
Stultus ego, huic nostræ similem*
                                            VIRG.

Fool that I was, I thought imperial Rome
Like Mantua   DRYDEN

THE first and most obvious reflections which arise in a man who changes the city for the country, are upon the different manners of the people whom he meets with in those two different scenes of life. By manners I do not mean morals, but behaviour and good-breeding, as they shew themselves in the town and in the country.

And here, in the first place, I must observe a very great revolution that has happened in this article of good-breeding. Several obliging deferences, condescensions, and submissions, with many outward forms and ceremonies that accompany them, were first of all brought up among the politer part of mankind, who lived in courts and cities, and distinguished themselves from the rustic part of the species (who on all occasions acted bluntly and naturally) by such a mutual complaisance and intercourse of civilities. These forms of conversation by degrees multiplied and grew troublesome, the modish world found too great a constraint in them, and have therefore thrown most of them aside. Conversation, like the Romish religion, was so encumbered with show and ceremony, that it stood in need of a reformation to retrench its superfluities, and restore it to its natural good sense and beauty. At present therefore an unconstrained carriage, and a certain openness of behaviour, are the height of good-breeding. The fashionable world is grown free and easy, our manners sit more loose upon us: nothing is so modish as an agreeable negligence. In a word, good-breeding shews itself most where to an ordinary eye it appears the least.

If after this we look on the people of mode in the country, we find in them the manners of the last age. They have no sooner fetched themselves up to the fashion of the polite world, but the town has dropped them, and are nearer to the first state of nature than to those refinements which formerly reigned in the court, and still prevail in the country. One may now know a man that never conversed in the world, by his excess of good-breeding. A polite country squire shall make you as many bows in half an hour as would serve a courtier for a week. There is infinitely more to do about place and precedency in a meeting of justices' wives, than in an assembly of duchesses.

This rural politeness is very troublesome to a man of my temper, who generally take the chair that is next me, and walk first or last, in the front or in the rear, as chance directs. I have known my friend Sir Roger's dinner almost cold before the company could adjust the ceremonial, and be prevailed upon to sit down, and have heartily pitied my old friend, when I have seen him forced to pick and cull his guests, as they sat at the several parts of his table, that he may drink their healths according to their respective ranks and qualities. Honest Will Wimble, who I should have thought had been altogether uninfected with ceremony, gives me abundance of trouble in this particular. Though he has been fishing all the morning, he will not help himself at dinner till I am served. When we are going out of the hall, he runs behind me; and last night, as we were walking in the fields, he stopped short at a style until I came up to it, and upon my making signs to him to get over, told me, with a serious smile, that sure I believed they had no manners in the country.

There has happened another revolution in the point of good-breeding, which relates to the conversation among men of mode, and which I cannot but look upon as very extraordinary. It was certainly one of the first distinctions of a well-bred man, to express every thing that had the most remote appearance of being obscene in modest terms and distant phrases, whilst the clown, who had no such delicacy of conception and expression, clothed his ideas in those plain homely terms that are the most obvious and natural. This kind of good manners was perhaps carried to an excess, so as to make conversation too stiff, formal, and precise; for which reason (as hypocrisy in one age is generally succeeded by atheism in another) conversation is in a great measure relapsed into the first extreme: so that at present several of our men of the town, and particularly those who have been polished in France, make use of the most coarse uncivilized words in our language, and utter themselves often in such a manner as a clown would blush to hear.

This infamous piece of good-breeding, which reigns among the coxcombs of the town, has not yet made its way into the country; and as it is impossible for such an irrational way of conversation to last long among a people that make any profession of religion or shew of modesty, if the country gentlemen get into it, they will certainly be left in the lurch. Their good-breeding will come too late to them, and they will be thought a parcel of lewd clowns, while they fancy themselves talking together like men of wit and pleasure.

As the two points of good-breeding which I have hitherto insisted upon, regard behaviour and conversation, there is a third which turns upon dress. In this too the country are very much behind hand. The rural beaux are not yet got out of the fashion that took place at the time of the revolution, but ride about the country in red coats and laced hats, while the women, in many parts, are still trying to outvie one another in the height of their head-dresses

But a friend of mine, who is now upon the western circuit, having promised to give me an account of the several modes and fashions that prevail in the different parts of the nation through which he passes, I shall defer the enlarging upon this last topic until I have received a letter from him, which I expect every post. L.

No CXX. WEDNESDAY, JULY 18.

> Equidem credo, quia sit divinitus illis
> Ingenium .... VIRG.
>
> I think their breasts with heav'nly souls insp'r'd.
> DRYDEN.

My friend Sir Roger is very often merry with me upon my passing so much of my time among his poultry. He has caught me twice or thrice looking after a bird's nest, and several times sitting an hour or two together near a hen and chickens. He tells me, he believes I am personally acquainted with every fowl about his house; calls such a particular cock my favourite, and frequently complains that his ducks and geese have more of my company than himself.

I must confess I am infinitely delighted with those speculations of nature which are to be made in a country-life; and as my reading has very much lain among books of natural history, I cannot forbear recollecting upon this occasion the several remarks which I have met with in authors, and comparing them with what falls under my own observation, the arguments for Providence drawn from the natural history of animals being in my opinion demonstrative.

The make of every kind of animal is different from that of every other kind, and yet there is not the least turn in the muscles or twist in the fibres of any one, which does not render them more proper for that particular animal's way of life than any other cast or texture of them would have been

The most violent appetites in all creatures are lust and hunger: the first is a perpetual call upon them to propagate their kind, the latter to preserve themselves.

It is astonishing to consider the different degrees of care that descend from the parent to the young, so far as is absolutely necessary for the leaving a posterity. Some creatures cast their eggs as chance directs them, and think of them no farther, as insects and several kinds of fish; others of a nicer frame find out proper beds to deposite them in, and there leave them, as the serpent, the crocodile, and ostrich; others hatch their eggs and tend the birth till it is able to shift for itself

What can we call the principle which directs every different kind of bird to observe a particular plan in the structure of its nest, and directs all of the same species to work after the same model? It cannot be imitation; for though you hatch a crow under a hen, and never let it see any of the works of its own kind, the nest it makes shall be the same, to the laying of a stick, with all the other nests of the same species It cannot be reason; for were animals endued with it to as great a degree as man, their buildings would be as different as ours, according to the different conveniences that they would propose to themselves.

Is it not remarkable, that the same temper of weather which raises this genial warmth in animals should cover the trees with leaves, and the fields with grass, for their security and concealment, and produce such infinite swarms of insects for the support and sustenance of their respective broods?

Is it not wonderful, that the love of the parent should be so violent while it lasts, and that it should last no longer than is necessary for the preservation of the young?

The violence of this natural love is exemplified by a very barbarous experiment; which I shall quote at length, as I find it in an excellent author, and hope my readers will pardon the mentioning such an instance of cruelty, because there is nothing can so effectually shew the strength of that principle in animals of which I am here speaking. "A person who was well skilled in dissections opened a bitch, and, as she lay in the most exquisite tortures, offered her one of her young puppies, which she immediately fell a licking, and for the time seemed insensible of her own pain: on the removal, she kept her eye fixed on it, and began a wailing sort of cry, which seemed rather to proceed from the loss of her young one than the sense of her own torments."

But notwithstanding this natural love in brutes is much more violent and intense than in rational creatures, Providence has taken care that it should be no longer troublesome to the parent than it is useful to the young; for so soon as the wants of the latter cease, the mother withdraws her fondness, and leaves them to provide for themselves: and what is a very remarkable circumstance in this part of instinct, we find that the love of the parent may be lengthened out beyond its usual time, if the preservation of the species requires it; as we may see in birds that drive away their young as soon as they are able to get their livelihood, but continue to feed them if they are tied to the nest, or confined within a cage, or by any other means appear to be out of a condition of supplying their own necessities.

This natural love is not observed in animals to ascend from the young to the parent, which is not at all necessary for the continuance of the species, nor indeed in reasonable creatures does it rise in any proportion, as it spreads itself downwards; for in all family affection, we find protection granted and favours bestowed, are greater motives to love and tenderness, than safety, benefits, or life received.

One would wonder to hear sceptical men disputing for the reason of animals, and telling us it is only our pride and prejudices that will not allow them the use of that faculty.

Reason shews itself in all occurrences of life; whereas the brute makes no discovery of such a talent, but in what immediately regards his own preservation, or the continuance of his species. Animals, in their generation, are wiser than the sons of men, but their wisdom is confined to a few particulars, and lies in a very narrow compass. Take a brute out of his instinct, and you find him wholly deprived of understanding. To use an instance that comes often under observation.

With what caution does the hen provide herself a nest in places unfrequented, and free from noise and disturbance? When she has laid her eggs in such a manner that she can cover them, what care does she take in turning them frequently, that all parts may partake of the vital warmth? When she leaves them to provide for her necessary sustenance, how punctually does she return before they have time to cool, and become incapable of producing an animal? In the summer you see her giving herself greater freedoms, and quitting her care for above two hours together; but in winter, when the rigour of the season would chill the principles of life, and destroy the young one, she grows more assiduous in her attendance, and stays away but half the time. When the birth approaches, with how much nicety and attention does she help the chick to break its prison? Not to take notice of her covering it from the injuries of the weather, providing it proper nourishment, and teaching it to help itself; nor to mention her forsaking the nest, if, after the usual time of reckoning, the young one does not make its appearance. A chemical operation could not be followed with greater art or diligence than is seen in the hatching of a chick, though there are many other birds that shew an infinitely greater sagacity in all the forementioned particulars.

But, at the same time, the hen, that has all this seeming ingenuity (which is indeed absolutely necessary for the propagation of the species), considered in other respects, is without the least glimmerings of thought or common sense. She mistakes a piece of chalk for an egg, and sits upon it in the same manner: she is insensible of any increase or diminution in the number of those she lays; she does not distinguish between her own and those of another species, and when the birth appears of never so different a bird, will cherish it for her own. In all these circumstances, which do not carry an immediate regard to the subsistence of herself or her species, she is a very idiot.

There is not in my opinion any thing more mysterious in nature than this instinct in animals, which thus rises above reason, and falls infinitely short of it. It cannot be accounted for by any properties in matter, and at the same time works after so odd a manner, that one cannot think it the faculty of an intellectual being. For my own part, I look upon it as upon the principle of gravitation in bodies, which is not to be explained by any known qualities inherent in the bodies themselves, nor from any laws of mechanism, but, according to the best notions of the greatest philosophers, is an immediate impression from the first Mover, and the Divine energy acting in the creatures. L.

No CXXI. THURSDAY, JULY 19.

Jovis omnia plena. VIRG.

All things are full of Jove.

As I was walking this morning in the great yard that belongs to my friend's country house, I was wonderfully pleased to see the different workings of instinct in a hen followed by a brood of ducks. The young, upon the sight of a pond, immediately ran into it, while the step-mother, with all imaginable anxiety, hovered about the borders of it, to call them out of an element that appeared to her so dangerous and destructive. As the different principle which acted in these different animals cannot be termed reason, so when we call it instinct, we mean something we have no knowledge of. To me, as I hinted in my paper, it seems the immediate direction of Providence, and such an operation of the Supreme Being, as that which determines all the portions of matter to their proper centres. A modern philosopher, quoted by Monsieur Bayle, in his learned Dissertation on the Souls of Brutes, delivers the same opinion, though in a bolder form of words, where he says, Deus est anima brutorum, "God himself is the soul of brutes." Who can tell what to call that seeming sagacity in animals, which directs them to such food as is proper for them, and makes them naturally avoid whatever is noxious or unwholesome? Tully has observed, that a lamb no sooner falls from its mother but immediately and of its own accord applies itself to the teat. Dampier, in his Travels, tells us, that when seamen are thrown upon any of the unknown coasts of America, they never venture upon the fruit of any tree, how tempting soever it may appear, unless they observe that it is marked with the pecking of birds, but fall on without any fear or apprehension where the birds have been before them

But notwithstanding animals have nothing like the use of reason, we find in them all the lower parts of our nature, the passions and senses in their greatest strength and perfection. And here it is worth our observation, that all beasts and birds of prey are wonderfully subject to anger, malice, revenge, and all the other violent passions that may animate them in search of their proper food, as those that are incapable of defending themselves, or annoying others, or whose safety lies chiefly in their flight, are suspicious, fearful, and apprehensive of every thing they see or hear, whilst others that are of assistance and use to man, have their natures softened with something mild and tractable, and by that means are qualified for a domestic life. In this case the passions generally correspond with the make of the body. We do not find the fury of a lion in so weak and defenceless an animal as a lamb, nor the meekness of a lamb in a creature so armed for battle and assault as the lion. In the same manner, we find that particular animals have a more or less exquisite sharpness and sagacity in those particular senses which most turn to their advantage, and in which their safety and welfare is the most concerned.

Nor must we here omit that great variety of arms with which nature has differently fortified the bodies of several kinds of animals, such as claws, hoofs and horns, teeth and tusks, a tail, a sting, a trunk, or a proboscis. It is likewise observed by naturalists, that it must be some hidden principle distinct from what we call reason, which instructs animals in the use of these their arms, and teaches them to manage them to the best advantage; because they naturally defend themselves with that part in which their strength lies, before the weapon be formed in it: as is remarkable in lambs, which though they are bred within doors, and never saw the actions of their own species, push at those who approach them with their foreheads, before the first budding of a horn appears.

I shall add to these general observations, an instance which Mr. Locke has given us of Providence, even in the imperfections of a creature which seems the meanest and most despicable in the whole animal world. 'We may, (says he) from the make of an oyster, or cockle, conclude, that it has not so many, nor so quick senses as a man, or several other animals: nor if it had, would it, in that state and incapacity of transferring itself from one place to another, be bettered by them. What good would sight and hearing do to a creature that cannot move itself to or from the object, wherein at a distance it perceives good or evil? And would not quickness of sensation be an inconvenience to an animal that must be still where chance has once placed it, and there receive the afflux of colder or warmer, clean or foul water, as it happens to come to it?'

I shall add to this instance out of Mr. Locke another out of the learned Dr. More, who cites it from Cardan, in relation to another animal which Providence has left defective, but at the same time has shown its wisdom in the formation of that organ in which it seems chiefly to have failed. 'What is more obvious and ordinary than a mole? and yet what more palpable argument of Providence than she? The members of her body are so exactly fitted to her nature and manner of life; for her dwelling being under ground, where nothing is to be seen, Nature has so obscurely fitted her with eyes, that naturalists can hardly agree whether she has any sight at all or not. But for amends, what she is capable of for her defence and warning of danger, she has very eminently conferred upon her, for she is exceeding quick of hearing. And then her short tail and short legs, but broad fore-feet, armed with sharp claws, we see by the event to what purpose they are, she so swiftly working herself under ground, and making her way so fast in the earth, as they that behold it cannot but admire it. Her legs therefore are short, that she need dig no more than will serve the mere thickness of her body; and her fore-feet are broad, that she may scoop away much earth at a time; and little or no tail she has, because she courses it not on the ground, like the rat or mouse, of whose kindred she is, but lives under the earth, and is fain to dig herself a dwelling there. And she making her way through so thick an element, which will not yield easily, as the air or the water, it had been dangerous to have drawn so long a train behind her; for her enemy might fall upon her rear, and fetch her out, before she had completed or got full possession of her works.'

I cannot forbear mentioning Mr. Boyle's remark upon this last creature, who, I remember, somewhere in his works observes, that though the mole be not totally blind (as it is commonly thought), she has not sight enough to distinguish particular objects. Her eye is said to have but one humour in it, which is supposed to give her the idea of light, but of nothing else, and is so formed that this idea is probably painful to the animal. Whenever she comes up into broad day, she might be in danger of being taken, unless she were thus affected by a light striking upon her eye, and immediately warning her to bury herself in her proper element. More sight would be useless to her, as none at all might be fatal.

I have only instanced such animals as seem the most imperfect works of Nature; and if Providence shows itself even in the blemishes of these creatures, how much more does it discover itself in the several endowments which it has variously bestowed upon such creatures as are more or less finished and completed in their several faculties, according to the condition of life in which they are posted.

I could wish our royal Society would compile a body of natural history, the best that could be gathered together from books and observations. If the several writers among them took each his particular species, and gave us a distinct account of its original, birth, and education; its policies, hostilities, and alliances, with the frame and texture of its inward and outward parts, and particularly those that distinguish it from all other animals, with their peculiar aptitudes for the state of being in which Providence has placed them...it would be one of the best services their studies could do mankind, and not a little redound to the glory of the all-wise Contriver.

It is true, such a natural history, after all the disquisitions of the learned, would be infinitely short and defective. Seas and deserts hide millions of animals from our observation. Innumerable artifices and stratagems are acted in the howling wilderness and in the great deep, that can never come to our knowledge. Besides that, there are infinitely more species of creatures which are not to be seen without, nor indeed with the help of the finest glasses, than of such as are bulky enough for the naked eye to take hold of. However, from the consideration of such animals as lie within the compass of our knowledge, we might easily form a conclusion of the rest, that the same variety of wisdom and goodness runs through the whole creation, and puts every creature in a condition to provide for its safety and subsistence in its proper station.

Tully has given us an admirable sketch of natural history, in his second book concerning the nature of the gods; and that in a style so raised by metaphors and descriptions, that it lifts the subject above raillery and ridicule, which frequently fall on such nice observations, when they pass through the hands of an ordinary writer.

L

No. CXXII.   FRIDAY, JULY 20.

Comes jucundus in via pro vehiculo est.   PUBL.

An agreeable companion upon the road is as good as a coach.

A MAN's first care should be to avoid the reproaches of his own heart; his next, to escape the censures of the world: if the last interferes with the former, it ought to be entirely neglected; but otherwise there cannot be a greater satisfaction to an honest mind, than to see those approbations which it gives itself, seconded by the applauses of the public. A man is more sure of his conduct, when the verdict which he passes upon his own behaviour is thus warranted and confirmed by the opinion of all who know him.

My worthy friend Sir Roger is one of those who is not only at peace within himself, but beloved and esteemed by all about him. He receives a suitable tribute for his universal benevolence to mankind, in the returns of affection and good-will, which are paid him by every one that lives within his neighbourhood. I lately met with two or three odd instances of that general respect which is shown to the good old Knight. He would needs carry Will Wimble and myself with him to the county assizes. As we were upon the road, Will Wimble joined a couple of plain men who rid before us, and conversed with them for some time: during which my friend Sir Roger acquainted me with their characters.

The first of them (says he), that has a spaniel by his side, is a yeoman of about a hundred pounds a-year, an honest man: he is just within the game-act, and qualified to kill a hare or a pheasant. He knocks down a dinner with his gun twice or thrice a-week, and by that means lives much cheaper than those who have not so good an estate as himself. He would be a good neighbour if he did not destroy so many partridges: in short, he is a very sensible man; shoots flying; and has been several times foreman of the petty jury.

The other that rides along with him is Tom Touchy, a fellow famous for taking the law of every body. There is not one in the town where he lives that he has not sued at a quarter-sessions. The rogue had once the impudence to go to law with the Widow. His head is full of costs, damages, and ejectments: he plagued a couple of honest gentlemen so long for a trespass in breaking one of his hedges, till he was forced to sell the ground it enclosed, to defray the charges of the prosecution. His father left him fourscore pounds a-year; but he has cast, and been cast so often, that he is not now worth thirty. I suppose he is going upon the old business of the willow-tree.

As Sir Roger was giving me this account of Tom Touchy, Will Wimble and his two companions stopped short till we came up to them. After having paid their respects to Sir Roger, Will told him that Mr. Touchy and he must appeal to him upon a dispute that arose between them. Will it seems had been giving his fellow-travellers an account of his angling one day in such a hole; when Tom Touchy, instead of hearing out his story, told him, that Mr. such-a-one, if he pleased, might take the law of him for fishing in that part of the river. My friend Sir Roger heard them both, upon a round trot; and after having paused some time, told them, with the air of a man who would not give his judgment rashly, that " much might be said on both sides." They were neither of them dissatisfied with the Knight's determination, because neither of them found himself in the wrong by it. Upon which we made the best of our way to the assizes.

The court was set before Sir Roger came, but notwithstanding all the justices had taken their places upon the bench, they made room for the old Knight at the head of them; who for his reputation in the country took occasion to whisper in the judge's ear, "That he was glad his lordship had met with so much good weather in his circuit." I was listening to the proceeding of the court with much attention, and infinitely pleased with that great appearance of solemnity which so properly accompanies such a public administration of our laws, when, after about an hour's sitting, I observed, to my great surprise, in the midst of a trial, that my friend Sir Roger was getting up to speak. I was in some pain for him, till I found he had acquitted himself of two or three sentences, with a look of much business and great intrepidity.

Upon his first rising, the court was hushed, and a general whisper ran among the country people that "Sir Roger was up." The speech he made was so little to the purpose, that I shall not trouble my readers with an account of it; and I believe was not so much designed by the knight himself to inform the court, as to give him a figure in my eye, and keep up his credit in the country.

I was highly delighted when the court rose, to see the gentlemen of the country gathering about my old friend, and striving who should compliment him most; at the same time that the ordinary people gazed upon him at a distance, not a little admiring his courage, that was not afraid to speak to the judge.

In our return home we met with a very odd accident, which I cannot forbear relating, because it shews how desirous all who know Sir Roger are of giving him marks of their esteem. When we were arrived upon the verge of his estate, we stopped at a little inn to rest ourselves and our horses. The man of the house had, it seems, been formerly a servant in the Knight's family; and to do honour to his old master, had some time since, unknown to Sir Roger, put him up in a signpost before the door; so that the Knight's head had hung out upon the road about a week before he himself knew any thing of the matter. As soon as Sir Roger was acquainted with it, finding that his servant's indiscretion proceeded wholly from affection and good will, he only told him that he had made him too high a compliment; and when the fellow seemed to think that could hardly be, added, with a more decisive look, that it was too great an honour for any man under a duke; but told him at the same time, that it might be altered with a very few touches, and that he himself would be at the charge of it. Accordingly, they got a painter, by the Knight's directions, to add a pair of whiskers to the face, and by a little aggravation of the features, to change it into the Saracen's Head. I should not have known this story, had not the inn-keeper, upon Sir Roger's alighting, told him in my hearing, that his honour's head was brought back last night with the alterations that he had ordered to be made in it. Upon this, my friend, with his usual cheerfulness, related the particulars above-mentioned, and ordered the head to be brought into the room. I could not forbear discovering greater expressions of mirth than ordinary, upon the appearance of this monstrous face, under which, notwithstanding it was made to frown and stare in a most extraordinary manner, I could still discover a distant resemblance of my old friend. Sir Roger, upon seeing me laugh, desired me to tell him truly if I thought it possible for people to know him in that disguise. I at first kept my usual silence: but upon the Knight's conjuring me to tell him whether it was not still more like himself than a Saracen, I composed my countenance in the best manner I could, and replied, "That much might be said on both sides."

These several adventures, with the Knight's behaviour in them, gave me as pleasant a day as ever I met with in any of my travels. L.

No. CXXIII   SATURDAY, JULY 21.

Doctrina sed vim promovet insitam,
Rectique cultus pectora roborant
  Utcunque defecere mores,
  Dedecorant bene nata culpæ.   Hor.

Yet the best blood by learning is refin'd,
  And virtue arms the solid mind,
Whilst vice will stain the noblest race,
  And the paternal stamp efface   Oldisworth

As I was yesterday taking the air with my friend Sir Roger, we were met by a fresh coloured ruddy young man, who rode by us full speed, with a couple of servants behind him. Upon my inquiry who he was, Sir Roger told me that he was a young gentleman of a considerable estate, who had been educated by a tender mother, that lived not many miles from the place where we were. She is a very good lady, says my friend, but took so much care of her son's health, that she has made him good for nothing. She quickly found that reading was bad for his eyes, and that writing made his head ache. He was let loose among the woods, as soon as he was able to ride on horseback, or to carry a gun upon his shoulder. To be brief, I found by my friend's account of him, that he had got a great stock of health, but nothing else; and that if it were a man's business only to live, there would not be a more accomplished young fellow in the whole country.

The truth of it is, since my residing in these parts, I have seen and heard innumerable instances of young heirs and elder brothers, who, either from their own reflecting upon the estates they are born to, and therefore thinking all other accomplishments unnecessary, or from hearing these notions frequently inculcated to them by the flattery of their servants and domestics, or from the same foolish thought prevailing in those who have the care of their education, are of no manner of use but to keep up their families, and transmit their lands and houses in a line to posterity.

This makes me often think on a story I have heard of two friends, which I shall give my reader at large, under feigned names. The moral of it may, I hope, be useful, though there are some circumstances which make it rather appear like a novel, than a true story.

Eudoxus and Leontine began the world with small estates. They were both of them men of good sense and great virtue. They prosecuted their studies together in their earlier years, and entered into such a friendship as lasted to the end of their lives. Eudoxus, at his first setting out in the world, threw himself into a court, where, by his natural endowments, and his acquired abilities, he made his way from one post to another, till at length he had raised a very considerable fortune. Leontine, on the contrary, sought all opportunities of improving his mind, by study, conversation, and travel. He was not only acquainted with all the sciences, but with the most eminent professors of them throughout Europe. He knew perfectly well the interests of its princes, with the customs and fashions of their courts, and could scarce meet with the name of an extraordinary person in the gazette, whom he had not either talked to or seen. In short, he had so well mixed and digested his knowledge of men and books, that he made one of the most accomplished persons of his age. During the whole course of his studies and travels, he kept up a punctual correspondence with Eudoxus, who often made himself acceptable to the principal men about court, by the intelligence which he received from Leontine. When they were both turned of forty (an age in which, according to Mr. Cowley, " there is no dallying with life") they determined, pursuant to the resolution they had taken in the beginning of their lives, to retire, and pass the remainder of their days in the country. In order to this, they both of them married much about the same time. Leontine, with his own and his wife's fortune, bought a farm of three hundred a year, which lay within the neighbourhood of his friend Eudoxus, who had purchased an estate of as many thousands. They were both of them fathers about the same time, Eudoxus having a son born to him, and Leontine a daughter; but to the unspeakable grief of the latter, his young wife (in whom all his happiness was wrapped up) died in a few days after the birth of her daughter. His affliction would have been insupportable, had not he been comforted by the daily visits and conversation of his friend. As they were one day talking together with their usual intimacy, Leontine, considering how incapable he was of giving his daughter a proper education in his own house, and Eudoxus reflecting on the ordinary behaviour of a son who knows himself to be the heir of a great estate, they both agreed upon an exchange of children, namely, that the boy should be bred up with Leontine, as his son, and that the girl should live with Eudoxus, as his daughter, till they were each of them arrived at the years of discretion. The wife of Eudoxus, knowing that her son could not be so advantageously brought up as under the care of Leontine, and considering at the same time that he would be perpetually under her own eye, was by degrees prevailed upon to fall in with the project. She therefore took Leonilla, for that was the name of the girl, and educated her as her own daughter. The two friends on each side had wrought themselves to such an habitual tenderness for the children who were under their direction, that each of them had the real passion of a father, where the title was but imaginary. Florio, the name of the young heir that lived with Leontine, though he had all the duty and affection imaginable for his supposed parent, was taught to rejoice at the sight of Eudoxus, who visited his friend very frequently, and was dictated by his natural affection, as well as by the rules of prudence, to make himself esteemed and beloved by Florio. The boy was now old enough to know his supposed father's circumstances, and that therefore he was to make his way in the world by his own industry. This consideration grew stronger in him every day, and produced so good an effect, that he applied himself with more than ordinary attention to the pursuit of every thing which Leontine recommended to him. His natural abilities, which were very good, assisted by the directions of so excellent a counsellor, enabled him to make a quicker progress than ordinary through all the parts of his education. Before he was twenty years of age, having finished his studies and exercises with great applause, he was removed from the University to the Inns of Court, where there are very few that make themselves considerable proficients in the studies of the place, who know they shall arrive at great estates without them. This was not Florio's case: he found that three hundred a-year was but a poor estate for Leontine and himself to live upon; so that he studied without intermission till he gained a very good insight into the constitution and laws of his country.

I should have told my reader, that whilst Florio lived at the house of his foster-father, he was always an acceptable guest in the family of Eudoxus, where he became acquainted with Leonilla from her infancy. His acquaintance with her by degrees grew into love, which in a mind trained up in all the sentiments of honour and virtue became a very uneasy passion. He despaired of gaining an heiress of so great a fortune, and would rather have died than attempted it by any indirect methods. Leonilla, who was a woman of the greatest beauty, joined with the greatest modesty, entertained at the same time a secret passion for Florio but conducted herself with so much prudence, that she never gave him the least intimation of it. Florio was now engaged in all those arts and improvements that are proper to raise a man's private fortune, and give him a figure in his country, but secretly tormented with that passion which burns with the greatest fury in a virtuous and noble heart, when he received a sudden summons from Leontine to repair to him in the country the next day. For it seems Eudoxus was so filled with the report of his son's reputation, that he could no longer withhold making himself known to him. The morning after his arrival at the house of his supposed father, Leontine told him that Eudoxus had something of great importance to communicate to him; upon which the good man embraced him and wept. Florio was no sooner arrived at the great house that stood in his neighbourhood, but Eudoxus took him by the hand, after the first salutes were over, and conducted him into his closet. He there opened to him the whole secret of his parentage and education, concluding after this manner: "I have no other way left of acknowledging my gratitude to Leontine than by marrying you to his daughter. He shall not lose the pleasure of being your father by the discovery I have made to you. Leonilla too shall be still my daughter; her filial piety, though misplaced, has been so exemplary, that it deserves the greatest reward I can confer upon it. You shall have the pleasure of seeing a great estate fall to you, which you would have lost the relish of had you known yourself born to it. Continue only to deserve it in the same manner you did before you were possessed of it. I have left your mother in the next room. Her heart yearns towards you. She is making the same discoveries to Leonilla which I have made to yourself." Florio was so overwhelmed with this profusion of happiness, that he was not able to make a reply, but threw himself down at his father's feet, and amidst a flood of tears kissed and embraced his knees, asking his blessing, and expressing in dumb show those sentiments of love, duty, and gratitude, that were too big for utterance. To conclude, the happy pair were married, and half Eudoxus's estate settled upon them, Leontine and Eudoxus passed the remainder of their lives together, and received, in the dutiful and affectionate behaviour of Florio and Leonilla, the just recompense as well as the natural effects of that care which they had bestowed upon them in their education. L.

No. CXXIV. MONDAY, JULY 23.

Μέγα βίβλιον, μέγα κακόν.

A great book is a great evil.

A MAN who publishes his works in a volume, has an infinite advantage over one who communicates his writings to the world in loose tracts and single pieces. We do not expect to meet with any thing in a bulky volume, till after some heavy preamble, and several words of course, to prepare the reader for what follows: nay, authors have established it as a kind of rule, that a man ought to be dull sometimes; as the most severe reader makes allowances for many rests and nodding places in a voluminous writer. This gave occasion to the famous Greek proverb which I have chosen for my motto, "that a great book is a great evil."

On the contrary, those who publish their thoughts in distinct sheets, and as it were by piece-meal, have none of these advantages. We must immediately fall into our subject, and treat every part of it in a lively manner, or our papers are thrown by as dull and insipid: our matter must lie close together, and either be wholly new in itself, or in the turn it receives from our expressions. Were the books of our best authors thus to be retailed to the public, and every page submitted to the taste of forty or fifty thousand readers, I am afraid we should complain of many flat expressions, trivial observations, beaten topics, and common thoughts, which go off very well in the lump. At the same time, notwithstanding some papers may be made up of broken hints and irregular sketches, it is often expected that every sheet should be a kind of treatise, and make out in thought what it wants in bulk: that a point of humour should be worked up in all parts, and a subject touched upon in its most essential articles, without the repetitions, tautologies, and enlargements, that are indulged to longer labours. The ordinary writers of morality prescribe to their readers after the Galenic way; their medicines are made up in large quantities. An essay writer must practise in the chemical method, and give the virtue of a full draught in a few drops. Were all books reduced thus to their quintessence, many a bulky author would make his appearance in a penny paper: there would be scarce such a thing in nature as a folio: the works of an age would be contained on a few shelves, not to mention millions of volumes that would be utterly annihilated.

I cannot think that the difficulty of furnishing out separate papers of this nature has hindered authors from communicating their thoughts to the world after such a manner: though I must confess I am amazed that the press should be only made use of in this way by news-writers and the zealots of parties, as if it were not more advantageous to mankind to be instructed in wisdom and virtue, than in politics; and to be made good fathers, husbands, and sons, than counsellors and statesmen. Had the philosophers and great men of antiquity, who took so much pains in order to instruct mankind, and leave the world wiser and better than they found it; had they, I say, been possessed of the art of printing, there is no question but they would have made such an advantage of it in dealing out their lectures to the public. Our common prints would be of great use were they thus calculated to diffuse good sense through the bulk of a people, to clear up their understandings, animate their minds with virtue, dissipate the sorrows of a heavy heart, or unbend the mind from its more severe employments with innocent amusements. When knowledge, instead of being bound up in books, and kept in libraries and retirements, is thus obtruded upon the public; when it is canvassed in every assembly, and exposed upon every table;... I cannot forbear reflecting upon that passage in the Proverbs, "Wisdom crieth without, she uttereth her voice in the streets; she crieth in the chief place of concourse, in the openings of the gates. In the city she uttereth her words, saying, How long, ye simple ones, will ye love simplicity? and the scorners delight in their scorning? and fools hate knowledge?"

The many letters which come to me from persons of the best sense in both sexes (for I may pronounce their characters from their way of writing), do not a little encourage me in the prosecution of this my undertaking: besides that, my bookseller tells me the demand for these my papers increases daily. It is at his instance that I shall continue my rural speculations to the end of this month; several having made up separate sets of them as they have done before of those relating to wit, to operas, to points of morality, or subjects of humour.

I am not at all mortified, when sometimes I see my works thrown aside by men of no taste nor learning. There is a kind of heaviness and ignorance that hangs upon the minds of ordinary men, which is too thick for knowledge to break through. Their souls are not to be enlightened.

> .... Nox atra cavâ circumvolat umbrâ. VIRG

Dark night surrounds them with her hollow shade

To these I must apply the fable of the mole, that after having consulted many oculists for the bettering of his sight, was at last provided with a good pair of spectacles, but upon his endeavouring to make use of them, his mother told him very prudently, "That spectacles, though they might help the eye of a man, could be of no use to a mole." It is not therefore for the benefit of moles that I publish these my daily essays.

But besides such as are moles through ignorance, there are others who are moles through envy. As it is said in the Latin proverb, "That one man is a wolf to another," so, generally speaking, one author is a mole to another author. It is impossible for them to discover beauties in one another's works; they have eyes only for spots and blemishes. they can indeed see the light, as it is said of the animals which are their namesakes, but the idea of it is painful to them; they immediately shut their eyes upon it, and withdraw themselves into a wilful obscurity. I have already caught two or three of these dark undermining vermin, and intend to make a string of them, in order to hang them up in one of my papers, as an example to all such voluntary moles. C

No. CXXV. TUESDAY, JULY 24.

Ne, pueri, ne tanta animis assuescite bella:
Neu patriæ validas in viscera vertite vires
                                        VIRG.

Embrace again, my sons, be foes no more,
Nor stain your country with her children's gore.
                                        DRYDEN.

My worthy friend Sir Roger, when we are talking of the malice of parties, very frequently tells us an accident that happened to him when he was a school-boy, which was at the time when the feuds ran high between the round-heads and cavaliers. This worthy knight being then but a stripling, had occasion to inquire which was the way to St. Anne's Lane: upon which the person whom he spoke to, instead of answering his question, called him a young popish cur, and asked him who had made Anne a saint? The boy, being in some confusion, inquired of the next he met, which was the way to Anne's Lane; but was called a prick-eared cur for his pains, and, instead of being shewn the way, was told, that she had been a saint before he was born, and would be one after he was hanged. Upon this, says Sir Roger, I did not think fit to repeat the former question, but going into every lane of the neighbourhood, asked what they called the name of that lane. By which ingenious artifice he found out the place he inquired after, without giving offence to any party. Sir Roger generally closes this narrative with reflections on the mischief that parties do in the country; how they spoil good neighbourhood, and make honest gentlemen hate one another: besides that they manifestly tend to the prejudice of the land-tax and the destruction of the game.

There cannot a greater judgment befal a country than such a dreadful spirit of division as rends a government into two distinct people, and makes them greater strangers and more averse to one another, than if they were actually two different nations. The effects of such a division are pernicious to the last degree, not only with regard to those advantages which they give the common enemy, but to those private evils which they produce in the heart of almost every particular person. This influence is very fatal both to men's morals and their understandings; it sinks the virtue of a nation, and not only so, but destroys even common sense.

A furious party spirit, when it rages in its full violence, exerts itself in civil war and bloodshed, and when it is under its greatest restraints, naturally breaks out in falsehood, detraction, calumny, and a partial administration of justice. In a word, it fills a nation with spleen and rancour, and extinguishes all the seeds of good nature, compassion, and humanity.

Plutarch says very finely, that a man should not allow himself to hate even his enemies; because, says he, if you indulge this passion in some occasions, it will rise of itself in others; if you hate your enemies, you will contract such a vicious habit of mind, as by degrees will break out upon those who are your friends, or those who are indifferent to you. I might here observe how admirably this precept of morality (which derives the malignity of hatred from the passion itself, and not from its object) answers to that great rule which was dictated to the world about an hundred years before this philosopher wrote: but instead of that, I shall only take notice, with a real grief of heart, that the minds of many good men among us appear soured with party-principles, and alienated from one another, in such a manner as seems to me altogether inconsistent with the dictates either of reason or religion. Zeal for a public cause is apt to breed passions in the hearts of virtuous persons, to which the regard of their own private interest would never have betrayed them.

If this party-spirit has so ill an effect on our morals, it has likewise a very great one upon our judgments. We often hear a poor insipid paper or pamphlet cried up, and sometimes a noble piece depreciated, by those who are of a different principle from the author. One who is actuated by this spirit is almost under an incapacity of discerning either real blemishes or beauties. A man of merit, in a different principle, is like an object seen in two different mediums, that appears crooked or broken, however straight and entire it may be in itself. For this reason, there is scarce a person of any figure in England who does not go by two contrary characters, as opposite to one another as light and darkness. Knowledge and learning suffer in a particular manner from this strange prejudice, which at present prevails amongst all ranks and degrees in the British nation. As men formerly became eminent in learned societies by their parts and acquisitions, they now distinguish themselves by the warmth and violence with which they espouse their respective parties. Books are valued upon the like considerations: an abusive scurrilous style passes for satire, and a dull scheme of party-notions is called fine writing.

There is one piece of sophistry practised by both sides, and that is the taking any scandalous story, that has been ever whispered or invented of a private man, for a known undoubted truth, and raising suitable speculations upon it. Calumnies that have been never proved, or have been often refuted, are the ordinary postulatums of these infamous scribblers, upon which they proceed as upon first principles granted by all men, though in their hearts they know they are false, or at best very doubtful. When they have laid these foundations of scurrility, it is no wonder that their superstructure is every way answerable to them. If this shameless practice of the present age endures much longer, praise and reproach will cease to be motives of action in good men.

There are certain periods of time in all governments when this inhuman spirit prevails. Italy was long torn in pieces by the Guelfes and Gibellines, and France by those who were for and against the League: but it is very unhappy for a man to be born in such a stormy and tempestuous season. It is the restless ambition of artful men that thus breaks a people into factions, and draws several well-meaning persons to their interest by a specious concern for their country. How many honest minds are filled with uncharitable and barbarous notions, out of their zeal for the public good? What cruelties and outrages would they not commit against men of an adverse party, whom they would honour and esteem, if, instead of considering them as they are represented, they knew them as they are? Thus are persons of the greatest probity seduced into shameful errors and prejudices, and made bad men even by that noblest of principles, the love of their country. I cannot here forbear mentioning the famous Spanish proverb, ' If there were neither fools nor knaves in the world, all people would be of one mind.'

For my own part, I could heartily wish that all honest men would enter into an association for the support of one another against the endeavours of those whom they ought to look upon as their common enemies, whatsoever side they may belong to. Were there such an honest body of neutral forces, we would never see the worst of men in great figures of life, because they are useful to a party, nor the best unregarded, because they are above practising those methods which would be grateful to their faction. We should then single every criminal out of the herd, and hunt him down, however formidable and overgrown he might appear: on the contrary, we should shelter distressed innocence, and defend virtue, however beset with contempt or ridicule, envy or defamation. In short, we should not any longer regard our fellow-subjects as Whigs or Tories, but should make the man of merit our friend, and the villain our enemy. C

No. CXXVI. WEDNESDAY, JULY 25.

Tros Rutulusve fuat, nullo discrimine habebo.   VIRG.

Rutulians, Trojans, are the same to me.   DRYDEN.

IN my yesterday's paper I proposed, that the honest men of all parties should enter into a kind of association for the defence of one another, and the confusion of their common enemies. As it is designed this neutral body should act with a regard to nothing but truth and equity, and divest themselves of the little heats and prepossessions that cleave to the parties of all kinds, I have prepared for them the following form of an association, which may express their intentions in the most plain and simple manner.

"WE whose names are hereunto subscribed, do solemnly declare, that we do in our conscience believe two and two make four; and that we shall adjudge any man whatsoever to be our enemy who endeavours to persuade us to the contrary. We are likewise ready to maintain, with the hazard of all that is near and dear to us, that six is less than seven in all times and all places; and that ten will not be more three years hence than it is at present. We do also firmly declare, that it is our resolution as long as we live, to call black black, and white white. And we shall upon all occasions oppose such persons that, upon any day of the year, shall call black white, or white black, with the utmost peril of our lives and fortunes."

Were there such a combination of honest men, who without any regard to places, would endeavour to extirpate all such furious zealots as would sacrifice one half of their country to the passion and interest of the other; as also such infamous hypocrites, that are for promoting their own advantage, under colour of the public good; with all the profligate immoral retainers to each side, that have nothing to recommend them but an implicit submission to their leaders; we should soon see that furious party-spirit extinguished, which may in time expose us to the derision and contempt of all the nations about us.

A member of this society, that would thus carefully employ himself in making room for merit, by throwing down the worthless and depraved part of mankind from those conspicuous stations of life to which they have been sometimes advanced, and all this without any regard to his private interest, would be no small benefactor to his country.

I remember to have read in Diodorus Siculus an account of a very active little animal, which I think he calls the Ichneumon, that makes it the whole business of his life to break the eggs of the crocodile, which he is always in search after. This instinct is the more remarkable, because the Ichneumon never feeds upon the eggs he has broken, nor any other way finds his account in them. Were it not for the incessant labours of this industrious animal, Egypt (says the historian) would be over-run with crocodiles; for the Egyptians are so far from destroying those pernicious creatures, that they worship them as gods.

If we look into the behaviour of ordinary partisans, we shall find them far from resembling this disinterested animal; and rather acting after the example of the wild Tartars, who are ambitious of destroying a man of the most extraordinary parts and accomplishments, as thinking that upon his decease the same talents, whatever post they qualified him for, enter of course into his destroyer

As in the whole train of my speculations I have endeavoured, as much as I am able, to extinguish that pernicious spirit of passion and prejudice which rages with the same violence in all parties, I am still the more desirous of doing some good in this particular, because I observe that the spirit of party reigns more in the country than in the town. It here contracts a kind of brutality and rustic fierceness, to which men of a politer conversation are wholly strangers. It extends itself even to the return of the bow and the hat, and at the same time that the heads of parties preserve towards one another an outward show of good-breeding, and keep up a perpetual intercourse of civilities, their tools that are dispersed in these outlying parts will not so much as mingle together at a cock-match. This humour fills the country with several periodical meetings of Whig jockies and Tory fox-hunters; not to mention the innumerable curses, frowns and whispers it produces at a quarter-sessions.

I do not know whether I have observed in any of my former papers, that my friend Sir Roger de Coverly and Sir Andrew Freeport are of different principles: the first of them inclined to the landed, and the other to the monied interest. This humour is so moderate in each of them, that it proceeds no further than to an agreeable raillery, which very often diverts the rest of the club. I find however that the knight is a much stronger Tory in the country than in town, which, as he has told me in my ear, is absolutely necessary for the keeping up his interest. In all our journey from London to his house we did not so much as bait at a Whig-inn, or if by chance the coachman stopped at a wrong place, one of Sir Roger's servants would ride up to his master full speed, and whisper to him that the master of the house was against such an one in the last election. This often betrayed us into hard beds and bad cheer; for we were not so inquisitive about the inn as the innkeeper; and provided our landlord's principles were sound, did not take any notice of the staleness of his provisions. This I found still the more inconvenient, because the better the host was, the worse generally were his accommodations; the fellow knowing very well, that those who were his friends would take up with coarse diet and a hard lodging. For these reasons, all the while I was upon the road I dreaded entering into a house of any one that Sir Roger had applauded for an honest man.

Since my stay at Sir Roger's in the country, I daily find more instances of this narrow party-humour. Being upon the bowling-green at a neighbouring market town the other day (for that is the place where the gentlemen of one side meet once a-week), I observed a stranger among them of a better presence and genteeler behaviour than ordinary; but was much surprised, that notwithstanding he was a very fair bettor, nobody would take him up. But upon inquiry, I found that he was one who had given a disagreeable vote in a former parliament; for which reason there was not a man upon the bowling-green who would have so much correspondence with him as to win his money of him.

Among other instances of this nature, I must not omit one that concerns myself. Will Wimble was the other day relating several strange stories that he had picked up, nobody knows where, of a certain great man, and upon my staring at him as one that was surprised to hear such things in the country, which had never been so much as whispered in the town, Will stopped short in the thread of his discourse, and after dinner asked my friend Sir Roger in his ear, if he was sure that I was not a fanatic.

It gives me a serious concern to see such a spirit of dissension in the country; not only as it destroys virtue and common sense, and renders us in a manner barbarians towards one another, but as it perpetuates our animosities, widens our breaches, and transmits our present passions and prejudices to our posterity. For my own part, I am sometimes afraid that I discover the seeds of a civil war in these our divisions: and therefore cannot but bewail, as in their first principles, the miseries and calamities of our children. C

No. CXXVII. THURSDAY, JULY 26.

.... Quantum est in rebus inane! PERS.

How much of emptiness we find in things!

It is our custom at Sir Roger's, upon the coming in of the post, to sit about a pot of coffee, and hear the old knight read Dyer's Letter, which he does with his spectacles upon his nose, and in an audible voice, smiling very often at those little strokes of satire which are so frequent in the writings of that author. I afterwards communicate to the knight such packets as I receive under the quality of "Spectator." The following letter chancing to please him more than ordinary, I shall publish it at his request.

'Mr SPECTATOR,

'You have diverted the town almost a whole month at the expense of the country, it is now high time that you should give the country their revenge. Since your withdrawing from this place, the fair sex are run into great extravagancies. Their petticoats, which began to heave and swell before you left us, are now blown up into a most enormous concave, and rise every day more and more: in short, Sir, since our women know themselves to be out of the eye of the Spectator, they will be kept within no compass. You praised them a little too soon for the modesty of their head-dresses, for as the humour of a sick person is often driven out of one limb into another, their superfluity of ornaments, instead of being entirely banished, seems only fallen from their heads upon their lower parts. What they have lost in height they make up in breadth, and, contrary to all rules of architecture, widen the foundations at the same time that they shorten the superstructure. Were they, like Spanish jennets, to impregnate by the wind, they could not have thought on a more proper invention. But as we do not yet hear any particular use in this petticoat, or that it contains any thing more than what was supposed to be in those of scantier make, we are wonderfully at a loss about it.

' The women give out, in defence of these wide bottoms, that they are airy, and very proper for the season: but this I look upon to be only a pretence, and a piece of art, for it is well known we have not had a more moderate summer these many years, so that it is certain the heat they complain of cannot be in the weather: besides, I would fain ask these tender constitutioned ladies, why they should require more cooling than their mothers before them?

' I find several speculative persons are of opinion, that our sex has of late years been very saucy, and that the hoop-petticoat is made use of to keep us at a distance. It is most certain that a woman's honour cannot be better intrenched than after this manner, in circle within circle, amidst such a variety of out-works and lines of circumvallation. A female who is thus invested in whalebone is sufficiently secured against the approaches of an ill-bred fellow, who might as well think of Sir George Etherege's way of making love in a tub, as in the midst of so many hoops.

'Among these various conjectures, there are men of superstitious tempers, who look upon the hoop-petticoat as a kind of prodigy. Some will have it that it portends the downfal of the French king, and observe that the farthingale appeared in England a little before the ruin of the Spanish monarchy. Others are of opinion that it foretels battle and bloodshed, and believe it of the same prognostication as the tail of a blazing star. For my part, I am apt to think it is a sign that multitudes are coming into the world rather than going out of it.

'The first time I saw a lady dressed in one of these petticoats, I could not forbear blaming her in my own thoughts for walking abroad when she was so near her time; but soon recovered myself out of my error, when I found all the modish part of the sex as far gone as herself. It is generally thought some crafty women have thus betrayed their companions into hoops, that they might make them accessary to their own concealments, and by that means escape the censure of the world; as wary generals have sometimes dressed two or three dozen of their friends in their own habit, that they might not draw upon themselves any particular attacks from the enemy. The strutting petticoat smooths all distinctions, levels the mother with the daughter, and sets maids and matrons, wives and widows, upon the same bottom. In the meanwhile, I cannot but be troubled to see so many well-shaped innocent virgins bloated up, and waddling up and down like big-bellied women.

'Should this fashion get among the ordinary people, our public ways would be so crowded, that we should want street-room. Several congregations of the best fashion find themselves already very much straitened; and if the mode increases, I wish it may not drive many ordinary women into meetings and conventicles. Should our sex at the same time take it into their heads to wear trunk breeches (as who knows what their indignation at this female treatment may drive them to,) a man and his wife would fill a whole pew

'You know, Sir, it is recorded of Alexander the Great, that in his Indian expedition, he buried several suits of armour, which by his directions were made much too big for any of his soldiers, in order to give posterity an extraordinary idea of him, and make them believe he had commanded an army of giants.' I am persuaded, that if one of the present petticoats happens to be hung up in any repository of curiosities, it will lead into the same error the generations that lie some removes from us; unless we can believe our posterity will think so disrespectfully of their great grandmothers, that they made themselves monstrous to appear amiable.

'When I survey this new-fashioned rotunda in all its parts, I cannot but think of the old philosopher, who after having entered into an Egyptian temple, and looked about for the idol of the place, at length discovered a little black monkey enshrined in the midst of it, upon which he could not forbear crying out (to the great scandal of the worshippers,) what a magnificent palace is here for such a ridiculous inhabitant!

'Though you have taken a resolution, in one of your papers, to avoid descending to particularities of dress, I believe you will not think it below you, on so extraordinary an occasion, to unhoop the fair sex, and cure this fashionable tympany that is got among them I am apt to think the petticoat will shrink of its own accord at your first coming to town; at least a touch of your pen will make it contract itself like the sensitive plant, and by that means oblige several who are either terrified or astonished at this portentous novelty, and among the rest,

Your humble servant, &c.'

C

No. CXXVIII. FRIDAY, JULY 27.

.........Concordia discors LUCAN

Harmonious discord

WOMEN in their nature are much more gay and joyous than men; whether it be that their blood is more refined, their fibres more delicate, and their animal spirits more light and volatile; or whether, as some have imagined, there may not be a kind of sex in the very soul, I shall not pretend to determine. As vivacity is the gift of women, gravity is that of men. They should each of them therefore keep a watch upon the particular bias which nature has fixed in their minds, that it may not draw too much, and lead them out of the paths of reason. This will certainly happen, if the one in every word and action affects the character of being rigid and severe, and the other of being brisk and airy. Men should beware of being captivated by a kind of savage philosophy, women by a thoughtless gallantry. Where these precautions are not observed, the man often degenerates into a cynic, the woman into a coquette; the man grows sullen and morose, the woman impertinent and fantastical.

By what I have said, we may conclude, men and women were made as counterparts to one another, that the pains and anxieties of the husband might be relieved by the sprightliness and good humour of the wife. When these are rightly tempered, care and cheerfulness go hand in hand; and the family, like a ship that is duly trimmed, wants neither sail nor ballast.

Natural historians observe (for whilst I am in the country I must fetch my allusions from thence), that only the male birds have voices; that their songs begin a little before breeding-time, and end a little after; that whilst the hen is covering her eggs, the male generally takes his stand upon a neighbouring bough within her hearing; and by that means amuses and diverts her with his songs during the whole time of her sitting.

This contract among birds lasts no longer than till a brood of young ones arises from it, so that in the feathered kind the cares and fatigues of the married state, if I may so call it, lie principally upon the female. On the contrary, as in our species the man and the woman are joined together for life, and the main burden rests upon the former, nature has given all the little arts of soothing and blandishment to the female, that she may cheer and animate her companion in a constant and assiduous application to the making a provision for his family, and the educating of their common children. This, however is not to be taken so strictly as if the same duties were not often reciprocal and incumbent on both parties, but only to set forth what seems to have been the general intention of nature, in the different inclinations and endowments which are bestowed on the different sexes.

But whatever was the reason that man and woman were made with this variety of temper, if we observe the conduct of the fair sex, we find that they choose rather to associate themselves with a person who resembles them in that light and volatile humour which is natural to them, than to such as are qualified to moderate and counterbalance it. It has been an old complaint, that the coxcomb carries it with them before the man of sense. When we see a fellow loud and talkative, full of insipid life and laughter, we may venture to pronounce him a female favourite: noise and flutter are such accomplishments as they cannot withstand. To be short, the passion of an ordinary woman for a man is nothing else but self-love diverted upon another object: she would have the lover a woman in every thing but the sex. I do not know a finer piece of satire on this part of woman-kind than those lines of Mr Dryden.

"Our thoughtless sex is caught by outward form
"And empty noise, and loves itself in man."

This is a source of infinite calamities to the sex, as it frequently joins them to men who, in their own thoughts, are as fine creatures as themselves; or if they chance to be good humoured, serve only to dissipate their fortunes, inflame their follies, and aggravate their indiscretions.

The same female levity is no less fatal to them after marriage than before: it represents to their imaginations the faithful prudent husband as an honest, tractable, and domestic animal; and turns their thoughts upon the fine gay gentleman that laughs, sings, and dresses so much more agreeably.

As this irregular vivacity of temper leads astray the hearts of ordinary women in the choice of their lovers and the treatment of their husbands, it operates with the same pernicious influence towards their children, who are taught to accomplish themselves in all those sublime perfections that appear captivating in the eye of their mother. She admires in her son what she loved in her gallant; and by that means contributes all she can to perpetuate herself in a worthless progeny.

The younger Faustina was a lively instance of this sort of women. Notwithstanding she was married to Marcus Aurelius, one of the greatest, wisest and best of the Roman emperors, she thought a common gladiator much the prettier gentleman, and had taken such care to accomplish her son Commodus according to her own notions of a fine man, that, when he ascended the throne of his father, he became the most foolish and abandoned tyrant that was ever placed at the head of the Roman Empire, signalizing himself in nothing but the fighting of prizes, and knocking out men's brains. As he had no taste of true glory, we see him in several medals and statues which are still extant of him, equipped like an Hercules with a club and a lion's skin.

I have been led into this speculation by the characters I have heard of a country gentleman and his lady, who do not live many miles from Sir Roger. The wife is an old coquette, that is always hankering after the diversions of the town; the husband a morose rustic, that frowns and frets at the name of it. The wife is over-run with affectation, the husband sunk into brutality; the lady cannot bear the noise of the larks and nightingales, hates your tedious summer days, and is sick at the sight of shady woods, and purling streams: the husband wonders how any one can be pleased with the fooleries of plays and operas, and rails from morning to night at essenced fops and tawdry courtiers. The children are educated in these different notions of their parents. The sons follow the father about his grounds, while the daughters read volumes of love-letters and romances to their mother. By this means it comes to pass, that the girls look upon their father as a clown, and the boys think their mother no better than she should be.

How different are the lives of Aristus and Aspasia? The innocent vivacity of the one is tempered and composed by the cheerful gravity of the other. The wife grows wise by the discourses of the husband, and the husband good-humoured by the conversations of the wife. Aristus would not be so amiable were it not for his Aspasia, nor Aspasia so much esteemed, were it not for her Aristus. Their virtues are blended in their children, and diffuse through the whole family a perpetual spirit of benevolence, complacency, and satisfaction

C

No. CXXIX. SATURDAY, JULY 28.

Vertentem sese frustra sectabere canthum,
Cùm rota posterior curras et in axe secundo. PERS.

Thou, like the hindmost chariot-wheels, art curst
Still to be near, but ne'er to be the first. DRYDEN.

GREAT masters in painting never care for drawing people in the fashion, as very well knowing that the head-dress or periwig that now prevails, and gives a a grace to their portraitures at present, will make a very odd figure, and perhaps look monstrous in the eyes of posterity. For this reason they often represent an illustrious person in a Roman habit, or in some other dress that never varies. I could wish, for the sake of my country friends, that there was such a kind of everlasting drapery to be made use of by all who live at a certain distance from the town, and that they would agree upon such fashions as should never be liable to changes and innovations. For want of this standing dress, a man who takes a journey into the country, is as much surprised as one who walks in a gallery of old family pictures, and finds as great a variety of garbs and habits in the persons he converses with. Did they keep to one constant dress, they would sometimes be in the fashion, which they never are as matters are managed at present. If, instead of running after the mode, they would continue fixed in one certain habit, the mode would sometime or other overtake them, as a clock that stands still is sure to point right once in twelve hours. In this case therefore I would advise them, as a gentleman did his friend, who was hunting about the whole town after a rambling fellow, if you follow him you will never find him, but if you plant yourself at the corner of any one street, I'll engage it will not be long before you see him.

I have already touched upon this subject in a speculation, which shews how cruelly the country are led astray in following the town; and equipped in a ridiculous habit, when they fancy themselves in the height of the mode. Since that speculation I have received a letter (which I there hinted at) from a gentleman who is now in the western circuit.

'Mr Spectator,

'Being a lawyer of the Middle-Temple, a Cornishman by birth, I generally ride the western circuit for my health; and as I am not interrupted with clients, have leisure to make many observations that escape the notice of my fellow-travellers.

'One of the most fashionable women I met with in all the circuit was my landlady at Staines, where I chanced to be on a holiday. Her commode was not half a foot high, and her petticoat within some yards of a modish circumference. In the same place I observed a young fellow with a tolerable periwig, had it not been covered with a hat that was shaped in the Ramilie cock. As I proceeded on my journey I observed the petticoat grew scantier and scantier, and about three-score miles from London was so very unfashionable, that a woman might walk in it without any manner of inconvenience.

'Not far from Salisbury I took notice of a justice of peace's lady, who was at least ten years behind-hand in her dress, but at the same time as fine as hands could make her. She was flounced and furbelowed from head to foot; every ribband was wrinkled, and every part of her garments in curl; so that she looked like one of those animals which in the country we call a Friezland hen.

'Not many miles beyond this place I was informed that one of the last year's little muffs had by some means or other straggled into those parts, and that all the women of fashion were cutting their old muffs in two, or retrenching them, according to the little model which was got among them. I cannot believe the report they have there; that it was sent down franked by a parliament-man in a little packet, but probably, by next winter, this fashion will be at the height in the country, when it is quite out at London.

'The greatest beau at our next county sessions was dressed in a most monstrous flaxen periwig, that was made in King William's reign The wearer of it goes, it seems, in his own hair when he is at home, and lets his wig lie in buckle for a whole half year, that he may put it on upon occasion to meet the Judges in it.

'I must not here omit an adventure which happened to us in a country church upon the frontiers of Cornwall. As we were in the midst of the service, a lady, who is the chief woman of the place, and had passed the winter at London with her husband, entered the congregation in a little head-dress and a hooped petticoat. The people, who were wonderfully startled at such a sight, all of them rose up Some stared at the prodigious bottom, and some at the little top, of this strange dress. In the mean time the lady of the manor filled the area of the church, and walked up to her pew with an unspeakable satisfaction, amidst the whispers, conjectures, and astonishments of the whole congregation.

'Upon our way from hence we saw a young fellow riding towards us full gallop with a bob-wig and a black silken bag tied to it. He stopt short at the coach to ask us how far the Judges were behind us. His stay was so very short, that we had only time to observe his new silk waistcoat, which was unbuttoned in several places, to let us see that he had a clean shirt on, which was ruffled down to his middle

'From this place, during our progress through the most western parts of the kingdom, we fancied ourselves in King Charles the second's reign, the people having made very little variations in their dress since that time. The smartest of the country 'squires appear still in the Monmouth cock, and when they go a-wooing (whether they have any post in the militia or not) they generally put on a red coat. We were, indeed, very much surprised, at the place we lay at last night, to meet with a gentleman that had accoutred himself in a night-cap wig, a coat with long pockets and slit sleeves, and a pair of shoes with high scollop-tops; but we soon found by his conversation that he was a person who laughed at the ignorance and rusticity of the country people, and was resolved to live and die in the mode.

'Sir, if you think this account of my travels may be of any advantage to the public, I will next year trouble you with such occurrences as I shall meet with in other parts of England. For I am informed there are greater curiosities in the northern circuit than in the western; and that a fashion makes its progress much slower into Cumberland than into Cornwall. I have heard in particular, that the Steenkirk arrived but two months ago at Newcastle, and that there are several commodes in those parts which are worth taking a journey thither to see.'

C

No CXXX. MONDAY, JULY 30.

>   Semperque recentes
> Convectare juvat prædas, et vivere rapto.
> VIRG.
>
> Hunting their sport, and plundering was their trade.
> DRYDEN.

As I was yesterday riding out in the fields with my friend Sir Roger, we saw at a little distance from us a troop of gypsies. Upon the first discovery of them, my friend was in some doubt whether he should not exert the Justice of the Peace upon such a band of lawless vagrants; but not having his clerk with him, who is a necessary counsellor on these occasions, and fearing that his poultry might fare the worse for it, he let the thought drop: but at the same time gave me a particular account of the mischiefs they do in the country, in stealing people's goods and spoiling their servants. If a stray piece of linen hangs upon an hedge, says Sir Roger, they are sure to have it; if a hog loses his way in the fields, it is ten to one but he becomes their prey; our geese cannot live in peace for them; if a man prosecutes them with severity, his hen-roost is sure to pay for it: they generally straggle into these parts about this time of the year, and set the heads of our servant-maids so agog for husbands, that we do not expect to have any business done as it should be whilst they are in the country. I have an honest dairy-maid who crosses their hands with a piece of silver every summer, and never fails being promised the handsomest young fellow in the parish for her pains. Your friend the butler has been fool enough to be seduced by them; and, though he is sure to lose a knife, a fork, or a spoon, every time his fortune is told him, generally shuts himself up in the pantry with an old gipsey for above half an hour, once in a twelvemonth. Sweethearts are the things they live upon, which they bestow very plentifully upon all those that apply themselves to them. You see now and then some handsome young jades among them: the sluts have very often white teeth and black eyes.

Sir Roger observing that I listened with great attention to his account of a people who were so entirely new to me, told me, that if I would they should tell us our fortunes. As I was very well pleased with the knight's proposal, we rode up and communicated our hands to them. A Cassandra of the crew, after having examined my lines very diligently, told me, "that I loved a pretty maid in a corner, that I was a good woman's man, with some other particulars which I do not think proper to relate. My friend Sir Roger alighted from his horse, and exposing his palm to two or three that stood by him, they crumpled it into all shapes, and diligently scanned every wrinkle that could be made in it; when one of them, who was older and more sun burnt than the rest, told him, that he had a widow in his line of life upon which the knight cried, Go, go, you are an idle baggage, and at the same time smiled upon me. The gipsy finding he was not displeased in his heart, told him after a farther inquiry into his hand, that his true love was constant, and that she should dream of him to-night. My old friend cried, Pish, and bid her go on. The gipsy told him that he was a bachelor, but would not be so long, and that he was dearer to somebody than he thought. The knight still repeated, she was an idle baggage, and bid her go on. Ah, master, says the gipsy, that roguish leer of your's makes a pretty woman's heart ache; you han't got that simper about the mouth for nothing..... The uncouth gibberish with which all this was uttered, like the darkness of an oracle made us the more attentive to it. To be short, the knight left the money with her that he had crossed her hand with, and got up again on his horse.

As we were riding away, Sir Roger told me, that he knew several very sensible people who believed these gypsies now and then foretold very strange things; and for half an hour together appeared more jocund than ordinary. In the height of his good-humour, meeting a common beggar upon the road, who was no conjurer, as he went to relieve him, he found his pocket was picked, that being a kind of palmistry at which this race of vermin are very dexterous.

I might here entertain my reader with historical remarks on this idle profligate people, who infest all the countries of Europe, and live in the midst of governments in a kind of commonwealth by themselves. But instead of entering into observations of this nature, I shall fill the remaining part of my paper with a story which is still fresh in Holland, and was printed in one of our monthly accounts about twenty years ago. " As the trekschuyt, or hackney-boat, which carries passengers from Leyden to Amsterdam, was putting off, a boy running along the side of the canal desired to be taken in, which the master of the boat refused, because the lad had not quite money enough to pay the usual fare. An eminent merchant being pleased with the looks of the boy, and secretly touched with compassion towards him, paid the money for him, and ordered him to be taken on board. Upon talking with him afterwards, he found that he could speak readily in three or four languages; and learned, upon farther examination, that he had been stolen away, when he was a child, by a gypsy, and had rambled ever since with a gang of those strollers up and down several parts of Europe. It happened that the merchant, whose heart seems to have inclined towards the boy by a secret kind of instinct, had himself lost a child some years before. The parents, after a long search for him, gave him for drowned in one of the canals with which that country abounds; and the mother was so afflicted at the loss of a fine boy, who was her only son, that she died for grief of it. Upon laying together all particulars, and examining the several moles and marks by which the mother used to describe the child when he was first missing, the boy proved to be the son of the merchant whose heart had so unaccountably melted at the sight of him. The lad was very well pleased to find a father who was so rich, and likely to leave him a good estate; the father, on the other hand, was not a little delighted to see a son return to him, whom he had given for lost, with such a strength of constitution, sharpness of understanding, and skill in languages." Here the printed story leaves off, but, if I may give credit to reports, our linguist, having received such extraordinary rudiments towards a good education, was afterwards trained up in every thing that becomes a gentleman; wearing off, by little and little, all the vicious habits and practices that he had been used to in the course of his peregrinations: nay it is said, that he has since been employed in foreign courts upon national business, with great reputation to himself and honour to those who sent him, and that he has visited several countries as a public minister, in which he formerly wandered as a gypsy. C

No. CXXXI. TUESDAY, JULY 31.

Ipsæ rursum concedite sylvæ
                                           VIRG.

Once more, ye woods, adieu

It is usual for a man who loves country sports to preserve the game in his own grounds, and divert himself upon those that belong to his neighbour. My friend Sir Roger generally goes two or three miles from his house, and gets into the frontiers of his estate, before he beats about in search of a hare or partridge, on purpose to spare his own fields, where he is always sure of finding diversion when the worst comes to the worst. By this means the breed about his house has time to increase and multiply; besides that the sport is the more agreeable where the game is the harder to come at, and where it does not lie so thick as to produce any perplexity or confusion in the pursuit. For these reasons the country gentleman, like the fox, seldom preys near his own home.

In the same manner I have made a month's excursion out of the town, which is the great field of game for sportsmen of my species, to try my fortune in the country, where I have started several subjects, and hunted them down with some pleasure to myself, and I hope to others. I am here forced to use a great deal of diligence before I can spring any thing to my mind; whereas, in town, whilst I am following one character, it is ten to one but I am crossed in my way by another, and put up such a variety of odd creatures in both sexes, that they foil the scent of one another, and puzzle the chace. My greatest difficulty in the country is to find sport, and in town to chuse it. In the mean time, as I have given a whole month's rest to the cities of London and Westminster, I promise myself abundance of new game upon my return thither.

It is indeed high time for me to leave the country, since I find the whole neighbourhood begin to grow very inquisitive after my name and character, my love of solitude, taciturnity, and particular way of life, having raised a great curiosity in all these parts.

The notions which have been framed of me are various: some look upon me as very proud, some as very modest, and some as very melancholy. Will Wimble, as my friend the butler tells me, observing me very much alone, and extremely silent when I am in company, is afraid I have killed a man. The country people seem to suspect me for a conjurer, and some of them hearing of the visit which I made to Moll White, will needs have it that Sir Roger has brought down a cunning man with him, to cure the old woman, and free the country from her charms. So that the character which I go under in part of the neighbourhood is what they here call a " white witch."

A justice of peace, who lives about five miles off, and is not of Sir Roger's party, has it seems said twice or thrice at his table, that he wishes Sir Roger does not harbour a Jesuit in his house; and that he thinks the gentlemen of the country would do very well to make me give some account of myself.

On the other side, some of Sir Roger's friends are afraid the old knight is imposed upon by a designing fellow, and as they have heard that he converses very promiscuously when he is in town, do not know but he has brought down with him some discarded whig, that is sullen, and says nothing because he is out of place.

Such is the variety of opinions which are here entertained of me; so that I pass among some for a disaffected person, and among others for a popish priest, among some for a wizard, and among others for a murderer; and all this for no other reason, that I can imagine, but because I do not hoot and halloo and make a noise. It is true, my friend Sir Roger tells them, " that it is my way," and that I am only a philosopher, but this will not satisfy them. They think there is more in me than he discovers, and that I do not hold my tongue for nothing.

For these and other reasons I shall set out for London to-morrow, having found by experience that the country is not a place for a person of my temper, who does not love jollity, and what they call good neighbourhood. A man that is out of humour when an unexpected guest breaks in upon him, and does not care for sacrificing an afternoon to every chance-comer, that will be the master of his own time, and the pursuer of his own inclinations, makes but a very unsociable figure in this kind of life. I shall therefore retire into the town, if I may make use of that phrase, and get into the crowd again as fast as I can, in order to be alone. I can there raise what speculations I please upon others without being observed myself, and at the same time enjoy all the advantages of company with all the privileges of solitude. In the mean while, to finish the month, and conclude these my rural speculations, I shall here insert a letter from my friend Will Honeycomb, who has not lived a month for these forty years out of the smoke of London, and rallies me after his way upon my country life.

'Dear Spec

'I suppose this letter will find thee picking of daisies, or smelling to a lock of hay, or passing away thy time in some innocent country diversion of the like nature. I have, however, orders from the club to summon thee up to town, being all of us cursedly afraid thou wilt not be able to relish our company, after thy conversations with Moll White and Will Wimble. Pr'ythee, don't send us up any more stories of a cock and a bull, nor frighten the town with spirits and witches. Thy speculations begin to smell confoundedly of woods and meadows. If thou dost not come up quickly, we shall conclude that thou art in love with one of Sir Roger's dairy-maids. Service to the Knight. Sir Andrew is grown the cock of the club since he left us; and if he does not return quickly, will make every mother's son of us commonwealth's men.

'Dear SPEC.
'Thine eternally,
'WILL HONEYCOMB.'

No CXXXII.—WEDNESDAY, AUGUST 1.

Qui, aut tempus quid postulet non videt, aut plura loquitur, aut se ostentat, aut eorum quibuscum est rationem non habet, is ineptus esse dicitur. TULL.

That man is guilty of impertinence, who considers not the circumstances of time, or engrosses the conversation, or makes himself the subject of his discourse, or pays no regard to the company he is in.

HAVING notified to my good friend Sir Roger, that I should set out for London the next day, his horses were ready at the appointed hour in the evening; and, attended by one of his grooms, I arrived at the county-town at twilight, in order to be ready for the stage-coach the day following. As soon as we arrived at the inn, the servant who waited upon me, inquired of the chamberlain, in my hearing, what company he had for the coach? The fellow answered, Mrs. Betty Arable, the great fortune, and the widow her mother; a recruiting officer (who took a place because they were to go;) young 'squire Quickset her cousin, that her mother wished her to be married to: Ephraim the quaker, her guardian; and a gentleman that had studied himself dumb, from Sir Roger de Coverley's. I observed, by what he said of myself, that according to his office, he dealt much in intelligence; and doubted not but there was some foundation for his reports of the rest of the company, as well as for the whimsical account he gave of me. The next morning at day-break we were all called: and I, who know my own natural shyness, and endeavour to be as little liable to be disputed with as possible, dressed immediately, that I might make no one wait. The first preparation for our setting out was, that the captain's half-pike was placed near the coachman, and a drum behind the coach. In the mean time, the drummer, the captain's equipage, was very loud, that none of the captain's things should be placed so as to be spoiled: upon which his cloak-bag was fixed in the seat of the coach; and the captain himself, according to a frequent, though invidious behaviour of military men, ordered his man to look sharp, that none but one of the ladies should have the place he had taken fronting to the coach-box.

We were in some little time fixed in our seats, and sat with that dislike which people not too good-natured, usually conceive of each other at first sight. The coach jumbled us insensibly into some sort of familiarity; and we had not moved above two miles when the widow asked the captain what success he had in his recruiting? The officer, with a frankness he believed very graceful, told her, "that indeed he had but very little luck, and had suffered much by desertion; and therefore should be glad to end his warfare in the service of her or her fair daughter. In a word, continued he, I am a soldier, and to be plain is my character: you see me, Madam, young, sound, and impudent: take me yourself, widow, or give me to her; I will be wholly at your disposal I am a soldier of fortune, ha!" This was followed by a vain laugh of his own, and a deep silence of all the rest of the company. I had nothing left for it but to fall fast asleep, which I did with all speed. "Come, said he, resolve upon it, we will make a wedding at the next town we will make this pleasant companion who is fallen asleep to be the brideman," and (giving the quaker a clap on the knee) he concluded, "This sly saint, who, I'll warrant, understands what's what as well as you or I, widow, shall give the bride as father." The quaker, who happened to be a man of smartness, answered, "Friend, I take it in good part that thou hast given me the authority of a father over this comely and virtuous child; and I must assure thee that if I have the giving her, I shall not bestow her on thee. Thy mirth, friend, savoureth of folly: thou art a person of a light mind; thy drum is a type of thee, it soundeth because it is empty. Verily, it is not from thy fulness, but thy emptiness, that thou hast spoken this day. Friend, friend, we have hired this coach in partnership with thee, to carry us to the great city; we cannot go any other way. This worthy mother must hear thee if thou wilt needs utter thy follies; we cannot help it, friend, I say; if thou wilt, we must hear thee; but if thou wert a man of understanding, thou wouldst not take advantage of thy courageous countenance, to abash us children of peace. Thou art, thou sayest, a soldier; give quarter to us who cannot resist thee. Why didst thou fleer at our friend, who feigned himself asleep? He said nothing, but how dost thou know what he containeth? If thou speakest improper things in the hearing of this virtuous young virgin, consider it is an outrage against a distressed person that cannot get from thee: To speak indiscreetly what we are obliged to hear, by being hasped up with thee in this public vehicle, is in some degree assaulting on the high road."

Here Ephraim paused, and the captain, with a happy and uncommon impudence (which can be convicted and support itself at the same time) cries, "Faith friend, I thank thee; I should have been a little impertinent, if thou hadst not reprimanded me. Come, thou art, I see, a smoky old fellow, and I'll be very orderly the ensuing part of the journey. I was going to give myself airs; but, ladies, I beg pardon."

The captain was so little out of humour, and our company was so far from being soured by this little ruffle, that Ephraim and he took a particular delight in being agreeable to each other for the future; and assumed their different provinces in the conduct of the company. Our reckonings, apartments, and accommodations, fell under Ephraim; and the captain looked to all disputes on the road, as the good behaviour of our coachman, and the right we had of taking place as going to London of all vehicles coming from thence. The occurrences we met with were ordinary, and very little happened which could entertain by the relation of them: but when I considered the company we were in, I took it for no small good fortune, that the whole journey was not spent in impertinences, which to one part of us might be an entertainment, to the other a suffering. What therefore Ephraim said when we were almost arrived at London, had to me an air not only of good understanding but good-breeding. Upon the young lady's expressing her satisfaction in the journey, and declaring how delightful it had been to her, Ephraim delivered himself as follows: "There is no ordinary part of human life which expresseth so much a good mind, and a right inward man, as his behaviour upon meeting with strangers, especially such as may seem the most unsuitable companions to him: such a man, when he falleth in the way with persons of simplicity and innocence, however knowing he may be in the ways of men, will not vaunt himself thereof; but will the rather hide his superiority to them, that he may not be painful unto them. My good friend (continued he, turning to the officer), thee and I are to part by and by, and peradventure we may never meet again; but be advised by a plain man: modes and apparels are but trifles to the real man, therefore do not think such a man as thyself terrible for thy garb, nor such an one as me contemptible for mine. When two such as thee and I meet, with affections as we ought to have towards each other, thou shouldst rejoice to see my peaceable demeanour, and I should be glad to see thy strength and ability to protect me in it." T

No. CXXXIII. THURSDAY, AUGUST 2.

Quis desiderio sit pudor, aut modus
  Tam cari capitis? Hor.

Who can grieve too much, what time shall end
  Our mourning for so dear a friend?
                            Creech.

There is a sort of delight, which is alternately mixed with terror and sorrow in the contemplation of death. The soul has its curiosity more than ordinarily awakened, when it turns its thoughts upon the conduct of such who have behaved themselves with an equal, a resigned, a cheerful, a generous or heroic temper in that extremity. We are affected with these respective manners of behaviour, as we secretly believe the part of the dying person imitable by ourselves, or such as we imagine ourselves more particularly capable of. Men of exalted minds march before us like princes, and are, to the ordinary race of mankind, rather subjects for their admiration than example. However, there are no ideas strike more forcibly upon our imaginations than those which are raised from reflections upon the exits of great and excellent men. Innocent men who have suffered as criminals, though they were benefactors to human society, seem to be persons of the highest distinction, among the vastly greater number of human race, the dead. When the iniquity of the times brought Socrates to his execution, how great and wonderful is it to behold him, unsupported by any thing but the testimony of his own conscience, and conjectures of hereafter, receive the poison with an air of mirth and good-humour, and, as if going on an agreeable journey, bespeak some deity to make it fortunate

When Phocion's good actions had met with the like reward from his country, and he was led to death with many others of his friends, they bewailing their fate, he walking composedly towards the place of execution; how gracefully does he support his illustrious character to the very last instant! One of the rabble spitting at him as he passed, with his usual authority he called to know, if no one was ready to teach this fellow how to behave himself. When a poor-spirited creature, that died at the same time for his crimes, bemoaned himself unmanfully, he rebuked him with this question, Is it no consolation to such a man as thou art to die with Phocion? At the instant when he was to die, they asked what commands he had for his son? he answered, "To forget this injury of the Athenians." Niocles, his friend, under the same sentence, desired he might drink the potion before him: Phocion said, "because he never had denied him any thing, he would not even this, the most difficult request he had ever made."

These instances were very noble and great; and the reflections of those sublime spirits had made death to them, what it is really intended to be by the Author of nature, a relief from a various being, ever subject to sorrows and difficulties.

Epaminondas, the Theban general, having received in fight a mortal stab with a sword, which was left in his body, lay in that posture till he had intelligence that his troops had obtained the victory, and then permitted it to be drawn out: at which instant he expressed himself in this manner, " This is not the end of my life, my fellow-soldiers; it is now your Epaminondas is born, who dies in so much glory."

It were an endless labour to collect the accounts with which all ages have filled the world with noble and heroic minds that have resigned this being, as if the termination of life were but an ordinary occurrence of it.

This common-place way of thinking I fell into from an awkward endeavour to throw off a real and fresh affliction, by turning over books in a melancholy mood; but it is not easy to remove griefs which touch the heart, by applying remedies which only entertain the imagination. As therefore this paper is to consist of any thing which concerns human life, I cannot help letting the present subject regard what has been the last object of my eyes, though an entertainment of sorrow.

I went this evening to visit a friend, with a design to rally him upon a story I had heard of his intending to steal a marriage without the privity of us his intimate friends and acquaintance. I came into his apartment with that intimacy which I have done for very many years, and walked directly into his bed-chamber, where I found my friend in the agonies of death. What could I do? The innocent mirth in my thoughts struck upon me like the most flagitious wickedness. I in vain called upon him, he was senseless, and too far spent to have the least knowledge of my sorrow, or any pain in himself. Give me leave then to transcribe my soliloquy, as I stood by his mother, dumb with the weight of grief for a son who was her honour and her comfort, and never till that hour since his birth had been an occasion of a moment's sorrow to her.

"How surprising is this change! from the possession of vigorous life and strength, to be reduced in a few hours to this fatal extremity! Those lips which look so pale and livid, within these few days gave delight to all who heard their utterance. it was the business, the purpose of his being, next to obeying Him to whom he is going, to please and instruct, and that for no other end but to please and instruct. Kindness was the motive of his actions, and with all the capacity requisite for making a figure in a contentious world, moderation, good-nature, affability, temperance and chastity, were the arts of his excellent life. There, as he lies in helpless agony, no wise man who knew him so well as I, but would resign all the world can bestow to be so near the end of such a life. Why does my heart so little obey my reason as to lament thee, thou excellent man!....Heaven receive him or restore him!. Thy beloved mother, thy obliged friends, thy helpless servants, stand around thee without distinction. How much wouldest thou, hadst thou thy senses, say to each of us!

"But now that good heart bursts, and he is at rest. With that breath expired a soul who never indulged a passion unfit for the place he is gone to. Where are now thy plans of justice, of truth, of honour? Of what use the volumes thou hast collated, the arguments thou hast invented, the examples thou hast followed? Poor were the expectations of the studious, the modest, and the good, if the reward of their labours were only to be expected from man. No, my friend, thy intended pleadings, thy intended good offices to thy friends, thy intended services to thy country, are already performed, as to thy concern in them, in His sight, before whom the past, present, and future, appear at one view....While others with thy talents were tormented with ambition, with vain-glory, with envy, with emulation, how well didst thou turn thy mind to its own improvement in things out of the power of fortune; in probity, in integrity, in the practice and study of justice! How silent thy passage, how private thy journey, how glorious thy end! 'Many have I known more famous, some more knowing, not one so innocent." R

No. CXXXIV. FRIDAY, AUGUST 3

.......Opiferque per orbem
Dicor...... OVID.

And am the great physician call'd below
DRYDEN.

During my absence in the country several packets have been left for me, which were not forwarded to me, because I was expected every day in town. The author of the following letter, dated from Tower-hill, having sometimes been entertained with some learned gentlemen in plush doublets,* who have vended their wares from a stage in that place, has pleasantly enough addressed to me, as no less a sage in morality, than those are in physic. To comply with his kind inclination to make my cures famous, I shall give you his testimonial of my great abilities at large in his own words.

" SIR,

"Your saying t'other day there is something wonderful in the narrowness of those minds which can be pleased, and be barren of bounty to those who please

* Meaning quack-doctors

them, makes me in pain that I am not a man of power. If I were, you should soon see how much I approve your speculations. In the mean time, I beg leave to supply that inability with the empty tribute of an honest mind, by telling you plainly I love and thank you for your daily refreshments. I constantly peruse your paper as I smoke my morning's pipe (though I can't forbear reading the motto before I fill and light,) and really it gives a grateful relish to every whiff; each paragraph is fraught either with useful or delightful notions, and I never fail of being highly diverted or improved. The variety of your subjects surprises me as much as a box of pictures did formerly, in which there was only one face, that by pulling some pieces of isinglas over it, was changed into a grave senator or a merry-andrew, a patched lady or a nun, a beau or a black-a-moor, a prude or a coquette, a country 'squire or a conjurer, with many other different representations, very entertaining (as you are) though still the same at the bottom. This was a childish amusement, when I was carried away with outward appearance, but you make a deeper impression, and affect the secret springs of the mind; you charm the fancy, sooth the passions, and insensibly lead the reader to that sweetness of temper that you so well describe; you rouse generosity with that spirit, and inculcate humanity with that ease, that he must be miserably stupid that is not affected by you. I can't say, indeed, that you have put impertinence to silence, or vanity out of countenance; but methinks you have bid as fair for it, as any man that ever appeared upon a public stage; and offer an infallible cure of vice and folly, for the price of one penny. And since it is useful for those who receive benefit by such famous operators, to publish an advertisement, that others may reap the same advantage, I think myself obliged to declare to all the world, that having for a long time been splenetic, ill-natured, froward, suspicious, and unsociable, by the application of your medicines, taken only with half an ounce of right Virginia tobacco, for six successive mornings, I am become open, obliging, officious, frank, and hospitable.

'I am,
'Your humble servant,
'and great admirer,

TOWER-HILL,
JULY 5, 1711.
'GEORGE TRUSTY.'

The careful father and the humble petitioner hereafter mentioned, who are under difficulties about the just management of fans, will soon receive proper advertisements relating to the professors in that behalf, with their places of abode, and methods of teaching.

JULY 5, 1711.
'SIR,

'IN your Spectator of June the 27th, you transcribe a letter sent to you from a new sort of muster-master, who teaches ladies the whole exercise of the fan. I have a daughter just come to town, who, though she has always held a fan in her hand at proper times, yet she knows no more how to use it according to true discipline, than an awkward school-boy does to make use of his new sword. I have sent for her on purpose to learn the exercise, she being already very well accomplished in all other arts which are necessary for a young lady to understand. My request is, that you will speak to your correspondent on my behalf, and, in your next paper, let me know what he expects either by the month or the quarter for teaching; and where he keeps his place of rendezvous. I have a son too, whom I would fain have taught to gallant fans; and should be glad to know what the gentleman will have for teaching them both, I finding fans for practice at my own expense. This information will in the highest manner oblige,
'Sir,
'Your most humble servant,
'WILLIAM WISEACRE.

'As soon as my son is perfect in this art (which I hope will be in a year's time, for the boy is pretty apt,) I design he shall learn to ride the great horse (although he is not yet above twenty years old) if his mother, whose darling he is, will venture him.'

TO THE SPECTATOR,

'THE HUMBLE PETITION OF BENJAMIN EASIE, GENT.

'SHEWETH,

'THAT it was your petitioner's misfortune to walk to Hackney Church last Sunday, where, to his great amazement, he met with a soldier of your own training; she furls a fan, recovers a fan, and goes through the whole exercise of it to admiration. This well-managed officer of yours has, to my knowledge, been the ruin of above five young gentlemen besides myself, and still goes on laying waste wheresoever she comes, whereby the whole village is in great danger. Our humble request is, therefore, that this bold Amazon be ordered immediately to lay down her arms, or that you would issue forth an order, that we who have been thus injured, may meet at the place of general rendezvous, and there be taught to manage our snuff-boxes in such manner as we may be an equal match for her:

'And your petitioner shall ever pray, &c.'

R.

No. CXXXV. SATURDAY, AUGUST 4.

Est brevitate opus, ut currat sententia.   Hor.

Express your sentiments with brevity.

I HAVE somewhere read of an eminent person, who used in his private offices of devotion to give thanks to heaven, that he was born a Frenchman: for my own part, I look upon it as a peculiar blessing that I was born an Englishman. Among many other reasons, I think myself very happy in my country, as the language of it is wonderfully adapted to a man who is sparing of his words, and an enemy to loquacity.

As I have frequently reflected on my good fortune in this particular, I shall communicate to the public my speculations upon the English tongue, not doubting but they will be acceptable to all my curious readers.

The English delight in silence more than any other European nation, if the remarks which are made on us by foreigners are true. Our discourse is not kept up in conversation, but falls into more pauses and intervals than in our neighbouring countries, as it is observed, that the matter of our writings is thrown much closer together, and lies in a narrower compass, than is usual in the works of foreign authors: for, to favour our natural taciturnity, when we are obliged to utter our thoughts, we do it in the shortest way we are able, and give as quick a birth to our conceptions as possible.

This humour shews itself in several remarks that we may make upon the English language. As, first of all, by its abounding in monosyllables, which gives us an opportunity of delivering our thoughts in few sounds. This indeed takes off from the elegance of our tongue, but at the same time expresses our ideas in the readiest manner, and consequently answers the first design of speech better than the multitude of syllables which make the words of other languages more tuneable and sonorous. The sounds of our English words are commonly like those of string music, short and transient, which rise and perish upon a single touch; those of other languages are like the notes of wind-instruments, sweet and swelling, and lengthened out into variety of modulation.

In the next place we may observe, that where the words are not monosyllables, we often make them so, as much as lies in our power, by our rapidity of pronunciation; as it generally happens in most of our long words which are derived from the Latin, where we contract the length of the syllable that gives them a grave and solemn air in their own language, to make them more proper for dispatch, and more conformable to the genius of our tongue. This we may find in a multitude of words, as liberty, conspiracy, theatre, orator, &c.

The same natural aversion to loquacity has of late years made a very considerable alteration in our language by closing in one syllable the termination of our præterperfect tense, as in the words drown'd, walk'd, arriv'd, for drowned, walked, arrived, which has very much disfigured the tongue, and turned a tenth part of our smoothest words into so many clusters of consonants. This is the more remarkable, because the want of vowels in our language has been the general complaint of our politest authors, who nevertheless are the men that have made these retrenchments, and consequently very much increased our former scarcity.

This reflection on the words that end in *ed*, I have heard in conversation from one of the greatest geniuses this age has produced[*]. I think we may add to the foregoing observation, the change which has happened

[*] Dean Swift.

VOL. II.

in our language by the abbreviation of several words that are terminated in *eth*, by substituting an *s* in the room of the last syllable, as in *drowns, walks, arrives,* and innumerable other words, which in the pronunciation of our forefathers were *drowneth, walketh, arriveth.* This has wonderfully multiplied a letter which was before too frequent in the English tongue, and added to that hissing in our language, which is taken so much notice of by foreigners; but at the same time humours our taciturnity, and eases us of many superfluous syllables.

I might here observe, that the same single letter on many occasions does the office of a whole word, and represents the *his* and *her* of our forefathers. There is no doubt but the ear of a foreigner, which is the best judge in this case, would very much disapprove of such innovations, which indeed we do ourselves in some measure, by retaining the old termination in writing, and in all the solemn offices of our religion.

As in the instances I have given we have epitomized many of our particular words to the detriment of our tongue, so on other occasions we have drawn two words into one, which has likewise very much untuned our language, and clogged it with consonants, as *mayn't, can't, shan't, won't,* and the like, for *may not, can not, shall not, will not, &c.*

It is perhaps this humour of speaking no more than we needs must, which has so miserably curtailed some of our words, that, in familiar writings and conversations, they often lose all but their first syllables, as in *mob. rep. pos. incog.* and the like; and as all ridiculous words make their first entry into a language by familiar phrases, I dare not answer for these, that they will not in time be looked upon as a part of our tongue. We see some of our poets have been so indiscreet as to imitate Hudibras's doggerel expressions in their serious compositions, by throwing out the signs of our substantives, which are essential to the English language

Nay, this humour of shortening our language, had once run so far, that some of our celebrated authors, among whom we may reckon Sir Roger L'Estrange in particular, began to prune their words of all superfluous letters, as they termed them, in order to adjust the spelling to the pronunciation, which would have confounded all our etymologies, and have quite destroyed our tongue.

We may here likewise observe that our proper names, when familiarized in English, generally dwindle to monosyllables; whereas in other modern languages they receive a softer turn on this occasion by the addition of a new syllable, *Nick* in Italian is *Nicolini*, *Jack* in French *Janot*: and so of the rest.

There is another particular in our language, which is a great instance of our frugality of words, and that is the suppressing of several particles which must be produced in other tongues to make a sentence intelligible, this often perplexes the best writers, when they find the relatives *whom*, *which*, or *they*, at their mercy whether they may have admission or not, and will never be decided till we have something like an acadamy, that by the best authorities and rules, drawn from the analogy of languages, shall settle all controversies between grammar and idiom.

I have only considered our language as it shews the genius and natural temper of the English, which is modest, thoughtful, and sincere, and which perhaps may recommend the people, though it has spoiled the tongue. We might perhaps carry the same thought into other languages, and deduce a great part of what is peculiar to them from the genius of the people who speak them. It is certain the light talkative humour of the French has not a little infected their tongue, which might be shewn by many instances, as the genius of the Italians, which is so much addicted to music and ceremony, has moulded all their words and phrases to those particular uses. The stateliness and gravity of the Spaniards shews itself to perfection in the solemnity of their language; and the blunt honest humour of the Germans sounds better in the roughness of the High-Dutch, than it would in a politer tongue.

C

No CXXXVI. MONDAY, AUGUST 6.

— Parthis mendacior...... HOR.

A greater liar Parthia never bred.

ACCORDING to the request of this strange fellow, I shall print the following letter.

' MR. SPECTATOR,

' I SHALL, without any manner of preface or apology, acquaint you that I am and ever have been, from my youth upward, one of the greatest liars this island has produced. I have read all the moralists upon the subject, but could never find any effect their discourses had upon me, but to add to my misfortune by new thoughts and ideas, and making me more ready in my language, and capable of sometimes mixing seeming truths with my improbabilities. With this strong passion towards falsehood in this kind, there does not live an honester man or a sincerer friend; but my imagination runs away with me, and whatever is started, I have such a scene of adventures appears in an instant before me, that I cannot help uttering them, though to my immediate confusion, I cannot but know I am liable to be detected by the first man I meet.

'Upon occasion of the mention of the battle of Pultowa, I could not forbear giving an account of a kinsman of mine, a young merchant who was bred at Moscow, that had too much mettle to attend books of entries and accounts, when there was so active a scene in the country where he resided, and followed the Czar as a volunteer, this warm youth, born at the instant the thing was spoken of, was the man who unhorsed the Swedish general, he was the occasion that the Muscovites kept their fire in so soldier-like a manner, and brought up those troops which were covered from the enemy at the beginning of the day; besides this, he had at last the good fortune to be the man who took Count Piper. With all this fire I knew my cousin to be the civilest creature in the world. He never made any impertinent show of his valour, and then he had an excellent genius for the world in every other kind. I had letters from him (here I felt in my pocket) that exactly spoke the Czar's character, which I knew perfectly well and I could not forbear concluding, that I lay with his imperial majesty twice or thrice a-week all the while he lodged at Deptford. What is worse than all this, it is impossible to speak to me, but you give me some occasion of coming out with one lie or other, that has neither wit, humour, prospect of interest, or any other motive that I can think of in nature. The other day, when one was commending an eminent and learned divine, what occasion in the world had I to say, methinks he would look more venerable if he were not so fair a man? I remember the company smiled. I have seen the gentleman since, and he is coal black. I have intimations every day in my life that nobody believes me, yet I am never the better. I was saying something the other day to an old friend at Will's coffee-house, and he made me no manner of answer: but told me that an acquaintance of Tully the orator, having two or three times together said to him, without receiving any answer, that upon his honour he was but that very month forty years of age; Tully answered, Surely you think me the most incredulous man in the world, if I don't believe what you have told me every day this ten years. The mischief of it is, I find myself wonderfully inclined to have been present at every occurrence that is spoken of before me: this has led me into many inconveniences, but indeed they have been the fewer, because I am no ill-natured man, and never speak things to any man's disadvantage. I never directly defame, but I do what is as bad in the consequence, for I have often made a man say such and such a lively expression, who was born a mere elder brother. When one has said in my hearing, such a one is no wiser than he should be; I immediately have replied, Now 'faith I can't see that, he said a very good thing to my lord such-a-one upon such an occasion, and the like. Such an honest dolt as this has been watched in every expression he uttered, upon my recommendation of him, and consequently been subject to the more ridicule. I once endeavoured to cure myself of this impertinent quality, and resolved to hold my tongue for seven days together. I did so, but then I had so many winks and unnecessary distortions of my face upon what any body else said, that I found I only forbore the expression, and that I still lied in my heart to every man I met with. You are to know one thing, (which I believe you'll say is a pity, considering the use I should have made of it) I never travelled in my life; but I do not know whether I could have spoken of any foreign country with more familiarity than I do at present, in company who are strangers to me. I have cursed the inns in Germany; commended the brothels at Venice, the freedom of conversation in France, and though I was never out of this dear town and fifty miles about it, have been three nights together dogged by bravoes for an intrigue with a cardinal's mistress at Rome.

'It were endless to give you particulars of this kind; but I can assure you, Mr. Spectator, there are about twenty or thirty of us in this town, I mean by this town the cities of London and Westminster, I say there are in town a sufficient number of us to make a society among ourselves; and since we cannot be believed any longer, I beg of you to print this my letter, that we may meet together, and be under such regulation as there may be no occasion for belief or confidence among us. If you think fit we might be called the Historians, for Liar is become a very harsh word. And that a member of this society may not hereafter be ill received by the rest of the world, I desire you would explain a little this sort of men, and not let us Historians be ranked, as we are in the imaginations of ordinary people, among common liars, make-bates, impostors, and incendiaries. For your instruction herein, you are to know, that a historian in conversation is only a person of so pregnant a fancy, that he cannot be contented with ordinary occurrences. I know a man of quality of our order, who is of the wrong side of forty-three, and has been of that age, according to Tully's jest, for some years since, whose vein is upon the romantic. Give him the least occasion, and he will tell you something so very particular that happened in such a-year, and in such company, where by the bye was present such a one, who was afterwards made such a thing. Out of all these circumstances, in the best language in the world, he will join together, with such probable incidents, an account, that shews a person of the deepest penetration, the honestest mind, and withal, something so humble when he speaks of himself, that you would admire. Dear Sir, why should this be lying! there is nothing so instructive. He has withal the gravest aspect; something so very venerable and great! Another of these historians is a young man whom we would take in, though he extremely wants parts, as people send children (before they can learn any thing) to school, to keep them out of harm's way. He tells things which have nothing at all in them, and can neither please nor displease, but merely take up your time to no manner of purpose, no manner of delight; but he is good-natured, and does it because he loves to be saying something to you and entertain you.

'I could name you a soldier that has done very great things without slaughter; he is prodigiously dull and slow of head, but what he can say is for ever false, so that we must have him.

'Give me leave to tell you of one more, who is a lover: he is the most afflicted creature in the world, lest what happened between him and a great beauty should ever be known. Yet again, he comforts himself, "Hang the jade her woman. If money can keep the slut trusty, I will do it, though I mortgage every acre: Antony and Cleopatra for that, All for love, and the world well lost."

'Then, Sir, there is my little merchant, honest Indigo of the Exchange: there is my man for loss and gain; there is tare and tret, there is lying all round the globe. He has such a prodigious intelligence he knows all the French are doing, and what we intend or ought to intend, and has it from such hands. But, alas, whither am I running! While I complain, while I remonstrate to you, even all this is a lie, and there is not one such person of quality, lover, soldier, or merchant, as I have now described in the whole world, that I know of. But I will catch myself once in my life, and in spite of nature speak one truth, to wit, that I am

T 'Your humble servant, &c.'

No. CXXXVII. TUESDAY, AUGUST 7.

At hæc etiam servis semper libera fuerunt, timerent, gauderent, dolerent, suo potius quàm alterius arbitrio. TULL

Even slaves were always at liberty to fear, rejoice, and grieve at their own, rather than another's pleasure.

It is no small concern to me, that I find so many complaints from that part of mankind whose portion it is to live in servitude, that those whom they depend upon will not allow them to be even as happy as their condition will admit of. There are, as these unhappy correspondents inform me, masters who are offended at a cheerful countenance, and think a servant is broke loose from them, if he does not preserve the utmost awe in their presence. There is one who says, if he looks satisfied, his master asks him what makes him so pert this morning? if a little sour, hark you, sirrah, are you not paid your wages? The poor creatures live in the most extreme misery together the master knows not how to preserve respect, nor the servant how to give it. It seems this person is of so sullen a nature that he knows but little satisfaction in the midst of a plentiful fortune, and secretly frets to see any appearance of content in one that lives upon the hundredth part of his income, while he is unhappy in the possession of the whole. Uneasy persons, who cannot possess their own minds, vent their spleen upon all who depend upon them; which I think is expressed in a lively manner in the following letters.

August 2, 1711.

"SIR,

"I have read your Spectator of the third of the last month, and wish I had the happiness of being preferred to serve so good a master as Sir Roger. The character of my master is the very reverse of that good and gentle knight's. All his directions are given, and his mind revealed by way of contraries; as when any thing is to be remembered, with a peculiar cast of face he cries, "Be sure to forget now." If I am to make haste back, "Don't come these two hours, be sure to call by the way on some of your companions." Then another excellent way of his is, if he sets me any thing to do, which he knows must necessarily take up half a day, he calls ten times in a quarter of an hour to know whether I have done yet. This is his manner, and the same perverseness runs through all his actions, according as the circumstances vary. Besides all this, he is so suspicious, that he submits himself to the drudgery of a spy. He is as unhappy himself as he makes his servants: he is constantly watching us, and we differ no more in pleasure and liberty, than as a gaoler and as a prisoner. He lays traps for faults, and no sooner makes a discovery, but falls into such language, as I am more ashamed of, for coming from him, than for being directed to me. This, Sir, is a short sketch of a master I have served upwards of nine years: and though I have never wronged him, I confess my despair of pleasing him has very much abated my endeavour to do it. If you will give me leave to steal a sentence out of my master's Clarendon, I shall tell you my case in a word, "Being used worse than I deserved, I cared less to deserve well than I had done."

"I am, Sir,
 "Your humble servant,
  "RALPH VALET."

"DEAR MR. SPECTER,

"I AM the next thing to a lady's woman, and am under both my lady and her woman. I am so used by them both, that I should be very glad to see them in the Specter. My lady herself is of no mind in the world, and for that reason her woman is of twenty minds in a moment. My Lady is one that never knows what to do with herself: she pulls on and puts off every thing she wears, twenty times before she resolves upon it for that day. I stand at one end of the room, and reach things to her woman. When my lady asks for a thing, I hear, and have half brought it, when the woman meets me in the middle of the room to receive it, and at that instant she says, No, she will not have it. Then I go back, and her woman comes up to her, and by this time she will have that, and two or three things more in an instant: the woman and I run to each other; I am loaded, and delivering the things to her, when my lady says she wants none of all these things, and we are the dullest creatures in the world, and she the unhappiest woman living, for she shan't be drest in any time. Thus we stand, not knowing what to do, when our good lady, with all the patience in the world, tells us as plain as she can speak, that she will have temper because we have no manner of understanding; and begins again to dress, and see if we can find out of ourselves what we are to do. When she is dressed, she goes to dinner, and, after she has disliked every thing there, she calls for the coach; then commands it in again; and then she will not go out at all, and then will go too, and orders the chariot. Now, good Mr. Specter, I desire you would, in the behalf of all who serve froward ladies, give out in your paper, that nothing can be done without allowing time for it, and that one cannot be back again with what one was sent for, if one is called back before one can go a step for that they want. And, if you please, let them know that all mistresses are as like as all servants.

"I am your loving friend,
"PATIENCE GIDDY."

These are great calamities; but I met the other day in the five fields towards Chelsea, a pleasanter tyrant than either of the above represented. A fat fellow was puffing on in his open waistcoat; a boy of fourteen in a livery, carrying after him his cloak, upper coat, hat, wig, and sword. The poor lad was ready to sink with the weight, and could not keep up with his master, who turned back every half furlong, and wondered what made the lazy young dog lag behind.

There is something very unaccountable, that people cannot put themselves in the condition of the persons below them, when they consider the commands they give. But there is nothing more common, than to see a fellow, (who, if he were reduced to it, would not be hired by any man living) lament that he is troubled with the most worthless dogs in nature.

It would, perhaps, be running too far out of common life to urge, that he who is not master of himself and his own passions, cannot be a proper master of another. Equanimity in a man's own words and actions, will easily diffuse itself through his whole family. Pamphilio has the happiest household of any man I know, and that proceeds from the humane regard he has to them in their private persons, as well as in respect that they are his servants. If there be any occasion, wherein they may in themselves be supposed to be unfit to attend their master's concerns, by reason of any attention of their own, he is so good as to place himself in their condition. I thought it very becoming in him, when at dinner the other day he made an apology for want of more attendants. He said, " One of my footmen is gone to the wedding of his sister, and the other I don't expect to wait, because his father died but two days ago."   T

No CXXXVIII. WEDNESDAY, AUGUST 8.

Utitur in re non dubiâ testibus non necessariis
                                            TULL.

He uses unnecessary proofs in an undisputable point.

ONE meets now and then with persons who are extremely learned and knotty in expounding clear cases. Tully tells us of an author that spent some pages to prove that generals could not perform the great enterprizes which have made them so illustrious, if they had not had men. He asserted also, it seems, that a minister at home, no more than a commander abroad, could do any thing without other men were his instruments and assistants. On this occasion he produces the example of Themistocles, Pericles, Cyrus, and Alexander himself, whom he denies to have been capable of effecting what they did, except they had been followed by others. It is pleasant enough to see such persons contend without opponents, and triumph without victory.

The author above-mentioned by the orator is placed for ever in a very ridiculous light; and we meet every day in conversation such as deserve the same kind of renown, for troubling those with whom they converse, with the like certainties. The persons that I have always thought to deserve the highest admiration in this kind are your ordinary story-tellers, who are most religiously careful of keeping to the truth in every particular circumstance of a narration, whether it concern the main end or not. A gentleman, whom I had the honour to be in company with the other day, upon some occasion that he was pleased to take, said, he remembered a very pretty repartee made by a very witty man in king Charles's time upon the like occasion. I remember (said he, upon entering into the tale), much about the time of Oates's plot, that a cousin-german of mine and I were at the Bear in Holborn: No, I am out, it was at the Cross-Keys; but Jack Thomson was there, for he was very great with the gentleman who made the answer. But I am sure it was spoken somewhere thereabouts, for we drank a bottle in that neighbourhood every evening: But no matter for all that, the thing is the same; but........ ..... .

He was going on to settle the geography of the jest when I left the room, wondering at this odd turn of head, which can play away its words, with uttering nothing to the purpose, still observing its own impertinencies, and yet proceeding in them. I do not question but he informed the rest of his audience, who had more patience than I, of the birth and parentage, as well as the collateral alliances of his family who made the repartee, and of him who provoked him to it.

It is no small misfortune to any who have a just value for their time, when this quality of being so very circumstantial, and careful to be exact, happens to shew itself in a man whose quality obliges them to attend his proofs, that it is now day and the like. But this is augmented when the same genius gets into authority, as it often does. Nay, I have known it more than once ascend the very pulpit. One of this sort taking it in his head to be a great admirer of Dr. Tillotson and Dr. Beveridge, never failed of proving, out of these great authors, things which no man living would have denied him upon his own single authority. One day, resolving to come to the point in hand, he said, According to that excellent divine, I will enter upon the matter, or in his words, in his fifteenth sermon of the folio edition, page 160.

"I shall briefly explain the words, and then consider the matter contained in them."

This honest gentleman needed not, one would think, strain his modesty so far as to alter his design of " entering upon the matter," to that " of briefly explaining." But so it was, that he would not even be contented with that authority, but added also the other divine to strengthen his method, and told us, with the pious and learned Dr Beveridge, page 4th of his 9th volume. " I shall endeavour to make it as plain as I can from the words which I have now read, wherein for that purpose we shall consider." This Wiseacre was reckoned by the parish, who did not understand him, a most excellent preacher, but that he read too much, and was so humble that he did not trust enough to his own parts.

Next to these ingenious gentlemen, who argue for what nobody can deny them, are to be ranked a sort of people who do not indeed attempt to prove insignificant things, but are ever labouring to raise arguments with you about matters you will give up to them without the least controversy. One of these people told a gentleman who said he saw Mr Such-a-one, go this morning at nine o'clock towards the Gravel-Pits, Sir, I must beg your pardon for that, for though I am very loth to have any dispute with you, yet I must take the liberty to tell you it was nine when I saw him at St James's. When men of this genius are pretty far gone in learning, they will put you to prove that snow is white, and when you are upon that topic, can say that there is really no such thing as colour in nature: in a word, they can turn what little knowledge they have into a ready capacity of raising doubts, into a capacity of being always frivolous and always unanswerable. It was of two disputants of this impertinent and laborious kind that the Cynic said, "One of these fellows is milking a ram, and the other holds the pail."

ADVERTISEMENT

'The exercise of the snuff-box, according to the most fashionable airs and motions, in opposition to the exercise of the fan, will be taught with the best plain or perfumed snuff, at Charles Lillie's, perfumer, at the corner of Beaufort-buildings in the Strand, and attendance given for the benefit of young merchants about the exchange for two hours every day at noon, except Saturdays, at a toy-shop near Garraway's coffee-house. There will be likewise taught " the ceremony of the snuff-box," or rules for offering snuff to a stranger, a friend, or a mistress, according to the degrees of familiarity or distance; with an explanation of the careless, the scornful, the polite, and the surly pinch, and the gestures proper to each of them.

'N B The undertaker does not question but in a short time to have formed a body of regular snuff-boxes ready to meet and make head against all the regiment of fans which have been lately disciplined, and are now in motion.' T

No. CXXXIX THURSDAY, AUGUST 9.

Vera gloria radices agit, atque etiam propagatur ficta omnia celeriter, tanquam flosculi, decidunt, nec simulatum potest quidquam esse diuturnum.

TULL.

True glory takes root, and even spreads: all false pretences, like flowers, fall to the ground; nor can any counterfeit last long.

Of all the affections which attend human life, the love of glory is the most ardent. According as this is cultivated in princes, it produces the greatest good or the greatest evil. Where sovereigns have it by impressions received from education only, it creates an ambitious rather than a noble mind; where it is the natural bent of the prince's inclination, it prompts him to the pursuit of things truly glorious. The two greatest men now in Europe (according to the common acceptation of the word great) are Louis king of France, and Peter emperor of Russia. As it is certain that all fame does not arise from the practice of virtue, it is, methinks, no unpleasing amusement to examine the glory of these potentates, and distinguish that which is empty, perishing, and frivolous, from what is solid, lasting, and important. Louis of France had his infancy attended by crafty and worldly men, who made extent of territory the most glorious instance of power, and mistook the spreading of fame for the acquisition of honour. The young monarch's heart was by such conversation easily deluded into a fondness for vain-glory, and upon these unjust principles to form or fall in with suitable projects of invasion, rapine, murder, and all the guilts that attend war when it is unjust. At the same time this tyranny was laid, sciences and arts were encouraged in the most generous manner, as if men of higher faculties were to be bribed to permit the massacre of the rest of the world. Every superstructure which the court of France built upon their first designs, which were in themselves vicious, was suitable to its false foundation. The ostentation of riches, the vanity of equipage, shame of poverty, and ignorance of modesty, were the common arts of life; the generous love of one woman was changed into gallantry for all the sex, and friendships among men turned into commerces of interest, or mere professions. 'While these were the rules of life, perjuries in the prince, and a general corruption of manners in the subject, were the snares in which France has entangled all her neighbours.' With such false colours have the eyes of Louis been enchanted, from the debauchery of his early youth, to the superstition of his present old age. Hence it is, that he has the patience to have statues erected to his prowess, his valour, his fortitude; and in the softness and luxury of a court, to be applauded for magnanimity and enterprise in military achievements.

Peter Alexowitz of Russia, when he came to the years of manhood, though he found himself emperor of a vast and numerous people, master of an endless territory, absolute commander of the lives and fortunes of his subjects, in the midst of this unbounded power and greatness turned his thoughts upon himself and people with sorrow. Sordid ignorance and a brute manner of life this generous prince beheld and contemned from the light of his own genius. His judgment suggested this to him, and his courage prompted him to amend it. In order to this, he did not send to the nation from whence the rest of the world has borrowed its politeness, but himself left his diadem to learn the true way to glory and honour, and application to useful arts, wherein to employ the laborious, the simple, the honest part of his people. Mechanic employments and operations were very justly the first objects of his favour and observation. With this glorious intention he travelled into foreign nations in an obscure manner, above receiving little honours where he sojourned, but prying into what was of more consequence, their arts of peace and of war. By this means has this great prince laid the foundation of a great and lasting fame, by personal labour, personal knowledge, personal valour. It would be injury to any of antiquity to name them with him. Who, but himself, ever left a throne to learn to sit in it with more grace? Who ever thought himself mean in absolute power till he had learned to use it?

If we consider this wonderful person, it is perplexity to know where to begin his encomium. Others may in a metaphorical or philosophic sense be said to command themselves, but this emperor is also literally under his own command. How generous and how good was his entering his own name as a private man in the army he raised, that none in it might expect to outrun the steps with which he himself advanced! By such measures this godlike prince learned to conquer, learned to use his conquests. How terrible has he appeared in battle, how gentle in victory! Shall then the base arts of the Frenchman be held polite, and the honest labours of the Russian barbarous? No: barbarity is the ignorance of true honour, or placing any thing instead of it. The unjust prince is ignoble and barbarous, the good prince only renowned and glorious.

Though men may impose upon themselves what they please by their corrupt imaginations, truth will ever keep its station; and as glory is nothing else but the shadow of virtue, it will certainly disappear at the departure of virtue. But how carefully ought the true notions of it to be preserved, and how industrious should we be to encourage any impulses towards it! The Westminster schoolboy that said the other day he could not sleep or play for the colours in the hall, ought to be free from receiving a blow for ever.

But let us consider what is truly glorious according to the author I have to-day quoted in the front of my paper

The perfection of glory, says Tully, consists in these three particulars: "That the people love us; that they have confidence in us; that being affected with a certain admiration towards us, they think we deserve honour." This was spoken of greatness in a commonwealth: but if one were to form a notion of consummate glory under our constitution, one must add to the above-mentioned felicities, a certain necessary inexistence and disrelish of all the rest without the prince's favour. He should, methinks, have riches, power, honour, command, glory; but riches, power, honour, command, and glory, should have no charms, but as accompanied with the affection of his prince. He should methinks, be popular because a favourite, and a favourite because popular. Were it not to make the character too imaginary, I would give him sovereignty over some foreign territory, and make him esteem that an empty addition without the kind regards of his own prince. One may merely have an idea of a man thus composed and circumstantiated; and if he were so made for power without an incapacity of giving jealousy, he would be also glorious without possibility of receiving disgrace. This humility and this importance, must make his glory immortal.

These thoughts are apt to draw me beyond the usual length of this paper, but if I could suppose such rhapsodies could outlive the common fate of ordinary things, I would say these sketches and faint images of glory were drawn in August 1711, when John Duke of Marlborough made that memorable march* wherein he took the French lines without bloodshed.   T

---

* Related in Kane's Memoirs

No. CXL. FRIDAY, AUGUST 10.

..... Animum nunc huc celerem, nunc dividit illuc.
VIRG.

This way and that he turns his anxious mind.
DRYDEN.

When I acquaint my reader, that I have many other letters not yet acknowledged, I believe he will own, that I have a mind he should believe, that I have no small charge upon me, but am a person of some consequence in this world. I shall therefore employ the present hour only in reading petitions, in the order as follows.

'Mr Spectator,

'I have lost so much time already, that I desire, upon the receipt hereof, you would sit down immediately and give me your answer. I would know of you whether a pretender of mine really loves me. As well as I can, I will describe his manners. When he sees me he is always talking of constancy, but vouchsafes to visit me but once a fortnight, and then is always in haste to be gone. When I am sick, I hear, he says he is mightily concerned, but neither comes nor sends, because, as he tells his acquaintance with a sigh, he does not care to let me know all the power I have over him, and how impossible it is for him to live without me. When he leaves the town, he writes once in six weeks, desires to hear from me, complains of the torment of absence, speaks of flames, tortures, languishings, and ecstasies. He has the cant of an impatient lover, but keeps the pace of a lukewarm one. You know I must not go faster than he does; and to move at this rate is as tedious as counting a great clock. But you are to know he is rich; and my mother says, As he is slow he is sure: he will love me long if he loves me little, but I appeal to you whether he loves at all.

'Your neglected humble servant,
'LYDIA NOVELL.'

'All these fellows who have money are extremely saucy and cold. Pray, Sir, tell them of it.'

'MR. SPECTATOR,

'I HAVE been delighted with nothing more through the whole course of your writings, than the substantial account you lately gave of wit, and I could wish you would take some other opportunity to express further the corrupt taste the age has run into; which I am chiefly apt to attribute to the prevalency of a few popular authors, whose merit in some respects has given a sanction to their faults in others. Thus the imitators of Milton, seem to place all the excellency of that sort of writing either in the uncouth or antique words, or something else which was highly vicious, though pardonable, in that great man. The admirers of what we call point, or turn, look upon it as the particular happiness to which Cowley, Ovid, and others, owe their reputation; and therefore imitate them only in such instances: what is just, proper, and natural, does not seem to be the question with them, but by what means a quaint antithesis may be brought about, how one word may be made to look two ways, and what will be the consequence of a forced allusion. Now, though such authors appear to me to resemble those who make themselves fine, instead of being well dressed or graceful; yet the mischief is, that these beauties in them, which I call blemishes, are thought to proceed from luxuriance of fancy and overflowing of good sense: in one word, they have the character of being too witty; but if you would acquaint the world they are not witty at all, you would, among many others, oblige, Sir,

'Your most benevolent reader,
'R. D.'

'SIR,

'I AM a young woman, and reckoned pretty; therefore you'll pardon me that I trouble you to decide a wager between me and a cousin of mine, who is always contradicting one because he understands Latin. Pray, Sir, is dimple spelt with a single or a double p?

'I am, Sir,
'Your very humble servant,
'BETTY SAUNTER.'

'Pray, Sir, direct thus, "To the kind Querist;" and leave it at Mr Lillie's; for I don't care to be known in the thing at all. I am, Sir, again, your humble servant.'

'MR. SPECTATOR,

'I MUST needs tell you there are several of your papers I do not much like. You are often so nice there is no enduring you; and so learned there is no understanding you. What have you to do with our petticoats?

'Your humble servant,
'PARTHENOPE.'

'MR. SPECTATOR,

'LAST night, as I was walking in the park, I met a couple of friends. Pry'thee, Jack, says one of them, let us go drink a glass of wine; for I am fit for nothing else. This put me upon reflecting on the many miscarriages which happen in conversation over wine, when men go to the bottle to remove such humours as it only stirs up and awakens. This I could not attribute more to any thing than to the humour of putting company upon others which men do not like themselves. Pray, Sir, declare in your papers, that he who is a troublesome companion to himself, will not be an agreeable one to others. Let people reason themselves into good humour, before they impose themselves upon their friends. Pray, Sir, be as eloquent as you can upon this subject, and do human life so much good, as to argue powerfully, that it is not every one that can swallow, who is fit to drink a glass of wine.

'Your most humble servant.'

'Sir,

'I this morning cast my eye upon your paper concerning the expense of time. You are very obliging to the women, especially those who are not young and past gallantry, by touching so gently upon gaming: therefore I hope you do not think it wrong to employ a little leisure time in that diversion; but I should be glad to hear you say something upon the behaviour of some of the female gamesters.

'I have observed ladies, who in all other respects are gentle, good-humoured, and the very pinks of good breeding; who, as soon as the ombre-table is called for, and set down to their business, are immediately transmigrated into the veriest wasps in nature.

'You must know I keep my temper, and win their money; but am out of countenance to take it, it makes them so very uneasy. Be pleased, dear Sir, to instruct them to lose with a better grace, and you will oblige

'Your's,
'Rachel Basto.'

'Mr Spectator,

'Your kindness to Eleonora, in one of your papers, has given me encouragement to do myself the honour of writing to you. The great regard you have so often expressed for the instruction and improvement of our sex, will, I hope, in your own opinion, sufficiently excuse me from making any apology for the impertinence of this letter. The great desire I have to embellish my mind with some of those graces which you say are so becoming, and which you assert reading helps us to, has made me uneasy till I am put in a capacity of attaining them: this, Sir, I shall never think myself in, till you shall be pleased to recommend some author or authors to my perusal.

'I thought, indeed, when I first cast my eye on Eleonora's letter, that I should have had no occasion for requesting it of you; but, to my very great concern, I found on the perusal of that Spectator, I was entirely disappointed, and am as much at a loss how to make use of my time for that end as ever. Pray, Sir, oblige me at least with one scene, as you were pleased to entertain Eleonora with your prologue. I write to you not only my own sentiments, but also those of several others of my acquaintance, who are as little pleased with the ordinary manner of spending one's time as myself: and if a fervent desire after knowledge, and a great sense of our present ignorance, may be thought a good presage and earnest of improvement, you may look upon your time you shall bestow in answering this request, not thrown away to no purpose. And I can't but add, that unless you have a particular and more than ordinary regard for Eleonora, I have a better title to your favour than she, since I do not content myself with a tea-table reading of your papers, but it is my entertainment very often when alone in my closet. To shew you I am capable of improvement, and hate flattery, I acknowledge I do not like some of your papers; but even there I am readier to call in question my own shallow understanding, than Mr. Spectator's profound judgment.

'I am, Sir, your already (and in hopes of
  'being more your) obliged servant,
    'PARTHENIA'

This last letter is written with so urgent and serious an air, that I cannot but think it incumbent upon me to comply with her commands, which I shall do very suddenly.

T.

No. CXLI. SATURDAY, AUGUST 11.

*... Migravit ab aure voluptas
Omnis*   Hor.

Pleasure no more arises from the ear.

In the present emptiness of the town, I have several applications from the lower part of the players, to admit suffering to pass for acting. They, in very obliging terms, desire me to let a fall on the ground, a stumble, or a good slap on the back, be reckoned a jest. These gambols I shall tolerate for a season, because I hope the evil cannot continue longer than till the people of condition and taste return to town. The method, some time ago, was to entertain that part of the audience who have no faculty above eye-sight, with rope-dancers and tumblers, which was a way discreet enough, because it prevented confusion, and distinguished such as could show all the postures which the body is capable of, from those who were to represent all the passions to which the mind is subject. But though this was prudently settled, corporeal and intellectual actors ought to be kept at a still wider distance than to appear on the same stage at all; for which reason, I must propose some methods for the improvement of the Bear-garden, by dismissing all bodily actors to that quarter.

In cases of greater moment, where men appear in public, the consequence and importance of the thing can bear them out. And though a pleader or preacher is hoarse or awkward, the weight of their matter commands respect and attention; but in theatrical speaking, if the performer is not exactly proper and graceful, he is utterly ridiculous. In cases where there is little else expected but the pleasure of the ears and eyes, the least diminution of that pleasure is the highest offence. In acting, barely to perform the part, is not commendable, but to be the least out is contemptible. To avoid these difficulties and delicacies, I am informed, that while I was out of town, the actors have flown in the air, and played such pranks, and run such hazards, that none but the servants of the fire-office, tilers, and masons could have been able to perform the like. The author of the following letter, it seems, has been of the audience at one of these entertainments, and has accordingly complained to me upon it, but I think he has been to the utmost degree severe against what is exceptionable in the play he mentions, without dwelling so much as he might have done on the author's most excellent talent of humour. The pleasant pictures he has drawn of life should have been more kindly mentioned, at the same time that he banishes his witches, who are too dull devils to be attacked with so much warmth.

'Mr. Spectator,

'Upon a report that Moll White had followed you to town, and was to act a part in the "Lancashire Witches," I went last week to see that play. It was my fortune to sit next to a country justice of the peace, a neighbour (as he said) of Sir Roger's, who pretended to shew her to us in one of the dances. There was witchcraft enough in the entertainment almost to incline me to believe him: Ben Johnson was almost lamed, young Bullock narrowly saved his neck; the audience was astonished, and an old acquaintance of mine, a person of worth, whom I would have bowed to in the pit, at two yards distance did not know me.

'If you were what the country people reported you, a white witch, I could have wished you had been there to have exorcised that rabble of broomsticks with which we were haunted for above three hours. I could have allowed them to set Clod in the tree, to have scared the sportsmen, plagued the justice, and employed honest Teague with his holy water. This was the proper use of them in comedy, if the author had stopped here, but I cannot conceive what relation the sacrifice of the black lamb, and the ceremonies of their worship to the devil, have to the business of mirth and humour.

'The gentleman who writ this play, and has drawn some characters in it very justly, appears to have been misled in his witchcraft by an unwary following the inimitable Shakspeare. The incantations in Macbeth have a solemnity admirably adapted to the occasion of that tragedy, and fill the mind with a suitable horror, besides that, the witches are a part of the story itself, as we find it very particularly related in Hector Boetius, from whom he seems to have taken it. This, therefore, is a proper machine where the business is dark, horrid, and bloody; but is extremely foreign from the affair of comedy. Subjects of this kind, which are in themselves disagreeable, can at no time become entertaining, but by passing through an imagination like Shakspeare's to form them, for which reason Mr Dryden would not allow even Beaumont and Fletcher capable of imitating him.

"But Shakspeare's magic could not copied be,
Within that circle none durst walk but he."

'I should not, however, have troubled you with these remarks, if there were not something else in this comedy, which wants to be exorcised more than the witches: I mean the freedom of some passages, which I should have overlooked, if I had not observed that those jests can raise the loudest mirth, though they are painful to right sense, and an outrage upon modesty.

'We must attribute such liberties to the taste of that age, but indeed by such representations a poet sacrifices the best part of his audience to the worst; and, as one would think, neglects the boxes, to write to the orange-wenches.

'I must not conclude till I have taken notice of the moral with which this comedy ends. The two young ladies having given a notable example of outwitting those who had a right in the disposal of them, and marrying without consent of parents, one of the injured parties, who is easily reconciled, winds up all with this remark;

"————Design whate'er we will,
There is a fate which over-rules us still."

'We are to suppose that the gallants are men of merit; but if they had been rakes, the excuse might have served as well. Hans Carvel's wife was of the same principle, but has expressed it with a delicacy which shews she is not serious in her excuse, but in a sort of humorous philosophy turns off the thought of her guilt, and says,

"That if weak women go astray,
Their stars are more in fault than they."

'This, no doubt, is a full reparation, and dismisses the audience with very edifying impressions.

'These things fall under a province you have partly pursued already, and therefore demand your animadversions for the regulating so noble an entertainment as that of the stage. It were to be wished, that all who write for it hereafter would raise their genius, by the ambition of pleasing people of the best understanding; and leave others who show nothing of the human species but risibility, to seek their diversions at the Bear-garden, or some other privileged place, where reason and good-manners have no right to disturb them.

T   'I am, &c.'
August 8, 1711

No. CXLII. MONDAY, AUGUST 13

Irrupta tenet copula .   Hor.

They equal move
In an unbroken yoke of faithful love.
                                                Glanvil.

The following letters being genuine, and the images of a worthy passion, I am willing to give the old lady's admonition to myself, and the representation of her own happiness, a place in my writings.

'Mr. Spectator,   August 9, 1711.

' I am now in the sixty-seventh year of my age, and read you with approbation, but methinks, you do not strike at the root of the greatest evil in life, which is the false notion of gallantry in love. It is, and has long been, upon a very ill foot; but I who have been a wife forty years, and was bred in a way that has made me ever since very happy, see through the folly of it.... In a word, Sir, when I was a young woman, all who avoided the vices of the age were very carefully educated, and all fantastical objects were turned out of our sight. The tapestry hangings, with the great and venerable simplicity of the scripture stories, had better effects than now the loves of Venus and Adonis, or Bacchus and Ariadne, in your fine present prints. The gentleman I am married to, made love to me in rapture, but it was the rapture of a Christian and a man of honour, not a romantic hero, or a whining coxcomb. this put our life upon a right basis. To give you an idea of our regard one to another, I inclose to you several of his letters, writ forty years ago, when my lover, and one writ t'other day, after so many years cohabitation.

'Your servant,
'ANDROMACHE.'

AUGUST 7, 1671.
'MADAM,

'IF my vigilance and ten thousand wishes for your welfare and repose could have any force, you last night slept in security, and had every good angel in your attendance. To have my thoughts ever fixed on you, to live in constant fear of every accident to which human life is liable, and to send up my hourly prayers to avert them from you, I say, Madam, thus to think, and thus to suffer, is what I do for her who is in pain at my approach, and calls all my tender sorrow impertinence. You are now before my eyes, my eyes that are ready to flow with tenderness, but cannot give relief to my gushing heart, that dictates what I am now saying, and yearns to tell you all its achings. How art thou, oh my soul, stolen from thyself! How is all my attention broken! My books are blank paper, and my friends intruders. I have no hope of quiet but from your pity. To grant it, would make more for your triumph. to give pain is the tyranny, to make happy the true empire, of beauty. If you would consider aright, you'd find an agreeable change in dismissing the attendance of a slave, to receive the complaisance of a companion. I bear the former, in hopes of the latter condition, as I live in chains without murmuring at the power which inflicts them, so I could enjoy freedom without forgetting the mercy that gave it.

'Madam, I am
'Your most devoted,
'most obedient servant.'

'Though I made him no declarations in his favour, you see he had hopes of me when he writ this in the month following.'

SEPTEMBER 3, 1671.
'MADAM,

'BEFORE the light this morning dawned upon the earth, I awaked, and lay in expectation of its return, not that it could give any new sense of joy to me, but as I hoped it would bless you with its cheerful face, after a quiet which I wished you last night. If my prayers are heard, the day appeared with all the influence of a merciful Creator upon your person and actions. Let others, my lovely charmer, talk of a blind Being that disposes their hearts, I contemn their low images of love. I have not a thought which relates to you, that I cannot with confidence beseech the all-seeing Power to bless me in. May He direct you in all your steps, and reward your innocence, your sanctity of manners, your prudent youth, and becoming piety, with the continuance of His grace and protection. This is an unusual language to ladies; but you have a mind elevated above the giddy notions of a sex ensnared by flattery, and misled by a false and short adoration into a solid and long contempt. Beauty, my fairest creature, palls in the possession, but I love also your mind; your soul is as dear to me as my own; and if the advantages of a liberal education, some knowledge, and as much contempt of the world, joined with the endeavours towards a life of strict virtue and religion, can qualify me to raise new ideas in a breast so well disposed as yours is, our days will pass away with joy, and old age, instead of introducing melancholy prospects of decay, give us hope of eternal youth in a better life. I have but few minutes from the duty of my employment to write in, and without time to read over what I have writ; therefore beseech you to pardon the first hints of my mind, which I have expressed in so little order.

'I am, dearest creature,
'Your most obedient,
'most devoted servant.'

'The two next were written after the day for our marriage was fixed.'

SEPTEMBER 25, 1671.
'MADAM,

'It is the hardest thing in the world to be in love, and yet attend business. As for me, all that speak to me find me out, and I must lock myself up, or other people will do it for me. A gentleman asked me this morning what news from Holland, and I answered, she's exquisitely handsome. Another desired to know when I had been last at Windsor, I replied, she designs to go with me. Pr'ythee allow me at least to kiss your hand before the appointed day, that my mind may be in some composure. Methinks I could write a volume to you; but all the language on earth would fail in saying how much, and with what disinterested passion,

'I am ever yours.'

SEPTEMBER 30, 1671.

'DEAR CREATURE, Seven in the morning.

'NEXT to the influence of heaven, I am to thank you that I see the returning day with pleasure. To pass my evenings in so sweet a conversation, and have the esteem of a woman of your merit, has in it a particularity of happiness no more to be expressed than returned. But I am, my lovely creature, contented to be on the obliged side, and to employ all my days in new endeavours to convince you, and all the world, of the sense I have of your condescension in choosing,

'Madam, your most faithful,
'most obedient humble servant.'

'He was when he writ the following letter as agreeable and pleasant a man as any in England.'

OCTOBER 20, 1671.

'MADAM,

'I BEG pardon that my paper is not finer, but I am forced to write from a coffee-house where I am attending about business. There is a dirty crowd of busy faces all around me talking of money, while all my ambition, all my wealth, is love: love which animates my heart, sweetens my humour, enlarges my soul, and affects every action of my life. It is to my lovely charmer I owe that many noble ideas are continually affixed to my words and actions: it is the natural effect of that generous passion to create in the admirer some similitude of the object admired. Thus, my dear, am I every day to improve from so sweet a companion. Look up, my fair one, to that heaven which made thee such, and join with me to implore its influence on our tender innocent hours, and beseech the Author of love to bliss the rites he has ordained, and mingle with our happiness a just sense of our transient condition, and a resignation to His will, which only can regulate our minds to a steady endeavour to please Him and each other,

'I am for ever your faithful servant.'

'I will not trouble you with more letters at this time, but if you saw the poor withered hand which sends you these minutes, I am sure you would smile to think that there is one who is so gallant as to speak of it still as so welcome a present, after forty year's possession of the woman whom he writes to.'

JUNE 23, 1711.
'MADAM,

'I heartily beg your pardon for my omission to write yesterday. It was no failure of my tender regard for you; but having been very much perplexed in my thoughts on the subject of my last, made me determine to suspend speaking of it till I came myself. But, my lovely creature, know it is not in the power of age, of misfortune, or any other accident which hangs over human life, to take from me the pleasing esteem I have for you, or the memory of the bright figure you appeared in when you gave your hand and heart to,

'Madam, your most grateful husband,
'and obedient servant'

T

No. CXLIII. TUESDAY, AUGUST 14.

Non est vivere sed valere vita. MART.

To breathe, is not to live, but to be well.

It is an unreasonable thing some men expect of their acquaintance. They are ever complaining that they are out of order, or displeased, or they know not how, and are so far from letting that be a reason for retiring to their own homes, that they make it their argument for coming into company. What has any body to do with accounts of a man's being indisposed but his physician? If a man laments in company, where the rest are in humour enough to enjoy themselves, he should not take it ill if a servant is ordered to present him with a porringer of caudle or posset-drink, by way of admonition that he go home to bed. That part of life which we ordinarily understand by the word conversation, is an indulgence to the sociable part of our make, and should incline us to bring our proportion of good-will or good-humour among the friends we meet with, and not to trouble them with relations which must of necessity oblige them to a real or feigned affliction. Cares, distresses, diseases, uneasinesses, and dislikes of our own, are by no means to be obtruded upon our friends. If we would consider how little of this vicissitude of motion and rest, which we call life, is spent with satisfaction, we should be more tender of our friends, than to bring them little sorrows which do not belong to them. There is no real life but cheerful life; therefore valetudinarians should be sworn before they enter into company, not to say a word of themselves till the meeting breaks up. It is not here pretended that we should be always sitting with chaplets of flowers round our heads, or be crowned with roses in order to make our entertainment agreeable to us; but if (as it is usually observed) they who resolve to be merry seldom are so, it will be much more unlikely for us to be well pleased, if they are admitted who are always complaining they are sad. Whatever we do, we should keep up the cheerfulness of our spirits, and never let them sink below an inclination at least to be well pleased; the way to this is, to keep our bodies in exercise, our minds at ease. That insipid state wherein neither are in vigour, is not to be accounted any part of our portion of being. When we are in the satisfaction of some innocent pleasure, or pursuit of some laudable design, we are in the possession of life, of human life. Fortune will give us disappointments enough, and nature is attended with infirmities enough, without our adding to the unhappy side of our account by our spleen or ill-humour. Poor Cottilus, among so many real evils, a chronical distemper and a narrow fortune, is never heard to complain: that equal spirit of his, which any man may have, that like him will conquer pride, vanity, and affectation, and follow nature, is not to be broken, because it has no points to contend for. To be anxious for nothing but what nature demands as necessary, if it is not the way to an estate, is the way to what men aim at by getting an estate. This temper will preserve health in the body as well as tranquillity in the mind. Cottilus sees the world in a hurry, with the same scorn that a sober person sees a man drunk. Had he been contented with what he ought to have been, how could, says he, such a one have met with such a disappointment? If another had valued his mistress for what he ought to have loved her, he had not been in her power: if her virtue had had a part of his passion, her levity had been his cure; she could not then have been false and amiable at the same time.

VOL. II.

Since we cannot promise ourselves constant health, let us endeavour at such a temper as may be our best support in the decay of it. Uranius has arrived at that composure of soul, and wrought himself up to such a neglect of every thing with which the generality of mankind is enchanted, that nothing but acute pains can give him disturbance; and against those too, he will tell his intimate friends, he has a secret which gives him present ease. Uranius is so thoroughly persuaded of another life, and endeavours so sincerely to secure an interest in it, that he looks upon pain but as a quickening of his pace to a home, where he shall be better provided for than in his present apartment. Instead of the melancholy views which others are apt to give themselves, he will tell you that he has forgot he is mortal, nor will he think of himself as such. He thinks at the time of his birth he entered into an eternal being, and the short article of death he will not allow an interruption of life, since that moment is not of half the duration as is his ordinary sleep. Thus is his being one uniform and consistent series of cheerful diversions and moderate cares, without fear or hope of futurity. Health to him is more than pleasure to another man, and sickness less affecting to him than indisposition is to others.

I must confess, if one does not regard life after this manner, none but idiots can pass it away with any tolerable patience. Take a fine lady, who is of a delicate frame, and you may observe from the hour she rises a certain weariness of all that passes about her. I know more than one who is much too nice to be quite alive: they are sick of such strange frightful people that they meet; one is so awkward, and another so disagreeable, that it looks like a penance to breathe the same air with them. You see this is so very true, that a great part of ceremony and good-breeding among the ladies turns upon their uneasiness: and I'll undertake, if the how-d'ye servants of our women were to make a weekly bill of sickness, as the parish-clerks do of mortality, you would not find, in an account of seven days, one in thirty that was not downright sick or indisposed, or but a very little better than she was, and so forth.

It is certain, that to enjoy life and health as a constant feast, we should not think pleasure necessary; but, if possible, to arrive at an equality of mind. It is as mean to be overjoyed upon occasions of good fortune, as to be dejected in circumstances of distress. Laughter in one condition is as unmanly as weeping in the other. We should not form our minds to expect transport on every occasion, but know how to make it enjoyment to be out of pain. Ambition, envy, vagrant desire, or impertinent mirth, will take up our minds, without we can possess ourselves in that sobriety of heart which is above all pleasures, and can be felt much better than described. But the ready way, I believe, to the right enjoyment of life, is by a prospect towards another, to have but a very mean opinion of it. A great author* of our time has set this in an excellent light, when with a philosophic pity of human life, he spoke of it in his 'Theory of the Earth' in the following manner.

'For what is this life but a circulation of little mean actions? We lie down and rise again, dress and undress, feed and wax hungry, work or play, and are weary, and then we lie down again, and the circle returns. We spend the day in trifles; and when the night comes, we throw ourselves into the bed of folly amongst dreams, and broken thoughts, and wild imaginations. Our reason lies asleep by us, and we are, for the time, as arrant brutes as those that sleep in the stalls or in the field. Are not the capacities of man higher than these? And ought not his ambition and expectations to be greater? Let us be adventurers for another world. 'tis at least a fair and noble chance; and there is nothing in this worth our thoughts or our passions. If we should be disappointed, we are still no worse than the rest of our

* Dr. Burnet.

fellow-mortals; and if we succeed in our expectations, we are eternally happy.'

No. CXLIV. WEDNESDAY, AUGUST 15.

Nôris quam elegans formarum spectator siem. TER.

You shall see how nice a judge of beauty I am.

BEAUTY has been the delight and torment of the world ever since it began. The philosophers have felt its influence so sensibly, that almost every one of them has left us some saying or other, which intimated that he too well knew the power of it. One has told us that a graceful person is a more powerful recommendation than the best letter that can be writ in your favour. Another desires the possessor of it to consider it as a mere gift of nature, and not any perfection of his own. A third calls it a short-lived tyranny, a fourth, a silent fraud, because it imposes upon us without the help of language: but I think Carneades spoke as much like a philosopher as any of them, though more like a lover, when he called it royalty without force. It is not indeed to be denied, that there is something irresistible in a beauteous form; the most severe will not pretend, that they do not feel an immediate prepossession in favour of the handsome. No one denies them the privilege of being first heard, and being regarded before others in matters of ordinary consideration. At the same time the handsome should consider that it is a possession, as it were, foreign to them. No one can give it himself, or preserve it when they have it. Yet so it is, that people can bear any quality in the world better than beauty. It is the consolation of all who are naturally too much affected with the force of it, that a little attention, if a man can attend with judgment, will cure them. Handsome people usually are so fantastically pleased with themselves, that if they do not kill at first sight, as the phrase is, a second interview disarms them of all their power. But I shall make this paper rather a warning-piece to give notice where the danger is, than to propose instructions how to avoid it when you have fallen in the way of it. Handsome men shall be the subject of another chapter, the women shall take up the present discourse

Amaryllis, who has been in town but one winter, is extremely improved with the arts of good-breeding without leaving nature. She has not lost the native simplicity of her aspect, to substitute that patience of being stared at, which is the usual triumph and distinction of a town lady. In public assemblies you meet her careless eye diverting itself with the objects around her, insensible that she herself is one of the brightest in the place.

Dulcissa is quite of another make; she is almost a beauty by nature, but more than one by art. If it were possible for her to let her fan or any limb about her rest, she would do some part of the execution she meditates; but though she designs herself a prey, she will not stay to be taken. No painter can give you words for the different aspects of Dulcissa in half a moment, where ever she appears; so little does she accomplish what she takes so much pains for, to be gay and careless.

Merah is attended with all the charms of woman and accomplishments of man. It is not to be doubted but she has a great deal of wit, if she were not such a beauty; and she would have more beauty had she not so much wit. Affectation prevents her excellencies from walking together. If she has a mind to speak such a thing, it must be done with such an air of her body, and if she has an inclination to look very careless, there is such a smart thing to be said at the same time, that the design of being admired destroys itself. Thus the unhappy Merab, though a wit and beauty, is allowed to be neither, because she will always be both.

Albacinda has the skill as well as the power of pleasing. Her form is majestic, but her aspect humble. All good men should beware of the destroyer. She will speak to you like your sister till she has you sure; but is the most vexatious of tyrants when you are so. Her familiarity of behaviour, her indifferent questions, and general conversation, make the silly part of her votaries full of hopes, while the wise fly from her power. She well knows she is too beautiful and too witty to be indifferent to any who converse with her, and therefore knows she does not lessen herself by familiarity, but gains occasions of admiration, by seeming ignorance of her perfections.

Eudosia adds to the height of her stature a nobility of spirit which still distinguishes her above the rest of her sex. Beauty in others is lovely, in others agreeable, in others attractive, but in Eudosia it is commanding: love towards Eudosia is a sentiment like the love of glory. The lovers of other women are softened into fondness, the admirers of Eudosia exalted into ambition.

Eucratia presents herself to the imagination with a more kindly pleasure, and as she is woman, her praise is wholly feminine. If we were to form an image of dignity in a man, we should give him wisdom and valour, as being essential to the character of manhood. In like manner, if you describe a right woman in a laudable sense, she should have gentle softness, tender fear, and all those parts of life which distinguish her from the other sex; with some subordination to it, but such an inferiority that makes her still more lovely. Eucratia is that creature; she is all over woman; kindness is all her art, and beauty all her arms. Her look, her voice, her gesture, and whole behaviour, is truly feminine. A goodness mixed with fear, gives a tincture to all her behaviour. It would be savage to offend her, and cruelty to use art to gain her. Others are beautiful, but Eucratia thou art beauty!

Omniamante is made for deceit; she has an aspect as innocent as the famed Lucrece, but a mind as wild as the more famed Cleopatra. Her face speaks a vestal, but her heart a Messalina. Who that beheld Omniamante's negligent unobserving air, would believe that she hid under that regardless manner the witty prostitute, the rapacious wench, the prodigal courtezan? She can, when she pleases, adorn those eyes with tears like an infant that is chid; she can cast down that pretty face in confusion, while you rage with jealousy, and storm at her perfidiousness; she can wipe her eyes, tremble and look frighted, till you think yourself a brute for your rage, own yourself an offender, beg pardon, and make her new presents.

But I go too far in reporting only the dangers in beholding the beauteous, which I design for the instruction of the fair as well as their beholders; and shall end this rhapsody with mentioning what I thought was well enough said of an ancient sage to a beautiful youth, whom he saw admiring his own figure in brass. What, said the philosopher, could that image of your's say for itself if it could speak? It might say, answered the youth, "That it is very beautiful." "And are not you ashamed (replied the cynic) to value yourself upon that only of which a piece of brass is capable?"

T

No. CXLV. THURSDAY, AUGUST 16.

Stultitiam patiuntur opes   Hor.

Their folly pleads the privilege of wealth.

If the following enormities are not amended upon the first mention, I desire farther notice from my correspondents.

' Mr. Spectator,

' I am obliged to you for your discourse the other day upon frivolous disputants, who with great warmth, and enumeration of many circumstances and authorities, undertake to prove matters which nobody living denies. You cannot employ yourself more usefully than in adjusting the laws of disputation in coffee-houses and accidental companies, as well as in more formal debates. Among many other things which your own experience must suggest to you, it will be very obliging if you please to take notice of wagerers. I will not here repeat what Hudibras says of such disputants, which is so true, that it is almost proverbial, but shall only acquaint you with a set of young fellows of the Inns of Court, whose fathers have provided for them so plentifully, that they need not be very anxious to get law into their heads for the service of their country at the bar; but are of those who are sent (as the phrase of parents is) to the Temple, to know how to keep their own. One of these gentlemen is very loud and captious at a coffee-house which I frequent; and being in his nature troubled with a humour of contradiction, though withal excessive ignorant, he has found a way to indulge this temper, go on in idleness and ignorance, and yet still give himself the air of a very learned and knowing man, by the strength of his pocket. The misfortune of the thing is, I have, as it happens sometimes, a greater stock of learning than of money. The gentleman I am speaking of takes advantages of the narrowness of my circumstances in such a manner, that he has read all that I can pretend to, and runs me down with such a positive air, and with such powerful arguments, that from a very learned person I am thought a mere pretender. Not long ago I was relating that I had read such a passage in Tacitus, up starts my young gentleman in a full company, and pulling out his purse offered to lay me ten guineas, to be staked immediately in that gentleman's hands (pointing to one smoking at another table) that I was utterly mistaken. I was dumb for want of ten guineas; he went on unmercifully to triumph over my ignorance how to take him up, and told the whole room he had read Tacitus twenty times over, and such a remarkable incident as that could not escape him. He has at this time three considerable wagers depending between him and some of his companions, who are rich enough to hold an argument with him. He has five guineas upon questions in geography, two that the Isle of Wight is a peninsula, and three guineas to one that the world is round. We have a gentleman comes to our coffeehouse, who deals mightily in antique scandal; my disputant has laid him twenty pieces upon a point of history, to wit, that Cæsar never lay with Cato's sister, as is scandalously reported by some people.

'There are several of this sort of fellows in town, who wager themselves into statesmen, historians, geographers, mathematicians, and every other art, when the persons with whom they talk have not wealth equal to their learning. I beg of you to prevent in these youngsters, this compendious way to wisdom, which costs other people so much time and pains, and you will oblige

'Your humble servant.'

CoFFEE-HOUSE NEAR THE TEMPLE.
AUGUST 12, 1711.

'Mr. SPECTATOR,

'Here's a young gentleman that sings opera-tunes or whistles in a full house. Pray let him know that he has no right to act here as if he were in an empty room. Be pleased to divide the spaces of a public room, and certify whistlers, singers, and common orators, that are heard further than their portion of the room comes to, that the law is open, and that there is an equity which will relieve us from such as interrupt us in our lawful discourse, as much as against such as stop us on the road. I take these persons, Mr. Spectator, to be such trespassers as the officer in your stage-coach, and am of the same sentiment with counsellor Ephraim. It is true the young man is rich, and, as the vulgar say, needs not care for any body; but sure that is no authority for him to go whistle where he pleases.

'I am, Sir,
'Your most humble servant.'

'P. S. I have chambers in the Temple, and here are students that learn upon the hautboy; pray desire the benchers, that all lawyers who are proficients in wind-music may lodge near to the Thames.'

'Mr. SPECTATOR,

'We are a company of young women who pass our time very much together, and obliged by the mercenary humour of the men to be as mercenarily inclined as they are. There visits among us an old bachelor whom each of us has a mind to. The fellow is rich, and knows he may have any of us, therefore is particular to none, but excessively ill bred. His pleasantry consists in romping, he snatches kisses by surprise, puts his hand in our necks, tears our fans, robs us of ribbands, forces letters out of our hands, looks into any of our papers, and a thousand other rudenesses. Now what I'll desire of you is, to acquaint him, by printing this, that if he does not marry one of us very suddenly, we have all agreed, the next time he pretends to be merry, to affront him, and use him like a clown as he is. In the name of the sisterhood I take my leave of you, and am, as they all are,

'Your constant reader and well wisher.'

'MR. SPECTATOR,

'I AND several others of your female readers have conformed ourselves to your rules, even to our very dress. There is not one of us but has reduced our outward petticoat to its ancient sizeable circumference, though indeed we retain still a quilted one underneath; which makes us not altogether unconformable to the fashion; but it is on condition Mr Spectator extends not his censure too far. But we find you men secretly approve our practice by imitating our pyramidical form. The skirt of your fashionable coats forms as large a circumference as our petticoats; as these are set out with whalebone, so are those with wire, to increase and sustain the bunch of fold that hangs down on each side; and the hat, I perceive, is decreased in just proportion to our head-dresses. We make a regular figure; but I defy your mathematics to give name to the form you appear in. Your architecture is mere Gothic, and betrays a worse genius than ours therefore if you are partial to your own sex, I shall be less than I am now

T   'Your humble servant.'

No. CXLVI. FRIDAY, AUGUST 17.

Nemò vir magnus sine aliquo afflatu divino unquam fuit.
TULL.

All great men are in some degree inspired.

WE know the highest pleasure our minds are capable of enjoying with composure, when we read sublime thoughts communicated to us by men of great genius and eloquence. Such is the entertainment we meet with in the philosophical parts of Cicero's writings. Truth and good sense have there so charming a dress, that they could hardly be more agreeably represented with the addition of poetical fiction and the power of numbers. This ancient author, and a modern one, have fallen into my hands within these few days; and the impressions they have left upon me have at the present quite spoiled me for a merry fellow. The modern is that admirable writer, the Author of the "Theory of the Earth." The subjects with which I have lately been entertained in them both bear a near affinity, they are upon inquiries into hereafter: and the thoughts of the latter seem to me to be raised above those of the former in proportion to his advantages of scripture and revelation. If I had a mind to it, I could not at present talk of any thing else: therefore I shall translate a passage in the one, and transcribe a paragraph out of the other, for the speculation of this day. Cicero tells us, that Plato reports Socrates upon receiving his sentence, to have spoken to his judges in the following manner.

' I have great hopes, O my judges, that it is infinitely to my advantage that I am sent to death; for it must of necessity be, that one of these two things must be the consequence. Death must take away all these senses, or convey me to another life. If all sense is to be taken away, and death is no more than that profound sleep without dreams, in which we are sometimes buried, oh heavens! how desirable is it to die! how many days do we know in life preferable to such a state? But if it be true that death is but a passage to places, which they who lived before us do now inhabit, how much happier still is it to go from those who call themselves judges, to appear before those that really are such; before Minos, Rhadamanthus, Æacus, and Triptolemus, and to meet men who have lived with justice and truth? Is this, do you think, no happy journey? Do you think it nothing to speak with Orpheus, Musæus, Homer, and Hesiod? I would, indeed, suffer many deaths to enjoy these things. With what particular delight should I talk to Palamedes, Ajax, and others, who like me have suffered by the iniquity of their judges! I should examine the wisdom of that great prince, who carried such mighty forces against Troy; and argue with Ulysses and Sisyphus, upon difficult points, as I have in conversation here, without being in danger of being condemned. But let not those among you who have pronounced me an innocent man be afraid of death. No harm can arrive at a good man whether dead or living, his affairs are always under the direction of the gods, nor will I believe the fate which is allotted to me myself this day to have arrived by chance, nor have I aught to say either against my judges or accusers, but that they thought they did me an injury... But I detain you too long; it is time that I retire to death, and you to your affairs of life, which of us has the better, is known to the gods, but to no mortal man.'

The divine Socrates is here represented in a figure worthy his great wisdom and philosophy, worthy the greatest mere man that ever breathed. But the modern discourse is written upon a subject no less than the dissolution of nature itself. Oh how glorious is the old age of that great man, who has spent his time in such contemplations as has made this being, what only it should be, an education for heaven! He has, according to the lights of reason and revelation, which seemed to him clearest, traced the steps of Omnipotence: he has, with a celestial ambition, as far as it is consistent with humility and devotion, examined the ways of Providence, from the creation to the dissolution of the visible world. How pleasing must have been the speculation, to observe nature and Providence move together, the physical and moral world march the same pace: to observe paradise and eternal spring the seat of innocence: troubled seasons and angry skies the portion of wickedness and vice. When this admirable author has reviewed all that has past or is to come which relates to the habitable world, and run through the whole fate of it, how could a guardian angel, that had attended it through all its courses or changes, speak more emphatically at the end of his charge, than does our author, when he makes, as it were, a funeral oration over this globe, looking to the point where it once stood?

' Let us only, if you please to take leave of this subject, reflect upon this occasion on the vanity and transient glory of this habitable world. How by the force of one element breaking loose upon the rest, all the varieties of nature, all the works of art, all the labours of men, are reduced to nothing. All that we admired and adored before as great and magnificent, is obliterated or vanished; and another form and face of things, plain, simple, and every where the same, overspreads the whole earth. Where are now the great empires of the world, and their great imperial cities? their pillars, trophies, and monuments of glory? Shew me where they stood, read the inscription, tell me the victor's name. What remains, what impressions, what difference, or distinction, do you see in this mass of fire? Rome itself, eternal Rome, the great city, the empress of the world, whose domination and superstition, ancient and modern, make a great part of the history of this earth, what is become of her now? She laid her foundations deep, and her palaces were strong and sumptuous; "She glorified herself, and lived deliciously, and said in her heart, I sit a queen, and shall see no sorrow:" but her hour is come, she is wiped away from the face of the earth, and buried in everlasting oblivion. But it is not cities only, and works of men's hands, but the everlasting hills, the mountains and rocks of the earth, are melted as wax before the sun, and their place is nowhere found. Here stood the Alps, the load of the earth, that covered many countries, and reached their arms from the ocean to the Black Sea; this huge mass of stone is softened and dissolved as a tender cloud into rain. Here stood the African mountains, and Atlas with his top above the clouds; there was frozen Caucasus, and Taurus, and Imaus, and the mountains of Asia; and yonder, towards the north, stood the Riphæan hills, clothed in ice and snow. All these are vanished, dropt away as the snow upon their heads. "Great and marvellous are thy works, just and true are thy ways, thou King of saints! Hallelujah!'   T

No. CXLVII. SATURDAY, AUGUST 18.

Pronunciatio est vocis et vultûs et gestûs moderatio cum venustate. TULL.

Good delivery is a graceful management of the voice, countenance, and gesture.

'MR. SPECTATOR,

'THE well reading of the common-prayer is of so great importance, and so much neglected, that I take the liberty to offer to your consideration some particulars on that subject. And what more worthy your observation than this! a thing so public, and of so high consequence. It is indeed wonderful, that the frequent exercise of it should not make the performers of that duty more expert in it. This inability, as I conceive, proceeds from the little care that is taken of their reading, while boys and at school, where when they are got into Latin, they are looked upon as above English, the reading of which is wholly neglected, or at least read to very little purpose, without any due observations made to them of the proper accent and manner of reading; by this means they have acquired such ill habits as will not easily be removed. The only way that I know of to remedy this is, to propose some person of great ability that way, as a pattern for them; example being most effectual to convince the learned, as well as instruct the ignorant.

'You must know, Sir, I have been a constant frequenter of the service of the Church of England for above these four years last past, and till Sunday was seven-night never discovered, to so great a degree, the excellency of the common-prayer. When being at St. James's Garlic-hill church, I heard the service read so distinctly, so emphatically, and so fervently, that it was next to an impossibility to be inattentive. My eyes and my thoughts could not wander as usual, but were confined to my prayers. I then considered I addressed myself to the Almighty, and not to a beautiful face. And when I reflected on my former performances of that duty, I found I had run it over as a matter of form, in comparison to the manner in which I then discharged it. My mind was really affected, and fervent wishes accompanied my words. The confession was read with such a resigned humility, the absolution with such a comfortable authority, the thanksgivings with such a religious joy, as made me feel those affections of the mind in a manner I never did before. To remedy therefore the grievance above complained of, I humbly propose, that this excellent reader, upon the next and every annual assembly of the clergy of Sion College, and all other conventions, should read prayers before them. For then those that are afraid of stretching their mouths, and spoiling their soft voices, will learn to read with clearness, loudness, and strength. Others that affect a rakish negligent air, by folding their arms, and lolling on their book, will be taught a decent behaviour and comely erection of body. Those that read so fast as if impatient of their work, may learn to speak deliberately. There is another sort of persons whom I call Pindaric readers, as being confined to no set measure: these pronounce five or six words with great deliberation, and the five or six subsequent ones with as great celerity: the first part of a sentence with a very exalted voice, and the latter part with a submissive one; sometimes again with one sort of a tone, and immediately after with a very different one. These gentlemen will learn of my admired reader an evenness of voice and delivery. And all who are innocent of these affectations, but read with such an indifferency as if they did not understand the language, may then be informed of the art of reading movingly and fervently, how to place the emphasis, and give the proper accent to each word, and how to vary the voice according to the nature of the sentence. There is certainly a very great difference between the reading a prayer and a gazette, which I beg of you to inform a set of readers who affect, forsooth, a certain gentleman-like familiarity of tone, and mend the language as they go on, crying, instead of pardoneth and absolveth, pardons and absolves. These are often pretty classical scholars, and would think it an unpardonable sin to read Virgil or Martial with so little taste as they do divine service.

‘ This indifference seems to me to arise from the endeavour of avoiding the imputation of cant, and the false notion of it. It will be proper therefore to trace the original and signification of this word. Cant is, by some people, derived from one Andrew Cant, who, they say, was a Presbyterian minister in some illiterate part of Scotland, who by exercise and use had obtained the faculty, alias gift, of talking in the pulpit in such a dialect, that it is said he was understood by none but his own congregation, and not by all of them. Since Mr Cant's time it has been understood in a larger sense, and signifies all sudden exclamations, whinings, unusual tones, and in fine, all praying and preaching like the unlearned of the Presbyterians. But I hope a proper elevation of voice, a due emphasis and accent, are not to come within this description: so that our readers may still be as unlike the Presbyterians as they please. The Dissenters (I mean such as I have heard) do indeed elevate their voices, but it is with sudden jumps from the lower to the higher part of them, and that with so little sense or skill, that their elevation and cadence is bawling and muttering. They make use of an emphasis, but so improperly, that it is often placed on some very insignificant particle, as upon if, or and. Now if these improprieties have so great an effect on the people, as we see they have, how great an influence would the service of our church, containing the best prayers that ever were composed, and that in terms most affecting, most humble, and most expressive of our wants and dependence on the object of our worship, disposed in most proper order, and void of all confusion: What influence (I say) would these prayers have, were they delivered with a due emphasis, an apposite rising and variation of voice, the sentence concluded with a gentle cadence, and, in a word, with such an accent and turn of speech as is peculiar to prayer?

'As the matter of worship is now managed, in dissenting congregations, you find insignificant words and phrases raised by a lively vehemence, in our own churches, the most exalted sense depreciated, by a dispassionate indolence. I remember to have heard Dr S——e say in his pulpit, of the Common prayer, that, at least, it was as perfect as any thing of human institution. If the gentlemen who err in this kind would please to recollect the many pleasantries they have read upon those who recite good things with an ill grace, they would go on to think that what in that case is only ridiculous, in themselves is impious. But leaving this to their own reflections, I shall conclude this trouble with what Cæsar said upon the irregularity of tone in one who read before him, 'Do you read or sing? if you sing, you sing very ill.'

T   'Your most humble servant.'

No. CXLVIII. MONDAY, AUGUST 20.

—— Exempta juvat spinis è pluribus una   Hor.

Better one thorn pluck'd out than all remain

My correspondents assure me that the enormities which they lately complained of, and I published an account of, are so far from being amended, that new evils arise every day to interrupt their conversation, in contempt of my reproofs. My friend who writes from the coffee-house near the Temple, informs me, that the gentleman who constantly sings a voluntary in spite of the whole company, was more musical than ordinary after reading my paper; and has not been contented with that, but has danced up to the glass in the middle of the room, and practised minuet-steps to his own humming. The incorrigible creature has gone still farther, and in the open coffee-house, with one hand extended as leading a lady in it, he has danced both French and country-dances, and admonished his supposed partner by smiles and nods to hold up her head and fall back, according to the respective facings and evolutions of the dance. Before this gentleman began this his exercise, he was pleased to clear his throat by coughing and spitting a full half hour; and as soon as he struck up, he appealed to an attorney's clerk in the room, whether he hit as he ought, "Since you from death have saved me?" and then asked the young fellow (pointing to a chancery bill under his arm) whether that was an opera score he carried or not? Without staying for an answer he fell into the exercise above-mentioned, and practised his airs to the full house who were turned upon him, without the least shame or repentance for his former transgressions

I am to the last degree at a loss what to do with this young fellow, except I declare him an outlaw, and pronounce it penal for any one to speak to him in the said house which he frequents, and direct that he be obliged to drink his tea and coffee without sugar, and not receive from any person whatsoever any thing above mere necessaries.

As we in England are a sober people, and generally inclined rather to a certain bashfulness of behaviour in public, it is amazing whence some fellows come whom one meets with in this town; they do not at all seem to be the growth of our island; the pert, the talkative, all such as have no sense of the observation of others, are certainly of foreign extraction. As for my part, I am as much surprised when I see a talkative Englishman, as I should be to see the Indian pine growing on one of our quick-set hedges. Where these creatures get sun enough to make them such lively animals and dull men, is above my philosophy.

There are another kind of impertinents which a man is perplexed with in mixed company, and those are your loud speakers: these treat mankind as if we were all deaf, they do not express but declare themselves. Many of these are guilty of this outrage out of vanity, because they think all they say is well; or that they have their own persons in such veneration, that they believe nothing which concerns them can be insignificant to any body else. For these people's sake, I have often lamented that we cannot close our ears with as much ease as we can our eyes: it is very uneasy that we must necessarily be under persecution. Next to these bawlers, is a troublesome creature who comes with the air of your friend and your intimate, and that is your whisperer. There is one of them at a coffee-house which I myself frequent, who observing me to be a man pretty well made for secrets, gets by me, and with a whisper tells me things which all the town knows. It is no very hard matter to guess at the source of this impertinence, which is nothing else but a method or mechanic art of being wise. You never see any frequent in it, whom you can suppose to have any thing in the world to do. These persons are worse than bawlers, as much as a secret enemy is more dangerous than a declared one. I wish this my coffee-house friend would take this for an intimation, that I have not heard one word he has told me for these several years; whereas he now thinks me the most trusty repository of his secrets. The whisperers have a pleasant way of ending the close conversation; with saying aloud, 'Do not you think so?' then whisper again, and then aloud, 'But you know that person,' then whisper again. The thing would be well enough, if they whispered to keep the folly of what they say among friends; but, alas, they do it to preserve the importance of their thoughts. I am sure I could name you more than one person, whom no man living ever heard talk upon any subject in nature, or ever saw in his whole life with a book in his hand, that, I know not how, can whisper something like knowledge of what has, and does pass in the world; which you would think he learned from some familiar spirit that did not think him worthy to receive the whole story. But in truth whisperers deal only in half accounts of what they entertain you with. A great help to their discourse is, 'That the town says, and people begin to talk very freely, and they had it from persons too considerable to be named, what they will tell you when things are riper.' My friend has winked upon me every day since I came to town last, and has communicated to me as a secret, that he designed in a very short time to tell me a secret; but I shall know what he means, he now assures me, in less than a fortnight's time.

But I must not omit the dearer part of mankind, I mean the ladies, who take up a whole paper upon grievances which concern the men only; but shall humbly propose, that we change fools for an experiment only. A certain set of ladies complain they are frequently perplexed with a visitant, who affects to be wiser than they are, which character he hopes to preserve by an obstinate gravity and great guard against discovering his opinion upon any occasion whatsoever. A painful silence has hitherto gained him no farther advantage, than that as he might, if he had behaved himself with freedom, been excepted against, but as to this and that particular he now offends in the whole. To relieve these ladies, my good friends and correspondents, I shall exchange my dancing outlaw for their dumb visitant, and assign the silent gentleman all the haunts of the dancer: in order to which, I have sent them by the penny-post the following letters for their conduct in their new conversations.

' Sir,

' I have, you may be sure, heard of your irregularities without regard to my observations upon you, but shall not treat you with so much rigour as you deserve. If you will give yourself the trouble to repair to the place mentioned in the postscript to this letter, at seven this evening, you will be conducted into a spacious room well lighted, where there are ladies and music. You will see a young lady laughing next the window to the street, you may take her out, for she loves you as well as she does any man, though she never saw you before. She never thought in her life, any more than yourself. She will not be suprised when you accost her, nor concerned when you leave her. Hasten from a place where you are laughed at, to one where you will be admired. You are of no consequence, therefore go where you will be welcome for being so.

' Your most humble servant.'

' Sir,

' The ladies whom you visit, think a wise man the most impertinent creature living: therefore you cannot be offended that they are displeased with you. Why will you take pains to appear wise, where you would not be the more esteemed for being really so? Come to us, forget the giglers; and let your inclination go along with you, whether you speak or are silent, and let all such women as are in a clan or sisterhood go their own way; there is no room for you in that company, who are of the common taste of the sex.

> ‘ For women born to be controll’d,
> ‘ Stoop to the forward and the bold,
> ‘ Affect the haughty and the proud,
> ‘ The gay, the frolic, and the loud.’

T
WALLER.

No CXLIX. TUESDAY, AUGUST 21.

Cui in manu sit quem esse dementem velit,
Quem sapere, quem sanari, quem in morbum injici,
Quem contrà amari, quem accersiri, quem expeti

CÆCIL.

Who has it in her power to make any man mad, or in his senses, sick, or in health; and who can choose the object of her affections at pleasure.

THE following letter and my answer shall take up the present speculation.

‘ MR. SPECTATOR,

‘ I AM the young widow of a country gentleman who has left me entire mistress of a large fortune, which he agreed to as an equivalent for the difference in our years. In these circumstances, it is not extraordinary to have a crowd of admirers; which I have abridged in my own thoughts, and reduced to a couple of candidates only, both young, and neither of them disagreeable in their persons: according to the common way of computing, in one the estate more than deserves my fortune, in the other my fortune more than deserves the estate. When I consider the first, I own I am so far a woman I cannot avoid being delighted with the thoughts of living great, but then he seems to receive such a degree of courage from the knowledge of what he has, he looks as if he was going to confer an obligation on me; and the readiness he accosts me with, makes me jealous I am only hearing a repetition of the same things he has said to a hundred women before. When I consider the other, I see myself approached with so much modesty and respect, and such a doubt of himself, as betrays, methinks, an affection within, and a belief at the same time that he himself would be the only gainer by my consent. What an unexceptionable husband could I make out of both! But since that is impossible, I beg to be concluded by your opinion; it is absolutely in your power to dispose of.

'Your most obedient servant,
'SYLVIA.'

MADAM,

You do me great honour in your application to me on this important occasion I shall therefore talk to you with the tenderness of a father, in gratitude for your giving me the authority of one. You do not seem to make any great distinction between these gentlemen as to their persons: The whole question lies upon their circumstances and behaviour. If the one is less respectful because he is rich, and the other more obsequious because he is not so, they are in that point moved by the same principle, the consideration of fortune; and you must place them in each other's circumstances, before you can judge of their inclination.

To avoid confusion in discussing this point, I will call the richer man Strephon and the other Florio. If you believe Florio with Strephon's estate would behave himself as he does now, Florio is certainly your man; but if you think Strephon, were he in Florio's condition, would be as obsequious as Florio is now, you ought for your own sake to choose Strephon; for where the men are equal, there is no doubt riches ought to be a reason for preference. After this manner, my dear child, I would have you abstract them from their circumstances, for you are to take it for granted, that he who is very humble, only because he is poor, is the very same man in nature with him who is haughty because he is rich.

When you have gone thus far, as to consider the figure they make towards you, you will please, my dear, next to consider the appearance you make towards them. If they are men of discerning, they can observe the motives of your heart, and Florio can see when he is disregarded only upon account of fortune, which makes you to him a mercenary creature, and you are still the same thing to Strephon, in taking him for his wealth only, you are therefore to consider whether you had rather oblige, than receive an obligation.

The marriage life is always an insipid, a vexatious, or a happy condition. The first is, when two people of no genius or taste for themselves meet together, upon such a settlement as has been thought reasonable by parents and conveyancers, from an exact valuation of the land and cash of both parties. In this case the young lady's person is no more regarded than the house and the improvements in the purchase of an estate; but she goes with her fortune, rather than her fortune with her. These make up the crowd or vulgar of the rich, and fill up the lumber of human race, without beneficence towards those below them, or respect towards those above them; and lead a despicable, independent, and useless life, without sense of the laws of kindness, good-nature, mutual offices, and the elegant satisfactions which flow from reason and virtue.

The vexatious life arises from a conjunction of two people of quick taste and resentment, put together for reasons well known to their friends, in which especial care is taken to avoid (what they think the chief of evils) poverty, and insure to them riches, with every evil besides. These good people live in a constant constraint before company, and too great familiarity alone. When they are within observation they fret at each other's carriage and behaviour; when alone they revile each others person and conduct: in company they are in purgatory; when only together in a hell.

The happy marriage is, where two persons meet, and voluntarily make choice of each other, without principally regarding or neglecting the circumstances of fortune or beauty. These may still love in spite of adversity or sickness; the former we may in some measure defend ourselves from, the other is the portion of our very make. When you have a true notion of this sort of passion, your humour of living great will vanish out of your imagination, and you will find love has nothing to do with state. Solitude, with the person beloved, has a pleasure, even in a woman's mind, beyond show or pomp. You are therefore to consider which of your lovers will like you best undressed, which will bear with you most when out of humour; and your way to this is to ask of yourself, which of them you value most for his own sake? and by that judge which gives the greater instances of his valuing you for yourself only.

After you have expressed some sense of the humble approach of Florio, and a little disdain at Strephon's assurance in his address, you cry out, " What an unexceptionable husband could I make out of both!" It would therefore, methinks, be a good way to determine yourself: take him in whom what you like is not transferable to another; for if you choose otherwise, there is no hopes your husband will ever have what you liked in his rival; but intrinsic qualities in one man may very probably purchase every thing that is adventitious in another. In plainer terms; he whom you take for his personal perfections will sooner arrive at the gifts of fortune, than he whom you take for the sake of his fortune attain to personal perfections. If Strephon is not as accomplished and agreeable as Florio, marriage to you will never make him so; but marriage to you may make Florio as rich as Strephon; therefore to make a sure purchase, employ fortune upon certainties, but do not sacrifice certainties to fortune. I am

T

Your most obedient
humble servant.

No CL. WEDNESDAY, AUGUST 22.

Nil habet infelix paupertas durius in se,
Quàm quòd ridiculos homines facit —. Juv.

Want is the scorn of every wealthy fool,
And wit in rags is turn'd to ridicule. Dryden.

As I was walking in my chamber the morning before I went last into the country, I heard the hawkers, with great vehemence, crying about a paper, intitled, "The ninety-nine Plagues of an empty Purse." I had indeed some time before observed, that the orators of Grub-street had dealt very much in plagues. They have already published in the same month, "The Plagues of Matrimony," "The Plagues of a single Life," "The nineteen Plagues of a Chambermaid," "The Plagues of a Coachman," "The Plagues of a Footman," and

"The Plague of Plagues." The success these several plagues met with, probably gave occasion to the abovementioned poem on an empty purse. However that be, the same noise so frequently repeated under my window, drew me insensibly to think on some of those inconveniences and mortifications which usually attend on poverty, and in short gave birth to the present speculation; for, after my fancy had run over the most obvious and common calamities which men of mean fortunes are liable to, it descended to those little insults and contempts which, though they may seem to dwindle into nothing when a man offers to describe them, are perhaps of themselves more cutting and unsupportable than the former. Juvenal, with a great deal of humour and reason, tells us, that nothing bore harder upon a poor man in his time, than the continual ridicule which his habit and dress afforded to the beaux of Rome.

> Quid, quod materiam præbet caussasque jocorum
> Omnibus hic idem, si fæda et scissa lacerna,
> Si toga sordidula est, et rupta calceus alter,
> Pelle patet, vel si consuto vulnere crassum
> Atque recens linum ostendit non una cicatrix. JUV.

> Add, that the rich have still a gibe in store,
> And will be monstrous witty on the poor,
> For the torn surtout and the tatter'd vest,
> The wretch and all his wardrobe are a jest;
> The greasy gown sully'd with often turning,
> Gives a good hint to say the man's in mourning;
> Or if the shoe be ript, or patch is put,
> He's wounded! see the plaster on his foot.
> DRYDEN.

It is on this occasion that he afterwards adds the reflection which I have chosen for my motto.

> 'Want is the scorn of ev'ry wealthy fool,
> 'And wit in rags is turn'd to ridicule.' DRYDEN.

It must be confessed, that few things make a man appear more despicable, or more prejudice his hearers against what he is going to offer, than an awkward or pitiful dress, insomuch that I fancy, had Tully himself pronounced one of his orations with a blanket about his shoulders, more people would have laughed at his dress than have admired his eloquence. This last reflection made me wonder at a set of men, who, without being subjected to it by the unkindness of their fortunes, are contented to draw upon themselves the ridicule of the world in this particular. I mean such as take it into their heads, that the first regular step to be a wit is to commence a sloven. It is certain nothing has so much debased that, which must have been otherwise so great a character; and I know not how to account for it, unless it may possibly be in complaisance to those narrow minds who can have no notion of the same person's possessing different accomplishments; or that it is a sort of sacrifice which some men are contented to make to calumny, by allowing it to fasten on one part of their character, while they are endeavouring to establish another. Yet, however unaccountable this foolish custom is, I am afraid it could plead a long prescription; and probably gave too much occasion for the vulgar definition still remaining among us of an heathen philosopher.

I have seen the speech of a Terræ-filius, spoken in King Charles II's reign, in which he describes two very eminent men, who were perhaps the greatest scholars of their age, and after having mentioned the entire friendship between them, concludes, that "they had but one mind, one purse, one chamber, and one hat." The men of business were also infected with a sort of singularity little better than this. I have heard my father say, that a broad-brimmed hat, short hair, and an unfolded handkerchief, were in his time absolutely necessary to denote a notable man, and that he had known two or three, who aspired to the character of very notable, wear shoe-strings with great success.

To the honour of our present age it must be allowed, that some of our greatest geniuses for wit and business have almost entirely broke the neck of these absurdities.

Victor, after having dispatched the most important affairs of the commonwealth, has appeared at an assembly, where all the ladies have declared him the genteelest man in the company, and, in Atticus, though every way one of the greatest geniuses the age has produced, one sees nothing particular in his dress or carriage to denote his pretensions to wit and learning: so that at present a man may venture to cock up his hat, and wear a fashionable wig, without being taken for a rake or a fool.

The medium between a fop and a sloven is what a man of sense would endeavour to keep; yet I remember Mr Osborn advises his son to appear in his habit rather above than below his fortune; and tells him that he will find an handsome suit of clothes always procure some additional respect. I have indeed myself observed that my banker ever bows lowest to me when I wear my full-bottomed wig, and writes me "Mr" or "Esq.," according as he sees me dressed.

I shall conclude this paper with an adventure which I was myself an eye-witness of very lately.

I happened the other day to call in at a celebrated coffee-house near the Temple. I had not been there long when there came in an elderly man very meanly dressed, and sat down by me; he had a thread-bare loose coat on, which it was plain he wore to keep himself warm, and not to favour his under-suit, which seemed to have been at least its contemporary: his short wig and hat were both answerable to the rest of his apparel. He was no sooner seated than he called for a dish of tea, but as several gentlemen in the room wanted other things, the boys of the house did not think themselves at leisure to mind him. I could observe the old fellow was very uneasy at the affront, and at his being obliged to repeat his commands several times to no purpose, till at last one of the lads presented him with some stale tea in a broken dish, accompanied with a plate of brown sugar, which so raised his indignation, that after several obliging appellations of dog and rascal, he asked him aloud before the whole company, "Why he must be used with less respect than that fop there?" pointing to a well dressed young gentleman who was drinking tea at the opposite table. The boy of the house replied, with a good deal of pertness, that his master had two sorts of customers, and that the gentleman at the other table had given him many a six-pence for wiping his shoes. By this time the young Templar, who found his honour concerned in the dispute, and that the eyes of the whole coffee-house were upon him, had thrown aside a paper he had in his hand, and was coming towards us, while we at the table made what haste we could to get away from the impending quarrel, but were all of us surprised to see him as he approached nearer put on an air of deference and respect. To whom the old man said, "Hark you, sirrah, I'll pay off your extravagant bills once more; but will take effectual care for the future, that your prodigality shall not spirit up a parcel of rascals to insult your father."

Though I by no means approve either the impudence of the servants or the extravagance of the son, I cannot but think the old gentleman was in some measure justly served for walking in masquerade; I mean appearing in a dress so much beneath his quality and estate.

X

No. CLI. THURSDAY, AUGUST 23.

Maximas virtutes jacere omnes necesse est voluptate dominante.
TULL.

In the pursuit of pleasure, the greatest virtues lie neglected.

I KNOW no one character that gives reason a greater shock, at the same time that it presents a good ridiculous image to the imagination, than that of a man of wit and pleasure about the town. This description of a man of fashion, spoken by some with a mixture of scorn and ridicule, by others with great gravity as a laudable distinction, is in every body's mouth that spends any time in conversation. My friend Will Honeycomb has this expression very frequently, and I never could understand by the story which follows, upon his mention of such a one, but that his man of wit and pleasure was either a drunkard too old for wenching, or a young lewd fellow with some liveliness, who would converse with you, receive kind offices of you, and at the same time debauch your sister, or lie with your wife. According to his description, a man of wit when he could have wenches for crowns a-piece which he liked quite as well, would be so extravagant as to bribe servants, make false friendships, fight relations: I say, according to him, plain and simple vice was too little for a man of wit and pleasure, but he would leave an easy and accessible wickedness, to come at the same thing with only the addition of certain falsehood and possible murder. Will thinks the town grown very dull, in that we do not hear so much as we used to do of those coxcombs, whom (without observing it) he describes as the most infamous rogues in nature, with relation to friendship, love, or conversation.

When pleasure is made the chief pursuit of life, it will necessarily follow that such monsters as these will arise from a constant application to such blandishments as naturally root out the force of reason and reflection, and substitute in their place a general impatience of thought, and a constant pruriency of inordinate desire.

Pleasure, when it is a man's chief purpose, disappoints itself; and the constant application to it, palls the faculty of enjoying it, though it leaves the sense of our inability for that we wish, with a disrelish of every thing else. Thus the intermediate seasons of the man of pleasure, are more heavy than one would impose upon the vilest criminal. Take him when he is awaked too soon after a debauch, or disappointed in following a worthless woman without truth, and there is no man living whose being is such a weight or vexation as his is. He is an utter stranger to the pleasing reflections in the evening of a well-spent day, or the gladness of heart or quickness of spirit in the morning after profound sleep or indolent slumbers. He is not to be at ease any longer than he can keep reason and good sense without his curtains; otherwise he will be haunted with the reflection, that he could not believe such a one the woman that upon trial he found her. What has he got by his conquest, but to think meanly of her, for whom a day or two before he had the highest honour? and of himself for, perhaps, wronging the man whom of all men living he himself would least willingly have injured.

Pleasure seizes the whole man who addicts himself to it, and will not give him leisure for any good office in life which contradicts the gaiety of the present hour. You may indeed observe in people of pleasure a certain complacency and absence of all severity, which the habit of a loose unconcerned life gives them, but tell the man of pleasure your secret wants, cares, or sorrows, and you will find he has given up the delicacy of his passions to the cravings of his appetites. He little knows the perfect joy he loses, for the disappointing gratifications which he pursues. He looks at pleasure as she approaches, and comes to him with the recommendation of warm wishes, gay looks, and graceful motion, but he does not observe how she leaves his presence with disorder, impotence, down-cast shame, and conscious imperfection. She makes our youth inglorious, our age shameful.

Will Honeycomb gives us twenty intimations in an evening, of several hags whose bloom was given up to his arms; and would raise a value to himself for having had, as the phrase is, very good women. Will's good women are the comfort of his heart, and support him, I warrant, by the memory of past interviews with persons of their condition. No, there is not in the world an occasion wherein vice makes so fantastical a figure, as at the meeting of two old people who have been partners in unwarrantable pleasure. To tell a toothless old lady that she once had a good set, or a defunct wencher that he once was the admired thing of the town, are satires instead of applauses, but on the other side, consider the old age of those who have passed their days in labour, industry, and virtue, their decays make them but appear the more venerable, and the imperfections of their bodies are beheld as a misfortune to human society that their make is so little durable.

But to return more directly to my man of wit and pleasure. In all orders of men where this is the chief character, the person who wears it is a negligent friend, father, and husband, and entails poverty on his unhappy descendants. Mortgages, diseases, and settlements, are the legacies a man of wit and pleasure leaves to his family. All the poor rogues that make such lamentable speeches after every sessions at Tyburn, were, in their way, men of wit and pleasure, before they fell into the adventures which brought them thither.

Irresolution and procrastination in all a man's affairs are the natural effects of being addicted to pleasure: dishonour to the gentleman, and bankruptcy to the trader, are the portion of either, whose chief purpose of life is delight. The chief cause that this pursuit has been in all ages received with so much quarter from the soberer part of mankind, has been that some men of great talents have sacrificed themselves to it: the shining qualities of such people have given a beauty to whatever they were engaged in, and a mixture of wit has recommended madness. For let any man who knows what it is to have passed much time in a series of jollity, mirth, wit, or humorous entertainments, look back at what he was all that while a-doing, and he will find that he has been at one instant, sharp to some man he is sorry to have offended, impertinent to some one it was cruelty to treat with such freedom, ungracefully noisy at such a time, unskilfully open at such a time, unmercifully calumnious at such a time: and from the whole course of his applauded satisfactions, unable in the end to recollect any circumstance which can add to the enjoyment of his own mind alone, or which he would put his character upon with other men. Thus it is with those who are best made for becoming pleasures, but how monstrous is it in the generality of mankind who pretend this way, without genius or inclination towards it! The scene then is wild to an extravagance: this is as if fools should mimic madmen. Pleasure of this kind is the intemperate meals and loud jollities of the common rate of country gentlemen, whose practice and way of enjoyment is to put an end, as fast as they can, to that little particle of reason they have when they are sober: these men of wit and pleasure dispatch their senses as fast as possible, by drinking till they cannot taste, smoking till they cannot see, and roaring till they cannot hear. T.

No CLII. FRIDAY, AUGUST 24.

Οἴη περ φύλλων γενεὴ τοιήδε καὶ ἀνδρῶν. Hom.

Like leaves on trees the race of man is found
POPE.

THERE is no sort of people whose conversation is so pleasant as that of military men, who derive their courage and magnanimity from thought and reflection. The many adventures which attend their way of life makes their conversation so full of incidents, and gives them so frank an air in speaking of what they have been witnesses of, that no company can be more amiable than that of men of sense who are soldiers. There is a certain irregular way in their narrations or discourse, which has something more warm and pleasing than we meet with among men who are used to adjust and methodise their thoughts.

I was this evening walking in the fields with my friend Captain Sentry, and I could not, from the many relations which I drew him into of what passed when he was in the service, forbear expressing my wonder, that the fear of death, which we, the rest of mankind, arm ourselves against with so much contemplation, reason, and philosophy, should appear so little in camps, that common men march into open breaches, meet opposite battalions, not only without reluctance, but with alacrity. My friend answered what I said in the following manner: 'What you wonder at may very naturally be the subject of admiration to all who are not conversant in camps; but when a man has spent some time in that way of life, he observes a certain mechanic courage, which the ordinary race of men become masters of from acting always in a crowd. They see indeed many drop, but then they see many more alive, they observe themselves escape very narrowly, and they do not know why they should not again. Besides which general way of loose thinking, they usually spend the other part of their time in pleasures, upon which their minds are so entirely bent, that short labours or dangers are but a cheap purchase of jollity, triumph, victory, fresh quarters, new scenes, and uncommon adventures. Such are the thoughts of the executive part of an army, and indeed of the gross of mankind in general; but none of these men of mechanical courage have ever made any great figure in the profession of arms. Those who are formed for command, are such as have reasoned themselves, out of a consideration of greater good than length of days, into such a negligence of their being, as to make it their first position that it is one day to be resigned; and since it is, in the prosecution of worthy actions and service of mankind, they can put it to habitual hazard. The event of our designs, say they, as it relates to others is uncertain, but as it relates to ourselves it must be prosperous, while we are in the pursuit of our duty, and within the terms upon which Providence has insured our happiness whether we die or live. All that Nature has prescribed must be good, and as death is natural to us, it is absurdity to fear it. Fear loses its purpose when we are sure it cannot preserve us, and we should draw resolution to meet it from the impossibility to escape it. Without a resignation to the necessity of dying, there can be no capacity in man to attempt any thing that is glorious; but when they have once attained to that perfection, the pleasures of a life spent in martial adventures are as great as any of which the human mind is capable. The force of reason gives a certain beauty, mixed with the conscience of well-doing and thirst of glory, to all which before was terrible and ghastly to the imagination. Add to this, that the fellowship of danger, the common good of mankind, the general cause, and the manifest virtue you may observe in so many men, who made no figure till that day, are so many incentives to destroy the little consideration of their own persons. Such are the heroic part of soldiers who are qualified for leaders. As to the rest whom I before spoke of, I know not how it is, but they arrive at a certain habit of being void of thought, insomuch that on occasions of the most imminent danger they are still in the same indifference. Nay, I remember an instance of a gay Frenchman, who was led on in battle by a superior officer (whose conduct it was his custom to speak of always with contempt and raillery), and in the beginning of the action received a wound he was sensible was mortal. His reflection on this occasion was, " I wish I could live another hour, to see how this blundering coxcomb will get clear of this business."

' I remember two young fellows who rode in the same squadron of a troop of horse, who were ever together; they ate, they drank, they intrigued; in a word, all their passions and affections seemed to tend the same way, and they appeared serviceable to each other in them. We were in the dusk of the evening to march over a river, and the troop these gentlemen belonged to were to be transported in a ferry-boat as fast as they could. One of the friends was now in the boat, while the other was drawn up with others by the water-side waiting the return of the boat. A disorder happened in the passage by an unruly horse; and a gentleman who had the rein of his horse negligently under his arm, was forced into the water by his horse jumping over. The friend on the shore cried out,

"Who's that is drowned, trow!" He was immediately answered, "your friend Harry Thomson." He very gravely replied, "Ay, he had a mad horse." This short epitaph from such a familiar, without more words, gave me, at that time under twenty, a very moderate opinion of the friendship of companions. Thus is affection, and every other motive of life, in the generality rooted out by the present busy scene about them; they lament no man whose capacity can be supplied by another; and where men converse without delicacy, the next man you meet, will serve as well as he whom you have lived with half your life. To such the devastation of countries, the misery of inhabitants, the cries of the pillaged, and the silent sorrow of the great unfortunate, are ordinary objects; their minds are bent upon the little gratifications of their own senses and appetites, forgetful of compassion, insensible of glory, avoiding only shame; their whole heart is taken up with the trivial hope of meeting and being merry. These are the people who make up the gross of the soldiery: but the fine gentleman in that band of men is such a one as I have now in my eye, who is foremost in all danger to which he is ordered. His officers are his friends and companions, as they are men of honour and gentlemen: the private men his brethren, as they are of his species. He is beloved of all that behold him: they wish him in danger as he views their ranks, that they may have occasions to save him at their own hazard. Mutual love is the order of the files where he commands; every man afraid for himself and his neighbour, not lest their commander should punish them, but lest he should be offended. Such is his regiment who knows mankind, and feels their distresses so far as to prevent them. Just in distributing what is their due, he would think himself below their taylor to wear a snip of their clothes in lace upon his own; and below the most rapacious agent, should he enjoy a farthing above his own pay. Go on, brave man, immortal glory is thy fortune, and immortal happiness thy reward.' T

No. CLIII. SATURDAY, AUGUST 25.

Habet natura ut aliarum omnium rerum sic vivendi modum; senectus autem peractio ætatis est tanquam fabulæ. Cujus defatigationem fugere debemus præsertim adjuncta satietate. TULL.

Life, as well as all other things, has its bounds assigned by nature; and its conclusion, like the last act of a play, is old age; the fatigue of which we ought to shun, especially when our appetites are fully satisfied.

OF all the impertinent wishes which we hear expressed in conversation, there is not one more unworthy a gentleman, or a man of a liberal education, than that of wishing one's self younger. I have observed this wish is usually made upon sight of some object which gives the idea of a past action, that it is no dishonour to us that we cannot now repeat, or else on what was in itself shameful when we performed it. It is a certain sign of a foolish or a dissolute mind, if we want our youth again only for the strength of bones and sinews which we once were masters of. It is (as my author has it) as absurd in an old man to wish for the strength of a youth, as it would be in a young man to wish for the strength of a bull or a horse. These wishes are both equally out of nature, which should direct in all things that are not contradictory to justice, law, and reason. But though every old man has been young, and every young one hopes to be old, there seems to be a most unnatural misunderstanding between those two stages of life. This unhappy want of commerce arises from the insolent arrogance or exaltation in youth, and the irrational despondency or self-pity in age. A young man whose passion and ambition is to be good and wise, and an old one who has no inclination to be lewd or debauched, are quite unconcerned in this speculation; but the cocking young fellow who treads upon the toes of his elders, and the old fool who envies the saucy pride he sees him in, are the objects of our present contempt and derision. Contempt and derision are harsh words, but in what manner can one give advice to a youth in the pursuit and possession of sensual pleasures, or afford pity to an old man in the impotence and desire of enjoying them? When young men in public places betray in their deportment an abandoned resignation to their appetites, they give to sober minds a prospect of a despicable age, which, if not interrupted by death in the midst of their follies, must certainly come. When an old man bewails the loss of such gratifications which are passed, he discovers a monstrous inclination to that which it is not in the course of Providence to recal. The state of an old man, who is dissatisfied merely for his being such, is the most out of all measures of reason and good sense of any being we have any account of, from the highest angel to the lowest worm. How miserable is the contemplation, to consider a libidinous old man (while all created things, besides himself and devils, are following the order of Providence) fretting at the course of things, and being almost the sole malecontent in the creation! But let us a little reflect upon what he has lost by the number of years: the passions which he had in youth are not to be obeyed as they were then, but reason is more powerful now without the disturbance of them. An old gentleman the other day, in discourse with a friend of his (reflecting upon some adventures they had in youth together,) cried out, 'Oh Jack, these were happy days!' 'that is true,' replied his friend, 'but methinks we go about our business more quietly than we did then.' One would think it should be no small satisfaction to have gone so far in our journey, that the heat of the day is over with us. When life itself is a fever, as it is in licentious youth, the pleasures of it are no other than the dreams of a man in that distemper; and it is as absurd to wish the return of that season of life, as for a man in health to be sorry for the loss of gilded palaces, fairy walks, and flowery pastures, with which he remembers he was entertained in the troubled slumbers of a fit of sickness.

As to all the rational and worthy pleasures of our being, the conscience of a good fame, the contemplation of another life, the respect and commerce of honest men, our capacities for such enjoyments are enlarged by years. While health endures, the latter part of life, in the eye of reason, is certainly the more eligible. The memory of a well-spent youth gives a peaceable, unmixed, and elegant pleasure to the mind; and to such who are so unfortunate as not to be able to look back on youth with satisfaction, they may give themselves no little consolation that they are under no temptation to repeat their follies, and that they at present despise them. It was prettily said, ' He that would be long an old man, must begin early to be one.' It is too late to resign a thing after a man is robbed of it, therefore it is necessary, that before the arrival of age, we bid adieu to the pursuits of youth, otherwise sensual habits will live in our imaginations when our limbs cannot be subservient to them. The poor fellow who lost his arm last siege, will tell you, he feels the fingers that were buried in Flanders ach every cold morning at Chelsea.

The fond humour of appearing in the gay and fashionable world, and being applauded for trivial excellencies, is what makes youth have age in contempt, and makes age resign with so ill a grace the qualifications of youth: but this in both sexes is inverting all things, and turning the natural course of our minds, which should build their approbations and dislikes upon what nature and reason dictate into chimera and confusion.

Age in a virtuous person, of either sex, carries in it an authority which makes it preferable to all the pleasures of youth. If to be saluted, attended, and consulted with deference, are instances of pleasure, they are such as never fail a virtuous old age. In the enumeration of the imperfections and advantages of the younger and later years of man, they are so near in their condition, that, methinks, it should be incredible we see so little commerce of kindness between them. If we consider youth and age with Tully, regarding the affinity to death, youth has many more chances to be near it than age. What youth can say more than an old man, 'He shall live till night?' Youth catches distempers more easily, its sickness is more violent, and its recovery more doubtful. The youth indeed hopes for many more days, so cannot the old man. The youth's hopes are ill-grounded, for what is more foolish than to place any confidence upon an uncertainty? But the old man has not room so much as to hope; he is still happier than the youth, he has already enjoyed what the other does but hope for: one wishes to live long, the other has lived long. But, alas! is there any thing in human life, the duration of which can be called long? there is nothing which must end to be valued for its continuance. If hours, days, months, and years, pass away, it is no matter what hour, what day, what month, or what year we die. The applause of a good actor is due to him at whatever scene of the play he makes his exit. It is thus in the life of a man of sense, a short life is sufficient to manifest himself a man of honour and virtue: when he ceases to be such, he has lived too long, and while he is such, it is of no consequence to him how long he shall be so, provided he is so to his life's end.

T.

No. CLIV. MONDAY, AUGUST 27.

Nemo repentè fuit turpissimus....... Juv.

No man e'er reach'd the heights of vice at first. Tate.

'Mr. Spectator,

'You are frequent in the mention of matters which concern the feminine world, and take upon you to be very severe against men upon all those occasions: but all this while I am afraid you have been very little conversant with women, or you would know the generality of them are not so angry as you imagine at the general vices among us. I am apt to believe, begging your pardon, that you are still what I myself was once, a queer modest fellow; and therefore, for your information, shall give you a short account of myself, and the reasons why I was forced to wench, drink, play, and do every thing which are necessary to the character of a man of wit and pleasure, to be well with the ladies.

'You are to know then that I was bred a gentleman, and had the finishing part of my education under a man of great probity, wit, and learning, in one of our universities I will not deny but this made my behaviour and mien bear in it a figure of thought rather than action; and a man of a quite contrary character, who never thought in his life, rallied me one day upon it, and said, he believed I was still a virgin. There was a young lady of virtue present, and I was not displeased to favour the insinuation; but it had a quite contrary effect from what I expected. I was ever after treated with great coldness both by that lady and all the rest of my acquaintance. In a very little time I never came into a room but I could hear a whisper, 'here comes the maid,'

A girl of humour would on some occasion say, 'why, how do you know more than any of us?' An expression of that kind was generally followed by a loud laugh; in a word, for no other fault in the world than that they really thought me as innocent as themselves, I became of no consequence among them, and was received always upon the foot of a jest. This made so strong an impression upon me, that I resolved to be as agreeable as the best of the men who laughed at me; but I observed it was nonsense for me to be impudent at first among those who knew me: my character for modesty was so notorious wherever I had hitherto appeared, that I resolved to show my new face in new quarters of the world. My first step I chose with judgment; for I went to Astrop, and came down among a crowd of academics at one dash, the impudentest fellow they had ever seen in their lives. Flushed with this success, I made love and was happy. Upon this conquest, I thought it would be unlike a gentleman to stay long with my mistress, and crossed the country to Bury. I could give you a very good account of myself at that place also. At these two ended my first summer of gallantry. The winter following you would wonder at it, but I relapsed into modesty upon coming among people of figure in London, yet not so much but that the ladies who had formerly laughed at me, said, " Bless us, how wonderfully that gentleman is improved?" Some familiarities about the playhouses towards the end of the ensuing winter, made me conceive new hopes of adventures; and instead of returning the next summer to Astrop or Bury, I thought myself qualified to go to Epsom, and followed a young woman, whose relations were jealous of my place in her favour, to Scarborough. I carried my point, and in my third year aspired to go to Tunbridge, and in the autumn of the same year made my appearance at Bath. I was now got into the way of talk proper for ladies, and was run into a vast acquaintance among them, which I always improved to the best advantage. In all this course of time, and some years following, I found a sober modest man was always looked upon by both sexes as a precise unfashionable fellow of no life or spirit. It was ordinary for a man who had been drunk in good company, or passed a night with a wench, to speak of it next day before women for whom he had the greatest respect. He was reproved, perhaps, with a blow of the fan, or an 'Oh fy!' but the angry lady still preserved an apparent approbation in her countenance. He was called a strange wicked fellow, a sad wretch: he shrugs his shoulders, swears, receives another blow, swears again he did not know he swore, and all was well. You might often see men game in the presence of women, and throw at once for more than they were worth, to recommend themselves as men of spirit. I found, by long experience, that the loosest principles, and most abandoned behaviour, carried all before them in pretensions to women of fortune. The encouragement given to people of this stamp, made me soon throw off the remaining impressions of a sober education. In the above-mentioned places, as well as in town, I always kept company with those who lived most at large; and in due process of time, I was a pretty rake among the men, and a very pretty fellow among the women. I must confess, I had some melancholy hours upon the account of the narrowness of my fortune; but my conscience at the same time gave me the comfort that I had qualified myself for marrying a fortune.

'When I had lived in this manner for some time, and became thus accomplished, I was now in the twenty-seventh year of my age, and about the forty-seventh of my constitution, my health and estate wasting very fast, when I happened to fall into the company of a very pretty young lady in her own disposal. I entertained the company, as we men of gallantry generally do, with the many haps and disasters, watchings under windows, escapes from jealous husbands, and several other perils. The young thing was wonderfully charmed with one that knew the world so well, and talked so fine; with Desdemona, all her lover said affected her, " it was strange, it was wondrous strange." In a word, I saw the impression I had made upon her, and, with a very little application, the pretty thing has married me. There is so much charm in her innocence and beauty, that I do now as much detest the course I have been in for many years, as I ever did before I entered into it.

'What I intend, Mr. Spectator, by writing all this to you, is, that you would, before you go any further with your panegyrics on the fair sex, give them some lectures upon their silly approbations. It is, that I am weary of vice, and that it was not my natural way, that I am now so far recovered as not to bring this believing dear creature to contempt and poverty for her generosity to me. At the same time tell the youth of good education of our sex, that they take too little care of improving themselves in little things: a good air at entering into a room, a proper audacity in expressing himself with gaiety and gracefulness, would make a young gentleman of virtue and sense capable of discountenancing the shallow impudent rogues that shine among the women.

'Mr. Spectatator, I do not doubt but you are a very sagacious person; but you are so great with Tully of late, that I fear you will contemn these things as matters of no consequence: but believe me, Sir, they are of the highest importance to human life: and if you can do any thing towards opening fair eyes, you will lay an obligation upon all your contemporaries who are fathers, husbands, or brothers to females.

'Your most affectionate humble servant,
'SIMON HONEYCOMB.'

T

No. CLV. TUESDAY, AUGUST 28.

... Hæ nugæ feria ducunt
In mala. HOR.

These things, which now seem frivolous and slight,
Will prove of serious consequence. ROSCOMMON

I HAVE more than once taken notice of an indecent licence taken in discourse, wherein the conversation on one part is involuntary, and the effect of some necessary circumstance. This happens in travelling together in the same hired coach, sitting near each other in any public assembly, or the like. I have, upon making observations of this sort, received innumerable messages from that part of the fair sex, whose lot in life it is to be of any trade or public way of life. They are all to a woman urgent with me to lay before the world the unhappy circumstances they are under, from the unreasonable liberty which is taken in their presence, to talk on what subject it is thought fit by every coxcomb who wants understanding or breeding. One or two of these complaints I shall set down.

'MR SPECTATOR,

'I KEEP a coffee-house, and am one of those whom you have thought fit to mention as an Idol some time ago. I suffered a good deal of raillery upon that occasion, but shall heartily forgive you, who are the cause of it, if you will do me justice in another point. What I ask of you is, to acquaint my customers, who are otherwise very good ones, that I am unavoidably hasped in my bar, and cannot help hearing the improper discourses they are pleased to entertain me with. They strive who shall say the most immodest things in my hearing. At the same time half a dozen of them loll at the bar, staring just in my face, ready to interpret my looks and gestures according to their own imaginations. In this passive condition I know not where to cast my eyes, place my hands, or what to employ myself in; but this confusion is to be a jest, and I hear them say in the end, with an insipid air of mirth and subtlety, "Let her alone, she knows as well as we, for all she looks so." Good Mr. Spectator, persuade gentlemen that it is out of all decency: say, it is possible a woman may be modest, and yet keep a public-house. Be pleased to argue, that in truth the affront is the more unpardonable, because I am obliged to suffer it, and cannot fly from it. I do assure you, Sir, the cheerfulness of life which would arise from the honest gain I have, is utterly lost to me, from the endless, flat, impertinent pleasantries which I hear from morning to night. In a word, it is too much for me to bear; and I desire you to acquaint them, that I will keep pen and ink at the bar and write down all they say to me, and send it to you for the press. It is possible when they see how empty what they speak, without the advantage of an impudent countenance and gesture, will appear, they may come to some sense of themselves, and the insults they are guilty of towards me. I am, Sir,

'Your most humble servant,

'THE IDOL.'

This representation is so just, that it is hard to speak of it without an indignation which perhaps would appear too elevated to such as can be guilty of this inhuman treatment, where they see they affront a modest, plain, and ingenuous behaviour. This correspondent is not the only sufferer in this kind, for I have long letters both from the Royal and New Exchange on the same subject. They tell me, that a young fop cannot buy a pair of gloves, but he is at the same time straining for some ingenious ribaldry to say to the young woman who helps them on. It is no small addition to the calamity that the rogues buy as hard as the plainest and modestest customers they have: besides which they loll upon their counters half an hour longer than they need, to drive away other customers, who are to share their impertinencies with the milliner, or go to another shop. Letters from 'Change-Alley are full of the same evil; and the girls tell me, except I can chace some eminent merchants from their shops they shall in a short time fail. It is very unaccountable, that men can have so little deference to all mankind who pass by them, as to bear being seen toying by two's and three's at a time, with no other purpose but to appear gay enough to keep up a light conversation of commonplace jests, to the injury of her whose credit is certainly hurt by it, though their own may be strong enough to bear it. When we come to have exact accounts of these conversations, it is not to be doubted but that their discourses will raise the usual style of buying and selling: instead of the plain downright lying, and asking and bidding so unequally to what they will really give and take, we may hope to have from these fine folks an exchange of compliments. There must certainly be a great deal of pleasant difference between the commerce of lovers, and that of all other dealers, who are, in a kind, adversaries. A sealed bond, or a bank note, would be a pretty gallantry to convey unseen into the hands of one whom a director is charmed with, otherwise the city-loiterers are still more unreasonable than those at the other end of the town. At the New-Exchange they are eloquent for want of cash, but in the city they ought with cash to supply their want of eloquence.

If one might be serious on this prevailing folly, one might observe, that it is a melancholy thing when the world is mercenary even to the buying and selling our very persons, that young women, though they have never so great attractions from nature, are never the nearer being happily disposed of in marriage: I say, it is very hard under this necessity, it shall not be possible for them to go into a way of trade for their maintenance, but their very excellencies and personal perfections shall be a disadvantage to them, and subject them to be treated as if they stood there to sell their persons to prostitution. There cannot be a more melancholy circumstance to one who has made any observation in the world, than one of those erring creatures exposed to bankruptcy. When that happens, none of these toying fools will do any more than any other man they meet to preserve her from infamy, insult, and distemper. A woman is naturally more helpless than the other sex; and a man of honour and sense should have this in his view in all manner of commerce with her. Were this well weighed, inconsideration, ribaldry, and nonsense, would not be more natural to entertain women with than men; and it would be as much impertinence to go into a shop of one of these young women without buying, as into that of any other trader. I shall end this speculation with a letter I have received from a pretty milliner in the city.

' Mr. Spectator,

' I have read your account of beauties, and was not a little surprised to find no character of myself in it. I do assure you I have little else to do but to give audience as I am such. Here are merchants of no small consideration, who call in as certainly as they go to 'Change, to say something of my roguish eye: and here is one who makes me once or twice a week tumble over all my goods, and then owns it was only a gallantry to see me act with these pretty hands; then lays out three-pence in a little ribband for his wrist-bands, and thinks he is a man of great vivacity. There is an ugly thing not far off me, whose shop is frequented only by people of business, that is all day long as busy as possible. Must I that am a beauty be treated with for nothing but my beauty? Be pleased to assign rates to my kind glances, or make all pay who come to see me, or I shall be undone by my admirers for want of customers. Albacinda, Eudosia, and all the rest, would be used just as we are, if they were in our condition; therefore pray consider the distress of us the lower order of beauties, and I shall be

T   'Your obliged humble servant.'

No. CLVI. WEDNESDAY, AUGUST 29.

...... Sed tu simul obligâsti
Perfidum votis caput, enitescis
Pulchrior multo ....   HOR.

..... But thou,
Since perjur'd, dost more charming grow.   DUKE.

I DO not think any thing could make a pleasanter entertainment, than the history of the reigning favourites among the women from time to time about this town. In such an account we ought to have a faithful confession of each lady for what she liked such and such a man, and he ought to tell us by what particular action or dress he believed he should be most successful. As for my part I have always made as easy a judgment when a man dresses for the ladies, as when he is equipped for hunting or coursing. The woman's man is a person in his air and behaviour quite different from the rest of our species: his garb is more loose and negligent, his manner more soft and indolent, that is to say, in both these cases there is an apparent endeavour to appear unconcerned and careless. In catching birds the fowlers have a method of imitating their voices to bring them to the snare; and your women's men have always a similitude of the creature they hope to betray in their own conversation. A woman's man is very knowing in all that passes from one family to another, has little pretty officiousnesses, is not at a loss what is good for a cold, and it is not amiss if he has a bottle of spirits in his pocket in case of any sudden indisposition.

Curiosity having been my prevailing passion, and indeed, the sole entertainment of my life, I have sometimes made it my business to examine the course of intrigues, as well as the manners and accomplishments, of such as have been most successful that way. In all my observation, I never knew a man of good understanding a general favourite; some singularity in his behaviour, some whim in his way of life, and what would have made him ridiculous among the men, has recommended him to the other sex. I should be very sorry to offend a people so fortunate as these of whom I am speaking; but let any one look over the old beaux, and he will find the man of success was remarkable for quarrelling impertinently for their sakes, for dressing unlike the rest of the world, or passing his days in an insipid assiduity about the fair sex, to gain the figure he made amongst them. Add to this, that he must have the reputation of being well with other women, to please any one woman of gallantry; for you are to know that there is a mighty ambition among the light part of the sex to gain slaves from the dominion of others. My friend Will Honeycomb says it was a common bite with him, to lay suspicions that he was favoured by a lady's enemy, that is, some rival beauty, to be well with herself. A little spite is natural to a great beauty: and it is ordinary to snap up a disagreeable fellow lest another should have him. That impudent toad Bareface fares well among all the ladies he converses with, for no other reason in the world but that he has the skill to keep them from explanation with one another. Did they know there is not one who likes him in her heart, each would declare her scorn of him the next moment; but he is well received by them because it is the fashion, and opposition to each other brings them insensibly into an imitation of each other. What adds to him the greatest grace is, that the pleasant thief, as they call him, is the most inconstant creature living, has a wonderful deal of wit and humour, and never wants something to say, besides all which, he has a most spiteful dangerous tongue if you should provoke him.

To make a woman's man, he must not be a man of sense, or a fool, the business is to entertain: and it is much better to have a faculty of arguing than a capacity of judging right. But the pleasantest of all the women's equipage are your regular visitants, these are volunteers in their service, without hopes of pay or preferment, it is enough that they can lead out from a public place, that they are admitted on a public day, and can be allowed to pass away part of that heavy load, their time, in the company of the fair. But commend me above all others to those who are known for your ruiners of ladies, these are the choicest spirits which our age produces. We have several of these irresistible gentlemen among us when the company is in town. These fellows are accomplished with the knowledge of the ordinary occurrences about court and town, have that sort of good breeding which is exclusive of all morality, and consists only in being publicly decent, privately dissolute.

It is wonderful how far a fond opinion of herself can carry a woman, to make her have the least regard to a professed known woman's man: but as scarce one of all the women who are in the tour of gallantries ever hears any thing of what is the common sense of sober minds, but are entertained with a continual round of flatteries, they cannot be mistresses of themselves enough to make arguments for their own conduct from the behaviour of these men to others. It is so far otherwise, that a general fame for falsehood in this kind, is a recommendation, and the coxcomb, loaded with the favours of many others, is received like a victor that disdains his trophies, to be a victim to the present charmer

If you see a man more full of gesture than ordinary in a public assembly, if loud upon no occasion, if negligent of the company round him, and yet laying wait for destroying by that negligence, you may take it for granted that he has ruined many a fair one. The woman's man expresses himself wholly in that motion which we call strutting, an elevated chest, a pinched hat, a measurable step, and a sly surveying eye, are the marks of him. Now and then you see a gentleman with all these accomplishments; but alas, any one of them is enough to undo thousands. When a gentleman with such perfections adds to it suitable learning, there should be public warning of his residence in town, that we may remove our wives and daughters. It happens sometimes that such a fine man has read all the miscellany poems, a few of our comedies, and has the translation of Ovid's epistles by heart ' Oh if it were possible that such a one could be as true as he is charming, but that is too much, the women will share such a dear false man: ' A little gallantry to hear him talk, one would indulge one's self in, let him reckon the sticks of one's fan, say something of the cupids in it, and then call one so many soft names which a man of his learning has at his fingers' ends. There sure is some excuse for frailty, when attacked by such force against a weak woman.' Such is the soliloquy of many a lady one might name, at the sight of one of those who makes it no iniquity to go on from day to day in the sin of woman-slaughter.

It is certain that people are got into a way of affectation, with a manner of overlooking the most solid virtues, and admiring the most trivial excellencies. The woman is so far from expecting to be contemned for being a very injudicious silly animal, that while she can preserve her features and her mien, she knows she is still the object of desire; and there is a sort of secret ambition, from reading frivolous books, and keeping as frivolous company, each side to be amiable in imperfection, and arrive at the characters of the dear deceiver and the perjured fair. T

No. CLVII. THURSDAY, AUGUST 30.

  Genius, natale comes qui temperat astrum,
Naturæ Deus humanæ, mortalis in unumquodque caput. ...   Hor.

IMITATED
  .... That directing power,
Who forms the genius in the natal hour,
That God of nature, who, within us still,
Inclines our action, not constrains our will
          Pope.

I am very much at a loss to express by any word that occurs to me in our language, that which is understood by indoles in Latin. The natural disposition to any particular art, science, profession, or trade, is very much to be consulted in the care of youth, and studied by men for their own conduct when they form to themselves any scheme of life. It is wonderfully hard indeed for a man to judge of his own capacity impartially, that may look great to me which may appear little to another, and I may be carried by fondness towards myself so far as to attempt things too high for my talents and accomplishments. but it is not, methinks, so very difficult a matter to make a judgment of the abilities of others, especially of those who are in their infancy. My common-place book directs me on this occasion to mention the dawning of greatness in Alexander, who being asked in his youth to contend for a prize in the Olympic games, answered he would, if he had kings to run against him Cassius, who was one of the conspirators against Cæsar, gave as great a proof of his temper, when in his childhood he struck a playfellow, the son of Sylla, for saying his father was master of the Roman people. Scipio is reported to have answered (when some flatterers at supper were asking him what the Romans should do for a general after his death,) Take Marius. Marius was then a very boy, and had given no instances of his valour but it was visible to Scipio, from the manners of the youth, that he had a soul formed for the attempt and execution of great undertakings. I must confess I have very often with much sorrow bewailed the misfortune of the children of Great Britain, when I consider the ignorance and undiscerning of the generality of school-masters. The boasted liberty we talk of, is but a mean reward for the long servitude, the many heart-aches and terrors, to which our childhood is exposed in going through a grammar-school: many of these stupid tyrants exercise their cruelty without any manner of distinction of the capacities of children, or the intention of parents in their behalf. There are many excellent tempers which are worthy to be nourished and cultivated with all possible diligence and care, that were never designed to be acquainted with Aristotle, Tully, or Virgil; and there are as many who have capacities for understanding every word those great persons have writ, and yet were not born to have any relish of their writings.

For want of this common and obvious discerning in those who have the care of youth, we have so many hundred unaccountable creatures every age whipped up into great scholars, that are for ever near a right understanding, and will never arrive at it. These are the scandal of letters, and these are generally the men who are to teach others' The sense of shame and honour is enough to keep the world itself in order without corporal punishment, much more to train the minds of uncorrupted and innocent children. It happens, I doubt not, more than once in a year, that a lad is chastised for a blockhead, when it is a good apprehension that makes him incapable of knowing what his teacher means. A brisk imagination very often may suggest an error, which a lad could not have fallen into, if he had been as heavy in conjecturing as his master in explaining: but there is no mercy even towards a wrong interpretation of his meaning; the sufferings of the scholar's body are to rectify the mistakes of his mind.

I am confident that no boy who will not be allured to letters without blows, will ever be brought to any thing with them. A great or good mind must necessarily be the worse for such indignities; and it is a sad change to lose of its virtue for the improvement of its knowledge. No one who has gone through what they call a great school, but must remember to have seen children of excellent and ingenious natures (as has afterwards appeared in their manhood); I say no man has passed through this way of education, but must have seen an ingenious creature expiring with shame, with pale looks, beseeching sorrow, and silent tears, throw up its honest eyes, and kneel on its tender knees to an inexorable blockhead, to be forgiven the false quantity of a word in making a Latin verse: the child is punished, and the next day he commits a like crime, and so a third with the same consequence. I would fain ask any reasonable man, whether this lad, in the simplicity of his native innocence, full of shame, and capable of any impression from that grace of soul, was not fitter for any purpose in this life, than after that spark of virtue is extinguished in him, though he is able to write twenty verses in an evening?

Seneca says, after his exalted way of talking, 'As the immortal gods never learnt any virtue, though they are endued with all that is good; so there are some men who have so natural a propensity to what they should follow, that they learn it almost as soon as they hear it.' Plants and vegetables are cultivated into the production of finer fruits than they would yield without that care; and yet we cannot entertain hopes of producing a tender conscious spirit into acts of virtue, without the same methods as are used to cut timber, or give new shape to a piece of stone.

It is wholly to this dreadful practice that we may attribute a certain hardiness and ferocity which some men, though liberally educated, carry about them in all their behaviour. To be bred like a gentleman, and punished like a malefactor, must, as we see it does, produce that illiberal sauciness which we see sometimes in men of letters.

The Spartan boy who suffered the fox (which he had stolen and hid under his coat) to eat into his bowels, I dare say, had not half the wit or petulance which we learn at great schools among us: but the glorious sense of honour, or rather fear of shame, which he demonstrated in that action, was worth all the learning in the world without it.

It is, methinks, a very melancholy consideration, that a little negligence will spoil us, but great industry is necessary to improve us; the most excellent natures are soon depreciated, but evil tempers are long before they are exalted into good habits. To help this by punishments, is the same thing as killing a man to cure him of a distemper: when he comes to suffer punishment in that one circumstance he is brought below the existence of a rational creature, and is in the state of a brute that moves only by the admonition of stripes. But since this custom of educating by the lash is suffered by the gentry of Great Britain, I would prevail only, that honest heavy lads may be dismissed from slavery sooner than they are at present, and not whipped on to their fourteenth or fifteenth year, whether they expect any progress from them or not. Let the child's capacity be forthwith examined, and he sent to some mechanic way of life, without respect to his birth, if nature designed him for nothing higher; let him go before he has innocently suffered, and is debased into a dereliction of mind for being what it is no guilt to be, a plain man. I would not here be supposed to have said, that our learned men of either robe who have been whipt at school, are not still men of noble and liberal minds, but I am sure they had been much more so than they are, had they never suffered that infamy.

But though there is so little care, as I have observed, taken, or observation made, of the natural strain of men, it is no small comfort to me, as a Spectator, that there is any right value set upon the bona indoles of other animals; as appears by the following advertisement handed about the county of Lincoln, and subscribed by Enos Thomas, a person whom I have not the honour to know, but suppose to be profoundly learned in horse-flesh.

'A chesnut horse called Cæsar, bred by James Darcy, Esq; at Sedbury, near Richmond in the county of York; his grandam was his old royal mare, and got by Blunderbuss, which was got by Hemsly-Turk, and he got by Mr. Courant's Arabian, which got Mr. Minshul's Jew's-Trump. Mr Cæsar sold him to a nobleman (coming five years old, when he had but one sweat) for three hundred guineas. A guinea a leap and trial, and a shilling the man.

T

'ENOS THOMAS.'

No. CLVIII. FRIDAY, AUGUST 31.

. . . Nos hæc novimus esse nihil   MART.

We know these things to be mere trifles.

OUT of a firm regard to impartiality, I print these letters, let them make for me or not.

'MR SPECTATOR,

'I HAVE observed through the whole course of your rhapsodies (as you once very well called them), you are very industrious to overthrow all that many your superiors who have gone before you have made their rule of writing. I am now between fifty and sixty, and had the honour to be well with the first men of taste and gallantry in the joyous reign of Charles the Second; we then had, I humbly presume, as good understandings among us as any now can pretend to. As for yourself, Mr Spectator, you seem with the utmost arrogance to undermine the very fundamentals upon which we conducted ourselves. It is monstrous to set up for a man of wit, and yet deny that honour in a woman is any thing else but peevishness, that inclination is the best rule of life, or virtue and vice any thing else but health and disease. We had no more to do but to put a lady in good humour, and all we could wish followed in course. Then again, your Tully, and your discourses of another life, are the very bane of mirth and good humour. Pr'ythee do not value thyself on thy reason at that exorbitant rate, and the dignity of human nature: take my word for it, a setting dog has as good reason as any man in England. Had you (as by your diurnals one would think you do) set up for being in vogue in town, you should have fallen in with the bent of passion and appetite, your songs had then been in every pretty mouth in England, and your little distiches had been the maxims of the fair and the witty to walk by: but alas, Sir, what can you hope for, from entertaining people with what must needs make them like themselves, worse than they did before they read you? Had you made it your business to describe Corinna charming, though inconstant, to find something in human nature itself to make Zoilus excuse himself for being fond of her; and to make every man in good commerce with his own reflections, you had done something worthy our applause; but, indeed, Sir, we shall not commend you for disapproving us. I have a great deal more to say to you, but I shall sum it up in this one remark, In short, Sir, you do not write like a gentleman.

'I am, Sir,
'Your most humble servant'

'Mr. Spectator,

'The other day we were several of us at a tea-table, and according to custom and your own advice had the Spectator read among us: it was that paper wherein you are pleased to treat with great freedom that character which you call a woman's man. We gave up all the kinds you have mentioned, except those who, you say, are our constant visitants. I was upon the occasion commissioned by the company to write to you and tell you, that we shall not part with the men we have at present, till the men of sense think fit to relieve them, and give us their company in their stead. You cannot imagine but that we love to hear reason and good sense, better than the ribaldry we are at present entertained with, but we must have company, and among us very inconsiderable is better than none at all. We are made for the cements of society, and came into the world to create relations among mankind; and solitude is an unnatural being to us. If the men of good understanding would forget a little of their severity, they would find their account in it, and their wisdom would have a pleasure in it, to which they are now strangers. It is natural among us, when men have a true relish of our company and our value, to say every thing with a better grace; and there is, without designing it, something ornamental in what men utter before women, which is lost or neglected in conversations of men only. Give me leave to tell you, Sir, it would do you no great harm if you yourself came a little more into our company; it would certainly cure you of a certain positive and determining manner in which you talk sometimes. In hopes of your amendment,

'I am, Sir,
' Your gentle reader.'

' Mr. Spectator,

' Your professed regard to the fair sex may perhaps make them value your admonitions, when they will not those of other men. I desire, you, Sir, to repeat some lectures upon subjects which you have now and then in a cursory manner only just touched. I would have a Spectator wholly writ upon good-breeding; and after you have asserted that time and place are to be very much considered in all our actions, it will be proper to dwell upon behaviour at church. On Sunday last a grave and reverend man preached at our church: there was something particular in his accent, but without any manner of affectation. This particularity a set of giglers thought the most necessary thing to be taken notice of in his whole discourse, and made it an occasion of mirth during the whole time of sermon. You should see one of them ready to burst behind a fan; another pointing to a companion in another seat;

and a thrid with an arch composure, as if she would, if possible, stifle her laughter. There were many gentlemen who looked at them steadfastly; but this they took for ogling and admiring them: there was one of the merry ones in particular, that found out but just then that she had but five fingers, for she fell a reckoning the pretty pieces of ivory over and over again, to find herself employment and not laugh out. Would it not be expedient, Mr. Spectator, that the churchwarden should hold up his wand on these occasions, and keep the decency of the place, as a magistrate does the peace in a tumult elsewhere?'

' MR. SPECTATOR,

' I AM a woman's man, and read with a very fine lady your paper, wherein you fall upon us whom you envy. What do you think I did? you must know she was dressing, I read the Spectator to her, and she laughed at the places where she thought I was touched. I threw away your moral, and taking up her girdle cried out,

"Give me but what this ribband bound,
Take all the rest the sun goes round.*"

' She smiled, Sir, and said you were a pedant. So say of me what you please, read Seneca, and quote him against me if you think fit.
' I am, Sir,
' Your humble servant.'

* Waller's verses on a Lady's girdle.

No CLIX. SATURDAY, SEPTEMBER 1.

> ———Omnem, quæ nunc obducta tuenti
> Mortales habetat visus tibi, et humida circum
> Caligat, nubem eripiam——— VIRG.

> The cloud, which, intercepting the clear light,
> Hangs o'er the eyes, and blunts thy mortal sight,
> I will remove.

'WHEN I was at Grand Cairo, I picked up several oriental manuscripts, which I have still by me. Among others I met with one intitled, 'The Visions of Mirza,' which I have read over with great pleasure. I intend to give it to the public when I have no other entertainment for them, and shall begin with the first vision, which I have translated word for word as follows:

'On the fifth day of the moon, which, according to the custom of my forefathers, I always keep holy, after having washed myself, and offered up my morning devotions, I ascended the high hills of Bagdat, in order to pass the rest of the day in meditation and prayer. As I was here airing myself on the tops of the mountains, I fell into a profound contemplation on the vanity of human life, and passing from one thought to another, Surely (said I) man is but a shadow, and life a dream. Whilst I was thus musing, I cast my eyes towards the summit of a rock that was not far from me, where I discovered one in the habit of a shepherd, with a little musical instrument in his hand. As I looked upon him he applied it to his lips, and began to play upon it. The sound of it was exceeding sweet, and wrought into a variety of tunes that were inexpressibly melodious, and altogether different from any thing that I had ever heard: they put me in mind of those heavenly airs that are played to the departed souls of good men upon their first arrival in paradise, to wear out the impressions of their last agonies, and qualify them for the pleasures of that happy place. My heart melted away in secret raptures.

'I had been often told that the rock before me was the haunt of a genius; and that several had been entertained with music, who passed by it, but never heard that the musician had before made himself visible. When he had raised my thoughts by those transporting airs which he played, to taste the pleasures of his conversation, as I looked upon him like one astonished, he beckoned to me, and by the waving of his hand directed me to approach the place where he sat. I drew near with that reverence which is due to a superior nature; and as my heart was entirely subdued by the captivating strains I had heard, I fell down at his feet and wept. The genius smiled upon me with a look of compassion and affability that familiarized him to my imagination, and at once dispelled all the fears and apprehensions with which I approached him. He lifted me from the ground; and taking me by the hand, Mirza, said he, I have heard thee in thy soliloquies, follow me.

'He then led me to the highest pinnacle of the rock, and placing me on the top of it, Cast thy eyes eastward, said he, and tell me what thou seest. I see, said I, a huge valley, and a prodigious tide of water rolling through it. The valley that thou seest, said he, is the vale of misery, and the tide of water that thou seest, is part of the great tide of eternity. What is the reason, said I, that the tide I see rises out of a thick mist at one end, and again loses itself in a thick mist at the other? What thou seest, said he, is that portion of eternity which is called time, measured out by the sun, and reaching from the beginning of the world to its consummation. Examine now, said he, this sea, that is thus bounded with darkness at both ends, and tell me what thou discoverest in it. I see a bridge, said I, standing in the midst of the tide. The bridge thou seest, said he, is human life: consider it attentively. Upon a more leisurely survey of it, I found that it consisted of threescore and ten entire arches, with several broken arches, which, added to those that were entire, made up the number about an hundred. As I was counting the arches, the genius told me that this bridge consisted at first of a thousand arches, but that a great flood swept away the rest, and left the bridge in the ruinous condition I now beheld it. But tell me further, said he, what thou discoverest on it. I see multitudes of people passing over it, said I, and a black cloud hanging on each end of it. As I looked more attentively, I saw several of the passengers dropping through the bridge into the great tide that flowed underneath it; and upon farther examination, perceived there were innumerable trap-doors that lay concealed in the bridge, which the passengers no sooner trod upon but they fell through them into the tide, and immediately disappeared. These hidden pit-falls were set very thick at the entrance of the bridge; so that throngs of people no sooner broke through the cloud but many of them fell into them. They grew thinner towards the middle, but multiplied and lay closer together towards the end of the arches that were entire.

'There were indeed some persons, but their number was very small, that continued a kind of hobbling march on the broken arches, but fell through one after another, being quite tired and spent with so long a walk.

'I passed some time in the contemplation of this wonderful structure, and the great variety of objects which it presented. My heart was filled with a deep melancholy to see several dropping unexpectedly in the midst of mirth and jollity, and catching at every thing that stood by them to save themselves. Some were looking up towards the heavens in a thoughtful posture, and in the midst of a speculation stumbled and fell out of sight. Multitudes were very busy in the pursuit of bubbles that glittered in their eyes and danced before them; but often when they thought themselves within the reach of them, their footing failed and down they sunk. In this confusion of objects, I observed some with scimitars in their hands, and others with urinals, who ran to and fro upon the bridge, thrusting several persons on trap-doors which did not seem to lie in their way, and which they might have escaped had they not been thus forced upon them.

'The genius seeing me indulge myself in this melancholy prospect, told me I had dwelt long enough upon it: take thine eyes off the bridge, said he, and tell me if thou yet seest any thing thou dost not comprehend. Upon looking up, What mean, said I, those great flights of birds that are perpetually hovering about the bridge, and settling upon it from time to time? I see vultures, harpies, ravens, cormorants, and, among many other feathered creatures, several little winged boys, that perch in great numbers upon the middle arches. These, said the genius, are envy, avarice, superstition, despair, love, with the like cares and passions that infest human life.

'I here fetched a deep sigh. Alas, said I, man was made in vain! how is he given away to misery and mortality! tortured in life, and swallowed up in death! The genius being moved with compassion towards me, bid me quit so uncomfortable a prospect. Look no more, said he, on man in the first stage of his existence, in his setting out for eternity; but cast thine eye on that thick mist into which the tide bears the several generations of mortals that fall into it. I directed my sight as I was ordered, and (whether or no the good genius strengthened it with any supernatural force, or dissipated part of the mist that was before too thick for the eye to penetrate) I saw the valley opening at the farther end, and spreading forth into an immense ocean, that had a huge rock of adamant running through the midst of it, and dividing it into two equal parts. The clouds still rested on one half of it, insomuch that I could discover nothing in it: but the other appeared to me a vast ocean planted with innumerable islands, that were covered with fruits and flowers, and interwoven with a thousand little shining seas that ran among them. I could see persons dressed in glorious habits, with garlands upon their heads, passing among the trees, lying down by the sides of fountains, or resting on beds of flowers; and could hear a confused harmony of singing birds, falling waters, human voices, and musical instruments. Gladness grew in me upon the discovery of so delightful a scene. I wished for the wings of an eagle, that I might fly away to those happy seats; but the genius told me there was no passage to them, except through the gates of death that I saw opening every moment upon the bridge. The islands, said he, that lie so fresh and green before thee, and with which the whole face of the ocean appears spotted as far as thou canst see, are more in number than the sands on the sea-shore; there are myriads of islands behind those which thou here discoverest, reaching farther than thine eye, or even thine imagination can extend itself. These are the mansions of good men after death, who, according to the degree and kinds of virtue in which they excelled, are distributed among these several islands, which abound with pleasures of different kinds and degrees, suitable to the relishes and perfections of those who are settled in them; every island is a paradise accommodated to its respective inhabitants. Are not these, O Mirza, habitations worth contending for? Does life appear miserable that gives thee opportunities of earning such a reward? Is death to be feared, that will convey thee to so happy an existence? think not man was made in vain, who has such an eternity reserved for him. I gazed with inexpressible pleasure on these happy islands. At length, said I, shew me now, I beseech thee, the secrets that lie hid under those dark clouds which cover the ocean on the other side of the rock of adamant. The genius making me no answer, I turned about to address myself to him a second time, but I found that he had left me; I then turned again to the vision which I had been so long contemplating, but instead of the rolling tide, the arched bridge, and the happy islands, I saw nothing but the long hollow valley of Bagdat, with oxen, sheep, and camels grazing upon the sides of it.'

The end of the first Vision of Mirza.

No. CLX. MONDAY, SEPTEMBER 3.

...... Cùi mens divinior, atque os
Magna sonaturum, des nominis hujus honorem. Hor.

——He alone can claim this name, who writes
With fancy high, and bold and daring flights. Creech.

There is no character more frequently given to a writer than that of being a genius. I have heard many a little sonneteer called a fine genius. There is not an heroic scribbler in the nation, that has not his admirers who think him a great genius; and as for your smatterers in tragedy, there is scarce a man among them who is not cried up by one or other a prodigious genius.

My design in this paper is to consider what is properly a great genius, and to throw some thoughts together on so uncommon a subject.

Among great geniuses, those few draw the admiration of all the world upon them, and stand up as the prodigies of mankind, who, by the mere strength of natural parts, and without any assistance of art or learning, have produced works that were the delight of their own times, and the wonder of posterity. There appears something nobly wild and extravagant in these great natural geniuses, that is infinitely more beautiful than all the turn and polishing of what the French call a bel esprit; by which they would express a genius refined by conversation, reflection, and the reading of the most polite authors. The greatest genius which runs through the arts and sciences, takes a kind of tincture from them, and falls unavoidably into imitation.

Many of these great natural geniuses that were never disciplined and broken by rules of art, are to be found among the ancients, and in particular among those of the more eastern parts of the world. Homer has innumerable flights that Virgil was not able to reach; and in the Old Testament we find several passages more elevated and sublime than any in Homer. At the same time that we allow a greater and more daring genius to the ancients, we must own that the greatest of them very much failed in, or if you will, that they were much above the nicety and correctness of the moderns. In their similitudes and allusions, provided there was a likeness, they did not much trouble themselves about the decency of the comparison. Thus Solomon resembles the nose of his beloved to the tower of Lebanon which looketh toward Damascus, as the coming of a thief in the night is a similitude of the same kind in the New Testament. It would be endless to make collections of this nature: Homer illustrates one of his heroes encompassed with the enemy, by an ass in a field of corn that has his sides belaboured by all the boys of the village without stirring a foot for it; and another of them tossing to and fro in his bed and burning with resentment, to a piece of flesh broiled on the coals. This particular failure in the ancients opens a large field of raillery to the little wits, who can laugh at an indecency, but not relish the sublime in these sort of writings. The present Emperor of Persia, conformable to this eastern way of thinking, amidst a great many pompous titles, denominates himself " the Sun of glory," and " the Nutmeg of delight." In short, to cut off all cavilling against the ancients, and particularly those of the warmer climates, who had most heat and life in their imaginations, we are to consider that the rule of observing what the French call the bienseance in an allusion, has been found out of later years, and in the colder regions of the world; where we would make some amends for our want of force and spirit, by a scrupulous nicety and exactness in our compositions. Our countryman Shakespeare was a remarkable instance of this kind of great geniuses.

I cannot quit this head without observing, that Pindar was a great genius of the first class, who was hurried on by a natural fire and impetuosity to vast conceptions of things, and noble sallies of the imagination. At the same time, can any thing be more ridiculous than for men of a sober and moderate fancy to imitate this poet's way of writing, in those monstrous compositions which go among us under the name of Pindarics? When I see people copying works which, as Horace has represented them, are singular in their kind, and inimitable; when I see men following irregularities by rule, and by the little tricks of art straining after the most unbounded flights of nature—I cannot but apply to them that passage in Terence:

>   ..Incerta hæc si tu postules
> Ratione certa facere, nihilo plus agas,
> Quam si des operam, ut cum ratione insanias.   EUN.

' You may as well pretend to be mad and in your senses at the same time, as to think of reducing these uncertain things to any certainty by reason.'

In short, a modern Pindaric writer, compared with Pindar, is like a sister among the Camisars compared with Virgil's Sybil: there is the distortion, grimace, and outward figure, but nothing of that divine impulse which raises the mind above itself, and makes the sounds more than human.

There is another kind of great geniuses which I shall place in a second class, not as I think them inferior to the first, but only for distinction's sake, as they are of a different kind. This second class of great geniuses are those that have formed themselves by rules, and submitted the greatness of their natural talents to the corrections and restraints of art. Such among the Greeks were Plato and Aristotle, among the Romans, Virgil and Tully; among the English, Milton and Sir Francis Bacon.

The genius in both these classes of authors may be equally great, but shews itself after a different manner. In the first it is like a rich soil in a happy climate, that produces a whole wilderness of noble plants rising in a thousand beautiful landscapes, without any certain order or regularity. In the other it is the same rich soil under the same happy climate, that has been laid out in walks and parterres, and cut into shape and beauty by the skill of the gardener.

The great danger in these latter kind of geniuses is, lest they cramp their own abilities too much by imitation, and form themselves altogether upon models, without giving the full play to their own natural parts. An imitation of the best authors is not to compare with a good original; and I believe we may observe that very few writers make an extraordinary figure in the world, who have not something in their way of thinking or expressing themselves that is peculiar to them, and entirely their own.

It is odd to consider what great geniuses are sometimes thrown away upon trifles.

I one saw a shepherd, says a famous Italian author, who used to divert himself in his solitudes with tossing up eggs and catching them again without breaking them, in which he had arrived to so great a degree of perfection that he would keep up four at a time for several minutes together playing in the air, and falling into his hands by turns. I think, says the author, I never saw a greater severity than in this man's face, for by his wonderful perseverance and application, he had contracted the seriousness and gravity of a privy-counsellor, and I could not but reflect with myself, that the same assiduity and attention, had they been rightly applied, might have made him a greater mathematician than Archimedes. C

No. CLXI. TUESDAY, SEPTEMBER 4.

Ipse dies agitat festos: fususque per herbam,
Ignis ubi in medio, et socii cratera coronant,
Te libans, Lenæe, vocat pecorisque magistris
Velocis jaculi certamina ponit in ulmo,
Corporaque agresti nudat prædura palæstrâ
  Hanc olim veteres vitam coluere Sabini,
Hanc Remus et frater; sic fortis Etruria crevit,
Scilicet et rerum facta est pulcherrima Roma.
                                           VIRG.

Himself, in rustic pomp, on holy days,
To rural powers a just oblation pays,
And on the green his careless limbs displays
The hearth is in the midst the herdsmen, round
The cheerful fire, provoke his health in goblets crown'd.
He calls on Bacchus, and propounds the prize
The groom his fellow-groom at *butts* defies,
And bends his bow, and levels with his eyes;
Or, stript for wrestling, smears his limbs with oil,
And watches with a trip his foe to foil
Such was the life the frugal Sabines led
So Remus and his brother-god were bred
From whom the austere Etrurian virtue rose;
And this rude life our homely fathers chose
Old Rome from such a race deriv'd her birth,
The seat of empire, and the conquer'd earth
                                           DRYDEN.

I AM glad that my late going into the country has increased the number of my correspondents; one of whom sends me the following letter.

' SIR,

' THOUGH you are pleased to retire from us so soon into the city, I hope you will not think the affairs of the country altogether unworthy of your inspection for the future. I had the honour of seeing your short face at Sir Roger de Coverley's, and have ever since thought your person and writings both extraordinary. Had you staid there a few days longer, you would have seen a country-wake, which you know, in most parts of England, is the Eve-feast of the dedication of our churches. I was last week at one of these assemblies, which was held in a neighbouring parish; where I found their green covered with a promiscuous multitude of all ages and both sexes, who esteem one another more or less the following part of the year, according as they distinguish themselves at this time. The whole company were in their holy-day clothes, and divided into several parties, all of them endeavouring to shew themselves in those exercises wherein they excelled, and to gain the approbation of the lookers-on.

'I found a ring of cudgel-players, who were breaking one another's heads, in order to make some impression on their mistresses' hearts. I observed a lusty young fellow who had the misfortune of a broken pate: but what considerably added to the anguish of the wound, was his overhearing an old man, who shook his head and said, 'That he questioned now if Black Kate would marry him these three years.' I was diverted from a farther observation of these combatants by a foot-ball match, which was on the other side of the green; where Tom Short behaved himself so well, that most people seemed to agree, 'it was impossible that he should remain a batchelor till the next wake.' Having played many a match myself, I could have looked longer on this sport, had I not observed a country girl who was posted on an eminence at some distance from me, and was making so many odd grimaces, and writhing and distorting her whole body in so strange a manner, as made me very desirous to know the meaning of it. Upon my coming up to her, I found that she was overlooking a ring of wrestlers, and that her sweetheart, a person of small stature, was contending with an huge brawny fellow, who twirled him about, and shook the little man so violently, that by a secret sympathy of hearts it produced all those agitations in the person of his mistress, who, I dare say, like Celia in Shakspeare on the same occasion, could have 'wished herself invisible, to catch the strong fellow by the leg.' The 'squire of the parish treats the whole company every year with a hogshead of ale, and proposes a beaver hat as a recompense to him who gives most falls. This has raised such a spirit of emulation in the youth of the place, that some of them have rendered themselves very expert at this exercise; and I was often surprised to see a fellow's heels fly up, by a trip which was given him so smartly that I could scarce discern it. I found that the old wrestlers seldom entered the ring, till some one was grown formidable by having thrown two or three of his opponents; but kept themselves as it were in a reserved body to defend the hat, which is always hung up by the person who gets it, in one of the most conspicuous parts of the house, and looked upon by the whole family as something redounding much more to their honour than a coat of arms. There was a fellow who was so busy in regulating all the ceremonies, and seemed to carry such an air of importance in his looks, that I could not help inquiring who he was; and was immediately answered, 'That he did not value himself upon nothing, for that he and his ancestors had won so many hats, that his parlour looked like a haberdasher's shop.' However, this thirst of glory in them all, was the reason that no one man stood 'lord of the ring' for above three falls while I was among them.

'The young maids, who were not lookers-on at these exercises, were themselves engaged in some diversion; and upon my asking a farmer's son of my own parish what he was gazing at with so much attention, he told me, 'That he was seeing Betty

Welch, whom I knew to be his sweetheart, pitch a bar.'

' In short, I found the men endeavoured to shew the women they were no cowards, and that the whole company strived to recommend themselves to each other, by making it appear that they were all in a perfect state of health, and fit to undergo any fatigues of bodily labour.

' Your judgment upon this method of love and gallantry, as it is at present practised amongst us in the country, will very much oblige,

' Sir,
' Your's, &c.'

If I would here put on the scholar and politician, I might inform my readers how these bodily exercises or games were formerly encouraged in all the commonwealths of Greece; from whence the Romans afterwards borrowed their Pentathlum, which was composed of running, wrestling, leaping, throwing, and boxing, though the prizes were generally nothing but a crown of cypress or parsley, hats not being in fashion in those days. That there is an old statute, which obliges every man in England, having such an estate, to keep and exercise the long bow; by which means our ancestors excelled all other nations in the use of that weapon, and we had all the real advantages, without the inconvenience of a standing army, and that I once met with a book of projects, in which the author, considering to what noble ends that spirit of emulation, which so remarkably shews itself among our common people in these wakes, might be directed, proposes, that for the improvement of all our handicraft trades, there should be annual prizes set up for such persons as were most excellent in their several arts. But laying aside all these political considerations, which might tempt me to pass the limits of my paper, I confess the greatest benefit and convenience that I can observe in these country festivals, is the bringing young people together, and giving them an opportunity of shewing themselves in the most advantageous light. A country fellow that throws his rival upon his back, has generally as good success with their common mistress; as nothing is more usual than for a nimble-footed wench to get a husband at the same time she wins a smock. Love and marriages are the natural effects of these anniversary assemblies. I must therefore very much approve the method by which my correspondent tells me each sex endeavours to recommend itself to the other, since nothing seems more likely to promise a healthy offspring or a happy cohabitation. And I believe I may assure my country friend, that there has been many a court lady who would be contented to exchange her crazy young husband for Tom Short, and several men of quality who would have parted with a tender yoke-fellow for Black Kate.

I am the more pleased with having love made the principal end and design of these meetings, as it seems to be most agreeable to the intent for which they were at first instituted, as we are informed by the learned Dr. Kennet, with whose words I shall conclude my present paper.

'These wakes, says he, were in imitation of the ancient ἀγάπαι, or love feasts; and were first established in England by Pope Gregory the Great, who, in an epistle to Melitus the Abbot, gave order that they should be kept in shades or arbories made up with branches and boughs of trees round the church.'

He adds, 'That this laudable custom of wakes prevailed for many ages, till the nice Puritans began to exclaim against it as a remnant of popery; and by degrees the precise humour grew so popular, that at an Exeter assizes the lord chief baron Walter made an order for the suppression of all wakes; but, on bishop Laud's complaining of this innovating humour, the king commanded the order to be reversed.'

X

No CLXII. WEDNESDAY, SEPTEMBER 5.

—————Servetur ad imum,
Qualis ab incœpto processerit, et sibi constet
HOR.

Preserve consistency throughout the whole

NOTHING that is not a real crime makes a man appear so contemptible and little in the eyes of the world as inconstancy, especially when it regards religion or party. In either of these cases, though a man perhaps does but his duty in changing his side, he not only makes himself hated by those he left, but is seldom heartily esteemed by those he comes over to.

In these great articles of life therefore a man's conviction ought to be very strong, and if possible so well timed that worldly advantages may seem to have no share in it, for mankind will be ill-natured enough to think he does not change sides out of principle, but either out of levity of temper or prospects of interest. Converts and renegadoes of all kinds should take particular care to let the world see they act upon honourable motives, or whatever approbations they may receive from themselves, and applauses from those they converse with, they may be very well assured that they are the scorn of all good men, and the public marks of infamy and derision.

Irresolution on the schemes of life, which offer themselves to our choice, and inconstancy in pursuing them, are the greatest and most universal causes of all our disquiet and unhappiness. When ambition pulls one way, interest another, inclination a third, and perhaps reason contrary to all, a man is likely to pass his time but ill who has so many different parties to please. When the mind hovers among such a variety of allurements, one had better settle on a way of life that is not the very best we might have chosen, than grow old without determining our choice, and go out of the world, as the greatest part of mankind do, before we have resolved how to live in it. There is but one method of setting ourselves at rest in this particular, and that is by adhering stedfastly to one great end as the chief and ultimate aim of all our pursuits. If we are firmly resolved to live up to the dictates of reason, without any regard to wealth, reputation, and the like considerations, any more than as they fall in with our principal design, we may go through life with steadiness and pleasure; but if we act by several broken views, and will not only be virtuous but wealthy, popular, and every thing that has a value set upon it by the world, we shall live and die in misery and repentance.

One would take more than ordinary care to guard one's self against this particular imperfection, because it is that which our nature very strongly inclines us to: for if we examine ourselves thoroughly, we shall find that we are the most changeable beings in the universe. In respect of our understanding, we often embrace and reject the very same opinions; whereas beings above and beneath us have probably no opinions at all, or at least no wavering and uncertainties in those they have. Our superiors are guided by intuition, and our inferiors by instinct. In respect of our wills, we fall into crimes and recover out of them, are amiable or odious in the eyes of our great Judge, and pass our whole life in offending and asking pardon. On the contrary, the beings underneath us are not capable of sinning, nor those above us of repenting. The one is out of the possibilities of duty, and the other fixed in an eternal course of sin, or an eternal course of virtue

There is scarce a state of life, or stage in it, which does not produce changes and revolutions in the mind of man. Our schemes of thought in infancy are lost in those of youth; those too take a different turn in manhood, till old age often leads us back into our former infancy. A new title or an unexpected success throws us out of ourselves, and in a manner destroys our identity. A cloudy day, or a little sun-shine, have as great an influence on many constitutions as the most real blessings or misfortunes. A dream varies our being, and changes our condition while it lasts, and every passion, not to mention health and sickness, and the greater alterations in body and mind, makes us appear almost different creatures. If a man is so distinguished among other beings by this infirmity, what can we think of such as make themselves remarkable for it, even among their own species? It is a very trifling character to be one of the most variable beings of the most variable kind, especially if we consider that He who is the great standard of perfection has in him no shadow of change, but is the same yesterday, to-day, and for ever

As this mutability of temper and inconsistency with ourselves is the greatest weakness of human nature, so it makes the person who is remarkable for it, in a very particular manner, more ridiculous than any other infirmity whatsoever, as it sets him in a greater variety of foolish lights, and distinguishes him from himself by an opposition of party-coloured characters. The most humorous character in Horace is founded upon this unevenness of temper and irregularity of conduct,

.⸺Sardus habebat
Ille Tigellius hoc.⸺Cæsar, qui cogere posset,
Si peteret per amicitiam patris atque suam, non
Quidquam proficeret: si collibuisset, ab ovo
Usque ad mala citaret, Io Bacche, modo summâ
Voce, modo hâc, resonat quæ chordis quatuor imâ.
Nil æquale homini fuit illi; sæpè velut qui
Currebat fugiens hostem: persæpè velut qui
Junonis sacra ferret: hebebat sæpè ducentos,
Sæpè decem servos: Modò reges atque tetrarchas,
Omnia magna loquens; modo, Sit mihi mensa tripes, et
Concha salis puri, et toga, quæ defendere frigus,
Quamvis crassa, queat: Deciès centena dedisses
Huic parco paucis contento, quinque diebus
Nil erat in loculis: Noctes vigilabat ad ipsum
Manè, diem totum stertebat; nil fuit unquam
Sic impar sibi. ⸺ ⸺ Hor.

Instead of translating this passage in Horace, I shall entertain my English reader with the description of a parallel character, that is wonderfully well finished by Mr. Dryden, and raised upon the same foundation,

'In the first rank of these did Zimri stand!
A man so various, that he seem'd to be
Not one, but all mankind's epitome.
Stiff in opinions, always in the wrong:
Was every thing by starts, and nothing long;
But in the course of one revolving moon,
Was chemist, fidler, statesman, and buffoon:
Then all for women, painting, rhiming, drinking;
Besides ten thousand freaks that dy'd in thinking.
Blest madman, who could every hour employ,
With something new to wish, or to enjoy!'

C

No. CLXIII. THURSDAY, SEPTEMBER 6.

> Si quid ego adfuero, curamve levasso,
> Quæ nunc te coquit, et versat sub pectore fixa,
> Ecquid erit pretii? ENN.

> Say, will you thank me if I bring you rest,
> And ease the torture of your lab'ring breast?

INQUIRIES after happiness, and rules for attaining it, are not so necessary and useful to mankind, as the arts of consolation, and supporting one's self under affliction. The utmost we can hope for in this world is contentment; if we aim at any thing higher, we shall meet with nothing but grief and disappointment. A man should direct all his studies and endeavours at making himself easy now, and happy hereafter.

The truth of it is, if all the happiness that is dispersed through the whole race of mankind in this world were drawn together, and put into the possession of any single man, it would not make a very happy being. Though, on the contrary, if the miseries of the whole species were fixed in a single person, they would make a very miserable one.

I am engaged in this subject by the following letter, which, though subscribed by a fictitious name, I have reason to believe is not imaginary.

'Mr SPECTATOR,

'I AM one of your disciples, and endeavour to live up to your rules, which I hope will incline you to pity my condition. I shall open it to you in a very few words. About three years since a gentleman, whom, I am sure, you yourself would have approved, made his addresses to me. He had every thing to recommend him but an estate; so that my friends, who all of them applauded his person, would not for the sake of both of us favour his passion. For my own part, I resigned myself up entirely to the direction of those who knew the world much better than myself, but still lived in hopes that some juncture or other would make me happy in the man whom, in my heart, I preferred to all the world; being determined, if I could not have him, to have nobody else. About three months ago I received a letter from him, acquainting me, that by the death of an uncle he had a considerable estate left him, which he said was welcome to him upon no other account, but as he hoped it would remove all difficulties that lay in the way to our mutual happiness. You may well suppose, Sir, with how much joy I received this letter, which was followed by several others, filled with those expressions of love and joy, which I verily believe nobody felt more sincerely, nor knew better how to describe, than the gentleman I am speaking of. But, Sir, how shall I be able to tell it you! by the last week's post I received a letter from an intimate friend of this unhappy gentleman, acquainting me, that as he had just settled his affairs, and was preparing for his journey, he fell sick of a fever and died. It is impossible to express to you the distress I am in upon this occasion. I can only have recourse to my devotions, and to the reading of good books for my consolation; and as I always take a particular delight in those frequent advices and admonitions which you give the public, it would be a very great piece of charity in you to lend me your assistance in this conjuncture. If after the reading of this letter you find yourself in a humour rather to rally and ridicule, than to comfort me, I desire you would throw it into the fire, and think no more of it; but if you are touched with my misfortune, which is greater than I know how to bear, your counsels may very much support, and will infinitely oblige, the afflicted

'LEONORA'

A disappointment in love is more hard to get over than any other; the passion itself so softens and subdues the heart, that it disables it from struggling or bearing up against the woes or distresses which befal it. The mind meets with other misfortunes in her whole strength, she stands collected within herself, and sustains the shock with all the force which is natural to her; but a heart in love has its foundation sapped, and immediately sinks under the weight of accidents that are disagreeable to its favourite passion.

In afflictions men generally draw their consolations out of books of morality, which indeed are of great use to fortify and strengthen the mind against the impressions of sorrow. Monsieur St. Evremond, who does not approve of this method, recommends authors who are apt to stir up mirth in the mind of the readers, and fancies Don Quixote can give more relief to a heavy heart than Plutarch or Seneca, as it is much easier to divert grief than to conquer it. This, doubtless, may have its effects on some tempers. I should rather have recourse to authors of a quite contrary kind, that give us instances of calamities and misfortunes, and shew human nature in its greatest distresses.

If the afflictions we groan under be very heavy, we shall find some consolation in the society of as great sufferers as ourselves, especially when we find our companions men of virtue and merit. If our afflictions are light, we shall be comforted by the comparison we make between ourselves and our fellow sufferers. A loss at sea, a fit of sickness, or the death of a friend, are such trifles when we consider whole kingdoms laid in ashes, families put to the sword, wretches shut up in dungeons, and the like calamities of mankind, that we are out of countenance for our own weakness, if we sink under such little strokes of fortune.

Let the disconsolate Leonora consider, that at the very time in which she languishes for the loss of her deceased lover, there are persons in several parts of the would just perishing in ship-wreck, others crying out for mercy in the terrors of a death-bed repentance; others lying under the tortures of an infamous execution, or the like dreadful calamities, and she will find her sorrows vanish at the appearance of those which are so much greater and more astonishing.

I would further propose to the consolation of my afflicted disciple, that possibly what she now looks upon as the greatest misfortune, is not really such in itself. For my own part, I question not but our souls in a separate state will look back on their lives in quite another view than what they had of them in the body, and that what they now consider as misfortunes and disappointments, will very often appear to have been escapes and blessings.

The mind that has any cast towards devotion, naturally flies to it in its afflictions.

When I was in France I heard a very remarkable story of two lovers, which I shall relate at length in my to-morrow's paper, not only because the circumstances of it are extraordinary, but because it may serve as an illustration to all that can be said on this last head, and shew the power of religion in abating that particular anguish which seems to lie so heavy on Leonora. The story was told me by a priest as I travelled with him in a stage-coach. I shall give it my reader, as well as I can remember, in his own words, after having premised, that if consolations may be drawn from a wrong religion, and a misguided devotion, they cannot but flow much more naturally from those which are founded upon reason, and established in good sense.

L

No. CLXIV. FRIDAY, SEPTEMBER 7.

Illa, quis et me, inquit, miseram, et te perdidit, Orpheu?
Jamque vale: feror ingenti circumdata nocte,
Invalidasque tibi tendens, heu! non tua palmas.
VIRG.

Then thus the bride. What fury seiz'd on thee,
Unhappy man! to lose thyself and me!
And now farewel! involv'd in shades of night,
For ever I am ravish'd from thy sight;
In vain I reach my feeble hands to join
In sweet embraces, ah! no longer thine!
DRYDEN.

CONSTANTIA was a woman of extraordinary wit and beauty, but very unhappy in a father, who having arrived at great riches by his own industry, took delight in nothing but his money. Theodosius was the younger son of a decayed family, of great parts and learning, improved by a genteel and virtuous education. When he was in the twentieth year of his age he became acquainted with Constantia, who had not then passed her fifteenth. As he lived but a few miles distant from her father's house, he had frequent opportunities of seeing her; and by the advantages of a good person and a pleasing conversation, made such an impression on her heart as it was impossible for time to efface. he was himself no less smitten with Constantia. A long acquaintance made them still discover new beauties in each other, and by degrees raised in them that mutual passion which had influence on their following lives. It unfortunately happened, that in the midst of this intercourse of love and friendship between Theodosius and Constantia, there broke out an irreparable quarrel between their parents, the one valuing himself too much upon his birth, and the other upon his possessions. The father of Constantia was so incensed at the father of Theodosius, that he contracted an unreasonable aversion towards his son, insomuch that he forbade him his house, and charged his daughter upon her duty never to see him more. In the mean time, to break off all the communication between the two lovers, who he knew entertained secret hopes of some favourable opportunity that should bring them together, he found out a young gentleman of a good fortune and an agreeable person, whom he pitched upon as a husband for his daughter. He soon concerted this affair so well, that he told Constantia it was his design to marry her to such a gentleman, and that her wedding should be celebrated on such a day. Constantia, who was over-awed with the authority of her father, and unable to object any thing against so advantageous a match, received the proposal with a profound silence, which her father commended in her, as the most decent manner of a virgin's giving her consent to an overture of that kind. The noise of this intended marriage soon reached Theodosius, who, after a long tumult of passions, which naturally rise in a lover's heart on such an occasion, writ the following letter to Constantia.

'THE thought of my Constantia, which, for some years has been my only happiness, is now become a greater torment to me than I am able to bear. Must I then live to see you another's? The streams, the fields and meadows, where we have so often talked together, grow painful to me, life itself is become a burden. May you long be happy in the world, but forget that there was ever such a man in it as
'THEODOSIUS.'

This letter was conveyed to Constantia that very evening, who fainted at the reading of it; and the next morning she was much more alarmed by two or three messengers that came to her father's house, one after another, to inquire if they had heard any thing of Theodosius, who it seems had left his chamber about midnight, and could nowhere be found. The deep melancholy which had hung upon his mind for some time before, made them apprehend the worst that could befal him. Constantia, who knew that nothing but the report of her marriage could have driven him to such extremities, was not to be comforted; she now accused herself for having so tamely given an ear to the proposal of a husband, and looked upon the new lover as the murderer of Theodosius. In short, she resolved to suffer the utmost effects of her father's displeasure, rather than comply with a marriage which appeared to her so full of guilt and horror. The father seeing himself entirely rid of Theodosius, and likely to keep a considerable portion in his family, was not very much concerned at the obstinate refusal of his daughter, and did not find it very difficult to excuse himself upon that account to his intended son-in-law, who had all along regarded this alliance rather as a marriage of convenience than of love. Constantia had now no relief but in her devotions and exercises of religion, to which her afflictions had so entirely subjected her mind, that after some years had abated the violence of her sorrows, and settled her thoughts in a kind of tranquillity, she resolved to pass the remainder of her days in a convent. Her father was not displeased with a resolution which would save money in his family, and readily complied with his daughter's intentions. Accordingly, in the twenty-fifth year of her age, while her beauty was yet in all its height and bloom, he carried her to a neighbouring city, in order to look out a sisterhood of nuns, among whom to place his daughter. There was in this place a father of a convent, who was very much renowned for his piety and exemplary life, and as it is usual in the Romish church for those who are under any great affliction, or trouble of mind, to apply themselves to the most eminent confessors for pardon and consolation, our beautiful votary took the opportunity of confessing herself to this celebrated father.

We must now return to Theodosius, who the very morning that the above-mentioned inquiries had been made after him, arrived at a religious house in the city, where now Constantia resided; and desiring that secrecy and concealment of the fathers of the convent, which is very usual upon any extraordinary occasion, he made himself one of the order, with a private vow never to inquire after Constantia, whom he looked upon as given away to his rival upon the day on which, according to common fame, their marriage was to have been solemnized. Having in his youth made a good progress in learning, that he might dedicate himself more entirely to religion, he entered into holy orders, and in a few years became renowned for his sanctity of life, and those pious sentiments which he inspired into all who conversed with him. It was this holy man to whom Constantia had determined to apply herself in confession, though neither she nor any other besides the prior of the convent knew any thing of his name or family. The gay, the amiable Theodosius, had now taken upon him the name of father Francis, and was so far concealed in a long beard, a shaven head, and a religious habit, that it was impossible to discover the man of the world in the venerable conventual.

As he was one morning shut up in his confessional, Constantia kneeling by him, opened the state of her soul to him; and after having given the history of a life full of innocence, she burst out in tears, and entered upon that part of her story in which he himself had so great a share. My behaviour, says she, has, I fear, been the death of a man who had no other fault but that of loving me too much. Heaven only knows how dear he was to me whilst he lived, and how bitter the remembrance of him has been to me since his death. She here paused, and lifted up her eyes that streamed with tears towards the father; who was so moved with the sense of her sorrows, that he could only command his voice, which was broke with sighs and sobbings, so far as to bid her proceed. She followed his directions, and in a flood of tears poured out her heart before him. The father could not forbear weeping aloud, insomuch that in the agonies of his grief the seat shook under him. Constantia, who thought the good man was thus moved by his compassion towards her, and by the horror of her guilt, proceeded with the utmost contrition to acquaint him with that vow of virginity in which she was going to engage herself, as the proper atonement for her sins, and the only sacrifice she could make to the memory of Theodosius. The father, who by this time had pretty well composed himself, burst out again in tears upon hearing that name to which he had been so long disused, and upon receiving this instance of an unparalleled fidelity from one who, he thought, had several years since given herself up to the possession of another. Amidst the interruptions of his sorrow, seeing his penitent overwhelmed with grief, he was only able to bid her from time to time be comforted....To tell her that her sins were forgiven her..... That her guilt was not so great as she apprehended.....That she should not suffer herself to be afflicted above measure. After which he recovered himself enough to give her the absolution in form; directing her at the same time to repair to him again the next day, that he might encourage her in the pious resolutions she had taken, and give her suitable exhortations for her behaviour in it. Constantia retired, and the next morning renewed her applications. Theodosius having manned his soul with proper thoughts and reflections, exerted himself on this occasion in the best manner he could, to animate his penitent in the course of life she was entering upon, and wear out of her mind those groundless fears and apprehensions which had taken possession of it, concluding, with a promise to her, that he would from time to time continue his admonitions when she should have taken upon her the holy veil. The rules of our respective orders, says he, will not permit that I should see you, but you may assure yourself not only of having a place in my prayers, but of receiving such frequent instructions as I can convey to you by letters. Go on cheerfully in the glorious cause you have undertaken, and you will quickly find such a peace and satisfaction in your mind which it is not in the power of the world to give.

Constantia's heart was so elevated with the discourse of father Francis, that the very next day she entered upon her vow. As soon as the solemnities of her reception were over, she retired, as it is usual, with the Abbess into her own apartment.

The Abbess had been informed the night before of all that had passed between her noviciate and father Francis: from whom she now delivered to her the following letter.

'As the first fruits of those joys and consolations which you may expect from the life you are now engaged in, I must acquaint you that Theodosius, whose death sits so heavy upon your thoughts, is still alive; and that the father to whom you have confessed yourself, was once that Theodosius whom you so much lament. The love which we have had for one another will make us more happy in its disappointment than it could have done in its success. Providence has disposed of us for our advantage, though not according to our wishes. Consider your Theodosius still as dead, but assure yourself of one who will not cease to pray for you in father

'FRANCIS.'

Constantia saw that the hand-writing agreed with the contents of the letter; and upon reflecting on the voice of the person, the behaviour, and above all the extreme sorrow of the father during her confession, she discovered Theodosius in every particular. After having wept with tears of joy, It is enough, says she, Theodosius is still in being: I shall live with comfort, and die in peace.

The letters which the father sent her afterwards are yet extant in the nunnery where she resided, and are often read to the young religious, in order to inspire them with good resolutions and sentiments of virtue. It so happened, that after Constantia had lived about ten years in the cloister, a violent fever broke out in the place, which swept away great multitudes, and among others, Theodosius. Upon his death-bed he sent his benediction in a very moving manner to Constantia, who at that time was herself so far gone in the same fatal distemper that she lay delirious. Upon the interval which generally precedes death in sicknesses of this nature, the abbess finding that the physicians had given her over, told her that Theodosius was just gone before her, and that he had sent her his benediction in his last moments. Constantia received it with pleasure, and now, says she, If I do not ask any thing improper, let me be buried by Theodosius. My vow reaches no farther than the grave. What I ask is, I hope, no violation of it. She died soon after, and was interred according to her request.

Their tombs are still to be seen, with a short Latin inscription over them to the following purpose.

‘ Here lies the bodies of father Francis and sister Constance. They were lovely in their lives, and in their deaths they were not divided.’ C

No. CLXV. SATURDAY, SEPTEMBER 8.

>   ———— Si forè necesse est,
> Fingere cinctutis non exaudita Cethegis,
> Continget dabiturque licentia sumpta pudenter.   HOR.

>   ———— If you would unheard of things express,
>   Invent new words, we can indulge a muse,
>   Until the licence rise to an abuse   CREECH

I HAVE often wished, that as in our constitution there are several persons whose business it is to watch over our laws, our liberties and commerce, certain men might be set apart as superintendants of our language, to hinder any words of a foreign coin from passing among us; and in particular to prohibit any French phrases from becoming current in this kingdom, when those of our own stamp are altogether as valuable. The present war has so adulterated our tongue with strange words, that it would be impossible for one of our great grandfathers to know what his posterity have been doing, were he to read their exploits in a modern newspaper. Our warriors are very industrious in propagating the French language, at the same time that they are so gloriously successful in beating down their power. Our soldiers are men of strong heads for action, and perform such feats as they are not able to express. They want words in their own tongue to tell us what it is they achieve, and therefore send us over accounts of their performances in a jargon of phrases which they learn among their conquered enemies. They ought however to be provided with secretaries, and assisted by our foreign ministers, to tell their story for them in plain English, and to let us know in our mother tongue what it is our brave countrymen are about. The French would indeed be in the right to publish the news of the present war in English phrases, and make their campaigns unintelligible. Their people might flatter themselves that things are not so bad as they really are, were they thus palliated with foreign terms, and thrown into shades and obscurity: but the English cannot be too clear in their narrative of those actions which have raised their country to a higher pitch of glory than it ever yet arrived at, and which will be still the more admired the better they are explained.

For my part, by that time a siege is carried on two or three days, I am altogether lost and bewildered in it, and meet with so many inexplicable difficulties, that I scarce know which side has the better of it, till I am informed by the Tower guns that the place is surrendered. I do indeed make some allowances for this part of the war, fortifications having been foreign inventions, and upon that account abounding in foreign terms. But when we have won battles which may be described in our own language, why are our papers filled with so many unintelligible exploits, and the French obliged to lend us a part of their tongue before we can know how they are conquered? They must be made accessary to their own disgrace, as the Britons were formerly so artificially wrought in the curtain of the Roman theatre, that they seemed to draw it up, in order to give the spectators an opportunity of seeing their own defeat celebrated upon the stage: for so Mr. Dryden has translated that verse in Virgil.

>   Purpuerea intexti tollunt aulæa Britanni.   GEORG.
>
>   Which interwoven Britons seem to raise,
>   And show the triumph that their shame displays.

The histories of all our former wars are transmitted to us in our vernacular idiom, to use the phrase of a great modern critic. I do not find in any of our chronicles, that Edward III ever reconnoitred the enemy, though he often discovered the posture of the French, and as often vanquished them in battle. The Black Prince passed many a river without the help of pontoons, and filled a ditch with faggots as successfully as the generals of our times do it with fascines. Our commanders lose half their praise, and our people half their joy, by means of those hard words and dark expressions in which our newspapers do so much abound. I have seen many a prudent citizen, after having read every article, inquire of his next neighbour what news the mail had brought?

I remember, in that remarkable year when our country was delivered from the greatest fears and apprehensions, and raised to the greatest height of gladness it had ever felt since it was a nation, I mean the year of Blenheim, I had the copy of a letter sent me out of the country, which was written from a young gentleman in the army to his father, a man of a good estate and plain sense. As the letter was very modishly chequered with this modern military eloquence, I shall present my reader with a copy of it.

'Sir,

'Upon the junction of the French and Bavarian armies, they took post behind a great morass, which they thought impracticable. Our general the next day sent a party of horse to reconnoitre them from a little hauteur, at about a quarter of an hour's distance from the army, who returned again to the camp unobserved through several defiles, in one of which they met with a party of French that had been marauding, and made them all prisoners at discretion. The day after a drum arrived at our camp, with a message which he would communicate to none but the general; he was followed by a trumpet, who they say behaved himself very saucily, with a message from the Duke of Bavaria. The next morning our army, being divided into two corps, made a movement towards the enemy: You will hear in the public prints how we treated them, with the other circumstances of that glorious day. I had the good fortune to be in that regiment that pushed the Gens d'Armes. Several French battalions, which some say were a corps de reserve, made a show of resistance, but it only proved a gasconade; for upon our preparing to fill up a little fossee, in order to attack them, they beat the chamade, and sent us a charte blanche. Their commandant with a great many other general officers, and troops without number, are made prisoners of war, and will I believe give you a visit in England, the cartel not being yet settled. Not questioning but these particulars will be very welcome to you, I congratulate you upon them, and am your most dutiful son, &c.'

The father of the young gentleman, upon the perusal of the letter found it contained great news, but could not guess what it was. He immediately communicated it to the curate of the parish, who, upon the reading of it, being vexed to see any thing he could not understand, fell into a kind of passion, and told him, that his son had sent him a letter that was neither fish, flesh, nor good red herring. I wish (says he) the captain may be compos mentis, he talks of a saucy trumpet, and a drum that carries messages, then who is the Charte Blanche? He must either banter us or he is out of his senses. The father, who always looked upon the curate as a learned man, began to fret inwardly at his son's usage, and producing a letter which he had written to him about three posts before, You see here (says he) when he writes for money he knows how to speak intelligibly enough, there is no man in England can express himself clearer, when he wants a new furniture for his horse. In short, the old man was so puzzled upon the point, that it might have fared ill with his son, had he not seen all the prints about three days after filled with the same terms of art, and that Charles only writ like other men.

L.

No CLXVI. MONDAY, SEPTEMBER 10.

..... Quod nec Jovis ira, nec ignis,
Nec poterit ferrum, nec edax abolere vetustas.
OVID.

Which nor dreads the rage
Of tempests, fire, or war, or wasting age. WELSTED.

ARISTOTLE tells us that the world is a copy or transcript of those ideas which are in the mind of the first Being, and that those ideas which are in the mind of man are a transcript of the world: to this we may add, that words are the transcript of those ideas which are in the mind of man, and that writing or printing are the transcript of words.

As the Supreme Being has expressed, and as it were printed, his ideas in the creation, men express their ideas in books, which by this great invention of these latter ages may last as long as the sun and moon, and perish only in the general wreck of nature. Thus Cowley, in his poem on the resurrection, mentioning the destruction of the universe, has those admirable lines.

'Now all the wide extended sky,
And all th' harmonious worlds on high,
And Virgil's sacred work, shall die.'

There is no other method of fixing those thoughts which arise and disappear in the mind of man, and transmitting them to the last periods of time; no other method of giving a permanency to our ideas, and preserving the knowledge of any particular person, when his body is mixed with the common mass of matter, and his soul retired into the world of spirits. Books are the legacies that a great genius leaves to mankind, which are delivered down from generation to generation, as presents to the posterity of those who are yet unborn.

All other arts of perpetuating our ideas continue but a short time; statues can last but a few thousands of years, edifices fewer, and colours still fewer than edifices. Michael Angelo, Fontana, and Raphael will hereafter be what Phidias, Vitruvius, and Apelles are at present, the names of great statuaries, architects, and painters whose works are lost. The several arts are expressed in mouldering materials, nature sinks under them, and is not able to support the ideas which are imprest upon it.

The circumstance which gives authors an advantage above all these great masters is this, that they can multiply their originals; or rather can make copies of their works, to what number they please, which shall be as valuable as the originals themselves. This gives a great author something like a prospect of eternity, but at the same time deprives him of those other advantages which artists meet with. The artist finds greater returns in profit, as the author in fame. What an inestimable price would a Virgil or a Homer, a Cicero or an Aristotle bear, were their works like a statue, a building, or a picture, to be confined only in one place and made the property of a single person?

If writings are thus durable, and may pass from age to age throughout the whole course of time, how careful should an author be of committing any thing to print that may corrupt posterity, and poison the minds of men with vice and error? Writers of great talents who employ their parts in propagating immorality, and seasoning vicious sentiments with wit and humour, are to be looked upon as the pests of society and the enemies of mankind: they leave books behind them (as it is said of those who die in distempers which breed an ill will towards their own species) to scatter infection and destroy their posterity. They act the counter-parts of a

Confucius or a Socrates, and seem to have been sent into the world to deprave human nature, and sink it into the condition of brutality.

I have seen some Roman Catholic authors who tell us that vicious writers continue in purgatory so long as the influence of their writings continues upon posterity: for purgatory (say they) is nothing else but a cleansing us of our sins, which cannot be said to be done away so long as they continue to operate and corrupt mankind. The vicious author (say they) sins after death, and so long as he continues to sin, so long must he expect to be punished. Though the Roman Catholic notion of purgatory be indeed very ridiculous, one cannot but think that if the soul after death has any knowledge of what passes in this world, that of an immoral writer would receive much more regret from the sense of corrupting, than satisfaction from the thought of pleasing, his surviving admirers.

To take off from the severity of this speculation, I shall conclude this paper with the story of an atheistical author, who at a time when he lay dangerously sick, and had desired the assistance of a neighbouring curate, confessed to him with great contrition, that nothing sat more heavy at his heart than the sense of his having seduced the age by his writings, and that their evil influence was likely to continue even after his death. The curate upon further examination finding the penitent in the utmost agonies of despair, and being himself a man of learning, told him, that he hoped his case was not so desperate as he apprehended, since he found that he was so very sensible of his fault, and so sincerely repented of it. The penitent still urged the evil tendency of his books to subvert all religion, and the little ground of hope there could be for one whose writings would continue to do mischief when his body was laid in ashes. The curate finding no other way to comfort him, told him, that he did well in being afflicted for the evil design with which he published his book; but that he ought to be very thankful that there was no danger of its doing any hurt: that his cause was so very bad, and his arguments so weak, that he did not apprehend any ill effects of it: in short, that he might rest satisfied his book could do no more mischief after his death than it had done whilst he was living. To which he added, for his farther satisfaction, that he did not believe any besides his particular friends and acquaintance had ever been at the pains of reading it, or that any body after his death would ever inquire after it. The dying man had still so much the frailty of an author in him, as to be cut to the heart with these consolations, and without answering the good man, asked his friends about him (with a peevishness that is natural to a sick person) where they had picked up such a blockhead? And whether they thought him a proper person to attend one in his condition. The curate finding that the author did not expect to be dealt with as a real and sincere penitent, but as a penitent of importance, after a short admonition withdrew; not questioning but he should be again sent for if the sickness grew desperate. The author, however, recovered, and has since written two or three other tracts with the same spirit, and very luckily for his poor soul with the same success.*

C

* Mr Toland is supposed to be here alluded to.

No. CLXVII. TUESDAY, SEPTEMBER 11.

    Fuit haud ignobilis Argis,
Qui se credebat miros audire tragœdos,
In vacuo lætus sessor plausorque theatro,
Cætera qui vitæ servaret munia recto
More, bonus sane vicinus, amabilis hospes,
Comis in uxorem; posset qui ignoscere servis,
Et signo læso non insanire lagenæ·
Posset qui rupem et puteum vitare patentem.
Hic, ubi cognatorum opibus curisque refectus,
Expulit elleboro morbum bilemque meraco,
Et redit ad sese pol me occidistis, amici,
Non servâstis, ait, cui sic extorta voluptas,
Et demptus per vim mentis gratissimus error
HOR.

IMITATED

There liv'd in Primo Georgii (they record)
A worthy member, no small fool, a lord,
Who, though the house was up, delighted sate,
Heard, noted, answer'd, as in full debate.
In all but this, a man of sober life,
Fond of his friend, and civil to his wife,
Not quite a madman, though a pasty fell,
And much too wise to walk into a well.
Him the damn'd doctor and his friends immur'd,
They bled, they cupp'd, they purg'd, in short they cur'd;
Whereat the gentleman began to stare....
My friends! he cry'd Pox take ye for your care!
That from a patriot of distinguish'd note,
Have bled and purg'd me to a single vote.
POPE

THE unhappy force of an imagination, unguided by the check of reason and judgment, was the subject of a former speculation. My reader may remember that he has seen in one of my papers a complaint of an unfortunate gentleman, who was unable to contain himself, when any ordinary matter was laid before him, from adding a few circumstances to enliven plain narrative. That correspondent was a person of too warm a complexion to be satisfied with things merely as they stood in nature, and therefore formed incidents which should have happened to have pleased him in the story. The same ungoverned fancy which pushed that correspondent on, in spite of himself, to relate public and notorious falsehoods, makes the author of the following letter do the same in private: one is a prating, the other a silent, liar.

There is little pursued in the errors of either of these worthies but mere present amusement: but the folly of him who lets his fancy place him in distant scenes untroubled and uninterrupted, is very much preferable to that of him who is ever forcing a belief, and defending his untruths with new inventions. But I shall hasten to let this liar in soliloquy, who calls himself a Castle-builder, describe himself with the same unreservedness as formerly appeared in my correspondent above-mentioned. If a man were to be serious upon this subject, he might give very grave admonitions to those who are following any thing in this life, on which they think to place their hearts, and tell them that they are really Castle-builders. Fame, glory, wealth, honour, have in the prospect pleasing illusions; but they who come to possess any of them will find they are ingredients towards happiness, to be regarded only in the second place, and that when they are valued in the first degree, they are as disappointing as any of the phantoms in the following letter.

SEPT. 6, 1711.

'MR SPECTATOR,

'I AM a fellow of a very odd frame of mind, as you will find by the sequel: and think myself fool enough to deserve a place in your paper. I am unhappily far gone in building, and am one of that species of men who are properly denominated Castle-builders, who scorn to be beholden to the earth for a foundation, or dig in the bowels of it for materials; but erect their structures in the most unstable of elements, the air, fancy alone laying the line, marking the extent, and shaping the model. It would be difficult to enumerate what august palaces and stately porticoes have grown under my forming imagination, or what verdant meadows and shady groves have started into being by the powerful feat of a warm fancy. A castle-builder is even just what he pleases; and as such I have grasped imaginary sceptres, and delivered uncontroulable edicts, from a throne to which conquered nations yielded obeisance. I have made I know not how many inroads into France, and ravaged the very heart of that kingdom; I have dined in the Louvre, and drank champaign at Versailles; and I would have you take notice, I am not only able to vanquish a people already cowed and accustomed to flight, but I could Almanzor-like, drive the British general from the field, were I less a Protestant, or had ever been affronted by the Confederates. There is no art or profession whose most celebrated masters I have not eclipsed. Wherever I have afforded my salutary presence, fevers have ceased to burn and agues to shake the human fabric. When an eloquent fit has been upon me, an apt gesture and proper cadence has animated each sentence, and gazing crowds have found their passions worked up into a rage or soothed into a calm. I am short, and not very well made; yet upon sight of a fine woman, I have stretched into proper stature, and killed with a good air and mien. These are the gay phantoms that dance before my waking eyes, and compose my day-dreams. I should be the most contented happy man alive, were the chimerical happiness which springs from the paintings of fancy less fleeting and transitory. But alas! it is with grief of mind I tell you, the least breath of wind has often demolished my magnificent edifices, swept away my groves, and left no more trace of them than if they had never been. My exchequer has sunk and vanished by a rap on my door; the salutation of a friend has cost me a whole continent, and in the same moment I have been pulled by the sleeve, my crown has fallen from my head. The ill consequence of these reveries is inconceivably great, seeing the loss of imaginary possessions makes impressions of real woe. Besides, bad economy is visible and apparent in builders of invisible mansions. My tenants' advertisements of ruins and dilapidations often cast a damp on my spirits, even in the instant when the sun, in all his splendour, gilds my eastern palaces. Add to this the pensive drudgery in building, and constant grasping aerial trowels, distracts and shatters the mind, and the fond builder of Babels is often cursed with an incoherent diversity and confusion of thoughts. I do not know to whom I can more properly apply myself for relief from this fantastical evil than to yourself, whom I earnestly implore to accommodate me with a method how to settle my head and cool my brain-pan. A dissertation on castle-building may not only be serviceable to myself, but to all architects who display their skill in the thin element. Such a favour would oblige me to make my next soliloquy not contain the praises of my dear self, but of the Spectator, who shall, by complying with this, make me

'His obliged, humble servant,

T 'VITRUVIUS.'

No. CLXVIII. WEDNESDAY, SEPTEMBER 12.

.... *Pectus præceptis format amicis.* HOR.

Forms the soft bosom with the gentlest art.
POPE.

IT would be arrogance to neglect the application of my correspondents so far, as not sometimes to insert their animadversions upon my paper. That of this day shall be therefore wholly composed of the hints which they have sent me.

'MR. SPECTATOR,

'I SEND you this to congratulate your late choice of a subject, for treating on which you deserve public thanks; I mean that on those licensed tyrants the schoolmasters. If you can disarm them of their rods, you will certainly have your old age reverenced by all the young gentlemen of Great-Britain, who are now between seven and seventeen years. You may boast that the incomparably wise Quintilian and you are of one mind in this particular. Si cui est (says he) mens tam illiberalis ut objurgatione non corrigatur, is etiam ad plagas, ut pessima quæque mancipia, durabitur, i. e. "If any child be of so disingenuous a nature as not to stand corrected by reproof, he, like the very worst of slaves, will be hardened even against blows themselves." And afterwards, Pudet dicere in quæ probra nefandi homines isto cædendi jure abutantur; i. e. "I blush to say how shamefully those wicked men abuse the power of correction."

'I was bred myself, Sir, in a very great school, of which the master was a Welchman, but certainly descended from a Spanish family, as plainly appeared from his temper as well as his name. I leave you to judge what sort of a schoolmaster a Welchman ingrafted on a Spaniard would make. So very dreadful had he made himself to me, that although it is above twenty years since I felt his heavy hand, yet still once a month at least I dream of him, so strong an impression did he make on my mind. It is a sign he has fully terrified me waking, who still continues to haunt me sleeping.

'And yet I may say without vanity, that the business of the school was what I did without great difficulty, and I was not remarkably unlucky. and yet such was the master's severity, that once a month, or oftener, I suffered as much as would have satisfied the law of the land for a petty larceny.

'Many a white and tender hand which the fond mother had passionately kissed a thousand and a thousand times, have I seen whipped until it was covered with blood; perhaps for smiling, or for going a yard and a-half out of a gate, or for writing an O for an A, or an A for an O. These were our great faults! Many a brave and noble spirit has been there broken. others have run from thence, and were never heard of afterwards. It is a worthy attempt to undertake the cause of distressed youth; and it is a noble piece of knight-errantry to enter the lists against so many armed pedagogues. It is pity but we had a set of men, polite in their behaviour and method of teaching, who should be put into a condition of being above flattering or fearing the parents of those they instruct. We might then possibly see learning become a pleasure, and children delighting themselves in that which now they abhor for coming upon such hard terms to them. What would be still a greater happiness arising from the care of such instructors, would be, that we should have no more pedants, nor any bred to learning who had not genius for it.

'I am, with the utmost sincerity, Sir,

'Your most affectionate humble servant,'

RICHMOND, SEPTEMBER 5, 1711.

'Mr. SPECTATOR,

'I AM a boy of fourteen years of age, and have for this last year been under the tuition of a doctor of divinity, who has taken the school of this place under his care. From the gentleman's great tenderness to me and friendship to my father, I am very happy in learning my book with pleasure. We never leave off our diversions any further than to salute him at hours of play when he pleases to look on. It is impossible for any of us to love our own parents better than we do him. He never gives any of us a harsh word, and we think it the greatest punishment in the world when he will not speak to any of us. My brother and I are both together inditing this letter: he is a year older than I am, but is now ready to break his heart that the doctor has not taken any notice of him these three days. If you please to print this, he will see it; and we hope, taking it for my brother's earnest desire to be restored to his favour, he will again smile upon him.

'Your most obedient servant,
'T. S.'

'Mr. SPECTATOR,

'You have represented several sorts of impertinents singly, I wish you would now proceed and describe some of them in sets. It often happens in public assemblies, that a party who came thither together, or whose impertinencies are of an equal pitch, act in concert, and are so full of themselves as to give disturbance to all that are about them. Sometimes you have a set of whisperers who lay their heads together in order to sacrifice every body within their observation; sometimes a set of laughers, that keep up an insipid mirth in their own corner, and by their noise and gestures shew they have no respect for the rest of the company. You frequently meet with these sets at the opera, the play, the water-works, and other public meetings, where their whole business is to draw off the attention of the spectators from the entertainment, and to fix it upon themselves; and it is to be observed that the impertinence is ever loudest when the set happens to be made up of three or four females who have got what you call a woman's man among them.

'I am at a loss to know from whom people of fortune should learn this behaviour, unless it be from the footmen who keep their places at a new play, and are often seen passing away their time in sets at all fours in the face of a full house, and with a perfect disregard to the people of quality sitting on each side of them.

'For preserving therefore the decency of public assemblies, methinks it would be but reasonable that those who disturb others should pay at least a double price for their places; or rather women of birth and distinction should be informed, that a levity of behaviour in the eyes of people of understanding degrades them below their meanest attendants; and gentlemen should know that a fine coat is a livery, when the person who wears it discovers no higher sense than that of a footman. I am,

'Sir,

'Your most humble servant.'

BEDFORDSHIRE, SEPTEMBER 1, 1711.

'Mr SPECTATOR,

'I AM one of those whom every body calls a poacher, and sometimes go out to course with a brace of greyhounds, a mastiff, and a spaniel or two; and when I am weary with coursing, and have killed hares enough, go to an ale-house to refresh myself. I beg the favour of you, as you set up for a reformer, to send us word how many dogs you will allow us to go with, how many full pots of ale to drink, and how many hares to kill in a day, and you will do a great piece of service to all the sportsmen. Be quick then, for the time of coursing is come on.

'Yours in haste,
T 'ISAAC HEDGEDITCH.'

No. CLXIX. THURSDAY, SEPTEMBER 13.

Sic vita erat: facilè omnes perferre ac pati
Cum quibus erat cunque unà, his sese dedere,
Eorum obsequi studiis, adversus nemini,
Nunquam præponens se aliis, ita facillimè
Sine invidia invenias laudem. TER.

His manner of life was this: to bear with every body's humours, to comply with the inclinations and pursuits of those he conversed with; to contradict nobody; never to assume a superiority over others. This is the ready way to gain applause, without exciting envy.

MAN is subject to innumerable pains and sorrows by the very condition of humanity, and yet, as if nature had not sown evils enough in life, we are continually adding grief to grief, and aggravating the common calamity by our cruel treatment of one another. Every man's natural weight of afflictions is still made more heavy by the envy, malice, treachery, or injustice of his neighbour. At the same time that the storm beats upon the whole species, we are falling foul upon one another.

Half the misery of human life might be extinguished, would men alleviate the general curse they lie under by mutual offices of compassion, benevolence, and humanity. There is nothing therefore which we ought more to encourage in ourselves and others, than that disposition of mind which in our language goes under the title of good-nature, and which I shall choose for the subject of this day's speculation.

Good nature is more agreeable in conversation than wit, and gives a certain air to the countenance which is more amiable than beauty. It shows virtue in the fairest light, takes off in some measure from the deformity of vice, and makes even folly and impertinence supportable.

There is no society or conversation to be kept up in the world without good nature, or something which must bear its appearance and supply its place. For this reason mankind have been forced to invent a kind of artificial humanity, which is what we express by the word good-breeding. For if we examine thoroughly the idea of what we call so, we shall find it to be nothing else but an imitation and mimicry of good nature, or, in other terms, affability, complaisance, and easiness of temper reduced into an art.

These exterior shows and appearances of humanity render a man wonderfully popular and beloved when they are founded upon a real good nature, but without it, are like hypocrisy in religion, or a bare form of holiness, which, when it is discovered, makes a man more detestable than professed impiety.

Good nature is generally born with us: health, prosperity, and kind treatment from the world, are great cherishers of it where they find it, but nothing is capable of forcing it up where it does not grow of itself. It is one of the blessings of a happy constitution, which education may improve but not produce.

Xenophon in the life of his imaginary prince, whom he describes as a pattern for real ones, is always celebrating the philanthropy or good nature of his hero, which he tells us he brought into the world with him, and gives many remarkable instances of it in his childhood, as well as in all the several parts of his life. Nay, on his death-bed he describes him as being pleased, that while his soul returned to him who made it, his body should incorporate with the great mother of all things, and by that means become beneficial to mankind. For which reason he gives his sons a positive order not to enshrine it in gold or silver, but to lay it in the earth as soon as the life was gone out of it.

An instance of such an overflowing of humanity, such an exuberant love to mankind, could not have entered into the imagination of a writer, who had not a soul filled with great ideas and a general benevolence to mankind.

In that celebrated passage of Sallust, where Cæsar and Cato are placed in such beautiful, but opposite lights, Cæsar's character is chiefly made up of good nature, as it showed itself in all its forms towards his friends or his enemies, his servants or dependants, the guilty or the distressed. As for Cato's character, it is rather awful than amiable. Justice seems most agreeable to the nature of God, and mercy to that of man. A Being who has nothing to pardon in himself, may reward every man according to his works; but he whose very best actions must be seen with grains of allowance, cannot be too mild, moderate, and forgiving. For this reason, among all the monstrous characters in human nature, there is none so odious, nor indeed so exquisitely ridiculous, as that of a rigid severe temper in a worthless man.

This part of good nature, however, which consists in the pardoning and overlooking of faults, is to be exercised only in doing ourselves justice, and that too in the ordinary commerce and occurrences of life; for, in the public administrations of justice, mercy to one may be cruelty to others.

It is grown almost into a maxim, that good natured men are not always men of the most wit. This observation, in my opinion, has no foundation in nature. The greatest wits I have conversed with are men eminent for their humanity. I take therefore this remark to have been occasioned by two reasons. First, because ill nature among ordinary observers passes for wit. A spiteful saying gratifies so many little passions in those who hear it, that it generally meets with a good reception. The laugh rises upon it, and the man who utters it is looked upon as a shrewd satirist. This may be one reason why a great many pleasant companions appear so surprisingly dull when they have endeavoured to be merry in print, the public being more just than private clubs or assemblies in distinguishing between what is wit and what is ill nature.

Another reason why the good natured man may sometimes bring his wit in question is, perhaps because he is apt to be moved with compassion for those misfortunes or infirmities which another would turn into ridicule, and by that means gain the reputation of a wit. The ill natured man, though but of equal parts, gives himself a larger field to expatiate in, he exposes those failings in human nature which the other would cast a veil over, laughs at vices which the other either excuses or conceals, gives utterance to reflections which the other stifles, falls indifferently upon friends or enemies, exposes the person who has obliged him, and, in short, sticks at nothing that may establish his character of a wit. It is no wonder therefore he succeeds in it better than the man of humanity, as a person who makes use of indirect methods is more likely to grow rich than the fair trader. L.

THE INDEX.

A

ACTION the felicity of the soul, No. 116.
Affliction and sorrow not always expressed by tears, No. 95. True affliction labours to be invisible, ibid.
Age, the unnatural misunderstanding between age and youth, No. 153. The authority of an aged virtuous person preferable to the pleasures of youth, ibid.
Albacinda, her character, No. 144.
Alexander, his artifice in his Indian expedition, No. 127. His answer to those who asked him if he would not be a competitor for the prize in the Olympic games, No. 157.
Amaryllis, her character, No. 144.
Ambition, the occasion of factions, No. 125.
Animals, the different make of every species, No. 120. The instinct of brutes, ibid. Exemplified in several instances, ibid. God himself the soul of brutes, 121. The variety of arms with which they are provided by nature, ibid.
Amusements of life, when innocent, necessary and allowable, No. 93.
Apparitions, the creation of weak minds, No. 110.
Arable, (Mrs), the great heiress, the Spectator's fellow-traveller, No. 132.
Aristotle, his account of the world, No. 166.
Aristus and Aspasia, a happy couple, No. 128.
Artist, wherein he has the advantage of an author, No. 166.
Association of honest men proposed by the spectator, No. 126.
Author, in what manner one author is a mole to another, No. 124. Wherein an author has the advantage of an artist, 166. The care an author ought to take of what he writes, ibid. A story of an atheistical author, ibid.

INDEX.

B

BAREFACE, his success with the ladies, and the reason for it, No 156

Bear-Garden, the Spectator's method for the improvement of it, No. 141

Beauties, whether male or female, very untractable, No. 87. and fantastical, 144. impertinent and disagreeable, ibid. The efficacy of beauty, ibid

Board-wages, the ill effects of it, No 88

Bodily exercises, of ancient encouragement, No 161

Books reduced to their quintessence, No 124 The legacies of great geniuses, 166

Burnet (Dr.) some passages in his 'Theory of the Earth' considered, No. 143 and 146

C

CÆSAR (Julius), his reproof to an ill reader, No. 147.

Cambray (the Bishop of,) his 'Education of a Daughter' recommended, No 95

Cant, from whence said to be derived, No 147.

Care what ought to be a man's chief care, No 122.

Carneades, the philosopher, his definition of beauty, No 144

Cassius, the proof he gave of his temper in his childhood, No 157

Castle-builders, who, and their follies exposed, No 167.

Censure, a tax, by whom paid to the public, and for what, No 101

Chaplain, the character of Sir Roger de Coverley's, No 106.

Chastity, the great point of honour in women, No 99

Cheerfulness of temper, how to be obtained and preserved, No. 143

Children; wrong measures taken in the education of the British children, No 157

Children in the Wood, a ballad, wherein to be commended, No 85

Church-yard, the country 'Change on Sunday, No 112.

Common-prayer, some considerations on the reading of it, No 147 the excellency of it, ibid

Compassion, the exercise of it would tend to lessen the calamities of life, No 169

Compliments in ordinary discourse censured, No. 103 Exchange of compliments, 155

Condè (Prince of,) his face like that of an eagle, No. 86.

INDEX.

Connecte (Thomas,) a monk in the fourteenth century, a zealous preacher against the womens' commodes in those days, No 98

Contentment the utmost good we can hope for in this life, No 163

Conversation, usually stuffed with too many compliments, No 103 What properly to be understood by the word conversation, 143

Cottilus, his great equanimity, No 143

Coverly (Sir Roger de,) he is something of an humorist, No 106 his choice of a chaplain, ibid his management of his family, 107 his account of his ancestors, 109 is forced to have every room in his house exorcised by his chaplain, 110 a great benefactor to his church in Worcestershire, 112 in which he suffers no one to sleep but himself, ibid He gives the Spectator an account of his amours, and the character of his widow, 113, 118 The trophies of his several exploits in the country, 115 a great fox-hunter, 116 an instance of his good-nature, ibid his aversion to confidants, 118 the manner of his reception at the assizes, 122 where he whispers the judge in the ear, ibid his adventure when a school-boy, 125 a man for the landed interest, 126 his adventure with some gypsies, 130 rarely sports near his own seat, 131

Country, the charms of it, No 118 Country gentleman and his wife, neighbours to Sir Roger, their different tempers described, 126 Country Sunday, the use of it, 112 Country wake described, 161

Courage recommends a man to the female sex more than any other quality, No 99 One of the chief topics in books of chivalry, ibid False courage, ibid Mechanic courage, what, No 152

Cowley, his magnanimity, No 114

Coxcombs, generally the women's favourites, No 128

D

DEATH, the contemplation of it affords a delight mixed with terror and sorrow, No 133 Intended for our relief, ibid

Deaths of eminent persons the most improving passages in history, ibid

Debt the ill state of such as run in debt, No 82

Decency, nearly related to virtue, No 104

Demurrers, what sort of women so to be called, No 89

INDEX.

Devotion, the great advantages of it, No 93. The most natural relief in our afflictions, No 163.
Dick Crastin challengeth Tom Tulip, No. 91.
Disappointments in love, the most difficult to be conquered of any other, No 163.
Dissenters, their canting way of reading, No. 147.
Dissimulation, the perpetual inconvenience of it, No 103.
Duelling, a discourse against it, No. 48. Pharamond's edict against it, 97.
Duration, the idea of it how obtained according to Mr Locke, No 94. Different beings may entertain different notions of the same parts of duration, ibid.

E

EDUCATION an ill method observed in the educating our youth, No 157.
Eminent men, the tax paid by them to the public, No. 101.
Englishmen, the peculiar blessing of being born one, No 135. The Spectator's speculations upon the English tongue, ibid. English not naturally talkative, ibid and 148. The English tongue much adulterated, 165.
Epaminondas, his honourable death, No. 133.
Ephraim, the Quaker, the Spectator's fellow-traveller in a stage-coach, No 132. His reproof to a recruiting officer in the same coach, ibid and advice to him at their parting, ibid.
Equanimity, without it we can have no true taste of life, No 143.
Equestrian order of ladies, No 104. Its origin, ibid.
Errors and prepossessions difficult to be avoided, No. 117.
Eternity, a prospect of it, No 159.
Eucrate, his conference with Pharamond, No 84.
Eucratia, her character, No 144.
Eudosia, her character, No 144.
Eudoxus and Leontine, their friendship, and education of their children, No 123.
Exercise, the great benefit and necessity of bodily exercise, No 116.

F

FALSEHOOD in man, a recommendation to the fair sex, No 156.
Families the ill measures taken by great families in the education of their younger sons, No 108.

INDEX.

Fan, the exercise of it, No 102
Fashion men of fashion, who, No 151.
Faustina the empress, her notions of a pretty gentleman, No 128
Female virtues, which the most shining, No 81
Flavia, her mother's rival, No 91
Flutter of the fan, the variety of motions in it, No 102
Freeport (Sir Andrew,) his moderation in point of politics, No 126
Frugality, the support of generosity, No 107

G.

GAMING, the folly of it, No 93
Genius, what properly a great one, No 160
Gentry of England, generally speaking, in debt, No 82
Geography of a jest settled, No 138
Gigglers in church reproved, No 158
Gypsies an adventure between Sir Roger, the Spectator, and some gypsies, No 130
Glaphyra, her story out of Josephus, No 110
Glory, the love of it, No 139 In what the perfection of it consists, ibid
Good-breeding, the great revolution that has happened in that article, No 119
Good-humour, the necessity of, No 100
Good-nature more agreeable in conversation than wit, No 169 The necessity of it, ibid Good-nature born with us, ibid
Grandmother Sir Roger de Coverley's great, great, great grandmother's receipt for an hasty-pudding and a white pot, No 109.
Great men, the tax paid by them to the public, No 101. Not truly known till some years after their deaths, ibid.

H.

HANDSOME people generally fantastical, No 144.
The Spectator's list of some handsome ladies, ibid
Harry Terset and his lady, their way of living, No 100
Hate why a man ought not to hate even his enemies, No 125
Head-dress, the most variable thing in nature, No 98 Extravagantly high in the fourteenth century, ibid With what success attacked by a monk of that age, ibid.
Heathen philosopher, No 150

VOL. II. K k

Heirs and elder brothers frequently spoiled in their education, No. 123

Historian in conversation, who, No. 136

Honeycomb (Will,) his knowledge of mankind, No. 105 his letter to the Spectator, 131 his notion of a man of wit, 151 his boasts, ibid. his artifice, 156

Honour, wherein commendable, No. 99 and when to be exploded, ibid.

Hunting, the use of it, No. 116

I.

ICHNEUMON, a great destroyer of crocodile's eggs, No. 126.

Idols: coffee-house idols, No. 87.

Immortality of the soul, arguments in proof of it, No. 111

Impertinents, several sorts of them described, No. 148 and 168

Indigo, the merchant, a man of prodigious intelligence, No. 136

Indisposition: a man under any, whether real or imaginary, ought not to be admitted into company, No. 143

Indolence, what, No. 100

Instinct, the power of it in brutes, No. 120

Irresolution, from whence arising, No. 151.

Irus's fear of poverty, and effects of it, No. 114.

K.

KENNET (Dr.), his account of the country wakes, No. 161

Knowledge, the pursuits of it long, but not tedious, No. 94 The only means to extend life beyond its natural dimensions, ibid

L.

LABOUR bodily labour of two kinds, No. 115

Laertes, his character in distinction from that of Irus, No. 114

Lancashire Witches, a comedy, censured, No. 141.

Language, the English, much adulterated during the war, No. 165.

Leontine and Eudoxus, their great friendship and adventures, No. 123

Letters to the Spectator, from Rosalinda, with a desire to be admitted into the Ugly Club, No. 87 from T. T. complaining of the idols in Coffee-houses, ibid from Philo-

INDEX.

Britannicus on the corruption of servants, 88. from Sam Hopewell, 89. from Leonora, reminding the Spectator of the catalogue, 92. from B D concerning real sorrow, 95. from Annabella, recommending the bishop of Cambray's education of a daughter, ibid. from Tom Trusty, a servant, containing an account of his life and services, 96. from the master of the fan-exercise, 102. from ..against the equestrian order of ladies, 104. from Will Wimble to Sir Roger de Coverley, with a jack, 108. to the Spectator from ..complaining of the new petticoat, 127. from a lawyer on the circuit, with an account of the progress of the fashions in the country, 129. from Will Honeycomb, 131. from George Trusty, thanking the Spectator for the great benefit he has received from his works, 134. from William Wiseacre, who desires his daughter may learn the exercise of the fan, ibid. from a professed liar, 136. from Ralph Valet, the faithful servant of a perverse master, 137. from Patience Giddy, the next thing to a lady's woman, ibid. from Lydia Novell, complaining of her lover's conduct, 140. from R D concerning the corrupt taste of the age, and the reasons of it, ibid. from Betty Saunter about a wager, ibid. from Parthenope, who is angry with the Spectator for meddling with the ladies' petticoats, ibid. from ...upon drinking, ibid. from Rachael Basto concerning female gamesters, ibid. from Parthenia, ibid. from....containing a reflection on a comedy called 'the Lancashire Witches,' 141. from Andromache, complaining of the false notion of gallantry in love, with some letters from her husband to her, 142. from . concerning wagerers, 145. from . complaining of impertinents in coffee-houses, ibid. from... complaining of an old batchelor, ibid. from...concerning the skirts in men's coats, ibid. from...on the reading of the common-prayer, 147. from the Spectator to a dancing outlaw, 148. from the same to a dumb visitant, ibid. to the Spectator from Sylvia a widow, desiring his advice in the choice of a husband, 149. the Spectator's answer, ibid. to the Spectator from Simon Honeycomb, giving an account of his modesty, impudence, and marriage, 154. from an Idol that keeps a coffee-house, 155. from a beautiful millener, complaining of her customers, ibid. from...with a reproof to the Spectator, 158. from concerning the ladies' visitants, ibid. from ...complaining of the behaviour of persons in church, ibid. from a woman's man, ibid. from . with a description of a country wake, 161. from Leonora, who had just lost her lover, 163 from a young officer to his father, 165 to the Spectator from a castle builder, 167 from....concerning the tyranny of school-masters, 168 from T S a schoolboy at Richmond, ibid from ...concerning impertinents, ibid. from Isaac Hedgeditch, a poacher, ibid

Lewis of France, compared with the Czar of Muscovy, No. 139

Lie given, a great violation of the point of honour, No 103

Life in what manner our lives are spent, according to Seneca, No 93. Life is not real but when cheerful, 143. in what manner to be regulated, ibid how to have a right enjoyment of it, ibid A survey of it in a vision, 159

Love, a passion never well cured, No 118 Natural love in brutes more intense than in reasonable creatures, 120. the gallantry of it on a very ill foot, 142. Love has nothing to do with state, 149.

M.

MACBETH, the incantations in that play vindicated, No 141

Mahometans, a custom among them, No 85

Males among the birds have only voices, No 128.

Man, variable in his temper, No 162

Marlborough (John Duke of) took the French lines without bloodshed, No 139

Marriage life, always a vexatious or happy condition, No. 149.

Master, a good one, a prince in his family, No 107 A complaint against some ill masters, No 137.

Merab, her character, No 144

Mirza, (the visions of,) No 159

Mode a standing mode or dress recommended, No 129

Modesty in men nowise acceptable to ladies, No 154.

Mourning the signs of true mourning generally misunderstood, No 95.

N.

NIGRANILLA, a party lady, forced to patch on the wrong side, No 81

Nutmeg of Delight, one of the Persian emperor's titles, No 160

INDEX.

O

OBSCURITY, the only defence against reproach, No 101.
Oeconomy, wherein compared to good-breeding, No 114.
Omniamante, her character, No 144.

P

PAMPHILIO, a good master, No 137.
Parties, an instance of the malice of parties, No 125.
The dismal effects of a furious party-spirit, ibid. it corrupts both our morals and judgment, ibid. and reigns more in the country than town, 126. Party patches, 81. Party scribblers reproved, No 125.
Passions of the fan, a treatise for the use of the author's scholars, No 102.
Pedants, who so to be reputed, No 105. The book pedant the most supportable, ibid.
Pericles, his advice to the women, No 81.
Persians, their instruction of their youth, No 99.
Petticoat, a complaint against the hoop petticoat, No 127. several conjectures upon it, ibid. compared to an Egyptian temple, ibid.
Pharamond, some account of him and his favourite, No 84. His edict against duels, No 97.
Phocion, his behaviour at his death, No 133.
Physiognomy, every man in some degree master of that art, No 86.
Place and precedence more contested among women of an inferior rank than ladies of quality, No 119.
Plato, his notion of the soul, No 90. wherein, according to him and his followers, the punishment of a voluptuous man consists, ibid.
Pleasure, when our chief pursuit disappoints itself, No 151. The deceitfulness of pleasure, ibid.
Pontignan (Monsieur,) his adventure with two women, No 90.
Posterity, its privilege, No 101.
Poverty, the inconveniences and mortifications usually attending it, No 150.
Prejudice, the prevalency of it, No 101.
Procrastination from whence proceeding, No 151.
Providence, demonstrative arguments for it, No 120.
Punishments in schools disapproved, No 157.

INDEX.

R

REASON not to be found in brutes, No. 120.
Riding a healthy exercise, No. 115.
Rival mother, the first part of her history, No. 91
Roman and Sabine ladies, their example recommended to the British, No. 81.
Rosalinda, a famous Whig partisan, her misfortune, No. 81.

S

SCHOOL-MASTERS, the ignorance and undiscerning of the generality of them, Nos. 157. 168.
Scipio, his judgment of Marius, when a boy, No. 157.
Sentry, his account of a soldier's life, No. 152.
Servants, the general corruption of their manners, No. 88. assume their masters' title, ibid. some good men among the many bad ones, 96. influenced by the example of their superiors, ibid. and 107. The great merit of some servants in all ages, ibid. The hard condition of many servants, 137.
Shakspere, wherein inimitable, No. 141.
Sincerity, the great want of it in conversation, No. 103.
Sloven, a character affected by some, and for what reason, No. 150. the folly and antiquity of it, ibid.
Snuff-box, the exercise of it, where taught, No. 138.
Socrates, his behaviour at his execution, No. 133. his speech to his judges, 146.
Soldiers, when men of sense, of an agreeable conversation, No. 152.
Sorrow, the outward signs of it very fallacious, No. 95.
Soul, the immortality of it evinced from several proofs, No. 111.
Spectator, his inquisitive temper, No. 85. his account of himself and his works to be written 300 years hence, 101. his great modesty, ibid. he accompanies Sir Roger de Coverley into the country, 106. his exercise when young, 115. he goes with Sir Roger a-hunting, 116. and to the assizes, 122. his adventure with a crew of gypsies, 130. The several opinions of him in the country, 131. his return to London, and fellow travellers in the stage-coach, 132. his soliloquy upon the sudden and unexpected death of a friend, 133.
Spirits, the appearance of them not fabulous, No. 110.

Squeezing the hand, by whom first used in making of love, No. 119
Story-tellers, their ridiculous punctuality, No. 138

T

TASTE (corrupt) of the age, to what attributed, No. 140
Tears, not always the signs of true sorrow, No. 95
Theodosius and Constantia, their adventures, No. 164
Time, our ill use of it, No. 93. The Spectator's direction how to spend it, ibid.
Tom Touchy, a quarrelsome fellow, No. 122
Tom Tulip challenged by Dick Crastin, No. 91 flies into the country, ibid.
Truepenny (Jack,) strangely good-natured, No. 82

V

VALETUDINARIANS in society, who, 100 not to be admitted into company, but on conditions, No. 143
Vapours in women, to what to be ascribed, No. 115
Varilas, his cheerfulness and good-humour make him generally acceptable, No. 100
Virgil, his beautiful allegories founded on the Platonic philosophy, No. 90
Virtue, the exercise of it recommended, No. 93 its influence ibid its near relation to decency, 104
Volumes, the advantages an author receives of publishing his works in volumes, rather than in single pieces, No. 124
Uranius, his great composure of soul, No. 143

W

WAGERING disputants exposed, No. 145
White (Moll) a notorious witch, No. 117
Widow (the,) her manner of captivating Sir Roger de Coverley, No. 113 her behaviour at the trial of her cause, ibid her artifices and beauty, ibid too desperate a scholar for a country gentleman, ibid her reception of Sir Roger, ibid whom she helped to some tansy in the eye of all the country, ibid she has been the death of several foxes, 115. Sir Roger's opinion of her that she either designs to marry, or she does not, 118
William and Betty, a short account of their amours, No. 118

INDEX

Wimble (Will,) his letter to Sir Roger de Coverley, No. 108. his character, ibid. his conversation with the Spectator, ibid. a man of ceremony, 119. thinks the Spectator a fanatic, 126. and fears he has killed a man, 131.

Wine, not proper to be drunk by every one that can swallow, No. 140.

Women, the English excel all other nations in beauty, No. 81. signs of their improvement under the Spectator's hand, 92. The real commendation of a woman, what, 95 and 104. their pains in all ages to adorn the outside of their heads, 98. more gay in their nature than men, 128. not pleased with modesty in men, 154. their ambition, 156.

Woman's man described, No. 156. his necessary qualifications, ibid.

World, the present, a nursery for the next, No. 111.

THE END.

M MAXWELL,
PRINTER.

BIBLIOLIFE

Old Books Deserve a New Life
www.bibliolife.com

Did you know that you can get most of our titles in our trademark **EasyScript**™ print format? **EasyScript**™ provides readers with a larger than average typeface, for a reading experience that's easier on the eyes.

Did you know that we have an ever-growing collection of books in many languages?

Order online:
www.bibliolife.com/store

Or to exclusively browse our **EasyScript**™ collection:
www.bibliogrande.com

At BiblioLife, we aim to make knowledge more accessible by making thousands of titles available to you – quickly and affordably.

Contact us:
BiblioLife
PO Box 21206
Charleston, SC 29413

Printed in Great Britain
by Amazon.co.uk, Ltd.,
Marston Gate.